Cold Kill

STEPHEN LEATHER

Cold Kill

HODDER &
STOUGHTON

First published in Great Britain in 2006 by Hodder & Stoughton
A division of Hodder Headline

A Hodder & Stoughton Book

5

A CIP catalogue record for this title
is available from the British Library

Hardback ISBN 0 340 83410 2
Trade Paperback ISBN 0 340 83411 0

Typeset in Plantin Light by Hewer Text UK Ltd, Edinburgh
Printed and bound by Mackays of Chatham Ltd, Chatham, Kent

Hodder Headline's policy is to use papers that are natural, renewable
and recyclable products and made from wood grown in sustainable forests.
The logging and manufacturing processes are expected to conform to the
environmental regulations of the country of origin.

Hodder & Stoughton Ltd
A division of Hodder Headline
338 Euston Road
London NW1 3BH

For Amelia

ACKNOWLEDGEMENTS

I am once again indebted to Alistair Cumming of the British Transport Police for keeping me on the straight and narrow regarding police procedure and to Lloyd Currie for his help and advice on matters nautical. Any errors of fact are mine and not theirs.

Denis O'Donoghue, Barbara Schmeling, Andrew Yates, Alex Bonham and Hazel Orme helped me get the manuscript into shape and Carolyn Mays was once again the perfect editor, always there for me when I needed support and encouragement.

The American folded his arms and watched without emotion as the electrodes were applied to the man's genitals. 'Tell us who gave you the satellite photographs,' he said. 'Tell us, and this will all be over.' He was wearing a lightweight headset, a silver-grey earpiece with a small curved mouthpiece.

The torturers on the other side of the two-way mirror were wearing similar headsets. They were in their early thirties with hard eyes and close-cropped hair. They wore dark sweatshirts with the sleeves pulled up to the elbows, jeans and heavy work-boots. The one attaching the electrodes had a broken nose; the other, standing by a table at the far end of the room, had a thick scar above his lip.

Broken Nose repeated the American's words.

The man in the plastic chair was also in his thirties. He hadn't shaved in three days and he had been fed infrequently with low-protein meals. His eyes were sunken, with dark patches beneath, and his black hair was matted and unkempt. 'I don't know what you're talking about,' he said.

Scarred Lip picked up a photograph from the table and waved it in front of the man's face. It was one of several satellite pictures that had been found in his apartment. Photographs of RAF Mildenhall, a base for bombers and tanker aircraft of the United States Air Force and headquarters of the 352nd Special Operations Group. It was a prime target. There could be no justifiable reason for a civilian to have the high-definition satellite images in his possession. Especially a civilian who had circled with black ink all the CCTV cameras that covered the base perimeter.

'Who gave you the pictures?' said the American, quietly.

Broken Nose repeated the question, word for word, but in a staccato scream, his mouth just inches from the bound man's ear.

'You can't do this!' shouted the man. He had a Manchester accent. He had been wearing a Manchester United shirt when he'd been dragged into the basement but he was naked now. He struggled, but the men who had tied him to the chair were professionals and the webbing straps held him tight.

'Yes, we can,' said Scarred Lip.

'I'm a British citizen. I've got rights.'

'Not here you haven't,' said Broken Nose. 'This is American soil. You've got no rights here.'

'I didn't do anything!' screamed the man, spittle spraying from his lips.

'That's a lie,' said Broken Nose. 'And you know what happens when you lie. Now, who gave you the photographs?'

'We know what you were planning,' said Scarred Lip. He threw the photograph back on to the table. 'All we need you to tell us is who was helping you.'

The man closed his eyes and shuddered in anticipation of the pain to come.

The American sighed. 'Do it,' he said softly.

Behind the chair a foot pedal connected the electrodes to the high-voltage batteries that would provide the charge. Direct current was much more painful than the mains alternating current. The American knew that from experience. Broken Nose put his foot on the pedal and the man went into spasm. Broken Nose kept his foot down for a full two seconds, then released it. The man sagged in the chair, gasping for breath. His body was bathed in sweat.

'Again,' said the American.

Broken Nose stamped on the pedal. The man went rigid, back arched like a bow, mouth wide in a silent scream. Urine pooled round the chair.

This time the current stayed on for a full five seconds. When

Broken Nose took his foot off the pedal, the man shuddered and was still.

Scarred Lip walked over and checked for a pulse in the neck. He nodded. The man was still alive. Unconscious, but alive.

'Let's take a break,' said the American.

The torturers grinned. Scarred Lip flashed the American a thumbs-up.

The American removed the headset and placed it on the table. He left the room, passing two marines with loaded carbines, and took the stairs to the ground floor. He swiped his security card through the reader and tapped his entry code into the keyboard. The door led to a long corridor that took him past storerooms and shredding rooms to a second security door. He swiped his card again and tapped in another four-digit code. The door opened into the main staff entrance where two more armed marines stood guard. They looked straight ahead as the American walked by.

The American went out into the sunshine. It was eleven o'clock, a fresh winter's day. He stood looking out over the square, enjoying the cool breeze that played across his face, took a deep breath and let it out slowly. It felt good to be out of the basement, which stank of sweat, urine and fear. He had been born on a farm and had always hated confined spaces. He walked along the metal fence to the gatehouse and showed his ID to the armed policeman, who flashed him a bored smile, then opened the gate. Across the square, two more policemen, in flak jackets, cradling carbines, watched him go past the statue of General Eisenhower.

He walked away from the fortress-like building behind him, surrounded by the blocks of concrete and metal barriers that prevented terrorists getting car bombs close to their target. Americans had enemies around the world, enemies who would love to wreak havoc on a high-profile embassy. Embassies didn't come more high profile than the one in London's Grosvenor Square.

The American liked London. It was a civilised city with good restaurants, a vibrant theatre district and well-tended parks. He headed down Upper Brook Street, past two more armed policemen standing beside a white Land Rover. The British made a big deal about their police force not being armed, but it seemed to the American that every policeman he came across had a gun these days. He smiled and nodded as he walked by, but they stared at him stonily. Everyone was a potential threat now, even a middle-aged white male. It was his regular walk whenever he wanted to clear his head and lungs. Down Park Lane to Hyde Park Corner, then a stroll through the park to the Serpentine. He'd stop off for a coffee at the café there and watch the swans glide by, then read the features pages of the *International Herald Tribune*. But eventually it would be back to the basement. And back to work.

It was difficult to believe she was a man. Tall, leggy, with a model's face, and breasts that were barely contained by the little black dress, she was dancing round a silver pole on a small podium in front of a beer bar packed with tourists, male and female. Alen sipped his mineral water and tried to avoid eye-contact. The Thai ladyboys were predatory and a simple side-long glance would result in one sitting at his side, massaging his upper thigh and asking him for a drink or offering a quick trip to a short-time hotel. There were more than a dozen working the tourists, all of them tall and lovely. Several were wearing Father Christmas hats and had trimmed their dresses with tinsel. The tourists were mainly British and German, middle-aged and overweight, the single guys flirting with the ladyboys, the married ones sneaking furtive glances whenever they thought their wives' attention was elsewhere. Every few minutes a lady-boy would leave with a customer, high heels clicking, her hips swinging, hair flicking in triumph. Alen wondered if the men knew they were going off for sex with a transsexual. Or if they cared.

The road throbbed with the beat of a dozen sound systems, all competing with each other. Tourists sat at roadside beer bars, knocking back bottles of Singha or Chang beer and fondling girls of half their age. Young Thai men in tight-fitting jeans lounged on gleaming motorcycles and smoked cigarettes as they watched their wives and girlfriends ply their trade.

Alen felt a tug at his shoulder. A small dark-skinned girl with impossibly large eyes thrust a handful of roses at him. Each flower had been carefully wrapped in polythene. 'Twenty baht,' she said. She couldn't have been more than eight.

'Where is your mother, child?' asked Alen.

The girl pointed to the right. A woman with skin the colour and texture of leather was standing at the side of the road with an armful of plastic-wrapped roses. She wore a brightly coloured headscarf and large gold hooped earrings. She grinned at Alen, showing a mouthful of blackened teeth.

'Twenty baht,' repeated the child, pushing the flowers closer to Alen's face.

'Don't encourage them,' said the girl sitting next to him. She was in her mid-twenties with shoulder-length blonde hair that blew round her face in the draught from the wall-mounted fan. She spoke in Bosnian, her second language, and Alen's too. Anna had been born in Italy, to an Italian mother and a Bosnian father. 'If no one bought from the kids, they wouldn't use them,' she said.

'And if they didn't work, maybe they wouldn't eat,' said Alen. 'Did you think of that?' He was also of mixed parentage: his mother was Polish and his father Russian, but his father had left before Alen had been born. Alen and Anna had met in Sarajevo. They had a lot in common. They had lived together for the last three years and, if everything went as planned, they would die together.

Anna ruffled the child's hair. 'She should be at home and asleep, not hanging around with prostitutes and whoremongers.'

'It's Christmas Day,' said Alen, his voice loaded with sarcasm. 'Where is your Christmas spirit?'

Anna snorted.

Alen pulled a rose from the little girl's hand and gave it to Anna, who took it and laughed at his sentimentality. He gave the child two ten-baht coins and winked at her. She ran over to her mother.

'You're too soft, Alen,' said Anna.

'You know that's not true,' said Alen. 'You, of all people, know that.'

There were around two dozen beer bars in the complex off Bangla Road, a hundred yards or so from Patong, Phuket's busiest beach. More than five hundred prostitutes worked in the bars, a fair number of whom were transsexuals, but even at ten o'clock at night a large number of families were around. Alen took another sip of mineral water. He would take no pleasure in killing children, but it was the will of Allah that the bombs were placed where they would do most damage and if the infidels chose to bring their children to a place of prostitution, then so be it.

He nodded at Anna, who smiled at him. She, too, was drinking mineral water. 'Happy?' he said.

'Perfect,' she replied. 'Merry Christmas. And thank you for my rose.'

Alen clinked his glass against hers. 'Merry Christmas,' he said loudly. He leaned across the table and planted a kiss on her cheek. She smelt of lemons and camomile. Her shampoo. '*Allahu akbar*,' whispered Alen.

'*Allahu akbar*,' echoed Anna. God is great.

Alen and Anna stayed in Bangla Road until the bars closed. They visited half a dozen but drank nothing stronger than mineral water. They saw other Muslims drinking alcohol and walking off with prostitutes, but their faces didn't betray the contempt they felt. Breaking the rules of Islam would bring its own reward. Alen and Anna walked arm in arm, laughing and smiling like any other holiday couple, but their eyes were watchful. It was the small details that would make or break their operation. Where were the police? How heavy was the traffic? What time did the shops and bars close? Were the streets busy? Did pedestrians walk down the middle of the road or stick to the pavements? Alen and Anna committed everything to memory.

They went down to the beach road to where they had parked their blue Suzuki Jeep, then Alen drove the short distance to the resort where they had been staying for the past three weeks. He drove up to their beach bungalow and parked on the cracked concrete strip by the door. The waves lapped the shore in the distance and the palm trees that surrounded the resort whispered in the night breeze.

They climbed out of the Jeep. Alen knocked on the door. Three quick knocks. Two slow knocks. Two taps with the flat of his hand. It opened, the security chain in place. Pale grey eyes squinted at him, then the door was closed, the chain removed and the door opened again. His name was Norbert, and at thirty-five he was the oldest of the group. He was wearing a red polo shirt and blue jeans, which he'd bought at a roadside stall that morning. His nose and forehead were sunburned and glistened with after-sun lotion. 'Okay?' he asked.

'Busy,' said Alen. 'The bars are packed.' He spoke in Bosnian. Norbert had been born in Luxembourg but, like Anna and Alen, he was fluent in Bosnian.

Another man, Emir, came out of the bedroom, his hair still wet from the shower. 'Tomorrow? Definitely tomorrow?' He was the only one of the four to have been born in Bosnia.

'Tomorrow,' said Alen. He went through to the second bedroom and pulled a grey Samsonite suitcase from under one of the two beds. He opened it, took out a rolled sheet of thick paper, then went with it into the sitting room. Emir and Anna had dropped down on to a bamboo sofa. Norbert helped Alen unroll the paper and weigh down the corners with saucers from the kitchen.

They all peered at the hand-drawn map. Alen ran his finger along Bangla Road. 'It is busy all day, but more so after eight p.m.,' he said. 'The bars shut at one. The best time will be at midnight.' Alen tapped a square some two-thirds of the way down the road. 'The first device will be here,' he said, 'outside the Ocean Plaza department store. It's always busy. Nearby there are dozens of parked motorcycles, which will add to the explosion. Immediately afterwards there will be panic. Most people will rush down the street towards the beach road.' He tapped the bar area where he had earlier been drinking with Anna. 'The second device will be detonated here precisely two minutes later. The street should be full and we will achieve maximum impact.' He smiled at Anna. They would be responsible for the second device.

Norbert took a deep breath and exhaled slowly. '*Allahu akbar*,' he said.

'*Allahu akbar*,' echoed his three companions.

Alen straightened up. 'Any questions?'

Three shaking heads. They knew what had to be done, and why they were doing it. They were prepared to give their lives to the *jihad*.

Alen went through to the first bedroom. It was larger than the second but had identical twin beds, which had been pushed to the side to give them room to work. A hundred and fifty kilos of Semtex had been packed inside metal petrol cans, with the handfuls of nails, screws and washers they had bought in Bangkok. More ironmongery had been taped around the cans. The Semtex had been manufactured in Czechoslovakia and shipped to Libya during the late 1980s. The Libyans had sold a batch to the Provisional Irish Republican Army a few years later and it had arrived in Dublin on a Spanish freighter. The consignment was split into four lots. The first batch was taken to London and formed the heart of a massive bomb that ripped through London's financial district in April 1993, killing one man and causing more than a billion pounds' worth of damage.

The remainder of the Semtex had stayed hidden for three years, until another batch was taken to London and used to detonate a half-tonne fertiliser-based bomb, left near the South Quay station on the Docklands Light Railway. It had killed one man, injured thirty-nine others and marked the end of a seventeen-month IRA ceasefire.

Four months later, another batch of the Semtex was used to destroy a busy shopping centre in Manchester, injuring more than two hundred. It was only because the IRA had issued a warning in advance of the explosion that no one was killed. There would be no warning when the two bombs exploded in Bangla

Road. Alen and his three colleagues were aiming to kill as many people as possible. It was only when the images of death and destruction were flashed round the world that policies would be changed, and the West would learn that it was time to treat the Muslim world with respect, not contempt.

The rest of the Semtex lay buried in a graveyard in Galway throughout the 1990s, under a tombstone that marked the resting-place of an eighty-three-year-old Catholic priest. In the wake of the Good Friday Agreement, the IRA High Command had decided to rid itself of the stockpile and sold it to a Bosnian gangster, who put it into a false compartment in the floor of a container and shipped it to Sarajevo. It remained hidden in a warehouse on the outskirts of the city until Alen had bought it, with a suitcase of euros still in their bank wrappers. The explosive went overland, past the country where it had been manufactured almost thirty years earlier and on to Thailand. Bribes were paid where necessary, and the truck carrying the deadly cargo arrived in Phuket without once having been examined by a Customs officer.

Norbert and Emir appeared in the doorway as Alen knelt to examine the petrol cans. He nodded his approval. 'Good work,' he said.

Norbert and Emir smiled, pleased at the compliment. 'What about the detonators?' asked Norbert.

'Tomorrow,' said Alen. 'They arrive tomorrow. *Inshaallah.*'
Insha allah. God willing.

The Saudi walked along the beach, enjoying the cool, early morning sea breeze. A well-muscled Thai man in a tight-fitting T-shirt jogged barefoot towards him, feet slapping on the wet sand. He smiled at the Saudi – the smile of a hooker searching for a client.

The Saudi looked away, more angry than embarrassed. He was wearing a cheap cotton shirt, baggy cotton pants, cheap plastic sandals, Ray-Ban sunglasses, and carried a knitted shoulder-bag embroidered with elephants. There were no vendors about – it was too early for them. Once the tourists started heading down to the beach, they would come, their skin burned black from years of touting their wares under the unforgiving sun – cheap towels, sarongs, cooked ears of corn, plastic toys from China, laminated maps of Thailand. A sunbathing tourist would be lucky to get a couple of minutes' peace before the next one blocked the rays.

The Saudi walked away from the sea towards the beach road. A few rusting red tuk-tuks were parked in front of a low-rise hotel, the drivers looking at him expectantly, but he avoided eye-contact. It seemed that every Thai he met in Phuket wanted to part him from his money. Indian tailors in long-sleeved shirts called to him whenever he went past their shops, bar-girls smiled suggestively, stallholders begged him to 'Take a look, please.' He had been in Phuket only eighteen hours but he had been proposi-tioned at least fifty times. It was wearisome to be constantly shaking his head.

He had driven down from Bangkok in a rented Toyota Corolla because after the bombs had exploded the police would check all flights into and out of the island. He had checked into the Hilton on Patong Beach, a hotel favoured by tourists from the Middle East. He had dined alone in its outdoor restaurant surrounded by Arab families, the women swathed in traditional black tent-like burkhas, the children running around unsupervised, the men huddled in groups over glasses of sweet tea.

Later in the evening he had gone past the resort where Alen and his three colleagues were staying. He had sat at a beer bar overlooking it, sipped 7-Up and played a dice game with a bar-girl while he satisfied himself that no one else had the resort under observation. He had seen Alen and Anna get into the Jeep and drive off to Bangla Road. No one had followed them. The Saudi had waited half an hour or so, then flagged down a tuk-tuk and sat in the back as it rattled down the beach road. He had rung the bell and climbed out at the intersection with Bangla Road.

He spent the evening keeping Alen and Anna under surveil-lance, sipping soft drinks and ignoring the advances of the young girls who assured him that he was a handsome man and they wanted to go back to his hotel with him. The Saudi had no interest in paying for sex – at least, not in Thailand: the Thai girls, with their brown skin and snub noses, held no attraction for him. He paid happily for female companionship in London or New York, and preferred leggy blondes, ideally in pairs. He had waited until Alen and Anna had left Bangla Road, then returned to the Hilton. He had slept dreamlessly, confident that everything was going to plan.

As the Saudi walked through the bungalows, he smiled to himself. The operation had been six months in the planning, and now it was all coming to fruition. The key to its success had been the three men and the woman who were holed up in the pretty bungalow with its steeply slanted roof and teak deck overlooking the sea.

Since the attack on the World Trade Center in New York, Arabs around the world had been regarded with suspicion, whether or not they were Muslims. The Saudi had seen the nervous way in which fellow passengers glanced at him whenever he boarded a plane. All Arabs were potential terrorists; anyone from the Middle East was capable of slashing a stewardess or grabbing the controls from the pilot or setting fire to his explosive-filled shoes. Arabs were scrutinised at check-in desks, at airport security, at hotels. They were all guilty until proven innocent, to be locked up in Guantanamo Bay or Belmarsh Prison and denied their basic human rights. It was hard for the Saudi to move round the world – and he had the luxury of a British passport and a public-school accent. For the foot-soldiers of al-Qaeda, post 9/11, it was almost impossible to operate in the West without attracting attention. The organisation needed terrorists who didn't look like terrorists. It needed fair-haired, white-skinned Muslims, who would be prepared to embrace martyrdom and die for Islam with smiles on their faces. The Saudi had found such men and women, and arranged for them to be trained. Now they were ready to give their lives for the *jihad*.

The Saudi took a mobile from his bag and tapped out a

number. It rang three times before Alen answered. 'Our meeting for tomorrow is still on schedule?' asked the Saudi.

'The following day would be better,' said Alen, in accented English. It was a prearranged phrase that meant everything was as it should be. If the operation had been compromised, Alen would simply have agreed with him.

'Excellent,' said the Saudi, and ended the call. He walked slowly round the resort until he was satisfied that there was no surveillance, then went over to the door of the beach bungalow and knocked on the door. Three quick knocks. Two slow knocks. Two taps with the flat of his hand.

The door opened and Alen embraced him as he stepped inside, kissing him on both cheeks. '*Allahu akbar,*' he said.

'*Allahu akbar,*' said the Saudi, kicking off his sandals. 'You are prepared?'

'We are all prepared,' said Alen.

They spoke in English, their common language: the common language of terrorists around the world.

Anna, Norbert and Emir stood at the entrance to the second bedroom, smiling nervously. None had met the Saudi before, but they knew of him.

The Saudi went over and embraced them one by one. '*Allahu akbar,*' he said, as he held them. 'God is great.'

'We have tea,' said Anna.

'I cannot stay,' said the Saudi, 'but thank you.'

He sat down on the bamboo sofa and removed a plastic-wrapped package from his bag. He laid it on the coffee table and unwrapped it carefully to reveal six pencil-sized metal tubes with plastic-coated wires attached to them. He placed them one by one on the table. The detonators had been brought into the country by a pilot with Emirates Airlines who had helped the Saudi before. Pilots, especially senior pilots with more than twenty years' experience, were searched thoroughly, but the detonators had been well hidden in a false compartment of the man's flight case. The Saudi had met him in the Shangri-la Hotel, overlooking the Chaoya Pra river. They had had coffee with cake and made small-talk. Then the Saudi had left with the detonators and the pilot had sat with an envelope containing a hundred thousand dollars in crisp new notes.

'Use three per vehicle,' said the Saudi. 'Where are the circuits?' Alen nodded at the bedroom. 'In there,' he said.

The Saudi eased himself up off the sofa and padded through to the bedroom. He gave the explosive-filled fuel cans a cursory glance. The wiring circuits were laid out on the two beds. He studied them carefully. Two batteries in each circuit. Two on-off switches, either of which would complete the circuit. Redundancy was essential. They could not afford a mistake at any level. There were flashlight bulbs, which could be used to test the circuit. The Saudi checked all four on-off switches. They worked perfectly.

He went back into the sitting room. The four *shahids* looked at him expectantly. 'Excellent,' he said. 'You have done well.'

The *shahids* were the front-line warriors of the *jihad*, the martyrs who would give their lives for Islam. The Koran promised the *shahids* unlimited sex with seventy-two black-eyed virgins. It said that martyrs went straight to heaven and that places would be saved for seventy of their relatives. There would be eighty thousand servants to take care of them. And they would see the face of Allah Himself. The Saudi didn't believe that, of course, and neither did the four *shahids* in the room. But they were still prepared to die. '*Allahu akbar*,' they said in unison.

Nine kilometres below the white-flecked waves of the Andaman Sea, the pressure had been building for hundreds of years. Tectonic stresses, pressure that dwarfed anything that could be produced by man. The huge stone plate on which India and Australia rested had been inching northwards for millennia, pushing against the equally massive Eurasian landmass near Indonesia. Millions upon millions of tonnes of rocks forced against each other as the continents drifted over the surface of the earth. Three days earlier there had been an earthquake in the

Macquarie Islands, but it had done nothing to alleviate the
pressure close to Sumatra.

No single event triggered the rupture. At one moment the plates
were jammed against each other as they had been for centuries, and
at the next they slipped. It happened at precisely fifty-eight minutes
past midnight, Greenwich Mean Time. The southern plate ripped
under the northern plate, like a bulldozer blade cleaving through
wet soil. Rocks ripped like cardboard. Pressure that had accumu-
lated over centuries was released in an instant. The forces at work
were almost unimaginable, equivalent to a million times the power
of the atom bomb that had destroyed Hiroshima.

A massive earthquake shook the island of Sumatra for more
than three minutes and registered 9.0 on the Richter scale. By the
time the shaking had subsided, hundreds were dead. There had
been only three bigger earthquakes in recorded history. But the
fatalities caused by the earthquake were only a taste of what was
to follow. The rupture in the ocean floor was twelve hundred
kilometres long and a hundred wide. It averaged twenty metres
deep and displaced millions of tonnes of water in a few seconds.
On the surface, there was little change in the white-flecked waves.
But deep underwater a tidal wave was racing outwards in all
directions, north, south, east and west, travelling at the speed of a
cruising airliner. Even at that velocity, the nearest landfall was
two hours away.

The floor trembled, a slight vibration that was little more than a
tickling sensation underfoot. Alen looked across at Anna. 'Can
you feel that?'

She nodded. 'Like it's shaking.'

Suddenly one of the framed pictures on the wall shifted. It was
a beach scene. White sand, palm trees blowing in the wind, a
fisherman tending his nets.

Norbert and Emir came out of the bedroom. 'What is it?' asked
Norbert.

The shaking stopped as suddenly as it had begun. 'An earthquake?' said Anna, frowning.

'They don't have earthquakes in Thailand,' said Alen.

Emir knelt and placed his hands on the tiled floor, as if preparing to pray. 'It's stopped now,' he said.

'It was nothing,' said Alen.

Norbert pushed open the blinds and peered outside. Tourists in swimsuits were walking along the beach. The first vendors were appearing. Stray dogs were scavenging around litter-bins. 'I'm going outside,' he said.

'It's the final day,' said Alen. 'We should stay indoors. We should pray and meditate on what we have to do tonight.'

'I know what we have to do tonight,' said Norbert. 'I need some air.'

Alen looked as if he was about to argue. Then he waved dismissively. 'Do as you want,' he said. 'Are the circuits ready?'

'They're fine. I've disconnected the switches but everything else is in place.' He unlocked the door, slipped outside and closed it behind him.

Alen went to the picture and adjusted it, then placed a hand flat against the wall. There was no vibration.

'It could have been a large truck passing,' said Emir.

Alen shrugged. 'Maybe,' he said. The vibration had felt too intense for that, but Thailand wasn't in an earthquake zone. Japan, maybe, but Japan was a thousand miles away.

Alen went into the bedroom. The completed circuits lay on the twin beds, one on each. He examined them but didn't touch them. Norbert knew what he was doing. Alen had met him in Bosnia, fighting the Serbs who were killing Muslim families and burying them in mass graves while the world watched and did nothing. In recognition of their services, both men had been given Bosnian citizenship, and passports in whatever name they chose. After the peacekeepers had moved into the former Yugoslavia, Alen and Norbert had stayed on, but while the killing had stopped, the Muslims had continued to be persecuted.

Alen had been approached first, by a representative of a Saudi-funded charity who asked if he would be prepared to continue his fight against the infidel. There was no pressure; it was a simple interview to see where his loyalties lay. Alen had left the man in no doubt that he served Islam. Norbert, too, was keen to continue the struggle. They had been taken into the al-Qaeda fold, then overland to Waziristan, a mountainous area along the Afghan border with Pakistan, where their training intensified. That was where they had met Anna and Emir. In Waziristan their training had moved to an even higher level: they were groomed to join the ranks of the *shahid*. Alen had no doubts about what he was going to do. He had almost died many times in Bosnia, and he would have died happily then, fighting the Serbs. He would die just as happily in Thailand, killing the infidels as they drank whiskey and partied with prostitutes.

All that was left to do was to transfer the explosive-filled cans into the two Jeeps and insert the detonators. That would have to wait until dark. Now all they could do was wait. Prepare themselves. And pray.

He showered first, then changed into clean clothes. He took a mat out of the wardrobe and spread it on the wooden floor, making sure that the top faced the direction of Mecca. Alen prayed five times each day, and washed himself before each prayer.

He faced Mecca, and raised his hands to his ears. He prayed in Arabic, the language of Allah. That was something he had been taught in Pakistan. It was not enough to recite a translation of the Koran: any translation was a poor imitation of the real thing. Arabic was the mother-tongue of the Prophet and his wives, and the wives of the Prophet were the mothers of the faithful so Arabic had to be the mother-tongue of every Muslim. Alen proclaimed his intention to worship, then lowered his hands to his knees and bent forward, head bowed. 'Subhaana rab-biyal azeem,' he said, three times. 'Glory to God, the Most Grand.'

Then he straightened up. 'Sami'al laahu liman hamidah, rab-banaa lakal hamd,' he said. 'Our Lord, praise be to Thee.'

Then he fell to his knees and placed his forehead, nose and palms on the mat. 'Subhaana rab-biyal a'laa,' he said, three times. 'Glory to my Lord, the Most High.'

He had just finished the third recitation when there was a sudden banging on the bungalow door. Alen scrabbled over to the bed nearest him and pulled a large automatic from under the mattress. He hurried into the sitting room. Anna had grabbed a handgun from her bag and was heading for the front door. Alen gestured for her to move to the left. Emir started to go to the main bedroom, but Alen clicked his fingers and motioned for him to stay where he was. If it was the police, they'd already have surrounded the bungalow and running wouldn't be an option.

'Who is it?' he called.

'Come and look at this!' It was Norbert.

Emir cursed and Anna exhaled through clenched teeth.

Alen opened the door but kept the security chain on. Norbert was shifting from foot to foot, head bobbing excitedly.

'We have a procedure,' said Alen. 'The code.'

'Screw the code,' said Norbert. 'You have to see this. Come on.'

Alen glared at Norbert, but removed the chain and went outside after him. Emir and Anna began to follow him but he waved them back. 'Stay there,' he said, 'and lock the door.'

Norbert was walking quickly towards the beach. Alen hurried after him. A sunburnt middle-aged couple were ahead, the man fumbling with a video camera. Other tourists were standing on the sand, gazing out to sea.

'Norbert, what the hell are you doing?' hissed Alen. 'You know how important today is. We have to stay inside.' His bare feet slipped in the sand as he walked.

Norbert stopped in the middle of the beach and pointed. 'Have you ever seen anything like it?' asked Norbert. 'It's just gone. The sea has gone.'

Where water should have been lapping at the beach, wet sand glistened under the early morning sun. Fish, large and small, were flapping about. Three old Thai men were scurrying to pick them up, putting them into plastic carrier-bags.

'It's a tide,' said Alen. 'That's all. The sea is out there – you can see it.'

Norbert shaded his eyes with a hand and peered at the horizon. There was blue water in the distance. 'The tide doesn't go that far out,' he said.

'How would you know?' said Alen. 'You're from Luxembourg. There's no sea there.'

'I'm just saying, the tide wouldn't go out more than thirty metres or so, at most.'

Alen looked out over the wet sand. It was hard to judge distance without landmarks and the seabed was flat to the horizon. More Thais hurried on to the beach to gather up the dying fish.

'We should go inside,' said Alen. 'All these tourists with their video cameras – it's dangerous.' He took his sunglasses from his top pocket and put them on.

Norbert shrugged and turned. The two men started to walk back to their bungalow.

'You are prepared?' asked Alen.

'Everything is ready,' said Norbert. 'You know that.'

'I mean in yourself. You, personally?'

'Of course,' said Norbert, defensively.

Alen looked at him over the top of his sunglasses. 'You are stronger than Emir, you know that. If he has doubts closer to the time . . .'

'I can handle Emir.'

Alen patted him on the back. 'Of course you can. But you must watch him. As I must watch Anna.'

'We're all willing to do what we have to do,' said Norbert.

Alen trusted Norbert. He had been trained by the best – by the Mujahideen in Afghanistan, by al-Qaeda in Pakistan. He was a late convert to Islam but he was physically and mentally prepared to die for Allah. As was Alen. Norbert would die first, with Emir. Their bomb would kill dozens and start a panic. Tourists would run away from the carnage, towards the sea, and that was when Alen and Anna would die, and with them hundreds of infidels.

A woman shouted somewhere behind them. Both men

stopped. There were more shouts. Men and women. Thai, English and German voices. They turned.

A wave was heading towards the shore, a big one, bigger than any Alen had ever seen before. The shouts turned to screams. The Thais dropped their fish and ran across the wet sand. Most of the tourists stood where they were, frozen in terror, their video cameras still trained on the approaching wave.

'Run!' yelled Alen, but Norbert was already sprinting across the sand, arms pumping furiously.

Alen could hear the wave now, a low, rumbling roar. The screams behind him intensified, then the roar drowned them and the water slammed into him. His legs were swept from under him and he fell backwards, spluttering salty water. He flailed, felt sand beneath his feet and kicked himself upright. He saw Norbert, caught in the surf, gasping for breath. Then Alen disappeared under the water again. He slammed into the sand and the impact forced the air out of his lungs. He tried to claw his way to the surface but the strength had gone from his arms. He took an involuntary breath and his lungs filled with water. His eyes were stinging and there was a burning pain in his chest. He broke through into the air again, coughing and spitting. He spun round in the raging torrent and saw Norbert slam into the trunk of a palm tree, like a broken doll, then disappear under the water.

Alen fought to hold his breath, but then his head banged on a hard surface. It was the road. The Tarmac ripped the skin from his left cheek and his eye popped out of its socket. He screamed and water flooded into his mouth. He burst into the air and saw, first, through his good eye, the clear blue sky, then a car that had been turned on to its side by the force of the water. He tried to kick round the car, but he was moving too fast and his head banged into the rear axle. His neck snapped and he died instantly.

The water ripped through the resort. The bungalows had been built cheaply, with little in the way of foundations and the contractors had scrimped on the concrete. They caved in as if they were made of plasterboard.

Emir died as he reached for the security chain on the door.

He'd heard the screams and the roar of the water and wanted to see what was happening. The wave demolished the front wall and the door smashed into him, crushing his nose. He fell backwards and crashed on to the coffee table as the water raced over him. The fall stunned him and the door pinned him to the floor. He drowned, trying to push the door off him.

Anna was in the shower in the main bathroom so she didn't hear the wave. She felt the bungalow shudder as the water hit, but before she could scream the torrent tore through the walls and the ceiling fell in. A thick teak roof timber slammed against her shoulders and she fell to the tiled floor. The glass shower door shattered and a shard sliced through her neck. Blood swirled round her, diluted by seawater, and she lost consciousness before the water had filled her lungs.

The explosives and detonating circuits were washed away with everything else in the bungalow. Five seconds after the wave had hit, there was nothing left but concrete outlines of where the building had once stood.

It was only a few hundred metres from the car park where he had left the rented Toyota to the international terminal and the Saudi walked at a brisk pace. He was carrying only a thin leather briefcase. It was all he had brought from Phuket. He had burned everything else in a rubber plantation before the eleven-hour drive north to Bangkok. He had taken the Sim card from the mobile phone he had used, and twisted it out of shape, then thrown it on to the fire. He had wiped the mobile phone with a handkerchief, then smashed it to pieces between two rocks. He had thoroughly cleaned the rental car, using a handkerchief to wipe the steering-wheel and door handle after he had got out for the last time. The Saudi was adept at covering his tracks. He had to be: his existence depended on no one suspecting what he was up to. In a world run by Americans, the merest suspicion of terrorist activity meant a one-way trip to a prison cell in Guantanamo Bay.

The Thai girl at the Qantas check-in desk greeted him with a cold smile and a mechanical '*Sawasdee ka*.' The Saudi knew that most Thais didn't like Arabs. It was nothing to do with the problems in the Middle East: it was racism, pure and simple. He enjoyed the confusion on her face as he handed her his British passport. She looked at the photograph, then at his face as if unable to believe that an Arab might be British. Then she examined his Australian visa. The Saudi smiled coldly. The Thais guarded their citizenship jealously and barely a handful of foreigners were granted a Thai passport each year, and only then after meeting strict criteria. The British had no such reservations. It was no longer a person's race or background that stipulated British citizenship: it was whether or not they had the correct paperwork. And the paperwork was for sale to anyone with enough money or the right connections. Russian asset-strippers, American conmen, Nigerian drug-dealers, Indian fraudsters, Muslim terrorists, the British had issued passports to them all. And they were making no move to stem the tide. It was politically incorrect even to mention that the proportion of foreigners holding British passports was growing, that the country's cultural identity was becoming so watered down that no one had any idea now of what it meant to be British.

It wasn't just the British who were committing cultural suicide, the Saudi mused. Most of Europe was following suit. Virtually all of his friends held European passports, and made good use of them. The Saudi had been British since he was a teenager: his father had invested heavily in high-profile companies and institutions, and made significant donations to the major political parties. There had been other payments, too, in cash and in secret, to politicians and bureaucrats who had smoothed the way for the family's citizenship application. Now the Saudi was British, and always would be. Once granted, British citizenship was almost impossible to lose. And with it came the freedom to travel the world.

The girl handed him his passport and boarding pass, and gave him a *wai*, her fingertips pressed together beneath her chin. 'The flight will be boarding soon, sir,' she said.

The Saudi headed for the gate. The metal detector bleeped as he walked through the security check. A girl in a dark blue suit motioned for him to stand on a small wooden plinth and he waited patiently as she ran a portable detector over his body. It buzzed as it went over his watch and he showed her his twenty-five-thousand-dollar diamond-encrusted watch, enjoying the jealousy that flashed across her face. The detector buzzed again as it passed over his wallet and he handed it to her. There was a thick wad of hundred-dollar bills inside, probably more than a year's salary for the girl, and all the credit cards were gold or platinum.

The Saudi stepped off the plinth, collected his briefcase and headed for the gate.

He walked by several television screens, all showing CNN. Groups of travellers were huddled in front of them. The Saudi frowned. A headline ran across the bottom of the nearest: HUNDREDS DEAD IN PHUKET. His mind whirled. Had the bomb gone off early? Had his people detonated the device by accident? Or had the police stormed the building, guns blazing? He frowned. There was a map of South East Asia on the screen now.

Another headline appeared: TSUNAMI KILLS THOUSANDS IN INDONESIA.

The frown deepened. A tsunami? His English was fluent but 'tsunami' looked like a Japanese word. Then he remembered. A tidal wave caused by an earthquake.

The map disappeared, replaced by two earnest newsreaders: a middle-aged man with blow-dried hair, and a woman ten years younger showing just enough cleavage to suggest that it wasn't solely her ability with the autocue that had got her the on-camera job. The man explained that a massive earthquake in the Andaman Sea had caused a tidal wave, which had hit beaches in Indonesia, Thailand and Malaysia. Thousands had been killed.

The Saudi went to a bank of payphones. He slotted in some coins and called the mobile number of his people in Phuket. A female Thai voice spoke for ten seconds, then repeated the information in accented English. The number was unobtainable.

The Saudi went to another television set and joined the throng of travellers watching the news. Another headline flashed up next to the CNN logo: DEATH TOLL ESTIMATED AT FIFTEEN THOUSAND.

Fifteen thousand? thought the Saudi. He had hoped to kill a few hundred at most, but nature had beaten him to the punch and killed thousands instead, including, probably, his four operatives. But nature would take credit for the death toll, not al-Qaeda. An act of terrorism that might have ignited a religious war in the south of Thailand had been replaced by a natural disaster that would unite the world in relief efforts. And, as always, the Americans would lead the charitable donations. It would do them no good in the long run, the Saudi knew. The Americans would always be hated for their arrogance, for the way they treated the world as if it were theirs by birthright, for the way they rode roughshod over cultures and civilisations millennia older than their own. But in the short term the news beamed round the world would show earnest American politicians pledging to do all they could to rebuild the region, American helicopters dropping supplies, American bankers offering financial aid.

The Saudi smiled wryly. He could do nothing to change what had happened. The Thais had a saying for it: *Jai yen*. Cool heart. Go with the flow. Nature had conspired to destroy his plans in Thailand. So be it. He couldn't fight nature.

As he reached the gate, passengers were already lining up to board the Qantas 747. The Saudi had never understood the urge to be first on to a plane. Even the first-class cabin wasn't an environment in which he was tempted to linger, but it was always those in Economy who seemed most eager to cram themselves into an uncomfortable seat in an aluminium tube where they would eat processed food on cue, watch poor-quality movies on a screen guaranteed to cause eyestrain, and breathe recycled air. The Saudi sat patiently until the last few passengers were boarding, then handed over his boarding card and passport to be checked and headed for the plane.

The seat next to his was empty. Most first-class passengers were seasoned travellers who would keep conversation to a minimum, but there were always exceptions and the Saudi was in no mood to make small-talk. He had a lot of thinking to do.

He was so deep in thought that he was barely aware of the huge plane powering along the runway, climbing into the sky and banking left over Bangkok as it headed south.

'Champagne, sir?'

The Saudi jerked as if he'd been stung. A blonde stewardess, wearing too much make-up, was holding a tray of filled champagne glasses. The Saudi thanked her and took one. He sipped. It wasn't a good vintage but, then, tastebuds lost most of their sensitivity at thirty thousand feet. The Saudi wasn't averse to alcohol. He had tried most drugs, out of curiosity rather than need. He ate pork: his favourite dish was the famous full English breakfast, complete with bacon, sausages and black pudding, ideally served at his regular table in the Grill Room at London's Savoy Hotel. So far as the Saudi was concerned, Islam wasn't about food choices, or whether one enjoyed a glass of champagne or a good malt whisky. Islam was about politics. And power.

The Saudi knew the Koran by heart, and could quote passages at length, word-perfect. But he didn't believe much of what the Holy Book contained. He didn't believe that martyrs to the cause were rewarded with seventy-two black-eyed virgins and that places in heaven were guaranteed for them and their relatives. There was much in the Koran that the Saudi didn't believe, in the same way that many Catholic priests did not believe in the literal truth of the Bible. The Koran was a tool for controlling people, as powerful as a gun or a bomb. The Saudi appreciated its power and he was as adept at using it as he was in the construction of bombs. So he sipped his champagne and felt not a twinge of guilt.

He listened to the couple in front of him talk about the tidal wave and the casualties. 'Those poor people,' said the woman, motioning for the stewardess to bring her more champagne.

'They're saying twenty thousand dead,' said the husband. 'Terrible. Thank God we weren't there.'

'Phuket's always too crowded this time of year.' The woman nodded at the stewardess as her glass was refilled. 'It's become too popular. Every man and his dog goes there, these days. Give me Koh Samui any day. Or the Maldives – at least there's still some exclusivity there.'

The Saudi closed his eyes and blocked out the inane chatter. Twenty thousand dead, he thought, killed by the forces of nature. Twenty thousand dead and for nothing.

It had been his decision to go for Phuket and he was sure it had been right. He had considered attacking the Khao San Road, Bangkok's backpacker centre, during Thai New Year, but had decided that the rich tourists of Phuket would be a more high-profile target.

He took a deep breath. What was done was done. It was time to move on. He already had his people in place for the next operation, and it dwarfed what he had planned for Phuket. Now he had to focus all his energy on what was to come. First Sydney. Then London. Both cities were about to discover what it was like to feel the wrath of Allah.

It was a smuggler's night, thick clouds scudding across the sky with only glimpses of a thin sliver of moon. The sea was rougher than the captain would have liked but the schedule had been fixed and he had already banked the advance payment. Ten thousand euros. Another ten thousand on delivery. Pretty good money for one night's work.

The stretch of water they were crossing was the busiest in the world, criss-crossed by thousands of craft every day. The captain knew it well, and that the odds on their boat being stopped were next to none. Neither the French government nor the British had the resources to check even a fraction of the boats that sailed between Britain and the Continent. The captain's name was Bernard Pepper – 'Bernie' to his aged mother, 'Skipper' to those who sailed with him, 'Chilli' to his friends. He was a big man, his cheeks mottled with broken veins from his years at sea, beard greying, wiry hair all but covered with a black wool hat.

There were two other men on the bridge. Tony Corke was in his thirties and, like Pepper, was wearing a dark blue pea coat, jeans and work boots. The third member of the crew was in his forties with a bullet-shaped shaven head and a British bulldog tattoo on his right forearm. His name was Andy Mosley and he'd done seven years in the Royal Navy, latterly as a communications specialist. Now he sat at a metal desk, monitoring the regular radio traffic on a receiver that was tuned to military and government frequencies. He was also watching a radar screen that showed all the traffic in their vicinity.

Corke took a stainless-steel hip flask from the back pocket of his jeans and sipped. The neat Jameson's whiskey slipped down his throat and spread a warming glow across his chest. He held it out to the captain.

Pepper scowled at the flask. 'What is it?'

'Whiskey.'

'Scotch or Irish?'

'Since when have you been so fussy?' Corke started to put it back into his pocket.

Pepper let go of the wheel with his left hand and gripped Corke's shoulder with thick fingers. 'I didn't say I didn't want it. I just wanted to know its heritage,' he growled.

Corke handed him the flask. Pepper took two big gulps, wiped his mouth on his sleeve, and gave it back. 'That's about all the Irish are good for,' he said. 'Guinness and Jameson's.'

'What about Joyce, Wilde, Shaw, Swift?'

'What?' Pepper belched, and Corke caught a whiff of garlic. They'd had lunch at a small café near Calais and Pepper had wolfed down two plates of calamari.

'Irish literary giants,' said Corke. 'Then there's the Irish poets. William Butler Yeats. Seamus Heaney. And the music – U2, the Corrs. Film directors like Sheridan and Jordan. Not bad for a population of three million.' He offered the flask to Mosley, who shook his head.

'Wouldn't have put you down as a Paddy-lover,' said Pepper. 'You said you were from Bristol.'

'Used to holiday in Galway when I was a kid,' said Corke. 'That's where I learned to sail.'

'You can't trust the Micks,' said Pepper. 'They'll steal the enamel from your teeth.'

'That's what you said about the Armenians,' said Corke.

'They're as bad as the Micks,' said Pepper.

'Let's face it, you hate pretty much everyone.'

Pepper laughed harshly. 'I met a Russian guy once and liked him. And you're okay, Tony, for a sheep-shagger.'

'I thought that was the Welsh.'

'Bristol's in Wales, innit?'

Corke shook his head. 'I give up,' he said. He unwrapped a stick of gum and popped it into his mouth.

'Why don't you check on the cargo?' said Pepper. He swung the wheel hard to the left, keeping the prow into the waves. 'Looks like we're going to beat the weather.'

Corke nodded. The forecast had been for squalls and showers but the rain had held off and with any luck it would stay that way until they reached the Northumberland coast. Not that heavy weather would make much of an impression on the sixty-five-foot trawler: it had been built to fish out in the Atlantic and was practically unsinkable. Its huge diesel engine would power the vessel through any weather and it was equipped with state-of-the-art navigation systems. Plus a few other tricks, courtesy of Andy Mosley.

Corke shoved his hip flask into his back pocket and pushed open the door that led to the deck. Spray flecked his face and he licked his lips, tasting salt. He swayed as he walked, trying to match his gait to the movement of the boat. He wasn't wearing a life-jacket. They were for wimps, said Pepper, and Pepper was the captain. Corke knelt down and pushed open the wooden hatch, the entrance to the hold where fishermen would store their catch, packed in ice.

Anxious faces gazed up at him, men, women and children: a catch far more profitable than fish. There were thirty-four in the hold and each was paying several thousand euros to be delivered safe and sound to Britain. Pepper and the men he worked for didn't care where the immigrants were from, how old they were, or why they wanted to get into the United Kingdom. All they cared about was that they had the money to pay for their passage. There were two girls among them who couldn't have been more than eight, and Pepper had told Corke they were charged the same rate as the adults. 'A body's a body,' the captain had said.

'Everybody okay?' Corke shouted down.

A few men nodded fearfully. They were all wrapped up against the cold in thick jackets and scarves, and the children were swathed in blankets that a woman had brought on board.

'We need more water,' said a middle-aged Oriental woman. She was probably Chinese, thought Corke. She was with her husband, teenage son and half a dozen nylon duffel bags, the first to complain when Pepper had told them there weren't any life-jackets. 'This is a trawler, not the *QE* bloody *Two*,' Pepper had shouted, adding that she could like it or lump it but she wouldn't get a refund if she stayed behind. She had glared at him and muttered something in her own language, but she and her family had climbed on.

'I'll get you some,' said Corke.

'And one of the women over there is sick,' she said.

Corke peered down to where she was pointing. Two women in headscarves were squatting against the bulkhead. The younger of them was coughing while the other had an arm round her and was dabbing at her head with a cloth. 'Are you okay there?' asked Corke.

'They don't speak English,' said the Chinese woman, scornfully. 'Why are they going to England if they cannot speak the language?'

Corke swung himself through the hatch and felt for the metal ladder. His boots found the rungs and he lowered himself into the belly of the boat. The stench of fish was almost overpowering and he had to fight to stop himself throwing up. He went over to the two women and knelt down beside the sick one. He felt her forehead with the back of his hand. It was hot and her skin was wet with sweat.

'Do you know what's wrong with her?' Corke asked her companion.

She said something in a language he couldn't understand and shrugged.

'She is seasick,' said a man in the shadows.

Corke beckoned him closer. He was in his thirties, olive-skinned with pockmarked cheeks and a thick moustache. An Afghan, maybe, or Iranian. 'She's your wife?' Corke asked.

The man nodded. 'She is seasick,' he said. 'That is all.'

'No, she has an infection,' said Corke. 'She's burning up.'

'If she's sick, she shouldn't be here,' the Chinese woman hissed. 'We could all get sick.'

Corke ignored her. 'Does anyone have any water?' he shouted. He had given them a pack of twelve litre bottles of mineral water before they had left port.

'It has all gone,' said the man.

'That's why I said we needed more,' said the Chinese woman. 'They drank it all. I said we should ration it, but they wouldn't listen.'

'Okay,' said Corke. He felt the woman's head again. She was way too hot. 'I'll see if we've got some medicine too.' He had no idea what was wrong with the woman, but such a high tempera-ture suggested an infection, and with any luck Pepper would have antibiotics in the boat's medical kit.

The boat swayed hard to the left and Corke stumbled against three black men who were squatting on the floor. They had been speaking French and Corke figured they were probably West Africans. He apologised, also in French, and they waved dis-missively.

Corke straightened up. 'Look, a few hours and we'll be in the UK,' he shouted. 'I'll get you some more water. Just relax, and you'll soon be on dry land.' He repeated it in French, then climbed back up the ladder and closed the hatch.

Pepper glanced over his shoulder as Corke walked into the bridge. 'Now what?' he said.

'They need more water, and there's a sick woman down there.'

'Fuck them,' said Pepper. 'They're paying for passage, not a bloody cruise.'

There was a first-aid kit on the wall by the door. Corke opened it and rifled through the contents. Bandages, plasters, antiseptic ointment, an emergency dental pack and a few plastic pill bottles. Corke read the labels. They were all painkillers of one form or another, aspirin, paracetamol, codeine. 'There's no antibiotics,' said Corke.

'What the fuck do you need antibiotics for?' snarled Pepper.

'She's got a temperature.' Corke took the paracetamol. It would be better than nothing. 'I need more water.'

'There's some in the galley,' said Mosley, 'and sodas in the fridge.'

Corke flashed him a thumbs-up. The ship rolled to the right and he staggered against the door, hard enough to wind him. He swore and rubbed his ribs.

'Where's your sea legs, Corke?' Pepper laughed.

Mosley frowned and twisted a dial on his receiver panel. 'Keep it down,' he said. 'I hear traffic.'

'What sort of traffic?' said Pepper.

'Coastguard, I think,' said Mosley. 'Talking to the navy.'

He pulled on his headphones and twisted another dial. Corke stood behind him.

'Shit!' hissed Pepper. 'That's all we need.'

Mosley's face screwed up as he concentrated. Then he took off his headphones. 'A navy frigate is looking for us as a possible drugs boat,' he said.

Pepper swore again.

'And there's a spotter plane on its way,' said Mosley.

'What's the radar show?'

'Nothing yet.'

Pepper looked at his GPS and did a few calculations in his head. 'There's no way we're going to make it,' he said. He slapped his gloved hand against the wheel.

'What do we do?' asked Mosley.

Pepper consulted his watch, then the GPS again. 'This is my nineteenth run,' he said. 'Eighteen without a hitch. Now this.'

'Can we outrun them?' asked Corke.

'We're not built for speed,' said Pepper. 'If the plane flies below the cloud layer we're sitting ducks.' He slapped the wheel again. 'I'm not going down for a hold full of asylum-seekers. Screw them.'

'We could say they're stowaways,' said Corke, 'that they sneaked on board before we left.'

'They'd talk,' said Pepper. 'They'd spill their guts to do a deal with Immigration. As soon as they set foot on UK soil all they have to do is say the magic word "asylum" and it's a free council house and cash in their hands while we go down for seven years.' He waved at Corke to step forward. 'Take the wheel,' he said. 'Keep her on this heading.'

'Where are you going?' said Corke.

'To talk to them,' said Pepper. 'Andy, you come with me.'

Mosley put his headphones on the metal table and followed him out on to the deck.

Corke bit down on his lower lip. He had a bad feeling about what was happening. A very bad feeling. He looked over his shoulder at the radar screen. There were several blips on the monitor but, to Corke's untrained eye, they meant nothing.

The boat lurched up, crashed down, and water surged over the prow. Corke turned the wheel to keep into the waves. He leaned forward and craned his neck to peer up through the windshield. He recognised several of the constellations overhead, but there was no sign of a spotter plane. Down below he saw Pepper walking along the deck, Mosley close behind.

He was drifting to starboard so he turned the wheel to the left. The trawler was responsive despite its bulk. An autopilot unit was set into the roof of the bridge, a simple enough piece of equipment that would keep the boat on whatever heading was keyed in. This stretch of water was too busy for boats to travel on autopilot, but he had no choice. He keyed in the heading, then hurried across the bridge and hauled open the door.

Half a dozen passengers had climbed out of the hold and were huddled together on the deck. Three men, two women and a little girl. East Europeans, by the look of them. The child couldn't have been more than ten and was clutching a blanket over her shoulders. One of the women had an arm around her. The mother, maybe.

Pepper had his back to the bridge. Mosley was standing a few feet away from him, his hands out to the side as if he was trying to soothe a panicky horse. Pepper was shouting down through the hatch, yelling at the rest of the passengers to get on to the deck.

Mosley saw Corke first. Pepper saw his reaction and turned. He was holding a large handgun. An automatic. 'What the hell are you doing?' he shouted.

'What's going on?' yelled Corke. The wind tore away his words.

'Get back to the wheel,' roared Pepper.

Corke walked towards the captain but stopped when he levelled the gun at his chest. Corke spat out his chewing-gum and the wind whipped it over the side of the boat.

'You heard what I said!' screamed Pepper. 'Back!'

A face appeared at the hatch. One of the Iranians. Pepper ordered him to climb out and join the others on the deck.

'Andy, you can't let him do this!' shouted Corke. The boat lurched to starboard and water spilled over the deck, soaking the legs of his jeans. The door to the bridge slammed behind him.

'He's the one with the gun!' bellowed Mosley.

'It's not about the gun,' said Corke. 'It's about throwing innocent men, women and children into the sea. That's murder, Andy. Cold-blooded murder, gun or no gun.'

'They're scum!' shouted Pepper. 'I'm not going to prison for scum. The navy are on the way – they'll pick them up.' He grabbed the Iranian by his coat collar. 'You! Over the side!'

'Even if they can swim the cold'll kill them in five minutes,' protested Corke.

Pepper waved the gun in his face. 'Do you want to join them? Because I'm easy either way.'

'I'm not going to let you kill them,' said Corke, taking a step towards him.

Pepper's finger tightened on the trigger.

Corke stared at him. 'You'd better be good with that thing,' he said, his voice barely audible over the sound of the waves hitting the side of the boat. 'Hard enough on a range, but hitting a target on a moving ship takes some doing. Doubt you'll do it with one shot. What's the clip hold? Thirteen? Thirteen shots, thirty-four people. Plus me, of course. The numbers don't work, Chilli.'

The captain grinned and reached into his pea coat with his left hand. He pulled out a loaded clip.

Corke's face tightened.

'Not so confident now, are we?' said Pepper. 'Now, you've got two choices. Back on the bridge and keep us heading west, or you take your chances over the side with them. With or without a bullet.'

Corke looked at Mosley, who was staring white-faced at the gun.

'Andy?'

He said nothing.

Pepper snarled and took step towards Corke. One of the men was pleading in a language that sounded like Russian. Pepper ignored him and kept the gun aimed at Corke. He knew the man was about to fire and that there was nothing he could do to stop him. He had no weapon, nothing to fight with, nothing to throw as a distraction, and the heavy clothing and boots he was wearing meant there was no way he could reach Pepper before he pulled the trigger.

His stomach heaved as the deck slammed upwards. He staggered back against the bridge door. Pepper almost lost his balance but stayed on his feet and kept the gun on him. The bow pointed almost straight up into the night sky and, for a second, Corke was weightless before it crashed into the sea. He fell to the deck and rolled over, slipped as he tried to get to his feet and hit the deck again.

The boat tipped to starboard and Corke slammed into the guardrail. He grabbed for it and hauled himself up.

'Get back to the bridge!' screamed Pepper. 'The sea's too

rough for the autopilot!' He fired the gun and a bullet cracked through the air. 'The next one is in your head!'

'Do as he says!' howled Mosley. 'He means it!'

The ship rolled to port and Corke gripped the rail, fighting to stay upright. Pepper laughed. 'Call yourself a sailor,' he sneered.

One of the male passengers yelled and Corke turned in time to see the little girl fall over the guardrail. Her mother shrieked and lunged for her but it was too late. The child was gone.

Corke rushed across the deck as the bow rose again. Pepper fired at him but the boat lurched and the shot went wide. Corke hit him with his shoulder, knocking him off-balance, then kicked out at his left leg, catching him behind the knee. As Pepper went down, Corke slashed him across the throat with the edge of his hand. Pepper pitched face down on to the deck.

The two women were screaming, eyes wide with horror. Corke reached them and looked over the side. He saw a flash of white. The child's face. Two white blurs. Her hands. He swore. Then he ripped off his pea coat and jumped over the side, arms flailing.

He hit the water, which engulfed him, so cold it numbed him immediately. He kicked for the surface, feeling his boots fill with water. He kicked harder, but his jeans were sticking to his legs, dragging him down. He took in a mouthful of water, then broke through to the surface and spat fiercely. He saw the child several metres away, kicked hard and swam towards her.

A wave crashed over him and his mouth filled with water again. He spat and gasped for breath. His pullover was hindering his movements so he trod water and pulled it off. The weight of his wet trousers was pulling him down. Despite the cold his leg muscles were burning. He let go of the pullover and swam on towards the little girl. Every stroke was an effort and his chest felt as if a clamp was squeezing the life from him.

He trod water again, trying to see where she was, then glanced over his shoulder at the trawler. Mosley was pointing at him, a woman at his side – the child's mother, maybe. Corke saw Pepper pull Mosley back, then lost sight of the boat in the swell.

He carried on swimming. The child was thrashing around in

the water and as he drew closer he heard her scream. It was cut short as she disappeared beneath a wave. Corke took a deep breath as a wave carried him up, then dropped him. His right hand slapped into something – the child. He grabbed her collar and pulled her to him. 'It's all right!' he shouted. 'I've got you!'

She was in shock. Her mouth was moving soundlessly, eyes blank and lifeless. Corke turned her so that her back was to him, then pushed his arm round her waist and kicked to keep himself upright in the heaving water. He could feel the strength draining from his legs and took a quick look over his shoulder. Through the swell he saw the trawler. Fifty metres away, maybe more. In a swimming-pool, he'd make it with ease, but in the freezing water, weighed down with wet clothing, he knew it might as well have been fifty miles. The current was carrying him away from the boat. And even if it hadn't been, it was all he could do to keep the child above water. There was no way he could swim for them both.

Water crashed over them and Corke pushed the child up, trying to keep her in the air.

It was hopeless. With every kick he felt weaker and he knew he was dying of hypothermia. The freezing water was sucking the life out of him, second by second. He held the child with his left arm and thrashed around with the right. His head went under and he coughed, spluttering. He didn't want to die, but he was so tired that he couldn't fight the water any longer. He held the child tighter. She was crying now, great sobs that racked her body. 'I'm sorry,' said Corke. 'I'm so sorry.'

He couldn't feel his legs now, couldn't tell if they were moving or not. He was impossibly cold, and more tired than he'd ever been before. He was breathing fast and shallow, and he knew that was bad because the stale air would stay deep in his lungs. His head went under and he closed his eyes. He knew that all he had to do was take in a lungful of water and it would be over. Drowning wasn't so bad. There was no panic, just tiredness and a gradual acceptance that he would die. It was the little girl he felt sorry for, with her whole life ahead of her. He'd been married, had a child, travelled the world. He'd lived a full life, and death was a natural part of it. But she hadn't even begun to live. It was so damned unfair. Corke roared and kicked with all the strength he had left. He didn't want the child to die but there was nothing he could do to save her. In his heart of hearts he'd known that from the moment he'd followed her into the water, but he'd had to try. And now he would die with her.

He leaned back in the water, holding her to his chest. Water washed over his face, stinging his eyes and filling his ears.

Suddenly a light shone on his face, so bright that it was blinding. He closed his eyes. His whole body was numb and he had no energy to swim. His body went limp in the water. At least he had tried. He felt totally relaxed, at peace with what was happening to him.

The blood was draining from his extremities, retreating to the body's core – the final stage of hypothermia. He would feel nothing in the final seconds. There were worse ways to die, he decided.

The light was still there, so intense that it burned through his eyelids. And now there was a roaring, thudding noise. He opened his eyes and gasped as a wave washed over him. He coughed, retched, then blinked up at the light. It was as bright as day. Brighter. An intense white light filled the night sky. Then he saw the figure dropping down towards him. A figure in orange with a white head like a giant insect. Corke smiled. It was an angel from heaven. He wanted to tell the angel that he didn't believe in heaven. Hell, maybe, but there was no such place as heaven. And if there was no heaven, there were no angels. The figure kept descending. An orange jumpsuit. Black boots. Corke's face went under the water, his eyes still open. It didn't sting any more. Nothing hurt. There was no pain, and no fear. Just acceptance.

The figure hit the water, and Corke felt arms surround him in an enveloping bear hug. He closed his eyes and slid into unconsciousness.

★   ★   ★

Sam Hargrove walked quickly along the hospital corridor, heels squeaking on the linoleum. His shoes were handmade and they shone under the overhead fluorescent lights. He was wearing a black wool overcoat over a dark blue pinstripe suit and a pale yellow shirt; his red tie was decorated with miniature cricket bats. He was carrying a bulging leather briefcase, scuffed at the corners, and he swung it in time with his walk. A middle-aged nurse stepped out of a side room and blocked his way. 'Can I help you?' she asked.

'I'm here to see Anthony Corke,' said Hargrove. He brushed his greying hair across his forehead. 'He was brought in about six hours ago.' He spelt out Corke's surname slowly, as if she had learning difficulties.

She frowned. 'And you are?'

'His solicitor,' said Hargrove, the lie coming as naturally as his smile.

'Visiting hours are between five and seven,' she said curtly.

Hargrove continued to smile, but his eyes hardened. 'My client has been arrested on a serious charge, and he has a right to legal representation. Any interference with it would result in a claim for damages laid against this hospital. I'm sure your NHS trust's administrator wouldn't want that, now, would he?'

'There's a policeman with him,' said the nurse.

'Which is why he needs my counsel,' said Hargrove. He made a show of looking at his watch. 'I don't have all day, Miss . . .' He peered at the nurse's name-tag. 'Miss Longworth. I know it's a frightful cliché, but my time really is money.'

The nurse pointed down the corridor. 'It's the third room on the left.'

'Thank you,' said Hargrove, and headed along the corridor. He opened the door without knocking. A young uniformed police-man was leaning against a large cast-iron radiator. As the door opened he jolted upright and straightened, hands behind his back. 'You're not supposed to be in here,' he said.

Hargrove looked round the room. There was only one bed.

The occupant's eyes were closed, his hands at his sides. He was wearing a pale blue surgical gown. There was monitoring equipment on the table next to the bed but it wasn't switched on. A thin chain ran from the man's ankle to the metal rail at the foot. 'I'm Mr Corke's solicitor,' said Hargrove. 'Can you explain to me why he's chained to the bed?'

'My chief inspector's orders, sir,' said the constable.

'My client has just been dragged out of the North Sea,' said Hargrove. 'He almost drowned.'

'I'm told he has to be restrained,' said the constable.

'It's an infringement of his human rights,' said Hargrove. 'My understanding is that Mr Corke hasn't been charged.'

'I'm just doing as I was told, sir,' said the constable.

'I need a word with my client,' said Hargrove. 'In private.'

'I'm supposed to stay with him,' said the constable.

'How long have you been in the job, son?'

'A year,' said the constable, defensively.

'That's long enough to know that lawyer–client conversations are confidential,' said Hargrove. 'He's not going anywhere with that chain on his leg. You can wait on the other side of the door. Or you can do the smart thing and take the opportunity to have a quick smoke or a coffee outside. Up to you.'

The constable held Hargrove's eye for several seconds, then left the room.

Hargrove put down his briefcase and stared at the man on the bed. 'Shepherd, do you always have to be so bloody heroic?' he asked. 'You almost gave me a heart-attack, throwing yourself into the sea. You're an undercover cop, not a bloody lifeguard.'

Shepherd opened his eyes. 'She was a kid,' he said.

Hargrove shook his head. 'I suppose I'm going to have to put you in for another commendation,' he said.

'Is she okay?'

'She's in ICU but she'll be fine.' Hargrove sat down on the metal chair and straightened the creases in his trousers. 'If the helicopter hadn't spotted you . . .'

'I couldn't let her die.'

'Pepper was going to throw them all into the sea. What was your plan? Save everybody?'

'She was a kid,' said Shepherd again.

'And what if the helicopter hadn't been there, Spider? What if I'd had to go and tell Liam his father wasn't coming home?'

'It was instinctive.'

'It was foolhardy,' said Hargrove. 'Brave, but foolhardy.'

'All's well that ends well,' said Shepherd. He sat up and pointed at the chain. 'Can you take that off me so I can get out of here?'

'We need to talk first,' said Hargrove.

'That sounds ominous.'

Hargrove examined the room. 'Not bad, considering it's NHS,' he said. 'Floor even looks as if it's been cleaned some time this century.'

'Do we know what went wrong?' asked Shepherd. 'I'm assuming you didn't send the navy to intercept us.'

'We were waiting to pick you up on Holy Island as planned. The local drugs squad had an informant in the French port. He thought the trawler was leaving with drugs and called his handler in Europol. By then it was in international waters but Europol were on the ball for once. They called Custom House and the night man took a decision. There was a Royal Navy frigate in the area, and Bob's your uncle.'

'What a cock-up.'

'Just one of those things,' said Hargrove. 'There was no way we could have tipped off everyone in advance.'

'What about Pepper?'

'He's under arrest for trafficking and attempted murder. The illegals are lining up to give evidence. If nothing else, it means they're guaranteed to stay in the country until the trial.'

'Mosley was going to help toss them overboard, but Pepper didn't give him much choice.'

'He's co-operating. Pepper pulling a gun on him changed his viewpoint and he's giving us all the info we need on the French end. Job well done, Spider. Not the way we planned it, but we've smashed their operation.'

Shepherd jiggled his leg, rattling the chain. 'So, I'm out of here, right?'

'Let me run something by you first,' said Hargrove. 'The parents of the girl you rescued were from Kosovo. They had a couple of suitcases with them. One contained three large cooking-oil cans filled with a hell of a lot of cash. Just under a million euros in five-hundred euro notes.'

'They could have gone first class for that,' said Shepherd, bought passports, new identities, the works.'

'The money's counterfeit, which is why we think they're couriers. They don't know that we've found it.'

'But why run counterfeit euros from Europe into the UK? The UK's about the only country left that doesn't use the euro.'

'Good question,' said the superintendent.

'You want me to talk to them – me being the hero and all?'

Hargrove flashed him a tight smile. 'They've been asking for you. They want to thank you. It'd be an opening.'

'Makes sense,' said Shepherd.

'We need to know where the notes were made, and where they were going.'

'And I stay in character?'

'Let's see how it works,' said Hargrove. 'We'll put you in the police station with them and give you a chance for a chat. If it doesn't work, we'll get Immigration to sweat them.'

'How good are the notes?' asked Shepherd.

'They're not good,' said Hargrove. 'They're perfect, the real McCoy. Watermark, ink, paper, all genuine. The only way to tell they're not real currency is by the numbers, which are sequential but haven't been issued by the European Bank.'

'Which means what?'

Hargrove shrugged. 'The only people with access to that sort of printing equipment are governments. North Korea, maybe. They did the US superbills a few years back. But that's hypothetical. Which is why I need you to talk to the girl's parents.'

'Okay. Where and when?'

Hargrove took a set of handcuffs from his pocket. 'We'll get them in here, just to start the ball rolling. Then we'll run them down to Newcastle nick and process them. We'll put you in a cell with the father and you can take it from there.'

Shepherd shook his left leg and the chain rattled. 'This is a pain,' he said.

'It's got to look like you're one of the bad guys,' said the superintendent.

'Some way to treat a hero,' Shepherd said ruefully. 'I told the woodentop outside that I needed to use the loo and they offered to give me a bottle to piss in. They haven't given me any food either.'

'I'll get it sorted,' promised Hargrove.

'I wouldn't mind a phone, too, so that I can call Liam.'

'Tomorrow. Soon as you're in the van to the station.' The superintendent stood up. 'I'm serious about the commendation.'

'I'm serious about the loo,' said Shepherd.

It was late evening when a female uniformed police officer brought the little girl's parents to Shepherd's room. A male nurse had brought him a cheese sandwich and a lukewarm cup of tea. Shepherd hadn't eaten anything since he'd left France and he'd wolfed it down.

The police officer opened the door and ushered the couple in. 'Five minutes,' she said brusquely. 'I'll wait outside.'

The young uniformed officer who had been guarding Shepherd all afternoon was sitting on a metal chair in the corner of the room, reading a copy of the *Sun*.

'Any chance of a bit of privacy?' said Shepherd.

'I'm not your bloody butler,' said the policeman.

'And I'm not going anywhere, chained to the bed, am I?' He jerked his head at the door. 'Besides, it'd give you a chance to chat her up, wouldn't it?'

The officer sighed, stood up and dropped his paper on to the chair. He glared at Shepherd as he left the room.

'Alone at last,' said Shepherd.

The man and woman frowned, not understanding. Shepherd hadn't paid them much attention on the boat. They'd been wrapped in warm clothes, their heads swathed in thick scarves, the man carrying two bulky suitcases, the woman fussing over their daughter. Without their heavy clothing and under the hospital's fluorescent lights he could see that they were in their early thirties. The man was square-jawed with a two-day growth of stubble, and the woman's face was pinched with deep worry lines etched into the forehead.

'How is your daughter?' Shepherd asked.

The woman stepped forward, took his left hand in hers and pressed it to her cheek. She spoke to him in a language he didn't understand. They were from Kosovo, Hargrove had said, which would make them economic migrants, rather than genuine refugees, Shepherd knew. The ethnic-cleansing horrors of the former Yugoslavia were a thing of the past, but few economic migrants travelled with a million euros.

'My wife says we owe you everything,' said her husband, in halting English.

'Is she okay, your little girl?'

The man's eyes glistened, as if he were close to tears. 'Her name is Jessica. The doctors say she will be good soon,' he said. 'Because of you she is alive.'

The woman spoke to Shepherd again, tears running down her cheeks. She looked into his eyes as she spoke, and even though Shepherd couldn't understand what she was saying he could feel gratitude pouring out of her.

'My wife says we can never thank you enough,' said her husband. 'She is Edita. I am Rudi.'

He stuck out a hand and Shepherd shook it. 'Tell her I'm a father,' said Shepherd. 'I'm just glad I was able to help.'

'You could have died,' said Rudi. 'You do not know us but you risked your life to save our daughter.' He translated for his wife. She nodded and kissed the back of Shepherd's hand.

'Where are you from?' asked Shepherd.

'Kosovo,' said Rudi. 'We want a new life in England. For us and for our daughter.'

The wife spoke to her husband and pointed at the chain attached to Shepherd's leg.

'Why are you chained?' he asked.

'The police did it,' said Shepherd. 'I'm under arrest.'

'But you saved our daughter.'

Shepherd forced a smile. 'They don't care,' he said. 'All they care about is that I was helping to bring you to England. I'll probably go to prison.'

Rudi spoke to his wife, then nodded sympathetically at him. 'I am sorry for what is happening to you,' he said.

'It's not your fault,' said Shepherd.

'The captain, he was trying to make us jump into the sea.'

'He'll be going to prison too.'

'He is an evil man.'

'No question about that,' said Shepherd. 'Have they said what will happen to you?'

'The police say they want us to go to court, to tell what happened. I am not sure that is a good idea.' Rudi glanced around nervously as if he feared being overheard. 'The men we paid to go on the boat, they are dangerous. If we help the police . . .' He left the sentence unfinished.

'The police can help you,' said Shepherd. 'They might let you stay in England.'

'That is what they said,' said Rudi. 'But I cannot risk my wife and daughter. We will say nothing and they will send us back to Kosovo. We will try again, maybe next year.' He put his arm round his wife's shoulders. 'We are very grateful,' he said. 'We will never forget you. What is your name?'

'Tony,' said Shepherd. 'Tony Corke.'

'We will never forget you, Tony Corke,' he said. 'And we will make sure that our daughter never forgets the name of the man who saved her life.'

'I'm just glad she's okay,' said Shepherd.

The female officer returned and took them away. Her colleague closed the door and stood at the end of the bed. 'You jumped into the sea to save a little girl?' he asked.

'Yeah,' said Shepherd.

'They said you nearly died.'

'It was pretty close.'

'Bloody brave.'

'Spur of the moment.'

'No life-jacket or anything?'

'There wasn't time,' said Shepherd. 'Like I said, it was a spur-of-the-moment thing. She went over the side and I went in after her.'

'There's not many would have done the same.'

'The kid was going to die. I couldn't stand by and watch.' Shepherd lay back and closed his eyes. He heard the officer walk to the chair and the legs scrape as he sat down.

'If you want anything, a coffee or whatever, let me know,' said the policeman. 'Or if there's anyone you want me to call, I'll pass on a message.'

'Thanks, but no thanks,' said Shepherd. 'Just fuck off and leave me be.' He could have done with some coffee but it was important to stay in character. He couldn't afford to give the impression that he was more than a criminal facing a jail term.

The Saudi toyed with his salad of seared tuna niçoise and looked over Circular Quay towards the Sydney Opera House, which squatted by the water like a huge beetle unfolding its wings. It would have been a superb target, but the area around it was too open, the tourists too spread out, and casualties, even from a large bomb, would be limited. He was sitting in a much better target, logistically and politically. The Hyatt Hotel was at the base of the Sydney Harbour Bridge, which spanned the entrance to Circular Quay and was one of the most recognisable structures in the world. A bomb in the hotel's restaurant on a Sunday lunch-time would kill up to a hundred people, and images of the devastation would be shown round the world, the aftermath of the explosion and, behind it, the bridge. It would be as powerful an image as that of the airliners flying into the Twin Towers in New York.

. Hotels were practically the perfect target, the Saudi knew, especially American-owned chains. Embassies were good for shock value, but generally more locals were killed than foreign nationals. Hotels were full of wealthy foreigners. The sort that newspaper editors liked to splash across their front pages. It was the way the world worked. Kill a hundred Pakistanis in Lahore and no one outside the country would care. Kill five hundred Nigerians in Lagos and the world's newspapers wouldn't devote more than a few paragraphs to the story. But kill a single American in Sydney and it would be on the front page of every newspaper in the United States, and a breaking story on every television channel.

The Saudi chewed a sliver of tuna, but barely tasted it. A young couple were sitting at a table by the window, drinking cappuccino and discussing whether or not to take one of the guided walking tours across the bridge. They had London accents, and the man was wearing a Chelsea football shirt. A German couple at the next table were drinking a bottle of white wine and encouraging their two young children to eat their pasta. One of the children, a chubby-faced toddler, smiled at the Saudi and waved a fork at him. The Saudi smiled back. He imagined a bomb going off in the middle of the restaurant. The flash of light, the explosion, the shrapnel ripping through bodies, the glass exploding across the walkway and into the blue-green waters of the harbour. Dismembered limbs, blood, entrails, the moans of the injured and dying, the screams of the living. The Saudi didn't make a habit of visiting the targets he intended to destroy, but sometimes it was too good an opportunity to miss. There was little police presence at the harbour, and he'd seen hardly any CCTV cameras. Not that it mattered. There was nothing to connect him with what was about to happen. By the time the bombs exploded he would already be out of the country. His flight to the United Kingdom left at just before five o'clock in the afternoon but the cell who would carry out the operation wouldn't arrive for another week.

They had all been trained and the explosives and detonators were already in the country, hidden in a self-storage facility in Melbourne.

The Saudi sipped his white wine. He liked Australian wine, especially the whites: it was unpretentious, like the Australian people.

A blonde woman in a beige *hijab* walked by, a flowing blue coat over her shirt and jeans. A convert after marriage, the Saudi was sure. An Australian, maybe. She was talking into a mobile phone, and laughing. The Saudi hoped there wouldn't be any Muslims in the vicinity when the bomb went off, but if there were, so be it. There were always casualties in a war, and the *jihad* was no exception. Hundreds of Muslims had died when the World Trade Center collapsed, but what had happened on that September morning had been a clarion call to the whole Muslim world.

The Saudi put down his fork, emptied his glass and paid his bill. His waitress was a cheerful girl with a bright smile, her dark brown hair held back from her face with a large blue plastic clip. The Saudi wished her a good day as he left the restaurant, and wondered whether she would be among the dead.

He strolled along the wooden boardwalk and watched the ferries ploughing through the water and behind them a flotilla of sailing boats, toys for the city's rich. It was a hot day and he walked slowly, seeking out shade where he could. The heat meant that the martyrs couldn't use vests packed with explosives so the bombs would be packed into rucksacks. There were plenty of backpackers around and no one was paying them any attention. He turned right in to George Street and walked up the sloping road through the weekend stalls of Rooks Market. Under tented canopies stallholders were selling things only tourists would want to buy: painted boomerangs, home-made fudge, soft toys, framed photographs of Sydney landmarks, bowls made from local wood.

It was another perfect target, thought the Saudi, with lots of wealthy tourists for the Western media to mourn. He paused by the Mercantile Hotel. The first bomb would go off there, detonated by a martyr sitting at one of the tables outside the Molly Malone bar. Nuts and bolts would be packed round the explosives to turn into deadly shrapnel that would rip through the stalls and the shoppers. Those who survived would run down the road towards the harbour. The second bomb would go off just a minute later, at the La Mela Café opposite the Old Sydney Holiday Inn, and catch them as they fled.

The Saudi looked at his watch. There was a concert at the Sydney Opera House later that night and he was looking forward to it. He always enjoyed Mozart. He had acquired his taste for classical music from his father, although the older man preferred Schubert and Brahms. The Saudi's father had taken him to concerts and the opera since he was seven. He remembered two things in particular of his childhood: his father's lectures on classical music, and his hatred of the West. The war to end all wars, his father had said, would be the battle between Islam and Christianity. And Islam would prevail. He had rubbed the back of his son's neck and told him that, one day, he would have a part to play in it. The Saudi's father had worked for the Saudi Royal Family, which had brought him his wealth and their British passports. He had insisted that a British education was the best in the world, even though it had meant that his son spent most of his childhood away from his family. The Saudi's father had beamed with pride when he had left Eton with a clutch of A levels, and on the day he'd graduated from the London School of Economics he'd presented him with a gleaming red Ferrari.

The Saudi had been with his father on 11 September 2001 in the family's compound in Riyadh, and they had watched the destruction of the World Trade Center on CNN. It was the start of the war, the Saudi's father had said, and it was time for the son to play his part. Introductions were made, oaths were sworn, and the Saudi had started on his path to *jihad*.

The Saudi would have liked to have taken his father to the concert that night, but he was old now and rarely left Riyadh. Besides, he refused to wear anything but traditional Arab garb and he would have attracted too much attention.

He walked through the stalls, listening to the different languages being spoken by the tourists: Chinese, French, German, British, a veritable smorgasbord of victims. He stopped by a stall selling didgeridoos. A middle-aged white man wearing a black and white bandana tied round his head was showing an American family how to play the Aboriginal instrument. A little blonde girl was jumping up and down, clapping her hands excitedly. 'Can we buy it, Daddy?' she pleaded. 'Can we?'

The Saudi took no pleasure in killing children – he took no pleasure in killing anyone, but there was no alternative. The Israelis had killed thousands of innocent Palestinians. The Americans had killed tens of thousands of men, women and children in Iraq with bombs and bullets. The Saudi saw no difference between what the Israelis and the Americans did and the actions of the *shahid*. Death was death, whether it was carried out by soldiers or martyrs.

The *jihad* was continuing in Iraq, with Allied soldiers dying almost every day. But it was only when civilian contractors were kidnapped and beheaded that the world took notice and governments acted. The death of a civilian was worth the death of a hundred paid soldiers. It was simple economics.

The father handed over the money for the didgeridoo and picked up his daughter. She squealed, threw her arms round his neck and kissed his cheek. The Saudi walked away towards the harbour. He had never married and had no children. What he was doing was too important to jeopardise with a family. Families were a weakness for soldiers of the *jihad*.

Superintendent Hargrove arrived at the hospital with two of his agents playing ordinary detectives. They flashed their warrant cards at the uniformed officer and told him they would be taking Corke to Newcastle police station and that they would be accompanied by his solicitor. Hargrove said nothing, playing the part of a solicitor who was about to break bad news to his client.

The men with him were wearing dark raincoats over shabby suits and the world-weary look of policemen who had been in the job long enough not to be surprised by anything. Shepherd knew one of them – Jimmy 'Razor' Sharpe, a twenty-year veteran of the Strathclyde Police. As soon as the uniform had left the room Sharpe winked and unlocked Shepherd's chain. 'Always the hero, Spider,' he said, in a heavy Glaswegian accent.

'Why is it they always call on you when I need a taxi service?' said Shepherd, slipping his legs over the side of the bed.

Sharpe grinned and nodded at his companion. 'Spider, this is DC Paul Joyce. Joycie, this is DC Dan Shepherd, Spider to his friends. Spider is ex-SAS so we use him whenever we need someone to jump out of a plane or a burning building or throw themselves into the North Sea in the middle of the night. Personally, I think he does it just to make the rest of us look bad.'

Joyce handed Shepherd a kitbag, containing the clothes he had been wearing when he had been dragged out of the water: a blue denim shirt, cheap jeans, boxer shorts and socks. They had been cleaned and pressed. His work boots had been stuffed with newspapers and dried out.

'I brought you a denim jacket and a pullover,' said the superintendent. 'I gather it's what the best-dressed human trafficker's wearing this season.'

Shepherd stood up. Sharpe and Joyce chuckled at his surgical gown. 'Maybe we should take him to the factory as he is,' said Joyce.

'Careful, Joycie,' said Sharpe. 'Spider's trained to kill.'

Shepherd flashed Hargrove a pained look. 'Did you have to bring Cannon and Ball with you?'

Hargrove smiled. 'Manpower shortage.'

The three men turned their backs while Shepherd changed.

'We're going to have to cuff you,' said Hargrove, once Shepherd was tying his bootlaces. 'It's got to look right.'

Shepherd held out his arm. Joyce cuffed the wrist and fastened the other end to himself. Then the four men walked along the corridor and out into the car park. They took Shepherd to a black

Vauxhall Vectra. Sharpe sat in the driver's seat next to Hargrove, while Shepherd and Joyce climbed into the back.

Joyce waited until Sharpe had driven away from the hospital, then removed the handcuffs. Hargrove opened the glove compartment and passed Shepherd a flask and a carrier-bag containing two plastic-wrapped sandwiches.

Shepherd unwrapped a sandwich and bit into it. Ham and mustard. He poured himself some coffee and settled back in the seat.

'They're going to drop me in town,' said Hargrove. 'I've got to get back to London. Anyway, there's no reason for your solicitor to be with you as you're not going to be interviewed.'

'No sweat,' said Shepherd.

'The local cops will transfer the father later this afternoon. I've cleared it with the local chief super that he's to be put into a holding cell with you.'

'He knows I'm undercover?'

'He's sound – Garth Carpenter. I've known him for years.'

Shepherd nodded. He was never happy about strangers knowing his true role, but there were times when it was necessary.

Sharpe wound down his window and showed the young uniformed constable his warrant card. 'He's expected,' said Sharpe, and waved at Shepherd, who was again handcuffed to Joyce.

The constable scrutinised Shepherd's face. 'Who is he?'

'Name's Corke. Floats like one, too. Pulled him out of the water after he jumped off a trawler full of illegal immigrants. He's here to be questioned before we put him up before a magistrate.'

Joyce held out his warrant card and the constable nodded. He straightened up and waved at his colleague, who was watching from a cubicle at the entrance to the car park. The metal gate rattled back and Sharpe edged the Vectra forward. 'Wonder if he joined the force so that he could be a bloody security guard,' he muttered.

'We can't all be high-flyers,' said Joyce, grinning at the constable as they drove past him.

They parked between two white vans with mesh-protected windows and walked into the rear entrance of the station. Sharpe flashed his warrant card and asked to speak to Chief Superintendent Carpenter. Then Shepherd was taken to a holding cell that contained a mattress on a concrete plinth, a single plastic and metal chair and a stainless-steel toilet.

He sat on the bunk and bent forward, arms resting on his legs, to run through his legend. Tony Corke. Fifteen years at sea, mostly on cross-Channel ferries, married but divorced, one child, a boy, a short spell inside for assault after a drunken brawl in a Portsmouth bar. Not a particularly nice guy, but not an outright villain. He lay back on the bed and relaxed, staring up at the ceiling. Someone had scraped 'ALL COPPERS ARE BASTARDS' into the plaster. He smiled to himself. Not all coppers were bastards, but he had met a fair few whose parentage might be called into question. He closed his eyes but didn't sleep.

Time seemed to crawl by. He wondered what was taking so long. An hour passed. Then another. The only light filtered in through a square of glass breeze blocks in the wall close to the ceiling. As the sky darkened, he stood up and switched on the light. Something must have gone wrong. He glanced at his watch. He'd been in the cell for almost five hours and all he'd had to eat were the sandwiches in the car. There was a bell push beside the door but Shepherd didn't want to start asking for favours.

He sat down on the bunk again. It wasn't his first time in a cell and he was no stranger to long waits. On SAS surveillance operations he'd spent days at a time lying in a rain-swept hide, pissing and shitting into plastic bags, so a few hours in a cell with plumbing was no real hardship. But that didn't make it any less boring. He should have asked Sharpe for a newspaper or magazine.

He lay back on the bed. The concrete was hard against his back through the thin plastic mattress but, considering the number of drunks who had probably spent the night here, the smell wasn't too bad.

Hargrove had definitely said that Rudi would be put in the cell that afternoon. Now it was evening. Hargrove wasn't the sort of man who made mistakes so something must have disrupted his plans. It happened on every operation, and Shepherd knew there was nothing he could do but ride it out.

It was almost seven o'clock when he heard footsteps, then the rattle of a key. The door was pushed open and Rudi stood on the threshold. Shepherd grinned at him. 'Hello again,' he said.

A uniformed constable gave Rudi a nudge and he stepped inside the cell. The door clanged shut behind him. 'You are not still in the hospital?' he asked.

'They said I'm okay,' said Shepherd, standing up. 'How's Jessica?'

'She's good. Not in danger any more.'

'Why didn't they let you stay in the hospital?' asked Shepherd.

'My wife is with her,' said Rudi. He sat down on the plastic chair. 'Everything will be okay. I have asked for asylum already. Now they have to get me a lawyer. Soon they will find us a place to live and then I can work.'

Shepherd smiled, but he knew it wouldn't be as easy as that. Even without the million euros of counterfeit currency in Rudi's bags, life as an asylum-seeker wasn't as rosy as Rudi seemed to imagine. 'Have they given you anything to eat?' he asked.

'Last night, but nothing today,' he said.

'You should tell them you want food,' said Shepherd, and sat on the bunk. 'They have to feed you. These people, they won't do anything for you unless you stand up for your rights.'

Rudi wiped his face with his hands. 'I want to be with my wife and daughter,' he said.

'You can ask your lawyer,' said Shepherd. 'They should at least let you see your daughter.'

'What about you?' asked Rudi. 'Have they said what will happen to you?'

'Prison,' said Shepherd.

'But you are a good man,' said Rudi. 'You saved my daughter.'

'I was smuggling people,' said Shepherd. 'They will send me to prison for that.'

'You have a wife?'

Shepherd nodded. 'But we are not together any more.'

'And you have children?'

'A boy.'

'It will not be easy for them if you go to prison.'

'It won't be for long,' said Shepherd. 'Two years, maybe three.'

'I am sorry.'

'It isn't your fault,' said Shepherd. 'It's nobody's fault but my own. I decided to break the law so I have to take the consequences.'

'It makes no sense,' said Rudi. 'I broke the law but your government will find me a place to live and take care of my family. You broke the law and you will go to prison.'

'Shit happens,' said Shepherd.

Rudi frowned. 'What do you mean?'

'Sometimes bad things happen. No matter what you do, no matter how carefully you make plans, things go wrong.'

'Shit happens,' Rudi repeated. 'It is true.'

Shepherd lay back on the bunk. Rudi was about to discover how true it was. Shepherd would take no pleasure in what he was about to do, but Rudi was a means to an end. 'I heard the police talking about you,' said Shepherd, quietly.

Rudi stiffened. 'What do you mean?'

'They found something on the boat,' said Shepherd. 'They think it belongs to you.'

The legs of the chair scraped along the floor as Rudi got up. 'What did they find?' he said. 'What did they say?'

Shepherd sat up again slowly and swung his feet to the floor. He shrugged. 'I just overheard two cops talking, that's all. About some cans in your luggage.'

'Cans? They said cans?'

'Cans of oil. Did you have some with you?'

Rudi had paled. 'Did they open them?' he said.

'I'm not sure,' said Shepherd. 'I was in the corridor and there were two policemen talking. Detectives, I think.'

'Detectives?'

'They weren't wearing uniforms. Why?'

Rudi began to pace up and down, his hands bunched into fists.

'What's wrong?' asked Shepherd.

'Nothing,' said Rudi.

'It doesn't look like nothing,' said Shepherd.

Rudi stopped pacing. 'Did they say anything else?'

'The detectives? No. But one of the cops was asking me about the bags.'

'Asking what?'

'He showed me photographs of all the baggage in the hold and asked me if I knew who they belonged to.'

'Why did they want to know that?'

'I guess they wanted to see who owned which bags.'

'And what did you tell them?'

'I didn't tell them anything. I'm waiting for my lawyer to get here.'

Rudi was pacing again.

'What's wrong?' asked Shepherd.

'They have no right to go through my bags,' said Rudi. 'My bags are private.'

'They can do what they want when you come into the country,' said Shepherd. 'Customs have the right to search you and all your possessions.' He paused. 'What was in the cans?' he asked.

'I don't know,' said Rudi.

'How can you not know?'

'I don't know!'

Shepherd held up his hands. 'Okay, okay,' he said. 'I was trying to help, that's all.'

Rudi walked over to the door and banged his forehead against the metal.

Shepherd went over to him. 'That won't help,' he said.

Rudi continued to bang his head.

'Rudi, they'll just come to see what you're doing, and if they think you're hurting yourself, they'll restrain you.'

Rudi stopped. 'What do you mean?'

'They'll handcuff you. They won't want you to hurt yourself.'

He put a hand on Rudi's shoulder. 'Sit down. Let's talk about it.' He guided the other man to the chair. 'Look, if you don't know what was in the cans, you can't be in trouble. The police will believe you.'

'It's true,' he said. 'I don't know.'

Shepherd sat on the bunk, facing him. 'So why did you have them in your luggage?'

Rudi shook his head. 'I can't tell you.'

'Maybe I can help.'

Rudi looked up fearfully. 'How can you? You're going to prison.'

'I'll get bail,' Shepherd said. 'I have money. My lawyer will get me released until I go to trial.'

'Will they release me?'

'It depends on what was in the cans,' said Shepherd. 'If it was drugs—'

'I told you, I don't know what was in them!'

'Yes – but if it was drugs they could send you to prison for a long time and you wouldn't be able to take care of your family.'

'They didn't tell me what was in the cans,' said Rudi. He propped his elbows on his knees and put his head into his hands.

'You were carrying them for someone else, then?' said Shepherd. 'Who?'

Rudi leaped to his feet. 'Why are you asking so many questions?'

'I just want to help you,' said Shepherd.

'No one can help me.' He began to bang his head on the door again. 'No one.'

It was just before ten when Sharpe and Joyce came to collect Shepherd. They handcuffed him and led him out to the Vectra. They showed their warrant cards to the guard at the gate, who made a note on his clipboard.

Sharpe drove out of the police car park and accelerated down the road.

'Home, James,' joked Shepherd, from the back seat.

'I'm dropping you in north London,' said Sharpe. 'The boss said he'll run you home. Joycie and I've got work to do – real work, as opposed to chauffeuring heroes.'

There was little traffic on the motorway and Sharpe kept the car in the outside lane at a steady 90 m.p.h. They left Shepherd at a service station on the outskirts of London where Hargrove was sitting in the back of his official Rover. The driver was already out of the car, holding the door open, as Shepherd walked over and climbed into the back. The superintendent was wearing a dinner jacket, with a scarlet cummerbund and a hand-tied black bow-tie.

'Been conjuring?' asked Shepherd, laconically.

'Awards ceremony,' said Hargrove. 'Bravery above and beyond, all that jazz. There wasn't a guy there who'd done a tenth of what you have over the past couple of years.'

'It's not about being brave,' said Shepherd. 'It's about getting the job done.'

The driver got behind the wheel and edged the car towards the M25.

'Be nice if you could step up and take a bow some time, though,' said Hargrove.

'I've got half a dozen photographs of me shaking hands with various police commissioners,' said Shepherd. 'I'm just not allowed to show them to anybody.'

'You know what I mean, Spider.'

'I'm not in this for the glory,' said Shepherd. He smiled ruefully. 'Or the money.'

'How did it go with your man?' asked Hargrove.

Shepherd shrugged. 'He wouldn't play ball. I'm not even sure he knows he was carrying money.'

'I'm sorry you were in there for so long. There was a manpower shortage. Local cops didn't have anyone to bring him over until the evening shift.'

'I figured something had gone wrong.' He stretched and groaned. He needed a shower.

'Wasn't as if we could call and tell you,' said Hargrove. 'So, you reckon he didn't know what was in the cans.'

'He says he didn't. I didn't tell him – thought that might be pushing it too far. I planted the idea that it might have been drugs and he didn't argue. We could use that as leverage, maybe. If he thinks he's facing ten years for bringing in a class-A drug, he might talk.'

'Did he say what he was supposed to do with the cans?'

Shepherd shook his head. 'Clammed up, pretty much. That was when he started the head-banging routine. I couldn't put him under pressure without stepping out of character.'

'How do you read him?'

'Just a guy trying to do the best for his family. Figured they'd have a better life in the UK. Probably thought the streets were paved with gold. Sad bastard.'

'No one forced him to come,' said Hargrove. 'Everyone on that boat was there by choice. They'd all paid for their passage.'

Shepherd sighed. The superintendent was right. But it was easy to talk about choice when you'd been born in England with the safety-net of a welfare state and a health system that might have its faults but was head and shoulders above what was on offer in the third world. He wondered how he'd feel if he had been born in a country with no prospects, no health care, no free education, no pension provision, no future, just a lifetime of toil with no prospect of anything better for his children. Would he grin and bear it? Shepherd was pretty sure he wouldn't stay put. He'd save whatever money he could, then take his family to a country where a man was paid a decent wage for his labour. 'Yeah, maybe you're right,' he said. He didn't want to argue politics with Hargrove. 'What happens next?'

'I'll get Immigration to speak with him and run through his options. He won't be able to claim asylum without giving us an explanation for the cash.'

'So, if he doesn't talk he gets sent back?'

'That's the way it works,' said Hargrove.

'And if he does talk, what'll his life be worth? Whoever gave him those cans isn't going to stand by and let a million euros go without repercussions.'

'If he helps us with the money, and gives evidence against Pepper, we can arrange witness protection for him,' said Hargrove, patiently. 'He's already opted for a new life so he might as well live it under a new name.'

'I hope he sees it that way,' said Shepherd.

At just before midnight the Rover pulled up in front of Shepherd's house. The drive from Newcastle had taken the best part of four hours. 'Take a few days off, Spider,' Hargrove said.

'I'm okay.'

'We've only just pulled you out of the sea,' said the superintendent, 'and you've been working for two weeks non-stop. Spend some time with Liam.'

'Okay.' It had been four days since Shepherd had been at home, but he had spoken to his son on his mobile.

'We'll sweat the father for a few days. When he tells us what he was supposed to do with the money, we'll work out how best to play it.' Hargrove patted Shepherd's shoulder. 'You did good, Spider.'

'Thanks.' Shepherd opened the door and climbed out. He waved as the Rover drove off, then let himself into the house. The kitchen light was on. 'It's me,' he called, not wanting to startle the au pair.

'I'm in the kitchen,' said Katra. She appeared in the doorway as he walked down the hall.

'Sorry I didn't call first. I thought you might be asleep,' he said.

Katra was wearing pink flannel pyjamas and her black hair was clipped up at the back. 'I was just getting some warm milk,' she said. 'Do you want me to cook something for you?' Her English had improved a lot during the year she had worked for Shepherd, but she still had the strong accent that betrayed her Slovenian origin.

'I'm fine,' said Shepherd. 'I've had a sandwich and I'll make myself a coffee. You get off to bed.'

'Sit down,' Katra said, and switched on the kettle. 'You look exhausted.'

'It's been a rough few days.' Shepherd pulled out a chair at the kitchen table. 'How's Liam?'

'Fine,' said Katra. 'He wants to start piano lessons.'

'What?'

'He wants to learn to play the piano. He can have lessons at school. He brought home a form for you to fill in.'

'I didn't know he liked music.'

Katra spooned coffee into a cafetière. 'One of his friends has started lessons.'

'A girl?'

Katra laughed. 'What makes you say that?'

'Because it's the way we guys operate. There's a girl he likes, she starts piano lessons so he wants piano lessons.'

'You are suspicious because you are a policeman,' she said.

'I'm suspicious because I know how guys think.'

'Liam is nine,' said Katra.

'Nine, nineteen, ninety-nine – guys are all the same. Trust me.'

'She *is* pretty,' admitted Katra.

Shepherd stood up again and stretched. 'I'll just go up and check on him,' he said. 'I'll be back in a minute for the coffee.'

He went upstairs and nudged open the door to Liam's bedroom. His son was asleep on his side, mouth slightly open, snoring softly. Shepherd knelt down next to the bed and stroked Liam's hair. He looked so like Sue when he was asleep, he thought, with a twinge of sadness. 'Sweet dreams,' he murmured. 'Sleep tight. Hope the bedbugs don't bite.'

'Hello, Mum,' whispered Liam.

'It's me,' said Shepherd.

Liam's eyes fluttered open. 'Oh. Hi, Dad. You're back.'

'I just got in,' said Shepherd. 'Sorry. It took longer than I thought.'

'Can I have a cuddle?'

'Sure you can.' He lay down next to Liam and put his arm round him. 'Goodnight,' he whispered.

'Goodnight, Dad,' said Liam. 'I love you.'

'I love you too,' said Shepherd.

'Three, four, five,' said Liam.

Shepherd closed his eyes, took a deep breath and was asleep.

'Dad?' Shepherd groaned and rolled over at the sound of his son's voice. He opened his eyes and blinked.

Liam was standing next to the bed in his school uniform, carrying his sports bag. 'Dad, I'm going to school.'

Shepherd sat up and rubbed his face. He was still wearing his Tony Corke clothes and they smelt foul. Katra appeared behind Liam. 'Why didn't you wake me up?' Shepherd asked her.

'I tried,' said Katra. 'You were fast asleep.'

'I'm sorry, Liam,' said Shepherd. 'I just came in to say good-night. I guess I was more tired than I thought.'

'That's okay,' said Liam. 'I'll see you tonight, yeah?'

'Sure.'

'Can we go to the park and play football?'

'Of course.'

'Promise?'

'Promise.' Liam held out his hand, little finger crooked.

Shepherd linked his own with it. 'Pinkie promise,' said Shepherd.

'I made coffee for you in the kitchen,' said Katra, and grinned. 'You and Liam were so cute, asleep together.'

'Thanks.' Shepherd rolled off the bed and ruffled Liam's hair. His son protested. 'Go on with you,' he said. 'You'll be late. We can talk about your piano lessons tonight.'

'Katra told you?'

'Oh, yes. She told me.'

Shepherd headed for the bathroom as they went downstairs. He shaved and showered, then put on his white towelling robe and went to his bedroom. There were three mobile phones on the bedside table. He hadn't wanted to risk taking them on the trawler. There'd be no reason for a sailor like Corke to have more than one. While he was away he'd missed a call on the phone he used for personal business. The caller had blocked their number, but there was a voicemail message. It was Major Allan

Gannon of the SAS. He didn't identify himself but Shepherd recognised the clipped tone and note of authority in the voice. 'Call me back when you get the chance, Spider.' Short and to the point.

Shepherd phoned the Major's mobile. Gannon answered on the second ring.

'What are you doing this evening?' asked the Major. 'Sixish?'

'Nothing special,' said Shepherd.

'Fancy a drink? The club?'

Shepherd knew that he could only mean the Special Forces Club, behind Harrods. 'Sure. Anything wrong?'

'Just a chat,' said the Major. 'It's been a while since we had a chinwag.' He cut the connection.

The Major wasn't one for small-talk and Shepherd doubted that it was a chinwag he wanted.

He changed into a faded T-shirt and shorts, then put on thick socks with his well-worn army boots and went downstairs. He poured some coffee, took a couple of gulps, then got his old canvas rucksack from the cupboard under the stairs. It contained half a dozen house bricks wrapped in newspaper. Shepherd always ran with the rucksack, a habit picked up from his army days. Before he had taken the SAS selection course he had spent many weekends running up and down the Brecon Beacons with a brick-filled rucksack, pushing the limits of his endurance and stamina. During SAS training all cross-country running was done with a full pack, and even though those days were behind him, he still felt that a run without a rucksack wasn't a run. He went back to the kitchen, finished his coffee, grabbed a plastic bottle of Evian from the fridge and headed for the door.

Rudi Pernaska was barely aware of the cold, hard concrete through the thin plastic mattress. From the moment that the Englishman had told him the detectives had been talking about the cans he'd known his life was over. Rudi had no idea what was inside them. He hadn't wanted to know. All he had cared about was delivering them to London. The men in France had told him that if he made any attempt to open them, he would pay with his life.

Now there was nothing he could do to make things right. If the police had the cans and there was something illegal inside, they would never give them back to him, so the men who had entrusted them to him would kill him. They would kill him and probably his family, too. His beloved Jessica – he couldn't bear her to suffer. Or his wife. She had been through enough already. They both had.

Tears ran down his face. He grabbed his hair and pulled it, cursing his stupidity. He should have stayed in Albania, should never have gambled on a new life in the West. They had barely scratched a living out of their smallholding on the outskirts of Tirana, but at least it had been a living. Now he had nothing. Less than nothing.

He slipped off the bed and paced round the cell. The window was made of glass blocks. The overhead fluorescent light was protected by a Perspex panel. There was a stainless-steel toilet in the corner with a button to operate the flush. Rudi knew what he had to do, but the cell had been designed to thwart any attempt at suicide. He'd asked for food, hoping they would give him a knife and fork, but he'd received a cheese sandwich, a handful of chips, two plain biscuits, a plastic cup of weak coffee, and no utensils. He could tear up his shirt to produce a home-made rope, but there was nothing in the cell to tie it to.

He paced up and down, faster and faster, and bellowed in frustration. If he ended his life, then maybe the men who had given him the cans would leave his family alone. It was the only solution, the only way his family stood a chance of any sort of life. He lifted up his right arm and stared at the pale green arteries under the skin. Just a few pints of blood and it would be over. He patted down his pockets for the hundredth time. They had taken away his belt, his shoelaces, his change, his wallet. There was nothing he could use to release his lifeblood and end his suffering.

Tears ran down his face. He had to take his life because if he didn't, his wife and child would die too. He raised his wrist to his lips, and kissed the flesh. He tasted the salt of his tears on his tongue as he bit, softly at first, then harder. Coppery-tasting blood spurted between his lips. He barely felt the pain. He opened his mouth and pushed his upper teeth harder into the wound, feeling them slip across the rubbery veins. He bit down hard, twisting his neck like a lion sacrificing its prey.

Shepherd's feet pounded on the pavement. He was breathing evenly, and although his T-shirt was soaked and his shoulders ached with the weight of the rucksack, he knew he could do at least another ten miles. When he saw the black Mazda sports car parked opposite his house he slowed and groaned.

Kathy Gift climbed out and waved. She was wearing a fawn raincoat with the collar turned up and carrying a black-leather briefcase. She brushed her chestnut hair behind an ear and locked her car. Shepherd forced a smile. He liked Kathy Gift but, as the unit's psychologist, she was a nuisance. 'Hey,' he said, stopping at the car.

'I thought that, rather than play phone-tag, I'd come to the mountain,' she said.

'I won't shake hands,' said Shepherd. 'I'm all sweaty.' He jogged past her and unlocked the front door. She followed him down the path. 'Make us both some coffee while I shower,' called Shepherd. 'You know where everything is.'

He tossed his rucksack into the cupboard under the stairs and went up to the bathroom. After he'd showered, he changed into a grey pullover and black jeans. He found Gift sitting at the kitchen table, her hands round a mug of coffee. She had hung her coat on the back of a chair and pushed up the sleeves of a pale blue cashmere polo-neck. A thin gold necklace with a Star of David hung over the sweater. She indicated a second mug on the table opposite her. 'Splash of milk and no sugar,' she said.

Shepherd grinned. 'You remembered. Or is it in my file?'

'I remembered,' she said. 'It isn't rocket science.'

Shepherd sat down. 'And to what do I owe the pleasure?'

Gift opened her case and took out a notepad and pen. 'It's your biannual. Last time it took us ages to schedule a meeting.'

'I was busy,' said Shepherd.

'Not a problem,' said Gift. 'Anyway, I'm here now. How's things?'

Shepherd smiled easily. 'Things is fine.'

Gift tapped her pen on the notebook.

'Aren't you going to write that down?' he teased.

'You've never liked these assessments, have you?' she said.

'I think they're a waste of time,' said Shepherd. 'No offence.'

'None taken.'

'If I didn't think I could do the job, I'd be the first to quit,' he said. 'It's my life on the line, remember.'

'I'm here to help you do your job better,' said Gift.

Shepherd smiled thinly. 'That's not strictly true, is it? You're also the one who decides whether or not I'm fit for duty.'

'And are you?'

'Definitely. Are you hungry?'

'I could eat.'

'Toast?'

'Why not?'

Shepherd went over to the toaster and slotted in two slices of wholemeal bread. He pressed the lever, then turned and leaned against the counter top. 'I'm fine. Really.'

'Still running, I see.'

'Keeps me fit.'

'How's Liam?'

'Doing well at school. No nightmares. He seems fine, too.'

'Does he talk about what happened to his mum? The accident?'

'He talks about her. We both do. He misses her, of course – he'll miss her for ever – but he doesn't talk about the crash.'

'Do you think he blames himself?'

'No,' said Shepherd, emphatically.

'He was in the back of the car, your wife was turning to help him when she jumped the red light. If wouldn't be unnatural for Liam to blame himself.'

'He doesn't.'

'What happens when you're away on a case?'

'We have the au pair. She lives in. Is this about me or my son?'

'It's about putting you in context, that's all. Are you in a relationship at the moment?'

'I'm a father,' said Shepherd. 'That's a relationship, right?' The toaster pinged and ejected the two slices. Shepherd put them on to a plate and arranged it on the table with butter, strawberry jam and marmalade.

'You know what I mean,' said Gift, as she picked up a slice of toast.

'I'm too busy for a relationship at the moment,' he said. 'When I'm working, I'm with villains or victims and neither would make suitable girlfriend material. When I'm not working, I'm at home with my son.'

'It can't be easy, being a single parent and an undercover policeman.' She was buttering her toast.

'Katra's a big help. She does the school run, same as his mum would have done. She cooks, cleans, helps him with his home-work if I'm not around.'

'Are you away much?'

'The unit operates all over the UK,' said Shepherd. 'You know that. We go where the work is.'

'And you were overseas recently?'

'France. But only for a few days.'

'And you're okay with that?'

Shepherd sighed. 'In a perfect world, I'd like to be able to spend more time with Liam. But in a perfect world, my wife wouldn't have died. Look, I don't see what Liam has to do with my ability to function under cover.'

'It's stress, Dan. Pressure.'

'I can take it.'

'Stress manifests in different ways.'

'I don't have nervous twitches and I sleep like a newborn babe.'

'Newborn babes tend to cry a lot and wet themselves,' said Gift, with a smile. 'So I'm told.'

Shepherd laughed and helped himself to a slice of toast. 'I know you're only doing your job,' he said, 'but, really, I'm fine.'

'What happened down the Tube last year. The suicide-bomber. Can we talk about that?'

'He was going to kill a lot of people. I shot him. End of story.'

'It's a big thing, to kill a man,' said the psychologist, then took a bite of toast.

'With respect, how the hell would you know?'

'I could take that as defensive,' she said.

'It's just such a glib thing to say,' said Shepherd. 'I know it's a big deal, but it needed doing. I'm not going to lose any sleep over a dead suicide-bomber. Anyway, he's up in heaven with his seventy-two virgins so I'm sure he's not complaining.'

'You believe in heaven, do you?'

Shepherd's eyes narrowed. He was silent for several seconds. 'No,' he said eventually. 'I don't believe in heaven, or hell, or God.'

'You've never been religious?'

'I was baptised as a kid,' said Shepherd, 'but it meant nothing to me.'

'The Catholic religion is based on guilt, pretty much.'

'I guess.'

'And confession, of course. The premise that, by confessing, your sins can be absolved.'

'Three Hail Marys and Jesus will forgive you. I don't see what I do as sinning, if that's what you're getting at.'

'Playing devil's advocate here. You do break a lot of com-mandments, don't you?'

'I'm one of the good guys, remember?'

'The end justifies the means?'

'That's the way I see it. Yes, I shot him dead, but he was wired up with enough explosives to blow himself to kingdom come. You can't expect me to feel guilty about that.'

'Just because what you did was right doesn't necessarily make it easier to deal with.'

'I disagree.'

'There are as many cases of post-traumatic stress disorder among troops on the winning side of a conflict as there are on the losing side. Stress is stress.'

'I was well trained,' said Shepherd.

'The best of the best?' There was a note of sarcasm in her voice.

'The selection procedure weeds out the guys who aren't up to it,' said Shepherd, 'and the training teaches you to cope with pretty much anything.'

'A high percentage of former SAS members end up killing themselves, don't they?' she said quietly.

'That's not stress,' said Shepherd. 'If it was stress, they'd do it while they were in the Regiment, not after they'd left.'

'So, if it's not stress, what is it?'

'They miss the action, I guess. They can't live without the adrenaline kick.' Suddenly Shepherd realised where the conversation was going. 'You always get back to this, don't you? You make it sound as if I'm addicted to violence.'

'We were talking about former members of the SAS.'

'We were talking about me – it's always about me but you take the long way round sometimes.'

'Honestly, I wasn't being that devious. But it's a fair question, isn't it? The men who do what you do: do they do it because it's a job, or because they enjoy it?'

'You enjoy your job, right?'

'It's challenging,' she said.

'So what's wrong with me enjoying my job?'

'I don't kill people, Dan,' said Gift, quietly.

'The only people who enjoy killing are psychopaths,' said Shepherd, firmly, 'and I'm not a psychopath.'

Gift opened her mouth to reply but before she could say anything they heard a key in the front door. Instead she finished her toast.

'Katra,' said Shepherd.

Gift nodded. The front door opened and Katra hurried down the hall. 'It's me!' she called, and burst into the kitchen. She frowned when she saw Gift at the kitchen table. 'Hello?' she said.

Gift smiled. 'Hi.'

'This is a friend of mine, Kathy,' Shepherd said, by way of introduction. 'Kathy, this is Katra, who looks after us.'

Katra smiled. Her hair was tied back in a ponytail and she was dressed for warmth in a quilted jacket over a thick pullover with horizontal rainbow stripes, brown cord jeans and Timberland boots. 'We have the same name, almost,' she said. 'Katra means Kathy. It was my grandmother's name.'

Gift laughed. 'I was named after a singer my father fancied,' she said. 'Where are you from? Your English is excellent.'

'Slovenia.'

'Where in Slovenia?'

'Portoroz,' said Katra. 'Do you know it?'

Gift shook her head. 'I've been to Croatia a few times but never Slovenia. I'm told it's a beautiful country.'

'It is. Very beautiful.' She turned to Shepherd. 'I'm going to the supermarket. Is there anything you need?'

'Shampoo,' said Shepherd. 'Head and Shoulders.' He grinned at Gift. 'Dandruff. And it's not stress-related.' Katra looked puzzled. 'I'll see you later,' Shepherd said to her. 'Can you pick Liam up from school?'

'Of course.'

'I've got to see someone at six, so I'll be leaving here at five.'

'I'll put your dinner in the oven,' said Katra. She waved goodbye and went out again.

Shepherd sat down opposite Gift. She was smiling at him. 'What?' he asked.

'What do you mean?'

'You know what I mean,' he said. 'That knowing smile. It says you think something's going on.'

'She's a pretty girl, that's all.'

'She's twenty-three.'

'You're . . . what? Thirty-five?'

'You know exactly how old I am,' said Shepherd. 'It's in my file.'

'It's been almost two years since your wife died,' said Gift, quietly.

'So?'

'It's a long time.' They heard Katra drive away.

'I'm not going to jump on the au pair, if that's what you mean. I already told you, the only relationship I'm concerned with is being a father.'

'She seems to have made herself at home,' said Gift.

'She lives in,' said Shepherd, then cursed himself inwardly – he had sounded defensive. Kathy Gift had the knack of making him feel guilty even when he knew there was no reason for it.

'Two years is a long time to grieve.'

'I'm not grieving,' said Shepherd, quickly. 'Sue died. Since then I've been working flat out. And when I'm not working, I'm with Liam. Anyway, you're the unit's psychologist, not a Relate counsellor.'

'I need to look at the whole person,' said Gift, patiently. 'When you're undercover you have to adopt a complete personality, don't you? If one thing isn't right, your cover can be blown.'

'And because I'm not going around bonking everything in a skirt, I've got a problem?'

'There's nothing wrong with being celibate, provided it's for the right reason.'

Shepherd leaned back and grinned. 'Is that what I am? A monk?'

'We're just talking here, Dan. I'd be more worried if you were having a string of one-night stands.'

'That's something,' said Shepherd. He finished his toast. 'You never ask about the important stuff, do you?'

'Such as?'

'My performance on the range. My fitness. I'm as good a shot as I was in the SAS, and I'm faster over five miles than I was a year ago.'

'You have an annual physical, don't you?' said Gift. 'I'm solely concerned with your mental well-being.'

'So, show me some ink blots or something.'

'You always use humour as a defence mechanism, don't you?'

'Damn right,' said Shepherd. 'Guns are just plain messy.'

Gift smiled. She put her notepad and pen into her briefcase, drank the last of her coffee and stood up.

'That's it?' said Shepherd.

'You seem fine to me,' said Gift, putting on her raincoat. 'As bloody-minded as always, but in your line of work . . .' She left the sentence unfinished, but extended her hand. Shepherd stood up and shook it, then walked her to the front door. 'Joking apart, Dan, you should get out more.'

'I run,' he said.

'You know what I mean. Socialise.'

'You're not asking me out, are you?' said Shepherd, with a grin.

Gift's cheeks reddened, but she laughed. 'There's your defence mechanism kicking in again,' she said.

Shepherd held open the door for her. 'What if I did ask you out?' he said.

'What do you mean?'

'Dinner. Or a movie.'

'Are you serious?'

'Sure. We never have a problem finding something to talk about, do we?'

Gift frowned, evidently trying to work out if he was serious or not. 'It's against protocol,' she said eventually.

'Really?'

'Really.'

'Okay.' He smiled ruefully. 'Pity.'

Her frown deepened. 'I've got to go,' she said.

Shepherd watched her walk down the path, high heels pecking at the flagstones. As she reached the car she dropped her keys and bent down hurriedly to retrieve them. She glanced over her shoulder as she straightened, then looked away quickly when she saw that Shepherd was watching her.

Shepherd smiled to himself as he walked back to the kitchen. He'd been joking at first, but once he saw that she was considering his offer he'd wanted her to say yes. She was right, of course: there was no way that a police psychologist could go out with a man she was monitoring. She had to be impartial and independent: a date would be a clear conflict of interest.

And she was right that it had been a long time since he'd gone out with a woman for anything other than professional reasons. The last time he'd seen a movie it had been with Sue. The last time he'd eaten Chinese food it had been with Sue. He hadn't been on holiday since Sue's death.

He made himself a fresh cup of coffee. As he put away the milk and closed the fridge, he gazed at a photograph of his wife and son stuck to the door with a magnet in the shape of an apple. Liam was in fancy dress, wearing a pirate's outfit and brandishing a plastic cutlass. Sue had her arm round him and she was smiling proudly at the camera. They'd taken the picture using a timer because Shepherd had been away on a job in the West Country. He had been away so much when Liam was growing up, always on some job or other. If he'd known then how little time he had left with Sue he'd have spent every minute with her. Now it was too late. She was gone and he and Liam had each other.

He took his mug of coffee out into the garden and sat down at the wooden table by the hedge. Sue had chosen it and the two wooden bench seats at the local garden centre, but the instructions for putting them together had been in Chinese or Japanese so it had taken him several attempts. The benches still weren't right and he had to stick pieces of folded cardboard under the legs to stop them wobbling. Sue had been pregnant with Liam and she'd used it as an excuse to avoid the heavy work, standing behind him with one hand on her swelling belly as she laughed at his D-I-Y efforts.

'Oh, Sue, I miss you,' Shepherd whispered. He remembered the last time he'd seen her as vividly as if it had been yesterday. He'd been undercover in a high-security prison, posing as an armed robber on remand so that he could get close to a drugs baron. Sue had come in with Liam for a visit, but to stay in character it had been vital to make it look as if they were having marital problems. As she left, she'd yelled at him, her voice loaded with venom, 'I hate you! I hope I never see you again, ever! You can rot in here for all I care!' They had been the last words she had ever said to him. Tears stung his eyes. He knew she had been playing a role, which he'd asked her to play, and he knew, too, that she had loved him and he loved her, and that she hadn't meant what she'd said, but it was so damned unfair that it was his last memory of her. He hadn't had the chance to say goodbye properly, to tell her how much he loved her and how important she was to him . . .

It was futile to accuse life of being unfair. Life wasn't fair or unfair, it was just life. You played the hand you were dealt, and that was it.

Shepherd looked around the garden. The grass had to be cut and the fruit trees pruned, while the rockeries that Sue had tended so lovingly needed weeding. The garden had always been Sue's province, and he hadn't touched it since her death. Katra had planted a few herbs by the kitchen and she'd told Shepherd that she'd mow the lawn but he'd said he'd take care of it. He would, too, as soon as he had time.

He looked at the unkempt lawn where Liam had taken his first steps, where he'd taught him to kick a football, where they'd played cowboys and Indians until Sue had said she didn't want Liam messing around with guns, even make-believe ones. Shepherd couldn't remember the last time he'd played with his son. Really played, the way they had when Sue was alive. He promised himself he'd spend more time with his boy. Quality time, as the TV psychologists put it. *And* he'd cut the grass. He sipped his coffee. Tomorrow.

He heard a mobile phone ring and hurried back into the kitchen. It was Hargrove.

'I've bad news, Spider,' said Hargrove. 'Rudi Pernaska's dead.'

'How?'

'He killed himself.'

'Why the hell did they let that happen?'

'They couldn't have stopped him. He bit his wrist open. Gnawed through a vein.'

Shepherd cursed under his breath.

'It wasn't your fault, Spider.'

'Like hell it wasn't,' hissed Shepherd. 'I told him we'd found the cans.'

'We're not sure that's why he did it.'

'What? You think he just got depressed and decided to top himself? He did it because he knew we were on to him. Which means he was more scared of them than he was of us.' Shepherd slammed his hand on the counter.

'We couldn't have known he'd react like that,' said Hargrove. 'And whether or not we told him we'd found the money, it would have come out eventually. It wasn't our fault. The moment the Pernaskas paid for passage on Pepper's boat, that money was going to turn up.'

Shepherd bit his lower lip. The superintendent was right. Shepherd had just been the bearer of the bad news. If Rudi hadn't heard it from him, he'd have heard it from someone else. But that didn't make the man's suicide any easier to accept. He remembered how grateful he had been when he came to see Shepherd in the hospital ward. And how the man's wife had kissed his hand. And how they'd promised that their daughter Jessica would never forget the name of the man who'd saved her life. Except that the name Shepherd had given them had been a lie. It had all been a lie.

'What's next?' he asked.

'We'll talk to the wife,' said Hargrove.

'Widow,' said Shepherd.

'What?'

'She's a widow now. You'll talk to the widow.'

Hargrove sighed. 'I know you're upset, Spider.'

'I'm sorry. They were nice people, that's all. They just wanted a better life and now he's dead and the kid's lost her father.'

'There's nothing we can do to change that. All we can do now is go after the guys he was afraid of. Chances are that he was coerced into carrying the money. The way you tell it, he might not have known there was cash in those cans. It's not a problem.

I'll get a female officer to talk to the wife, find out what she knows.'

'She doesn't speak English,' said Shepherd.

'We'll fix up an interpreter,' said Hargrove.

Shepherd sighed. 'Maybe I should be the one to talk to her,' he said.

'It's not your problem.'

'She might respond to me. She's grateful because I saved her daughter. And I doubt that she thinks I'm anything to do with her husband's suicide.'

'We haven't told her yet,' said Hargrove.

'What?'

'As soon as she knows he's dead, she'll shut down,' said Hargrove. 'We'll get nothing out of her. We'll interview her first, then tell her. It has to be that way.'

'It's one hell of a world, isn't it?' said Shepherd.

'We don't make the rules,' said Hargrove. 'We just play by them. There's nothing we can do to bring him back, but we can go after the men who put the family in harm's way.'

'And what happens then? She and her kid get sent back?'

'If she helps us, we can fast-track her to a residency visa,' said Hargrove.

'And if she can't?'

'Then we'll do what we can. If she's a genuine Kosovan, there's a good chance she'll get refugee status anyway.'

'We owe her,' said Shepherd. 'However this pans out, we owe her.'

'Agreed,' said Hargrove. 'I'll do what I can, I promise.'

'When do we do it?'

'The sooner the better,' said Hargrove. 'I'll get Sharpe to pick you up. She's still at the hospital so we can do the interview there. I'll find a room and an interpreter.'

Shepherd did the calculations. It was a four-hour run up to Newcastle, even if the traffic was good. An hour for the interview. Maybe two. Four hours back. With the best will in the world he wouldn't be home before midnight. He'd have to take a raincheck with the major. 'I'll be ready,' he said. 'How do I play it?'

'Dead straight,' said Hargrove. 'Short of telling her that you're an undercover cop, of course. Tell her you're co-operating with the police, tell her we'll help her stay in the country if she helps us.'

'Okay,' agreed Shepherd. 'Will you be there?'

'Your call.'

'I guess I don't need back-up,' said Shepherd. 'It's not as if she's likely to turn nasty. By the way, the lovely Doctor Gift dropped by this morning.'

'Must be that time of the year again.'

'Nothing to do with you?'

'You're due your biannual check, aren't you?'

'Just so long as that's all it is,' said Shepherd. 'I thought maybe you'd sent her to see if I was suicidal after my dip in the sea.'

'You're not, are you?'

'Of course not.'

'There you are, then. How did it go?'

'She thinks I should get out more.'

'She might be right. Call me when you've done the interview.'

Shepherd cut the connection and called the major. He asked if they could reschedule their meeting for the following evening and Gannon agreed. Then Shepherd went upstairs and changed back into his Tony Corke clothes.

The interpreter was waiting for them outside the hospital, sitting behind the wheel of a six-year-old Ford Ka. She was a middle-aged woman, with permed hair and thick-lensed glasses, and introduced herself as Lyn. She didn't offer a surname and Shepherd didn't ask. He and Sharpe shook hands with her.

'You speak Kosovan?' asked Shepherd.

'I speak seven languages fluently,' she said matter-of-factly, 'and I can get by in another four.'

Shepherd was impressed. His trick memory was good for facts and faces, but it was of little help when it came to languages. He could memorise vocabulary without any problems but speaking a foreign language was more about comprehension and grammar. 'We need to talk to a woman called Edita about some items that were found in her belongings.'

'Edita?' Lyn took a packet of Silk Cut from her coat pocket and lit a cigarette with a cheap plastic lighter.

'Something wrong?' asked Shepherd.

Lyn shrugged. 'It is not a usual Kosovan name,' she said, 'but never mind. She's an illegal?'

'What makes you say that?'

'That's usually why I'm called in,' she said. 'Immigration cases, mainly. Asylum-seekers.'

Shepherd had been trying to place her accent, but without success. She spoke English with the same clarity as a BBC newsreader but he had the feeling she was from somewhere in Central or Eastern Europe. 'She was trying to get into the country, but our interest is purely in what she had with her.'

Lyn took a long pull on her cigarette. 'Let me finish this first,' she said. 'They don't let you smoke in hospitals.'

Shepherd and Sharpe waited until she had stubbed out the cigarette, then walked into the hospital. Sharpe showed his warrant card at Reception and went back to Shepherd and Lyn. 'The little girl's out of Intensive Care,' he said. 'Her mother's with her, on the third floor.'

They took the lift and Sharpe led the way to the room. It was similar to the one Shepherd had been kept in, but there was no uniformed policeman standing guard.

Edita was sitting on the edge of the bed, holding her daughter's hand. She smiled when she saw Shepherd, who smiled back.

Jessica was lying on her back, asleep, her arms on top of the blankets. There were no monitoring instruments, no drips, just a little girl asleep in bed.

'Pretty girl,' said Lyn. 'What happened to her?'

'She nearly drowned,' said Sharpe, closing the door and standing with his back to it. 'The doctors say she'll be fine.'

Lyn spoke to Edita, but she turned away and brushed a lock of hair away from her daughter's face.

'Tell her we need to talk to her about some money that was found among her belongings,' said Shepherd.

Lyn translated. Edita didn't reply.

'Edita, please, if you co-operate with the police they'll do everything they can to let you stay in the country,' said Shepherd.

Again, Lyn translated. Once again, the woman refused even to acknowledge her presence.

Shepherd exhaled deeply. 'Ask her what's wrong.'

Lyn spoke again, but was ignored. She frowned and went to stand next to Edita. She put a hand gently on the woman's shoulder and spoke softly. Edita flinched, then shook her head. Lyn said something else and this time the woman replied.

Lyn walked back to Shepherd. 'I know what the problem is,' she said. 'She's not from Kosovo. She's Albanian.'

'Do you speak Albanian?'

'Enough to get by,' said Lyn. 'Probably enough for what you need.'

Shepherd nodded. The family had Kosovan passports: if they were Albanian their travel documents must be forgeries. Or stolen. 'Tell her we need to talk to her now. I'm happy to do it here so that she can be near her daughter, but if she doesn't start talking we'll take her to an office.' He forced a smile. 'Don't make it sound as threatening as that.'

Lyn spoke to Edita again. Edita turned to Shepherd and said something in Albanian. It sounded very different from Kosovan, but Shepherd couldn't understand a word of either language.

'She wants to know if you've spoken to her husband,' said Lyn.

'Yes,' said Shepherd, nodding.

Edita spoke again. 'You must speak to her husband about this,' said Lyn. 'She says it is nothing to do with her.'

'Tell her that the police need to check the information they have.'

Lyn translated, but Edita simply shrugged.

'Do you want to try good-cop-bad-cop?' asked Sharpe.

Shepherd shook his head. The woman had been through enough, and soon she would learn that her husband had killed himself. 'Ask her if she knew that there was money in the oil cans,' he told Lyn.

Lyn translated. Edita answered angrily.

'She says it was nothing to do with her. They met only her husband, and her husband told her not to talk about it.'

'They? Who does she mean?'

Lyn translated. Edita snapped back.

'Two men in France. They met her husband before they got on to the boat.'

'Why would he agree to take something on board? Did they threaten him? Or the little girl?'

This time the conversation went back and forth a few times before Lyn offered a translation: 'She doesn't know who the men were, but they were gangsters. There was no need to make any threats because they didn't have enough money to pay for their passage to England. The husband was told that if he carried the cans with him they would make up the difference. She guessed there wasn't oil in them but her husband said she was to mind her own business.'

'Would she recognise them if we showed her photographs?'

Lyn translated, and Edita shook her head firmly.

'And she didn't know what was in the cans?'

Lyn spoke to Edita, who waved her away. Lyn looked to Shepherd for guidance. He sighed. It was pointless asking her any more. And he didn't think there was any point in taking the woman away for further questioning. 'Let's call it a day,' he said. 'Tell her we're through here.'

Lyn spoke to Edita, who nodded, then got up and went to Shepherd. 'Mr Corke, we thank you,' she said, in halting English. She grabbed his hand and pressed the palm against her cheek. 'Thank you.' Then she said something to Lyn. 'She wants to see her husband,' said the interpreter.

'Later,' said Shepherd. 'Tell her later.'

Shepherd untangled his hand and followed Sharpe out of the room. A wave of guilt washed over him. He wanted to tell Edita the truth, that her husband was dead, but he knew that the job of breaking the bad news was better left to professionals, to men and women who could offer therapy and support. Even if he had told her, what would he have done when she'd broken down? Held her and told her that everything would be all right? Patted her back and told her that time healed all wounds? He was finding it hard enough to come to terms with the loss of his wife and had no idea what to say to a woman whose husband had just killed himself.

Lyn followed them out of the room. 'Why does she think your name's Corke?' she asked, as they walked down the corridor.

'It's a long story,' said Shepherd.

'He's a man of mystery,' growled Sharpe. 'Just leave it at that.'

Shepherd phoned Hargrove on his mobile as soon as he climbed into the Vectra. 'They're Albanians, not Kosovans,' he said. 'Their passports need a going-over with any other documents they had. They told me they're called Rudi and Edita, and the interpreter says they're Albanian names. I'm guessing they won't be the names on the passports.'

'Did she tell you anything else?'

'Her husband spoke to some men in France before they got on to the trawler. They gave him the oil cans. She asked him what they needed the oil for and he said it was nothing to do with her, and that it was helping to pay for their passage to England.'

'What did she think was in the cans? Drugs?'

'She says she didn't think anything. Her husband told her not to question him, and she's a woman who obeys her husband.'

'She's lucky it wasn't heroin. If it was, we'd have a hard job keeping her out of prison. So, she's no idea what he was supposed to do with the cans once they were in the UK?'

'She says not. She could be lying, but I doubt it. She just wanted a new life in the UK and didn't much care what she did to achieve it.'

'I'm going to get Forensics to examine everything. I can't see that they'd have expected her husband to remember the contact details, not with a million euros at stake, so there must be an address or phone number somewhere.'

'Who's going to tell her about her husband?' asked Shepherd.

'I've got someone from one of the refugee charities on their way,' said Hargrove. 'They'll break the news, fix her up with somewhere to stay, legal advice, the full monty. She'll be in good hands, Spider. I promise. Get a decent night's sleep and I'll call you tomorrow.'

Shepherd cut the connection, sat back and closed his eyes as Sharpe powered down the motorway. When he opened them again, they were driving up the road towards his house. All the lights were off. Shepherd cursed.

'What?' said Sharpe.

'I didn't call Liam. I promised I'd take him to play football.'

'He'll understand,' said Sharpe. 'He's a cop's son.' He brought the car to a gentle stop in front of Shepherd's house.

'It was a pinkie promise,' said Shepherd.

'What?'

'A pinkie promise. We linked little fingers.'

'Right . . .'

'The sort of promise you can't break.'

'Except you did.'

Shepherd smiled sarcastically. 'See? You do understand.'

'He's a kid,' said Sharpe. 'Kids know that dads do their best.'

'Cheers, Razor.' Shepherd punched his arm and climbed out of the Vectra. Sharpe drove away as he walked up to the front door and let himself in.

He switched on the hall light, padded upstairs and pushed open the door to Liam's bedroom. His heart lurched when he saw that his son's bed was empty, the quilt thrown to one side. He switched on the light and glanced round the room, then hurried to the bathroom. Liam wasn't there. Shepherd's heart raced and he fought to quell rising panic. If anything had happened, Katra would have phoned him. He took a deep breath, headed for her room and opened the door. Liam was curled up next to Katra, who was lying on top of the quilt in flannelette pyjamas, one arm round the child, her hair a dark curtain over the pillow. She opened her eyes as the light from the hallway fell across her face.

She opened her mouth to speak but Shepherd smiled and pressed his index finger to his lips, then closed the door. He went to his room, pulled off his clothes and showered. He still felt bad about not calling Liam, but at least he had until morning to think of some way to make it up to him.

It was just after eleven when Shepherd woke. He changed into his running gear and went downstairs. Katra had heard him and had a mug of strong coffee waiting for him. 'I didn't hear you guys get up,' he said.

'Liam went in to say good morning but you were fast asleep,' she said, as she unloaded the dishwasher. 'You must have been tired.'

'I've had a rough few days,' he said. He took several gulps of coffee. 'I had to go back up north. Unfinished business.'

'You work too hard,' she said.

'I don't know about hard, but I'm certainly putting in more than my fair share of hours.'

'Can't you transfer to an office job, with more regular hours?'

That was exactly what Sue had always said. Undercover work was dangerous and meant long hours away from home. But the overtime payments were generous and he knew he'd never get the same satisfaction sitting behind a desk. 'It's what I do, Katra,' he said. That had always been his answer to Sue, even though he knew it was more excuse than explanation. He could have done other jobs within the police – he still could. He could even go back to the SAS as an instructor. The major had made clear to him that an offer to join the Directing Staff was always on the table.

'I know Liam wishes he could spend more time with you,' said Katra.

'It's just been a busy period, that's all,' said Shepherd. 'I'll be around over the weekend. Most of it.' He drained his mug and put it into the sink.

'Do you want breakfast?' asked Katra.

Shepherd grabbed his rucksack and headed for the door. 'I'll eat when I get back,' he said.

★   ★   ★

Shepherd was lying on the sofa watching a black-and-white cowboy movie when he heard Katra walking down the hallway. He looked at his watch and realised she was going to pick up Liam from school. 'Katra!' he called. 'Hang on a minute.' He switched off the television and hurried into the hallway. 'I'll fetch Liam.' He held out his hands for the car keys.

'Are you sure?'

'I'm on a day off,' said Shepherd, 'and I owe him some quality time.'

'You are always busy,' said Katra. She was wearing a baggy denim shirt over a pair of khaki cargo pants and looked about fifteen.

'So are you,' he said. 'Have a few hours off. Don't bother cooking – I'll take Liam for fast food. You talk about me working long hours but you're always on the go. Kick back, watch some TV.'

Katra laughed. 'I've got ironing to do,' she said. 'And fast food is bad for you.'

'Once in a blue moon won't kill him.'

Katra frowned. 'A blue moon?'

Shepherd grinned. Katra's English had improved rapidly during the months she'd been with him and Liam, but she still didn't have too good a grasp of slang and idiom. Her English was still a hundred times better than Shepherd's Slovenian, though. 'It means rarely. Not often. You don't often see a blue moon.'

Katra's brow creased into a frown. 'I don't think I have ever seen the moon blue.'

'It's just an expression,' said Shepherd. He waved goodbye, went outside and climbed into the dark green Honda CRV. Parked next to it was the battered Land Rover he used when he was being Tony Corke.

He'd barely started the car when one of his mobiles rang. He fumbled in his pocket for it. It was his work phone and Hargrove was on the line. Shepherd slotted the phone into the hands-free socket. 'Can you talk?' asked the superintendent.

'I'm just heading to Liam's school,' said Shepherd. 'What's

up?' He slowed down to well under the speed limit – the main road was peppered with cameras.

'We found a telephone number under the insole of one of Rudi Pernaska's shoes,' said Hargrove. 'A throwaway mobile. There's a good chance it's the contact for the money. We've run a check on the phone and it's never been used.'

'Sounds like they're waiting for a call.' A set of traffic-lights ahead turned red and he brought the CRV to a stop. 'How do you want to play it?'

'Assuming the number is that of the contact who's expecting delivery of the cans, we should run with it. I've got our technical team resealing them and fitting a tracking device. We deliver them and see where they lead us.'

'You want me to handle the delivery?' said Shepherd.

'There's a number of options,' said Hargrove. 'You could switch roles, call up and say you were on the boat with Rudi, that he's been sent to an immigration centre and you've got the cans. It'd mean you pretending to be an asylum-seeker.'

'My language skills aren't up to that,' said Shepherd. 'If I say I'm from Kosovo and they wheel in a Kosovan speaker, it'll all be over.'

'Plan B would be to bring in someone who can pass themselves off as an asylum-seeker. We've got a Chinese guy on a long-term drugs play – I could pull him in.'

'Is there a Plan C?'

'You stick with the Tony Corke legend. Make a call, say you were on the crew and that you've got the cans. Tell them Pernaska gave you the number but you'll want paying.'

'And if they're hard cases, I get a bullet in the back of my head for my trouble.'

'You've got a million euros of their money,' said Hargrove. 'I would think they'll negotiate. Just make sure you arrange the handover in a public place.'

'Then you bust them?'

'I've had a word with Europol,' said Hargrove. 'They're keen to nail down both ends of this operation, Britain and France, and they'd like you to make contact with the British end, see if you can set up some sort of a deal to bring in more currency.'

'Offer to smuggle in more for them?'

'Find out why they're using refugees. And see if they'd be interested in you using a more direct method. We can set you up with a high-speed boat, which would fit in with your Corke legend.'

'I'm going to be sailing across the Channel on my own?'

'I'm told it's no more complicated than driving a car,' said Hargrove. 'We'll have you well trained, don't worry.'

'And you think they'll trust me?'

'You'll be handing over a million euros. That's got to buy you a lot of goodwill.'

'Why wouldn't Corke just do a runner with the cash?'

The lights turned green and Shepherd edged the car forward, looking both ways as he crossed the junction.

'Because he figured he was dealing with some very heavy people. And he's out on bail facing a prison sentence. He'd be looking for money to pay his lawyers.'

'Makes sense,' said Shepherd. 'Okay, when do I call them?'

'Sooner rather than later. We're keeping Pernaska's suicide under wraps. His wife and daughter will be held by Immigration in Croydon until the investigation's run its course – Pernaska's contact here will be expecting him to get in touch today so we don't want to go beyond tonight because they might start asking questions. Call this afternoon, but be cagey. It's going to take a day or two for us to get the tracker in place. Make contact, but tell them you'll need time to think about where to do the handover.'

'Do I tell them I know what's in the cans?'

'Best not – or maybe that you think it's drugs. Then play it by ear when you meet.'

'How do I explain that I'm footloose and fancy-free?'

'Tell them you've got a good lawyer and he got you bail. You used your house as security.'

'And you'll keep Pepper and Mosley out of the way?'

'It's already in hand. So, you're up for this?'

'Sure,' said Shepherd.

'I'll text you the number. Be handy if you could record the conversation with them.'

'I'll do it from home later tonight,' said Shepherd. He cut the connection.

He was still half a mile from Liam's school but already the traffic had slowed to a crawl. Ahead all he could see were middle-aged women at the wheel of expensive SUVs. As a kid Shepherd had spent thirty minutes on the bus to get to and from school, with a ten-minute walk at either end – his parents had been happy for him to go out on his own. At weekends he'd disappear on his bike for hours and they were perfectly happy, providing he was back before dark. Those days were long gone. Now Shepherd lived in Ealing, which was as safe as anywhere could be, but every year across the UK children were raped and murdered, or disappeared never to be seen again. Teenagers were out on the streets with knives and guns. Twelve-year-old crack addicts thought nothing of mugging a kid for his mobile phone and lunch money, while paedophiles were allowed to roam at will. There was no way Shepherd would allow Liam to use public transport to get about, and while he knew that the school run was a waste of time and fuel he, like most other parents, preferred it to the alternative.

Liam was waiting outside the school gates. He waved at the CRV and ran towards it, sports bag banging on his hip. He frowned when he saw that Shepherd was driving. He pulled open the passenger door, climbed into the front seat, dropped his bag in the back and fastened his seatbelt. 'Where's Katra?'

'I said I'd pick you up today. We can go and have a burger.' Shepherd put the CRV in gear and pulled away from the kerb.

'You said we'd play football yesterday,' said Liam sullenly.

'I got held up,' said Shepherd. 'I'm sorry.'

'Where were you?'

'I had to go and see someone and they were late.'

'It was a pinkie promise,' said Liam, folding his arms and staring straight ahead.

'I know.'

'Pinkie promises are real promises.'

'I meant it when I promised, I really did, but something happened.'

'And you didn't even get up this morning.'

'I was tired.'

'It's like you don't care.'

'I care, Liam. Of course I care – I'm your dad.'

'You don't always act like my dad.'

Shepherd felt as if he'd been punched in the stomach. He didn't know what to say, because he knew that Liam was right. Recently he hadn't been behaving much like a father. He was a policeman who happened to have a son, and more often than not his son ended up playing second fiddle to the job.

'Do you want McDonald's or Burger King? Or we could have KFC?'

'I don't like KFC much.'

'McDonald's, then? Or Burger King?'

'McDonald's, I guess.'

Shepherd drove to the nearest branch and they went inside. Liam ordered a Big Mac, fries and a Coke. Shepherd had a cheeseburger. They sat at a table by the window. 'How was school?'

'School's school,' said Liam.

'I was hoping for a bit more information than that,' said Shepherd.

'We did geography. And literature.'

'Yeah, what are you reading?'

'Anthony Horowitz's new Alex Rider book.'

'Alex Rider?'

'He's great. He's a kid who's a secret agent. He does the coolest stuff.'

'And you read that at school?'

'Yes.'

'In my day we did Dickens and Jane Austen.'

'Who?'

'Never mind,' said Shepherd. 'What does he do, this Alex Rider?'

'Fights bad guys and saves the world.'

'And how old is he?'

'He's a teenager.'

Shepherd grinned. 'And you believe that a teenager can save the world?'

Liam raised his eyebrows. 'They're books, Dad. Stories.'

Shepherd rarely spoke to his son about his work. He hadn't told Sue much, either. Not the details. Not that every now and again his life was on the line, that he'd looked down the barrels of several guns, and that while he hadn't actually saved the world he had fought more than a few bad guys. Part of him wanted to tell his son a few war stories, to see his eyes light up with excitement, but he didn't want Liam to know how dangerous his work was. In the real world, heroes didn't get shot in the chest and live to fight another day. Fist fights hurt like hell, and when you did shoot someone you never forgot the way the body slumped to the ground and the blood pumped out of them as they died. There was nothing glamorous about violence, although Shepherd couldn't deny the adrenaline rush it gave him.

'What about we go and play football tonight?' asked Liam.

'Sure,' said Shepherd. 'We can have a kickabout.' Liam grinned. Then Shepherd remembered Major Gannon. 'I'm sorry, Liam,' he said. 'I've got to meet someone.' Liam's face fell. 'I'm really sorry. It's important.'

'It's always important,' said Liam. He put down what was left of his burger.

'Come on, finish your Big Mac and we'll buy you some comics. Maybe a new game for your PlayStation.'

'I'm not hungry,' said Liam.

'Tomorrow's Saturday. We can play football then.'

'Whatever.'

Shepherd could see he was close to tears. 'Liam . . .'

'I want to go home.'

Shepherd reached over to ruffle his son's hair, but Liam leaned back, out of reach. Then he pushed himself out of his chair and headed for the door.

Shepherd walked through Harrods, taking a circuitous route through the perfumes department as he checked for a tail, then headed for the street behind the shop. The Special Forces Club was in a red-brick mansion block, typical of the upper-class residences in Knightsbridge. There was no plaque on the wall to identify it: it had been taken down in the wake of the terrorist attacks in America. The front door was never locked – the club was open twenty-four hours a day, seven days a week.

There was a small reception desk in the hallway, manned by a short, stocky former SAS staff sergeant who had once killed three men with his bare hands. Shepherd nodded at him as he signed in. 'How are they hanging, Sandy?'

'Fine, *sir*,' he said, with just a touch of irony. There were no ranks in the club.

Shepherd jogged upstairs to the first-floor bar. He saw Major Gannon sitting in a winged leather armchair by the window. Shepherd ordered a Jameson's and ice from the white-jacketed waiter and went over to shake hands. As he sat down in an armchair, he saw the Major's metal briefcase by the wall. It contained the secure satellite phone that those in the know called the Almighty.

'Working hard, Spider?' said Gannon.

'No rest for the wicked. Immigration scams. People-smuggling.'

'The new frontier,' said the Major. 'Last I heard there was more money to be made out of people-trafficking than there was from drugs.'

Shepherd grinned. 'I think that, pound for pound, cocaine still has the edge, but overall you're right. It's a bigger business.'

'With less of a downside,' said the Major.

'Yeah. Get caught with a few hundred kilos of a class-A drug and they'll throw away the key. Get caught with a containerload of Chinese workers and you'd be unlucky to get three years. Plus the traffickers get paid in advance, cash on the nail. The going rate into the UK is six thousand dollars. The drugs guys don't get their money until the drugs are delivered.'

'We're in the wrong business,' laughed the Major. 'Here we are, defending the free world for a pittance and the chance of a pension, while the bad guys live like princes.'

'We get the medals,' said Shepherd.

'Ah, yes, the medals,' said the Major.

'And we know we've got right on our side.' Shepherd raised his glass to the Major. 'So that's all right, then.'

The two men clinked their glasses.

'What about you?' asked Shepherd. 'Much on?'

'Still looking after the Increment,' said the Major. 'I'm doing such a good job, apparently, that they don't want me to do anything else.' The Increment was the government's best-kept secret: a group of highly trained special forces soldiers who were used on operations considered too dangerous for Britain's security services, MI5 and MI6. The Major headed the unit from the Duke of York Barracks in London, close to Sloane Square. Calls from MI5 and MI6, and the prime minister's office, came through on the satellite phone, which was never far from his side. The Major was able to draw on all the resources of the Special Air Service and the Special Boat Service, plus any other experts he required. 'I keep telling them I'm too long in the tooth for all this action stuff, but they just pat me on the back and say I'm the best man for the job.'

'It's good to be wanted,' said Shepherd.

'Which is why I asked you here,' said the Major. 'Somebody wants you. Or, at least, a chat with you.'

'About?'

'That's need-to-know, and apparently I don't need to know.'

'Terrific,' said Shepherd.

The Major sipped his drink. 'He's here now.'

Shepherd smiled tightly. 'The guy at the bar behind me? American, late forties, grey hair cut short, thin lips, class ring on his right hand, Rolex Submariner watch, the anniversary model with the green bezel, grey suit, pink shirt, blue tie with black stripes, black loafers with tassels, drinking gin and tonic?'

The Major grinned. 'You and your photographic memory,' he said. 'But it's vodka he's drinking, not gin. How did you know he was a Yank?'

'The class ring's very American. And he's reading the *International Herald Tribune*,' said Shepherd. 'Elementary, my dear Watson.'

The Major smiled. 'Oh, yes,' he said. 'He's very American.'

'FBI, CIA, DEA?'

'None of the above. He used to be CIA but now he's something in Homeland Security. A special unit answerable to someone at the White House.' The Major picked up his metal briefcase and stood up. 'I'll leave you to it,' he said. 'It's for your ears only, he says.'

'Secret Squirrel?'

The Major clapped Shepherd's shoulder and headed for the door. On the way out he nodded to the man at the bar, who slid off his stool and carried his drink to Shepherd's table. 'Thanks for this, Dan,' he said. He held out his hand. 'Richard Yokely.' He had a slight Southern drawl.

Shepherd shook his hand.

'Can I get you another drink?' asked Yokely.

'I'm fine,' said Shepherd. 'I'm surprised to see an American drinking alcohol. I thought, these days, you weren't allowed any vices.'

'I'm sure my secret's safe with you,' he said. 'Besides, I'm old school. I reckon it's more about the results a man gets than his appearance.' He leaned across the table. 'Don't tell anyone, but I still enjoy the odd cigar.' He chuckled, sat back in his chair and stretched out his legs. 'So, thanks for coming. I've heard a lot about you, Dan. All good.'

'That's a worry,' said Shepherd, 'since I'm supposed to be undercover.'

'We're on the same side,' said Yokely. 'I get to see some very secret files. And your name was mentioned in glowing terms.'

'And who is it you work for?'

The American shrugged carelessly. 'I don't have a business card, as such,' he said. 'Or an office. Truth be told, I'm more of a facilitator.'

'For whom?'

Another shrug. And a slight smile. 'For the government. In the same way that your Superintendent Hargrove is answerable to the Home Office, I answer directly to the head of Homeland Security. It's a very tight chain of command. I talk to my boss, he talks to the President. Sometimes I talk to the President direct. And in the same way that your unit doesn't have a name or any of those cute initials they like to give everything now, I don't have a designated department.' He grinned. 'I'm just little old me. The be-all and end-all.'

'And your brief?'

'To save the free world, Dan. To make the world a safer place.' He took a sip of his vodka and tonic, then swirled the ice round his glass with his index finger. 'What you did, down in the Tube, that was one hell of a thing.'

Shepherd said nothing.

'You saved a lot of lives,' said Yokely.

'I killed a man,' said Shepherd.

'Yes, you did,' said the American. 'You shot him in the back of the head. And some. Would you care to run it by me?'

Shepherd looked at Yokely for several seconds, then nodded slowly. That Gannon had arranged the meeting meant that Yokely could be trusted. Shepherd just wished he knew what the meeting was about. 'I was working undercover, infiltrating an armed-response unit,' he said. 'As part of that operation I was on the Underground. Armed. There were four suicide-bombers primed to detonate at the same time. One was killed above ground – by muggers, as it happened. One went off above ground. One deto-nated on a platform at Liverpool Street station. I killed the fourth.'

Yokely grinned.

'What's funny?' asked Shepherd, quickly. Too quickly. He'd sounded defensive.

'Your terminology is much more forthright than I'm used to,' said the American. 'The guys I work with would never be so up-front. They'd refer to it as "terminating the objective" or "managing the situation" or something equally banal.'

'I killed him,' said Shepherd flatly. 'Shot him seven times.'

'You didn't think that was overkill?'

'The two bombs that went off killed forty-seven people and injured more than a hundred others,' said Shepherd. 'You can't take any chances with suicide-bombers. Even mortally wounded, they can still press the trigger. You have to keep firing until you're sure, absolutely sure, they're dead. Or in a non-living situation, as your guys would probably say.'

'You shot him from behind,' said Yokely.

'Yes, I did.'

'So you couldn't see if he was holding the trigger?'

'It was a fair assumption.'

'In fact,' said Yokely, slowly, 'you couldn't even be sure that he was a suicide-bomber. Not from what you could see.'

'He was wearing a vest packed with explosives,' said Shepherd. 'There was a timing device too, so that if he was incapacitated, the device would still explode.'

Yokely held up a hand. 'Please don't get me wrong, Dan. I'm not suggesting it wasn't a totally righteous kill. You deserve a medal for what you did, no doubt about it. I'm just interested in the mechanics of what happened.'

'I identified the target. I killed him before he could detonate the bomb. End of story.'

'I suppose it would be trite to ask if you had any regrets.'

'Regrets?'

'About killing a man in cold blood.'

'No one kills in cold blood,' said Shepherd. 'That's a fallacy. The adrenaline courses through the system, the heart races, the hands shake. You can train to suppress the body's natural reactions, but no one kills coldly.'

'You've killed before, right?'

'In combat. Under fire.'

'So what happened on the Tube, that was the first time you'd shot an unarmed man?'

'Like I said, he wasn't exactly unarmed,' said Shepherd. 'He was wired up with a dozen pounds of high explosive.'

'Which you couldn't see from where you were.'

'What are you getting at?' said Shepherd.

'Stay with me for a while, Dan,' said Yokely. 'My point is that you made the kill without seeing the imminent threat for yourself.'

'Major Gannon had the area under observation through CCTV,' said Shepherd. 'He was in the British Transport Police observation centre.'

'But even he wasn't one hundred per cent sure,' said the American.

'Maybe. But all's well that ends well.'

'Absolutely,' said Yokely, enthusiastically. 'But tell me, how important was it to you that the Major was directing you?'

'I trust him totally,' said Shepherd.

'And if it had been someone else? Suppose it had been a Transport Police chief inspector who had made the call? Would you have been as willing to shoot?'

Shepherd sat back in his chair and considered the question. To an SAS trooper, obeying orders came naturally: rank commanded respect, even if the man who held it didn't. From time to time Shepherd had carried out orders he hadn't agreed with, but not often. In the police the situation was nowhere near as cut and dried. Promotion had more to do with politics and point-scoring than it did with ability, and Shepherd constantly came across officers whose judgement was questionable. Working for Superintendent Hargrove's undercover unit insulated him from having to follow orders given by men he didn't respect or trust, and that was the nub of the American's question. Would Shepherd have shot the terrorist if anyone other than the Major had given the order? At the time Shepherd had been working under-cover in SO19, the armed-response unit of the Metropolitan Police and while the officers he'd worked with had all been first rate, he doubted that he would have trusted them as much as he trusted the Major. He took a sip of whiskey. 'I might have hesitated if it had been anyone else,' he said.

'Nothing wrong with that,' said the American. 'You're paid to use your judgement. If you weren't you'd be in uniform handing out speeding tickets.'

'But if the scenario was the same, with a terrorist about to kill dozens of innocent bystanders, I'd shoot. Face to face, back of the head, wherever, whenever.'

'Okay. Let me run a different scenario by you. Suppose the terrorist had been on a train, heading to the station. You knew he didn't plan to detonate until he reached the destination, but suppose the Major had ordered you to shoot him on the train. Would you have done that?'

'Of course,' said Shepherd, emphatically. 'He could just as easily press the trigger on the train.'

'Now suppose he was walking towards the station to board the train, wearing the vest, fingers on the trigger. You'd shoot?'

'Yes.'

The American nodded thoughtfully. 'And if the terrorist was in his safe-house, preparing to don the vest. You burst in through the door. He looks at the vest. The trigger is close by. You'd shoot?'

Now Shepherd could see where the conversation was going. 'Yes,' he said.

The American smiled. 'Because your life was in imminent danger, or because he was a terrorist?'

'It wouldn't be an execution,' said Shepherd. 'The threat is that he would detonate the bomb. To use the phraseology of your guys, I would neutralise that threat.'

'Now, the sixty-four-thousand-dollar question—' said Yokely.

'Would I shoot him a month before the operation?' interrupted Shepherd. 'Would I kill him if I knew he was planning a terrorist incident?'

'Gannon said you were a sharp cookie.'

'Can cookies be sharp?' Shepherd smiled.

'Would you?' said the American, treating Shepherd's question as rhetorical. 'Would you shoot an unarmed man in anticipation of something he was going to do?'

'You mean, if someone had smothered Baby Hitler in his cradle, would millions of lives have been saved?'

The American shrugged. 'If you want to think of it that way.'

'You're talking about assassinations,' said Shepherd.

'I'm just shooting the breeze with you, Dan.'

'We tried it a few years ago,' said Shepherd. 'Gibraltar, 1988.' The SAS had mown down three unarmed IRA terrorists who had been planning to detonate a massive car bomb. 'Shit hit the fan with a vengeance. The media went for us. The European Court of Human Rights said our guys were wrong to shoot.'

'Easy for them to say,' said Yokely. 'Last I heard, the court wasn't anywhere near Gibraltar.'

'They had a point,' said Shepherd. 'We could have arrested them.'

'Lives were saved that day, Dan. A lot of lives. And we're in the position to start saving a lot more.'

'By killing people?'

'The world has changed, post 9/11. We've become more pre-emptive with our effects-based operations.' The American smiled thinly. 'In other words, we plan to get our defence in first.'

'Under whose authority?'

'We don't need anyone's authority any more,' said Yokely. 'It's like George W said. You're either with us or you're against us. We don't care what the European Court of Human Rights says. We shit on Amnesty and the rest of the misguided do-gooders. We do what we have to do.' He leaned closer to Shepherd. 'Forgive my French, Dan, but the world has gone fucking crazy and it's about time we brought some sanity to it.' He sat back and smiled easily. 'You've seen what's happening. They're hijacking planes full of women and children and flying them into buildings where decent people are doing nothing more than working to put food on their families' tables. They're cutting the heads off men and women who are begging for their lives. They're blowing up trains full of commuters. They're not fighting a war, these people, they're fighting a Crusade – with a capital C. They want us dead, Dan. They want us off the face of this earth. There's no draw being offered, no shaking hands and living together. They want us face down on a prayer mat five times a day or they want us dead. And it's time for us to start fighting back.'

'And who decides who shoots whom?'

'That'll come from the White House,' said Yokely. 'Decisions will be taken on the basis of all available intelligence. It's not a sanction that will be applied lightly, but it will be applied, and in my opinion it's about time. These people don't fight fair, Dan, they fight to win. And up to now we've been hampered by the fact that we've always played by the rules. Look what happened a while back when *Newsweek* ran the story that some interrogator at Guantanamo Bay had flushed a copy of the Koran down the toilet. Muslims go crazy in Afghanistan, the president of Pakistan gets on his high horse, and our own national security adviser, God bless his little cotton socks, stands up and says they'll investigate and take action. Excuse me, but it's a book. They're hacking the heads off charity workers in Baghdad, planning to poison our air with anthrax, doing everything they can to buy weapons of mass destruction, and we're worrying about a book. I was at Guantanamo Bay, and I can tell you that the story was horseshit. Never happened. But if I thought it would help damage al-Qaeda in any way I'd be first in line to wipe my arse with the bloody thing.' Yokely took a deep breath. 'Anyway, that's just me. I feel pretty strongly about what we're doing, Dan. Our way of life is under attack and I'm stepping up to defend it. End of story.'

Shepherd sipped his drink, his mind racing. The Special Forces Club was a place that had heard more than its fair share of tall stories, but this one took some beating. He was being sounded out for a job as a hired killer. Under other circumstances he'd have been wired up in anticipation of arresting Yokely and locking him up for a long time. 'You're putting together an assassination team?' he said, wanting the American to spell out exactly what he was planning.

'Not a team, exactly. More a group of individuals who may or may not work in co-operation on particular assignments.'

'So I'd just sit at home, waiting for the call?'

Yokely shook his head. 'You'd be placed with an official body, the Office of Anti-terrorism Assistance, for instance, as a consultant. You'd advise law-enforcement personnel from friendly governments on procedures to deal with terrorism. Bomb detection, crime-scene investigation, VIP protection. All the sort of techniques you're familiar with. And then, from time to time, we'd draw on you to utilise your particular talent.'

'You think killing people is a talent?'

'Most people can't do it, Dan,' said the American, in a low whisper. 'They reckon that up to half the soldiers who stormed the beaches on D-Day were firing high. And you're doing well if you can get a quarter of the men in a firing squad to hit the target. Human beings aren't natural killers of their own species. Few animals are. You're special, Dan. And in return for your services, you'd be very well paid. I'm not sure exactly what salary you're currently on, but I can guarantee that while you're working for us you'll be getting ten times as much. And as much downtime as you need. Full medical and psychiatric back-up.'

Shepherd grimaced. 'I already have a shrink on my case,' he said.

'They're necessary,' said Yokely. 'We're very well aware of the psychological damage that can be done by taking human life. You won't be on your own.'

'And if I get caught?'

'You'll have the full backing of the White House,' said the American. 'First of all, anything we do will be so well planned, so well thought out, that every eventuality will have been taken into account.'

'Yeah, and they said the *Titanic* was unsinkable,' said Shepherd.

'Second of all, in the unlikely event that any operative is in the least bit compromised, all it will take is a one-on-one phone call from our big guy to your big guy and it gets smoothed out.'

'As easy as that?'

'These are big boys' games, Dan,' said Yokely. 'Big boys' rules apply.' He sighed. 'No one expects you to make up your mind here and now,' he said. 'Think about it. Think about whether or not you're up to it. Whether or not you want to be involved. If so, we can talk again. If not, well, hell, it's been nice chewing the fat with you. But I want you to know one thing. The world now is a very dangerous place. A lot of innocent people are going to die. As a cop, you'll be putting away villains – drug-dealers, conmen, thieves. You come and work for us and you'll really be making a difference.' Yokely stood up. 'It's important work, Dan. It doesn't come any more important.'

Shepherd didn't turn to watch the American walk away. He stared at the wall, swirling his whiskey and ice in the glass, trying to pin down how he felt about Yokely's offer. Could he become a government-sanctioned assassin? Could he kill total strangers for no other reason than that he was told to? Didn't that put him on the same moral level as a terrorist? Didn't they kill for what they believed in? Hell, wouldn't he be worse than a terrorist? He'd be killing for cold, hard cash. He took a long pull at his drink. And it would mean lying to his friends and family. It had been bad enough when he was in the SAS and almost every-thing was classified. If he worked for Yokely, he'd never be able to tell anyone what he did for a living. It would be worse than working undercover. He'd be living a lie at every minute of every day.

He closed his eyes and leaned back, placing the cold glass against his forehead. The money would be useful, though. A few years at that level and he'd be set up for life. Assuming that men who worked for Yokely were allowed to retire. Any organisation that was geared up for execution without trial would have no qualms about disposing of former employees who knew too much. It would be a tough decision to make. He'd have to think about it. Long and hard. But he was sure of one thing already. He was certain he could the job. And do it well.

★   ★   ★

Shepherd waited until Liam was asleep before slotting an unused Sim card into one of his phones. He took it upstairs to his bedroom and pulled out the drawer in one of the bedside cabinets. Inside was a small digital recorder to which was attached a length of black-plastic-coated wire ending in a small suction cup. He licked the suction cup and pressed it to the back of the mobile. Then, on his work mobile, he called up the text message Hargrove had sent him. He tapped out the number and listened to the ringing tone, then pressed 'play' on the recorder. After half a dozen rings the call was answered but nobody spoke. 'Hello?' said Shepherd. No one answered. 'Is anyone there?'

'Who is this?' said a voice.

Shepherd couldn't place the accent. 'Who am I speaking to?' he asked.

The line went dead. 'Great,' Shepherd muttered. 'Play hard to get, why don't you?'

He pressed 'redial'. Three rings later, the call was answered. Again, no one spoke. 'Listen, I've got something you want,' said Shepherd. 'Hang up on me again and I'll keep it for myself.'

'Who is this?' said the voice. Indian, maybe, or Pakistani – even Bangladeshi. There were so many possibilities that it was pointless to guess.

'I'm the guy who's got the stuff you were expecting from France.'

'You're not Pernaska.'

'Do I sound like an asylum-seeker?'

'Where is Pernaska?'

'The cops have got him.'

The line went quiet as if someone had put a hand over the receiver. After a few seconds, the man spoke again: 'You have what Pernaska was carrying?'

'I have all his shit. Including the cans he was supposed to give you.'

'And how did you get this number?'

'Because I'm psychic,' said Shepherd, scornfully. 'How do you think I got the number?'

'Why don't you tell me?' said the man, patiently.

'Rudi gave it to me and told me to call you.'

'Because?'

'Because the immigration cops have got him under wraps and he was worried you might think he'd gone off with your drugs.'

'Drugs? What drugs?'

'Look, I wasn't born yesterday,' said Shepherd. 'It's not cooking oil you wanted brought into the country. Now, do you want it or not?'

'It is our property. Of course we want it,' said the man.

'Well, possession being nine-tenths of the law, strictly speaking it's my property at the moment.'

The line went quiet again. Then a second voice spoke, deeper than the first, the accent similar. 'Who is this?'

'Am I talking to the organ-grinder, finally?' asked Shepherd.

'What do you mean?'

'Are you the guy in charge?'

'Who are you?'

'We're going round in circles here,' said Shepherd. 'I've got the cans. I assume you want them. How much are you prepared to pay me?'

'Pay you? For what?'

'For the cans. For what's in them?'

'Have you opened them?'

'No. But if we don't get to the point, I will. Now, are we going to do business or not?'

'How much do you want?'

'How much are you prepared to pay?' asked Shepherd.

'Five thousand pounds.'

Shepherd laughed. 'I'm not Federal Express,' he said. 'If that's the best you can do, I'm going to get a can-opener.'

'Twenty,' said the man, hurriedly. 'Twenty thousand pounds. That's my final offer.'

'That's more like it.'

'Now, at least I should know the name of the man I'm giving twenty thousand pounds to.'

'No names,' said Shepherd. 'I don't need to know who you are, you don't need to know who I am.'

'But at least you can tell me why you're in possession of the cans.'

'I was on the ship. Part of the crew.'

'Okay,' said the man, thoughtfully. 'And what happened? Why do the police have Pernaska?'

'Not the police. Immigration. We were caught crossing the North Sea, on the way to the Northumberland coast. The cops took the crew but all the cargo claimed asylum. Pernaska managed to talk to me before Immigration took him away. I got back on the boat and picked up his bags.'

'When can I have my property?'

'Where are you?' asked Shepherd.

'Why do you want to know?'

'Because I've called a mobile so you could be anywhere in the country. Overseas, even. And I'm not keen to travel hundreds of miles.'

'Where are you?' The voice repeated Shepherd's question.

'London.'

'So are we.'

'We?'

'You have my property. I want it back.'

'Let me think about it,' said Shepherd. 'I'll call you.'

'When?'

'When I've thought about it,' said Shepherd. 'Have the twenty grand ready for when I call.' Shepherd cut the connection. He made a verbal note of the time and date, then switched off the recorder. He grinned at his reflection in the mirror above the dressing-table. 'That went well,' he said.

He picked up his personal mobile and phoned Hargrove. He relayed the conversation he'd had with the man on the throwaway mobile.

'What do you want to do? Let him sweat until tomorrow?' asked Hargrove.

'I think so,' said Shepherd. 'He's got to believe I'm a little nervous, right? I'll phone tomorrow and ask if he's got the money. Assuming he has, we could do the handover on Sunday. Would the tracker be ready by then?'

'Should be,' said Hargrove. 'They're working on it now. They've already resealed two of the cans and they've done a good job.'

'Day or night?' asked Shepherd.

'Afternoon,' said Hargrove. 'Gives the technical boys the morning and us the chance to run with it while it's still light.'

'Any thoughts on location?'

'For your safety, a public place is best – it'll give us more surveillance possibilities. But not near a motorway. The tracking device we'll be using is good, but we don't want to be belting down the fast lane after them. Ideally, close to where they're based. You didn't get a sense of who they are?'

'Asian, I'd guess.'

'Okay, I'll run a check through NCIS but let's not hold our breath. Maybe let them suggest a place. But no going up dark alleys. A million euros is worth killing for.'

'Yeah, but twenty thousand quid isn't.'

'Just be careful.'

'Careful is my middle name,' said Shepherd.

'I mean it. They won't be happy about an outsider knowing what they're up to. They might want to make sure there are no witnesses. We'll be watching your back, but I want you out in the open with lots of people around.'

'Message received,' said Shepherd.

'And what about the twenty grand? You don't think you pitched it too low?'

'All Corke knows is that the cans have to be delivered, not what's inside. Could just be a few kilos of dope.'

'True. But they agreed the twenty grand straight away. Corke might well figure he could up the ante.'

The superintendent was right. 'I'll make the call tomorrow,' said Shepherd.

He cut the connection and went downstairs, got a bottle of

Corona beer from the fridge, sat down in front of the television and began to flick through the channels with the remote control.

The little boy picked up the boomerang with a puzzled frown. 'How does it work?' he asked his father.

Derek Jewell took it from his six-year-old son. It was of reddish wood, thickly varnished, with koala bears painted on it. 'You throw it, and it comes back to you,' he said.

'Like remote control?' said the boy.

'No, it comes back because . . .' Jewell scratched his head. 'Honey, help me out here, will you?' he said to his wife.

Sally Jewell raised her eyebrows. 'You're the physicist.' She laughed. 'Didn't you do aerodynamics?' She was holding their two-year-old daughter, who was asleep.

'It was a long time ago,' he said.

'I don't think the laws of physics have changed much over the last ten years, have they?'

'Thanks, honey,' said Jewell. 'I knew I could rely on your support.'

'Actually, not all boomerangs come back,' said the teenager who was looking after the stall. 'The killing ones don't.'

'Can we have a killing one, Dad?' said the little boy. 'Can we?'

'I don't think so,' said Jewell. 'Anyway, they might not let you take it on the plane. It's probably classed as an offensive weapon.'

'What's offensive mean?'

Jewell gave the boomerang back to his son. 'It means danger-ous.'

'It doesn't look dangerous.'

'We can see it tomorrow,' said Sally, shifting the little girl from one shoulder to the other. 'We don't have to buy everything today. Anyway, we'll be back in Sydney next week after we've been to Brisbane.'

The Jewells lived in Portland, Maine, and had flown to Aus-tralia for the wedding of Derek's brother. He'd been living in Australia for the past three years and was marrying a local girl. Sally hadn't been keen on the idea of a twenty-eight-hour flight with two young children, but Derek had talked her into it. It had been a nightmare and neither of them was looking forward to the flight home. But it was still two weeks away. Before then they had the wedding and a list of things to do, culled from the Lonely Planet guide to Australia.

'Can I buy it now, Dad? Can I?'

The flash of light and the blast hit almost simultaneously. Jewell was slammed sideways by the force of the explosion. He hit the boomerang stall hard and felt his arm snap like dry wood, then slumped to the ground, ears ringing. The left side of his body was burning, his ears were running and something wet was pouring down his cheek. His mouth and nose were filled with a bitter, burned taste and his eyes stung.

His throat filled with something wet and treacly and he tried to spit it out, which made him choke. He got up on to his hands and knees. His son was lying on the road, chest ripped open by chunks of shrapnel, still clutching the boomerang. Jewel tried to scream but he couldn't breathe. Then he looked down and saw ribs sticking out through his shirt and the bloody pulpy mess that had once been his lungs.

Katra was watching the news on the portable television in the kitchen when Shepherd walked in. 'Have you heard what happened in Australia?' she said.

'No?' he said.

'Bombs,' she said. 'Three bombs.' She stood up and poured him a mug of coffee. 'More than a hundred people have died.'

Shepherd grabbed the remote and turned up the volume. The images on the screen were jerky, as if they had been filmed on a holidaymaker's video camera. Bloodstained bodies on the ground, men and women staggering around in shock, fires burning. A news reporter was explaining that, as Katra had said, three bombs had exploded within minutes of each other, two in a weekend market. The picture on the screen changed to a hotel, black smoke pluming from the central section, the arch of the Sydney Harbour Bridge behind it. The voiceover explained that the bomb in the restaurant at the Hyatt Hotel had killed or injured at least fifty people. No one had claimed responsibility but local law-enforcement officials were assuming it was the work of an al-Qaeda terrorist cell.

'All those people,' said Katra. 'It's terrible.'

'What's terrible?' said Liam, who had walked in and was bouncing a football.

'Not inside,' said Shepherd, pointing at the ball, 'I've told you before.'

Liam picked it up and hugged it to his chest. 'What are you watching?'

'The news,' said Shepherd. 'What do you want for breakfast?'

'Cheesy scrambled eggs,' said Liam.

'Is that all you ever eat?'

'I like it.'

'I'm not sure it's good for you. Too much cholesterol.'

'What's cholesterol?'

'Fat. And too much is bad for you.'

'There's fat in bacon and you eat bacon sandwiches all the time. And coffee's bad for you, too. That's what Mummy used to say.'

'She was probably right,' agreed Shepherd. 'What about some fruit? Or muesli?'

'Muesli's rabbit food,' said Liam.

'Cheesy scrambled eggs on toast,' said Katra. 'And I'll use wholemeal bread.' She smiled. 'Once in a blue moon won't hurt him.'

Shepherd grinned back. 'Yeah, but he has it every day. I'm surprised he's not bored with it.'

Liam sat down at the kitchen table and put the ball under his feet. 'Are we going to the park, Dad?'

'Sure,' said Shepherd, 'but let me watch this now.' He leaned against the counter and sipped his coffee. On the screen, paramedics with stretchers were rushing towards the wrecked hotel.

'Why do they blow things up, Dad?'

'It's a tough question, Liam.'

'What do they want, though, the men who did it?'

Another tough question, thought Shepherd. It had always been so much easier with the IRA. Their aims were clear. They wanted the British out, and a united Ireland. But the aims of Muslim terrorist groups, like al-Qaeda, were a lot harder to pin down. 'They want to frighten people,' he said.

'But why?'

Katra slotted slices of bread into the toaster and cracked eggs into a bowl.

'It's difficult to explain,' said Shepherd.

'But why would they blow up a hotel?'

'Because they think if they scare people enough they'll get what they want.'

'But what *do* they want?'

Shepherd sat down at the kitchen table opposite Liam. 'Okay, part of it is about Iraq. You know we went to war against Iraq?'

'Yes.'

'And our soldiers are still there, with American and Australian soldiers – soldiers from all over the world.'

'Yes.'

'Well, some people don't want the soldiers to be in Iraq. They want them to leave. And they think that if they scare people enough, the governments will tell their soldiers to leave.'

'But the people they killed aren't soldiers.'

'That's right.'

'It's not fair.'

Liam was right. But much of what went on in the world had nothing to do with fairness. Shepherd had seen that at first hand as an SAS trooper in Afghanistan and every day on the streets as a police officer. 'It's easier to kill members of the public than it is to kill soldiers,' he said.

'Because they don't have guns?'

'Partly. And partly because ordinary people don't expect to be attacked. Soldiers and policemen do.'

'Are we okay in London?' asked Liam. 'They won't do anything here again, will they?'

Shepherd had always tried to be truthful with his son. He'd never been the sort of parent who perpetuated the myths of the Tooth Fairy and Father Christmas. He was happy to go along with Sue when she'd slipped a pound coin under Liam's pillow in exchange for a milk tooth, but he'd always felt uncomfortable when she'd pretended that the Christmas presents had come from a man in a red suit who'd crawled down the chimney. When Liam was seven, he'd come home from school one day and said he'd been told by a classmate that Father Christmas wasn't real. Sue had said that Santa Claus was hard at work with the elves at the North Pole. She'd turned to Shepherd for support, but he had pulled a face and walked away. A lie was a lie, and he'd promised himself that he would never lie to his family. His entire undercover life was spent lying, and he didn't want to bring it home with him, even if it meant bursting the occasional bubble. 'They might try,' he said. 'They're bad men and they do bad things. But there's a lot of people working to stop them. And the chance of you or me or anyone we know being hurt is so small that you mustn't worry about it.'

There were two solemn newsreaders on screen, a pretty blonde girl and a man in his late forties, hair greying at the temples. Both had perfect teeth and a movie-star tan. The man was recapping earlier terrorist incidents – Madrid, Bali, New York.

'But if they did do something, people would die, wouldn't they?'

Katra stirred Liam's eggs and cheese. The toaster pinged, and she pulled out the toast.

'Maybe,' said Shepherd, 'but we can't let that worry us. If we're scared all the time the terrorists have won. That's what they want, to scare us. So if we aren't scared, they can't win.'

'But you're going to help catch them, aren't you?'

'I'm going to try.'

'And they'll go to prison, right?'

'Sure.'

'And you'll get a medal?'

Shepherd laughed. 'Maybe.'

There were more images on the screen. A Sydney hospital with ambulances unloading the injured. A voiceover saying that at least a hundred people had been killed but that the final death toll was likely to be much higher. Shepherd wondered what sort of men would set off a bomb to kill civilians. He could understand combat: man against man, weapon against weapon. Terrible things happened in wars, but it was always soldier against soldier. He'd killed in combat, but the men who had died might just as easily have killed him. He'd been shot, too, taken a sniper's bullet in the shoulder in Afghanistan and only survived because of the skill of an SAS medic and the fact that a chopper had been nearby. Shepherd felt no hatred for the guy who'd shot him: Shepherd had been doing his job and so had the sniper. Shepherd had been trained in the use of explosives, but only in military situations. He knew how to place a shaped charge to destroy a bridge or bring down a building, and he knew how to handle grenades. But if he had ever been ordered to plant a bomb that served no purpose other than to kill civilians, he would have refused, no matter what the circumstances.

Katra put down a plate of scrambled eggs and cheese on toast in front of Liam and he attacked it enthusiastically. 'Chew it properly,' said Shepherd.

'It's scrambled eggs,' said Liam. 'You can't chew scrambled eggs.'

'And don't talk with your mouth full.'

'What would you like, Dan?' asked Katra.

'Just toast, please,' said Shepherd. The newsreaders were back on screen. The woman was talking via a video link to a so-called terrorism expert, a balding, bespectacled academic in a turtleneck sweater who was trying to explain the aims and objectives of the various Muslim extremist groups around the world. To Shepherd, it was obvious: they wanted to kill as many Westerners as possible. They wanted to provoke a backlash against Muslims so that they could point the finger at the West and say, 'See? We told you they hated us.' The West was in an impossible situation. If it did nothing, the deaths would continue. But in invading Iraq, in locking people up without trial, it was playing into the hands of the enemy. It was a no-win situation for which Shepherd had no solution. That was for the politicians to work out. Shepherd was a policeman: his job was to uphold law and order. It was for politicians to solve the insoluble, but most of those he saw on television didn't have the intellectual skills necessary to programme a video recorder, never mind broker a peace with Islamic fundamentalists.

Shepherd scowled at the academic's woolly language and even woollier thinking. He seemed to have no clearer understanding of the aims of al-Qaeda than Shepherd did. What *did* al-Qaeda want? The dismantling of Israel? Death to all infidels? A world of Muslims? All women covered from head to foot in black and walking ten steps behind their men? If that was their aim, there would be no negotiating with them. And if negotiations were pointless, what then?

Katra put a plate of buttered toast in front of him. 'You look very serious,' she said.

Shepherd smiled up at her. 'Busy week,' he said.

'Can we watch cartoons?' asked Liam.

Shepherd pushed the remote control across the table to him. 'Watch whatever you want,' he said.

Liam flicked through the channels and stopped at a cartoon. Roadrunner was doing what he did best, running through the desert. A gleeful Wile E. Coyote was unwrapping an Acme bomb, a black sphere with a long fuse and 'BOMB' written on the side. Shepherd drank some coffee and wondered when bombs had stopped being funny. 'I've got to make a phone call,' he said and picked up a piece of toast. 'I'll be upstairs. You two stay down here, okay? I don't want to be disturbed.'

Liam nodded, his eyes on the television.

'It's a work call,' Shepherd said to Katra. 'I'll only be a few minutes.'

Shepherd went upstairs to his bedroom and took the Tony Corke mobile out of his bedside cabinet. He checked the call register. They hadn't rung back and there were no texts.

Shepherd pressed 'redial'. The call was answered on the third ring. 'Who are you?' said an Asian voice. Shepherd was fairly sure it was the second man he'd spoken to the last time he'd called. 'I can't deal with someone I don't know. You could be the police.'

'If you really thought I was a cop, you wouldn't be talking to me at all. Now, do you want these cans or not?'

'They are my property.'

'So, let me ask you a question,' said Shepherd. 'Who am I talking to?'

'You don't need to know my name,' said the man. 'I want what belongs to me.'

'So now it's "I", is it?'

'What do you mean?'

'Yesterday it was "we". Today it's "I". Am I talking to you or am I talking to a group?'

'You're talking to me.'

'So, I need a name. I need someone to ask for if I call again.'

'I will be the only one answering this phone from now on,' said the man, 'but you can call me Ben.'

'That's a start,' said Shepherd. 'You can call me Bill. That makes us Bill and Ben.'

'Bill,' repeated Ben. 'You are English?'

'As English as roast beef and Yorkshire pudding,' said Shepherd. 'Now, about my money.'

'We have it.'

'There's that "we" again,' said Shepherd.

'Please, do not play games with me,' said Ben.

'Where do I get my money?' asked Shepherd.

'We will meet you at Paddington station. You give us the cans, we give you the money. Providing the cans have not been opened.'

'Don't worry, they haven't,' said Shepherd. 'But Paddington isn't good for me.' Shepherd doubted that Hargrove would want the tracking device to disappear underground.

'Where, then?'

'What part of London are you in? Are you close to Paddington?'

'Why do you want to know?'

'I was trying to make it easy for you,' said Shepherd.

'What's wrong with Paddington?'

'I'm scared of trains,' said Shepherd. 'I choose the venue, okay? That's the way it's going to be. What about Hyde Park? Speaker's Corner. Sunday. Three o'clock. It'll be busy. Lots of people. Safety in numbers.'

'Okay.'

'We'll be out in the open, which means we'll have plenty of time to check each other out.'

'Agreed.'

'And come alone,' said Shepherd. 'One more thing. The price has gone up. To thirty thousand pounds.'

'You are a thief!'

'I haven't stolen anything,' said Shepherd. 'I'm the guy who's returning your property and I deserve a decent finder's fee.'

'You are a thief.'

'Call me all the names you want, Ben, but if you don't come up with thirty grand I'll open the cans and take my chances with what's inside.'

'Do that and we'll track you down and kill you. I swear on my children.'

'It's not nice to bring your kids into a business transaction. Are you going to come up with thirty grand or do I get me a can-opener?'

'We have a deal,' hissed Ben. 'But I warn you, my friend, if you increase the price again, you will die in agony.'

'Sticks and stones,' said Shepherd. 'Tomorrow. Three o'clock. Speaker's Corner.' He cut the connection and went downstairs.

Katra was standing in the kitchen waggling the landline receiver. 'It's Liam's grandmother,' she said, holding it out.

Shepherd smiled and took it from her. 'Moira, how are you?' he asked.

'We're fine, Daniel,' said Moira. She was the only person in the world who ever called him by his full first name. He'd long ago given up trying to persuade her to call him Dan. 'How's Liam?' she asked.

'He's great,' said Shepherd. 'We're just going out to play football.'

'It's been ages since we saw him. And you, of course. Tom and I were wondering when you'd be coming up here.'

'I'm sorry, Moira. Liam's got school and I've been up to my eyes in work.'

'We haven't seen you since Christmas.'

'I know.'

'Why not come today? Liam's old room is ready. You can stay overnight and drive back on Sunday.'

Shepherd grimaced. 'I'm so sorry, Moira. I'm working tomorrow.'

'Next weekend, then.'

'Okay.'

'Excellent!' said Moira. 'Tom will be delighted.'

'Do you want to chat with Liam now?' asked Shepherd. 'He's here.'

Shepherd gave the receiver to his son and went out into the garden to call Hargrove.

The Saudi liked the Savoy. It had been one of his favourite hotels since his father had taken him there as a child. The staff at the Oriental in Bangkok were more attentive, the rooms in the Hong Kong Peninsular were a touch more luxurious, the beds at the George V in Paris had the edge in comfort, but the Savoy was where he felt most at home. From the moment he walked up to the reception desk until the moment he checked out, all his needs and desires were taken care of. They knew the type of pillows he favoured, that he liked irises in his room, that he preferred white toast to wholemeal, took skimmed milk with his coffee, lemon with his tea, and wanted unscented soap in his bathroom.

He refilled the delicate china cup with Earl Grey and dropped in a slice of lemon. He could never understand why people put milk and sugar into Earl Grey. It destroyed the tea's delicate flavour. He sipped and watched the devastation on the television set in the corner of his suite. Everything had gone exactly as he'd planned. The bomb in the Hyatt had gone off at one o'clock on the dot, destroying the restaurant at its busiest time. He remembered the young waitress with the bright smile and wondered if she was among the dead. The first bomb in the street market had detonated at the same time, ripping through the throngs of tourists as they shopped for trinkets to take home to their families and friends. Those who hadn't been killed in the first market bomb had fled straight into the path of the second. CNN was saying that a hundred and twenty people had died, but the Saudi could tell from the pictures on the screen that the death toll would be much higher.

Sydney had been a good choice. It wasn't the capital city, but it was one that everyone identified as quintessentially Australian. Bringing the *jihad* to Australia would make the world realise that no one was safe. If the *shahids* could strike in Sydney, they could strike anywhere. CNN didn't refer to them as *shahids*, of course – or martyrs. They called them suicide-bombers, as if somehow it was their own deaths that had been the objective. It was always that way with American journalists. If the bombers were on the Americans' side, they were freedom-fighters; if they were against them, they were terrorists. They didn't bother to try to understand: they sought only to label.

The Saudi spread honey across his toast and took a bite. The use of *shahids* served two functions. It meant that there were no perpetrators to put on trial, and it brought home to the world that the fighters for the Muslim cause were prepared to die for their beliefs. It was easy for Western soldiers to go into battle with their weapons, armour and mobile hospitals: they were better-armed and equipped than their adversaries, and rarely went into battle without being sure that they would win. But at heart they were cowards, hiding behind walls as they fired their high-powered weapons, dropping bombs from planes high above the clouds and shooting artillery shells from afar, going in with tanks and armoured cars, only ever fighting from a position of strength. But the *shahids* fought alone: they went into battle knowing they would die, and died happily, knowing their death would serve the greater good. It was impossible to defeat such men and women. Nothing could be said or done to sway them from carrying out their mission. They were true heroes, but the Western media would never describe them as such.

The Saudi took another sip of tea. Already there were calls for the Australian government to pull their troops out of Iraq. The same thing had happened after the Madrid bombings: the Spanish had obeyed the calls and brought their soldiers home. The Saudi doubted that the Australians would pull out as easily. Not that he cared what happened in Iraq. This wasn't about the occupation of Iraq, who controlled the oil or decided who should or shouldn't hold elections. It was about the struggle between Islam and Christianity, between Allah and the infidels, and it was a struggle that could end with only one victor.

Liam kicked the ball hard and low, and Shepherd had to stretch to stop it going into the net. 'Nice shot,' he called, and threw the ball back. Liam caught it on his chest and let it drop to his feet. 'You're getting good at this,' said Shepherd.

'I scored two goals last week,' said Liam. He kicked the ball and this time it went straight past Shepherd into the back of the net.

'You play at school, yeah?'

'Every Thursday.'

'Is there a school team?'

'Yeah, but Mr Williams says I'm too small to play for it. I have to wait until next year.'

Shepherd retrieved the ball and tossed it to Liam. Liam headed it back.

'Are you going to get married again, Dad?' he asked.

Shepherd's jaw dropped. 'What makes you ask that?'

'Pete's dad's getting married next week and Pete says his new mum's really cool,' said Liam.

'What happened to Pete's old mum?'

'She and his dad got divorced. She went to live in America with her new husband and Pete got to live with his dad.'

Shepherd tried to spin the football on his right index finger but it fell to the ground. He trapped it with his foot. 'And you want a new mum, is that it?'

Liam shrugged awkwardly. 'It might be fun.'

'Do you have anyone in mind?'

Liam's cheeks reddened. 'Katra, maybe.'

Shepherd laughed. 'Katra? She's not much older than you.'

'She's twenty-three,' said Liam.

'And I'm thirty-five. I'm almost old enough to be her dad, too.'

'No, you're not,' said Liam. 'You'd have been twelve when she was born and you can't be a dad when you're twelve.'

'The way things are going, these days, you can,' said Shepherd.

'I like Katra,' said Liam.

'You marry her,' said Shepherd.

Liam pulled a face. 'I don't want to marry her,' he said. 'Anyway, I don't want a wife. I want a mum.'

'I miss your mum, too,' said Shepherd.

'All the time?'

'Of course.'

'I dream about her.'

'Me too,' said Shepherd.

'Sometimes I dream that she comes back. She says she's been away on holiday and now she's going to live with us again.'

Shepherd picked up the ball and tossed it back to his son. He had the same dreams, less often now, but they still came every few weeks. She'd be back with him and Liam, back in the house, back in his bed.

'When I dream about Mum, is it really her?' asked Liam. He sat on the ball, his hands on the ground to steady himself.

'It's just a dream,' said Shepherd.

'But it feels so real. Like it's really her.'

'I know, but it's not. It's just your subconscious trying to make you feel better.'

Liam frowned. 'What do you mean?'

Shepherd went and sat on the grass next to his son. 'First, there's the thinking bit of your brain, the bit you use to solve problems, the bit you use when you're talking, or when you just sit and think. But then there's another part that does its thinking in the background. Like your imagination.'

Liam's frown deepened and Shepherd realised he wasn't doing a good job of explaining himself. If he'd known in advance that he'd be going over the finer points of psychology with his son he'd have phoned Kathy Gift for a briefing.

'The subconscious does things without you thinking about it,' he continued. 'Sometimes you might feel sad but you don't know why, and that's because you're thinking about something subconsciously.'

'Thinking without thinking?' said Liam. 'Is that what you mean?'

'Sort of,' said Shepherd. His lecture was going from bad to worse he thought. 'It's, like, we know Mum's dead, and that she's not coming back. But part of us wants to believe she *will* come back. And that part of us is what makes the dreams.'

'But when I talk to her in the dreams, it's like I'm really talking to her.'

'I know what you mean.' Shepherd had conversations with Sue in his dreams. And more. They kissed and touched, and sometimes he entered her – and then he'd wake with a hard-on and his stomach would lurch when he remembered he'd never make love to her again. Sue was dead and she'd stay that way for all eternity. Shepherd didn't believe in God or in heaven, so he knew he'd never see her again. Ever. 'You're talking to her memory, Liam,' he went on. 'And you'll always have that. She'll always be in your heart and your head.'

Liam's lips quivered. 'Sometimes I forget what she looks like,' he said.

'That's not true,' said Shepherd.

'When I think about her, I can't remember her face. I look at the photographs and I know it's her and I can remember the photographs, but when I try to remember the things we did and the places we went sometimes I can't see her face. But when I dream it's like she's really there and I can see her and everything.'

'Hey, that's okay,' said Shepherd. 'You remember her and that's what matters. And you know how much she loved you. Your mum loved you more than anything.'

'More than you?' Liam wiped a tear from his cheek.

'You're her son. Her boy. You were the most important thing in her life.'

'So why am I forgetting her?'

'You're not,' said Shepherd.

'It's okay for you. You can remember everything,' said Liam bitterly.

Shepherd pulled the boy close to him. 'Not everything,' he said. But his photographic memory was virtually infallible and Shepherd could remember almost everything he'd ever done with Sue. Every conversation they'd had. Every place they'd been. Every argument they'd had. Liam wanted a new mother. Shepherd understood that. Every child needed a mother. But Shepherd didn't need or want another wife when his memories of Sue were as fresh as they had ever been. He could remember the glint in her eye when she wanted to make love, the tightening of her mouth when she was preparing for an argument, the way she bit her lower lip just before she laughed. Sue was a hard act to follow. In a way, fading memories could be a blessing: as they receded so did the pain. That was what Liam was going through. Every day the pain of losing his mother would get a little less. His heart wouldn't ache quite as much and one day the pain would have gone and he'd be able to think about her without crying. It seemed to Shepherd that, for most people, dealing with grief meant forgetting the pain, rather than coming to terms with it. And he knew that his pain would never go away. 'Sometimes forgetting can be a good thing,' Shepherd whispered. 'Like when you hurt yourself. You can remember that you were hurting, but you can't remember how much.'

'Like when you were shot?'

'That's right,' said Shepherd. 'I know it hurt, but I can't

remember the pain. It's the same with Mum. Every day it'll hurt less.'

'I don't want to forget her,' said Liam.

'You won't.' He patted his son's shoulder. 'So, what's with wanting a new mum?'

Liam shrugged. 'I don't know. I think I just want to be a family again.'

'You and I are a family.'

'We're half a family,' said Liam.

'There must be lots of kids at school with just one parent,' said Shepherd. 'Half of all marriages end in divorce, these days.'

'You weren't going to divorce Mum, were you?'

Shepherd smiled. 'Of course not.' He had loved Sue from the first moment he'd spoken to her in the pub in Hereford. He had been a cocky SAS trooper, the best of the best, and she had been a local girl who knew all about the heartbreak the soldiers caused in the town. Her friends had warned her of the danger in getting involved with one, and so had her parents. But Shepherd had won her over and when he'd married her he'd known he was married for life. 'Till death us do part,' he'd said, and he'd meant it. Sue was the love of his life, even when they'd argued and fought. They'd argued about his career with the SAS, and he'd let her talk him into leaving for the sake of their marriage and their son. And they'd argued about his career as an undercover cop because it kept him away from home for long periods. But divorce? Never.

'So it's not the same. If you and Mum weren't living together, we'd still be a family. We'd just be one that had split up. I'd still have a mum and a dad.'

Shepherd lay back on the grass and stared up at the pale grey sky. It was overcast but dry and not too cold.

'So, you won't marry Katra?' asked Liam.

Shepherd chuckled. 'It's not really on, Liam,' he said.

'She likes you.'

'And I like her. But I'm her boss. She works for us.'

'She does the same for us that Mum did. She cooks and cleans and takes me to school. She irons your shirts, same as Mum did.'

'That's her job.'

'But she likes you.'

Shepherd sighed. 'Someone liking you is no reason to get married. You have to love them. I loved your mum, and I love her as much now as I did when we got married. I'm going to have to wait until I meet someone I love as much as your mum. Maybe more . . . . I have a question for you,' he said, linking his fingers behind his head. 'How would you feel if we moved house?'

'Where to?'

'I don't know. Not far. You'd still go to the same school.'

'So why would we move?'

His son and Kathy Gift had one thing in common, Shepherd mused. The knack of asking questions he found difficult to answer. 'Okay, here's the thing,' he said. 'This house was our family house, for you, your mum and me. Your mum chose the decoration, she laid out the garden, she picked the furniture.'

'That's why it looks so good.'

'Right. But maybe we should get a new house – a house that belongs just to us.'

'And not Mum?'

'Mum doesn't need a house.'

'Because she's in heaven?'

That wasn't somewhere Shepherd wanted to go. He knew there was no such place as heaven and that Sue wasn't sitting on a cloud playing a harp. But although he'd been happy enough for Liam to know that Father Christmas didn't exist, it would serve no purpose to blow his faith in God and heaven out of the water.

'Yes, she's in heaven.' He'd promised himself that he would never to lie to his son but the truth, as Shepherd saw it, would have been far more hurtful. 'She's in heaven watching over you and helping me to take care of you.'

Liam nodded, and Shepherd knew he'd done the right thing. Perhaps some lies were acceptable.

'It's just that if we had somewhere new to live, maybe we

wouldn't miss her so much. I think that one of the reasons we think about her all the time is that we're still living in her house.' He sat up and rubbed his legs.

'So if we move, we'll forget her?'

'No, of course not,' said Shepherd. 'It's not about forgetting her. We won't ever forget her. But the house keeps reminding us that she's not here.'

'But I like that,' said Liam. 'Sometimes when I come in from school, it's like she's waiting for me in the kitchen.'

'But doesn't it make you feel bad when she's not?'

'I guess.'

'So if we were in a new house, maybe you wouldn't.'

Liam wiped his nose with his sleeve. 'Okay.'

Shepherd left Edgware Road Tube station and wandered round Marks & Spencer for five minutes to check that he wasn't being followed, then crossed the road and went into the Hilton Hotel. He was dressed as Tony Corke – cheap jeans, a roll-neck pull-over, work boots and a new pea coat to replace the one he'd lost on the trawler.

He took the lift to the seventh floor and went to Hargrove's suite. A dozen men and two women were with the superinten-dent, all in casual clothing. Jimmy Sharpe and Paul Joyce were among them, and an Asian guy in his late twenties, who grinned. 'If I'd known it was you, Spider, I would've used something more heavy duty.' Amar Singh worked for the National Criminal Intelligence Service but was often utilised by Hargrove's under-cover unit as he had access to state-of-the-art surveillance and tracking equipment.

'Good to see you again, Amar,' he said. 'Don't worry, I won't drop anything.'

'Right,' said the superintendent, raising his voice. 'Spider will be taking a rucksack with the three cans to Speaker's Corner. Amar, please.'

Amar picked up a blue canvas rucksack and heaved it on to a coffee table. He took out three large cooking-oil cans and held up one in both hands. 'This is the one with the transmitter, but hopefully you won't see the difference. We've built the power pack and electronics into the base and incorporated the aerial into the ridge round the bottom. Even when they cut open the can to get at the cash, they shouldn't find our gear.' He put the cans back into the rucksack.

'There's an outside chance that they'll pat Spider down so he won't be wearing any recording devices or transmitters,' the superintendent continued. 'We won't be using long-range eavesdropping either, but we will be taking photographs. This afternoon's meeting is solely to make contact with the targets. Spider will hand over the money, and we'll follow it. Our primary objective is to identify the men taking possession of it, but we will also be using the handover as an opportunity for a longer-term penetration of the gang. Spider's going to have to play that by ear. If he decides to go voluntarily with them, he'll pinch the bridge of his nose with his right hand. If we get that signal we follow – but at a distance. Everyone clear on that?'

They nodded.

'We doubt they'll bring firearms to such a public place, but he's wearing a Kevlar vest in case they do.'

Shepherd pulled up his pullover to reveal it.

'We're not sure how many will turn up, or how they'll react,' said Hargrove. 'Spider's to hand over the cans in exchange for thirty thousand pounds. It's just possible that they'll pull guns or knives and snatch the cans but, again, in view of the location it's unlikely. However, they might try to take Spider against his will. There's no way we can allow that to happen. We don't know who they are or what they're capable of, so if at any time Spider wants out, the signal will be for him to rub the back of his neck with his left hand.'

Shepherd demonstrated.

'If he can't make the signal for some reason, he'll yell for help,' said Hargrove. 'Inspector Steve Priestley will head up an armed unit dressed as park-keepers. They'll only move in if Spider's attacked or if the targets try to abduct him.'

Priestley raised a hand so that everyone could see who he was.

'We already have three long-range camera units in place covering Speaker's Corner and the main park exits,' continued the superintendent.

A large whiteboard had been propped against one wall with a map of the park and the surrounding roads, Park Lane, Knightsbridge, Bayswater Road, drawn on it. Hargrove tapped the area where 'Speaker's Corner' had been written in capital letters. 'The targets originally suggested Paddington station, but didn't protest when Hyde Park was suggested, which we think means they're local. They could, of course, have a car ready or be planning to use Marble Arch Tube station, so we're not making any assumptions. We have three vehicles ready to go, all with tracking equipment, whose range is up to a mile in the city, three or four miles outside. Our one worry is the Tube, so Blue Team will stay by the station entrance with day tickets for the whole network.' A man and a woman, who looked like a married couple, nodded.

'Green Team here.' Hargrove tapped the exit closest to Speaker's Corner. 'Red Team here. Yellow Team here.' More nodding. 'As you probably know, a network of underground tunnels connects the various roads around Marble Arch so bear in mind that we could lose the signal from time to time. But no rushing in to get close. We'll have all the options covered if and when that happens. Just be on your toes, and if I ask you to move, do it quickly. So, once more with the signals, Spider. Everything's okay and you're happy to go with them.'

Spider rubbed the bridge of his nose as if he had a headache.

'There's trouble and you want out.'

Shepherd rubbed the back of his neck with his left hand.

'Got that?' asked Hargrove. Everyone nodded again. Hargrove glanced at his watch. 'It's ten past twelve,' he said. 'Spider's on show at three, so you've got plenty of time to get bedded in. And remember, on your toes. We only get one crack at this.'

Jimmy Sharpe flashed Shepherd a thumbs-up as the surveillance teams filed out of the room.

'I didn't realise there'd be armed cops,' said Shepherd. 'I just hope no one knows me.' Shepherd had infiltrated an SO19 unit the previous year after rogue armed cops had ripped off a group of North London drug-dealers at gunpoint. It had been the first time he'd investigated cops and he hadn't enjoyed it.

'We're using local guys,' said Hargrove, 'and I cross-checked all the names with your SO19 operation. There's no possibility of any overlap. Now, how about a room-service coffee? We've plenty of time before you head off.'

On a Sunday morning Speaker's Corner was packed with orators standing on soapboxes or folding ladders, shouting their views on the world to anyone who cared to listen. Others wandered around grim-faced with sandwich boards, letting the written word do the shouting for them. But at three o'clock in the afternoon all the bastions of free speech had gone back to their hostels or lonely bedsits, leaving the park to tourists and joggers who preferred to do their running in the open air rather than sweating away on a treadmill watching Sky News.

Shepherd had the rucksack on just one shoulder. It wasn't as heavy as the brick-filled one he used to build up stamina on his regular fitness runs but the cans dug into his back. It was a cool day, with a soft wind blowing from the north, and leaden clouds threatened rain. He was chewing gum. It was Corke's habit, not his.

His eyes scanned the tourists wandering round the park – couples walking hand in hand, Japanese tourists clicking away with digital cameras, parents with nagging children queuing for ice-cream, an old tramp in a stained raincoat with a greyhound on a leash. He didn't see anyone who'd been at the hotel suite and didn't expect to. If he could spot them, the men he was going to meet might see them, too. Shepherd was sure that Ben wouldn't come alone. He'd have back-up – at least one heavy, probably more.

He saw an unoccupied bench and sat down, stretching out his legs and placing the rucksack next to him. It was exactly three o'clock, but that didn't mean Ben would be on time. If he knew what he was doing, he or someone else would be watching from a distance, until he was sure that Shepherd was alone. But Shepherd had to play the role: Tony Corke would get the jitters if everything didn't go exactly as he'd planned, so he looked at his watch again, then scanned the park. He saw two park-keepers walking along a path, deep in conversation. Shepherd couldn't tell if they were the real thing or armed police.

He felt the hairs stand up on the back of his neck and a tingle down his spine. He glanced about, trying to work out what had triggered the alarm signals, and saw a man to his left, walking along with his head down and his hands deep in his coat pockets. A squat, almost square Asian, with a fast-receding hairline and slightly bowed legs. He glanced in Shepherd's direction, then averted his eyes when he saw that Shepherd was staring at him. Shepherd suppressed a smile. Whoever the man was, he wasn't well versed in surveillance techniques. Shepherd made a point of consulting his watch again.

The Asian man was walking slowly, eyes on the ground now – Shepherd could feel the anxiety pouring out of him. He looked around, casually, for anything out of the ordinary. There were no other Asians nearby, but Shepherd regarded everyone over the age of ten as a potential threat. He took in faces, clothing, body language. Nothing. The Asian man had stopped and taken a handkerchief out of his coat pocket to wipe his brow. It was a cold afternoon so Shepherd figured he was sweating from nerves.

Shepherd checked his watch again. It was ten past three. The Asian started walking towards him, hands back in his pockets. Shepherd's mobile rang. He pulled it out of his pocket and studied the screen. It was Ben. Shepherd frowned and took the call. 'Hello?' he said. No one spoke. Then the line went dead. The Asian was still striding purposefully towards him. Shepherd realised what had happened: the Asian was Ben and he'd made the call to check that Shepherd was the man he was supposed to meet, keeping his own phone concealed in his pocket. It was a clever move.

Shepherd watched him walk over. 'You are Bill?' the Asian asked.

Shepherd put away his phone. 'Ben?' He stuck out his hand and Ben stared at it. 'You can shake hands, can't you?' he asked.

There was no strength in Ben's grip, and it was damp with sweat.

'The cans are in the rucksack?' he asked.

'Yes,' said Shepherd.

'I need to see them.'

'And I want the money,' said Shepherd. 'No thirty grand, no cans.' He grabbed the rucksack straps.

'I'm not trying to take them. I just want to check that they haven't been opened,' said Ben. 'For all I know they could be empty.'

Shepherd stared at him, playing the hard man. 'No money. No cans.'

'I understand that, but I have to be sure. For all I know you've emptied them and filled them with rocks.'

Shepherd continued to stare at Ben, then nodded slowly. 'Okay, but no tricks. Where's the money?'

'My associate has it. Once I've checked that the cans haven't been tampered with I'll phone him.'

Shepherd glared at him. 'That's not what we said. I said I'd bring the cans and you'd bring the money.'

'We don't know you,' said Ben. 'We didn't know you had the cans. For all we know you could be working for Customs. Or the police. So I make sure, first. Then I phone my associate. Would you take off your jacket, please?'

'What?'

'I want to check your jacket.'

Shepherd took off his coat and handed it to him. Ben went through the pockets. He examined Shepherd's mobile and flicked through the contacts file. 'You have only my number in this phone?'

'I bought the Sim card to call you,' he said. 'I didn't want you tracing me.'

Ben handed the phone back. 'Lift up your pullover, please.'

'Why?'

'I want to reassure myself that you are not recording our conversation.'

'You think I'm a cop?'

'I don't know who you are. But if you don't lift it, I'm walking away.'

Slowly Shepherd did as the man asked, revealing the Kevlar vest.

Ben frowned. 'What is that?'

'A bulletproof vest.'

Ben's frown deepened. 'Why?'

'Because I thought you might shoot me.'

'Why would I do that?'

'You might have thought a bullet was cheaper than thirty grand. I'm not wired for sound. I just want my money.'

Ben held out his hand. 'Give me your wallet.'

'Fuck you.'

'I need to see who you are.'

'It doesn't matter who I am. I'm the man with what you want, and that's all you need to know.'

'Your wallet,' repeated the Asian.

Shepherd cursed again, then pulled it out of his jeans and gave it to the man. Ben opened it and flicked through the contents. He pulled out a driving licence. 'Anthony Corke?'

'Tony to my friends.'

'And you live in Dover?'

'I'm a sailor. I used to work the ferries. Look, do you see a warrant card in there? No. So give me my wallet back and let's get on with this.'

'Why did the police let you go?' asked Ben, examining a Visa card.

'I'm on bail. If I run, I lose my house.'

'They've charged you?'

'I was up before a magistrate and I'm back in court in two weeks. I had the house so I got bail. But my solicitor's costing me an arm and a leg so I need the thirty grand.'

Ben sat down on Shepherd's left and gave him back his wallet. 'First let me see the cans.'

Shepherd pushed the rucksack towards him. Ben unfastened the straps and took out a can, looked at it closely, then set it on the ground. He checked the other two, running his fingers over the caps and seams, then put them back into the rucksack.

'Satisfied?' asked Shepherd.

Ben reached into his coat. Shepherd tensed but he knew there was next to no chance that the man would pull a gun in a public park, not when he'd have to run with a heavy rucksack. Ben's hand reappeared with a Nokia mobile. He made a call and said a few words in Bengali, then cut the connection.

'You'd better not try anything,' said Shepherd. 'If you do I'm out of here.'

'What happened to the boat?'

'Customs caught it.'

'What about the people on board?'

'The asylum-seekers? Immigration have got them. If they play it right and claim asylum they'll be back on the streets within days and have passports in three years.'

'And you?'

'Six months behind bars. Three years if I'm unlucky. Maybe a suspended sentence and a fine. Depends on the judge.'

'Why did Rudi Pernaska not wait until he was released? Why did he talk to you?'

'It's a long story.'

'I want to know.'

'Customs and Immigration went through the boat, but they were only interested in the passengers and crew. They weren't looking for contraband. I was put in a cell with Pernaska and he heard I was getting bail. He didn't know how long Immigration were going to hold him, and he wasn't sure they'd grant him asylum. His passport was fake, I think. He told them he was from Kosovo but really he's Albanian. I guess he was scared that either they'd send him straight back to Albania or that someone would open the cans before they let him out. Anyway, he gave me your number and asked me to phone you.'

'And the thirty thousand pounds was his idea?'

Shepherd grinned. 'I thought as I was doing you a favour I ought to get something out of it.' He saw an Asian man emerge from one of the pedestrian tunnels. He was almost six foot tall and had a long, loping stride. He was wearing a green anorak with the hood up, the sleeves several inches too short for his arms, and carried a black Adidas holdall.

Ben looked across at him. 'He has your money,' he said.

'No tricks,' said Shepherd.

'There won't be any,' said Ben. 'We want what's in those cans. You want your money. We exchange bags and go our separate ways.'

'Can I ask you a question?' said Shepherd.

'What?'

Shepherd patted the rucksack. 'You took a risk, giving them to an asylum-seeker. Why not just bring them in yourself?'

'Because all luggage on planes is X-rayed. The Eurostar, too. And Customs make spot-checks on the ferries. Asylum-seekers avoid all such checks.'

'Not on my boat they didn't.'

'That was bad luck,' said Ben. 'The chance of it happening was one in a million.'

'You do it a lot, then – bring cans from the Continent?'

Ben's eyes narrowed. 'Why are you so interested?'

'I might be able to help. What's in the cans?'

'That's none of your business.'

'I'm assuming drugs.'

'You can assume what you want. It's none of your business.'

The second Asian man drew level with the bench. Ben spoke to him in Bengali and pointed at the rucksack.

'I'd prefer it if you spoke English,' said Shepherd.

'I said that the cans are in good order,' said Ben.

The second man sat down on the other side of Shepherd and pushed the sports bag towards him. Shepherd unzipped it and peered inside. It contained bundles of twenty-pound notes held together with thick rubber bands. Shepherd glanced around to make sure that no one was watching, then pulled out a note at random. He checked the printing, the silver foil strip, then held it up to examine the watermark. 'Looks fine to me,' he said. He put the note back into the bag, then counted the bundles. There were thirty. He flicked through several as if to assure himself they were all made up of twenty-pound notes.

'Satisfied?' asked Ben.

Shepherd zipped up the bag and put it on his lap. 'We're done,' he said, and paused. 'I could help you bring more in, if you wanted,' he said quietly.

'Why should we trust you?' said Ben.

Shepherd lifted the holdall. 'Because we've just done a deal. You've got what you wanted and I've got my money. You had to pay me because your brilliant smuggling idea came a cropper. What if I could offer you a foolproof way of bringing in as many cans as you want?'

'Nothing is foolproof,' said Ben.

Shepherd grinned. 'I've got a boat that'll outrun anything in the Channel,' he said. 'I can get from the Continent to the English coast in under forty minutes.'

'A speedboat?'

'Faster than a speedboat, mate. It'll do eighty, and I've got night-vision gear, which means I can go out on a moonless night.'

'Where is it?'

'That's for me to know and you to find out,' said Shepherd. 'First we've got to talk about how much you're prepared to pay. And I need to know what you've got in those cans.'

'Why does it matter?'

Shepherd sneered. 'Because if it's heroin, I'll be taking a much bigger risk than if it's cannabis. I need to know what the risk is before we talk about the reward.'

The tall Asian said something in Bengali, but Ben cut him short with a wave. 'Let me think about it,' he said.

'Okay,' said Shepherd. 'You've got my mobile number, yeah?'

Ben nodded. 'You are an experienced sailor?'

'Fifteen years, man and boy,' said Shepherd. 'I've crossed the Channel more times than you've had hot dinners.'

'As I said, I will need time to consider your offer,' said Ben. He stood up and shouldered the rucksack.

'I'll wait for your call,' said Shepherd. He held up the bag. 'Thanks for this.'

The taller Asian stood up and the two men walked away. Shepherd sat and watched them go, tapping the strap of the holdall. Thirty thousand pounds. A year's salary, give or take.

Shepherd waited until the two Asians had left the park, then stood up. He walked towards Marble Arch, checking he wasn't being followed. Although the two men had left he had to stay in character because there was a chance that he was under surveillance. He walked down Bayswater Road, hailed a black cab and looked out of the back window as it sped west. He couldn't see a tail but he got out of the cab a mile later, dashed across the road and hailed another going in the opposite direction. He put the holdall on to the seat next to him and stretched. His mobile rang 'How did it go?' asked the superintendent.

'Fine,' said Shepherd. 'I think they'll bite.'

'He patted you down and went through your wallet.'

'It wasn't a problem,' said Shepherd. 'I was carrying a full set of ID. He asked why I wasn't in custody and I spun him the line about my house being collateral. We'll need to keep the Corke house running in case they check.' Hargrove had set Shepherd up with a two-bedroomed terraced house in Dover as part of his cover. He'd had several drunken nights there with Pepper and Mosley before they'd taken him on the smuggling run.

'Not a problem,' said Hargrove. 'I'll get some legal letters and stuff dropped around. A bail receipt as well. These guys, how do you rate them?'

'They don't seem like hardened villains,' said Shepherd, 'but they did everything right. I'm sure it's a regular run so they must be making a fortune. But the tall guy was wearing an army-surplus anorak by the look of it, and they both had cheap watches and no jewellery. Where are they headed?'

'East,' said Hargrove. 'Tower Hamlets way. They had a driver pick them up in a brand new Merc and they're not making it difficult so I think they bought your story. You're taking good care of the money, I hope?'

Shepherd patted the holdall. 'It's right by me.'

'I'll have Jimmy drop by and pick it up tonight,' said Hargrove.

'The guy who gave me the cash was wearing gloves,' said Shepherd.

'I saw that. But we'll need to check the notes. Good work, Spider.'

'Let me know what happens,' said Shepherd. 'If I don't hear from them within twenty-four hours, I'll make the call.'

It was just after five when Shepherd got home. Liam was in the sitting room, on his PlayStation. Shepherd patted his head. 'Have you had your dinner yet?' he asked.

'Katra's cooking.'

'What about homework?'

'Done it.'

'When?'

'This afternoon when you were out. I had maths, and I had a book report, and I had to write a poem.'

'What – "Roses are red, violets are blue"?'

Liam gave Shepherd a withering look. 'There's a bit more to it than that, Dad.'

'I didn't know you wrote poetry,' he said.

'I don't. But that was the homework. So I did.'

'Can I read it?'

'Da-ad!'

'What?'

'It's homework!'

Shepherd dropped down into an armchair. 'I just like to know what you're up to at school.'

'School's school.'

'You always say that.'

'Because it's true. What was school like when you were a kid?'

Shepherd shrugged. His son had a point: school was school. You went, they told you stuff, and then you went home.

'See?' said Liam. On the television screen, a high-powered car ran over two elderly pedestrians.

Shepherd raised his eyebrows. 'Did you just run over them?'

'You're supposed to,' said Liam. 'That's how you move up to the next level.'

'By killing people?'

'Dad! I'm trying to concentrate here.' The car squealed round a corner on two wheels and knocked a cyclist into the air.

Katra popped her head round the door. 'Hiya, Dan. I'm doing fried chicken, rosemary potatoes and broccoli.'

'Perfect,' said Shepherd. He expected the boy to quibble about the broccoli but Liam went on with his game. Sue had always had a problem getting any green vegetables into him, but he ate whatever Katra put in front of him.

The doorbell rang.

'I'll get it,' said Katra, and headed down the hallway.

'What's this about you wanting piano lessons?'

Liam shrugged.

'Why the piano? Why not the guitar?'

'I don't want to play the guitar.'

'Pianos are expensive.'

'We don't have to buy one. There's one at school and I'd have lessons there.'

'You know what's a great instrument?'

'What?'

'I don't know what it's called but it's shaped like a triangle and you hit it.'

'It's called a triangle,' said Liam. 'And you're taking the mickey.'

Katra reappeared at the door. 'It's one of your colleagues,' she said.

It was Jimmy Sharpe and Shepherd gave him the holdall.

'Nice,' said Sharpe, nodding towards the kitchen, where Katra had disappeared.

'She's a kid,' said Shepherd.

'I only said she was nice.'

'She's an au pair.'

'I don't care what her religion is – I'd give her one.'

'You're a real gentleman, Razor.' He jerked a thumb at the holdall. 'Be careful with that. It's been counted.'

'Very funny,' said Sharpe. He lowered his voice. 'Have you heard anything about Sam Hargrove moving on?'

'Moving on where?'

'Bigger and better things.'

'It's news to me.'

'It'll be a bugger if he goes,' said Sharpe.

'Why would he? The unit's his baby and we've had a string of successes.'

'I'm just telling you what I heard,' said Sharpe. 'Keep your ear to the ground. Forewarned is forearmed.'

'Any more clichés or are you done?'

Sharpe winked and headed for his car.

Shepherd went back into the sitting room. The car was driving at full speed along a crowded highway. The driver kept leaning out of the window to fire a shotgun. 'Is he doing what I think he is?'

'*Dad!*'

A mobile phone rang in the kitchen. 'Dan, it's one of yours!' shouted Katra.

Shepherd hurried into the kitchen. It was his work phone. Shepherd picked it up. It was Hargrove.

'How's it going?' asked Shepherd, by way of a greeting. He never used his boss's name or rank, either on the phone or when they were together in case he was overheard.

'We've got an address in Tower Hamlets,' said Hargrove. 'A three-bedroom council flat. We're working through the databases now but, as always at weekends, we're not getting much co-operation from the local council or the utility companies.'

'I can't believe they're smuggling in that much cash and living in a council flat,' said Shepherd.

'They might just be clever,' said Hargrove. 'Staying below the radar. Look, something's come up and we need to talk. Face to face.'

'Tonight?'

'Tomorrow will be soon enough. I've got to pop into the Yard, then see someone at Waterloo. How about I meet you by the London Eye at eleven?'

'I'll be there,' said Shepherd. 'Anything I should worry about?' Hargrove's tone had told him something was wrong.

'Nothing earth-shattering. I'll talk it through with you tomorrow.' He ended the call.

Shepherd put his phone on the kitchen counter. He hoped the investigation hadn't run into problems.

Shepherd took a Piccadilly Line train from South Ealing to South Kensington, where he changed platforms and waited for an eastbound Circle or District Line train. He let the first two trains go by to check that he wasn't being shadowed. The third was on the Circle Line and he sat opposite two Italian tourists, facing the platform. There was a copy of *Metro*, the free newspaper, on the seat next to him and he flicked through it as the train headed east, but couldn't concentrate and soon tossed it aside. The Italian couple were pointing at the Tube map above his head and murmuring to each other.

Shepherd folded his arms and closed his eyes. He knew why he was tense: Victoria station was down the line. It had been more than six months since he'd shot the would-be suicide-bomber on the westbound platform, then left the station unchallenged and been picked up by one of Gannon's men in an unmarked car. The CCTV footage of the fatal shooting had been erased, and the body removed by MI5 technicians, who had also sanitised the area. An hour after Shepherd's last shot had echoed around the tunnel it was as if nothing had happened.

The train stopped and Shepherd opened his eyes. Sloane

Square. The Italian tourists got off and three black teenagers got on, baseball caps, Puffa jackets and baggy jeans. They sat opposite Shepherd and started talking about football. Shepherd closed his eyes again. The killing ran through his mind in slow motion. Running through the tunnel on to the platform. The man, his back to Shepherd, wearing a brown raincoat, black trousers and black shoes, his hair jet black and glistening under the lights. Shepherd raising his Glock, the gun kicking, the front of the man's forehead exploding in a shower of blood, brain matter and bone fragments. Firing again. And again. The man slumping to the floor. Shepherd pumping more rounds into his head at close range.

The train moved off again. He didn't feel guilty about what he'd done. There was no way he could have called a warning, not when the terrorist had his finger on the trigger. He had done the only thing he could, and neutralised the threat. The American at the Special Forces Club sprang to his mind and he smiled. The terrorist had been well neutralised.

One of the youths glared at him, showing a gold tooth. 'What you laughing at?' he sneered.

Shepherd smiled amiably. 'Nothing, really,' he said.

'Someone might wipe that grin off your face,' said the youth, leaning forward. His companions were sniggering maliciously and clenching their fists.

Shepherd shrugged. 'You could try, I suppose,' he said.

A man in a suit with a shiny leather briefcase turned away pointedly, not wanting to get involved.

'That a real Rolex?' asked the young man, jerking his head at Shepherd's watch.

'I hope so,' said Shepherd.

'I want it!'

'I don't think so,' said Shepherd.

The train swayed as it rattled through the tunnel. The youth's hand disappeared into the pocket of his Puffa jacket and reappeared with a flick-knife. 'Give me your watch and your mobile,' he said, and got to his feet. His thumb depressed the silver button on the handle and a gleaming blade snapped out.

Shepherd's left hand grabbed the boy's wrist and twisted savagely. At the same time he hit his throat with the back of his right hand, hard enough to cause intense pain but not to splinter the cartilage. The knife dropped from the youth's fingers and clattered on the floor of the carriage. His hands went to his throat, as his mouth opened and closed like that of a stranded goldfish. Shepherd grabbed his jacket and lowered him on to his seat. The others sat where they were, too stunned by the violence to move. Shepherd kept his eyes on them as he bent to pick up the knife. He retracted the blade, then slid it into the back pocket of his jeans and sat down.

The train burst out of the tunnel and into Victoria. The injured youth's two friends helped him out on to the platform. They jeered at Shepherd as the doors closed and made obscene gestures, but he could see the fear in their eyes.

The train moved off. The businessman with the briefcase nodded approval but Shepherd ignored him: he took no pride in his ability to use violence, even when it was controlled – he could easily have put the youth in hospital, or worse. But now he'd attracted attention, and that was never a good thing. He felt the knife pressing into his backside. It was an offensive weapon: just carrying it could have earned the boy a prison sentence. Shepherd had seen from the look in his eyes that he would have used it without any thought of the consequences. It made no sense to stab someone on the Tube for a watch and a mobile: every platform and exit was covered by CCTV cameras.

The train plunged into the tunnel. Did he really make a difference? Shepherd wondered. Would anything he did as an undercover cop make the world a better place? He'd stopped a suicide-bomber, but al-Qaeda continued to wage war against the West. He'd put drug-dealers behind bars, but cocaine and heroin continued to flood into the country. He'd put away armed robbers, murderers and fraudsters, but for every one he put away there were a dozen more to take their place. As a soldier he'd fought in wars, and wars could be won and lost. But the war against crime was never-ending because the fight was against human nature. He sighed. What the hell? It was his job, and he could only do it to the best of his ability. If the world was going to hell in a basket, that was the world's problem, not his.

He got off the train at Embankment, walked out of the station and down to the Thames, where he stood and watched the London Eye, the huge ferris wheel that dominated the South Bank. He glanced around, searching for any faces he might recognise from the train but saw none and began to walk slowly across Westminster Bridge, with the Houses of Parliament to his right. The wind tugged at his hair and he turned up the collar of his leather jacket.

Hargrove preferred to meet in public places – sporting events were a favourite, or tourist attractions. In the unlikely event that either of them was followed, a watcher would stand out among sports fans or tourists.

Hargrove was sitting at a table outside a café with a cup of coffee, wrapped up against the cold in a long black coat and a scarlet scarf. Shepherd ordered a cappuccino and sat next to him.

'Everything okay?' asked Hargrove.

Shepherd told him what had happened on the Tube.

'Bastards,' said the superintendent.

'It's the way of the world,' said Shepherd. 'Kids with no hope and nothing to lose. Crime is pretty much their only option and once they take that route they either end up in prison or dead.'

'By choice, Spider. Let's not forget that. Everyone makes choices.'

'Maybe.' He sighed. 'He pulled a knife on me in a Tube train.'

'He was lucky you only winded him. You could have done a lot worse.'

Shepherd smiled. 'Yeah. I'm sure he sees it that way. He'll be on liquids for a week.' A pretty blonde waitress brought him his coffee and he waited until she'd left before he leaned towards Hargrove. 'Any joy identifying the guys from yesterday?'

The superintendent took two photographs from the inside

pocket of his coat and laid them in front of Shepherd. They were surveillance pictures, taken from high up with a long lens. In one the thickset Asian was taking the rucksack from Shepherd. In the other, the taller, thinner man was watching as Shepherd flicked through the banknotes in the sports bag. Hargrove tapped the man with the rucksack. 'Salik Uddin,' he said. 'British passport, but born in Bangladesh. Like ninety per cent of Bangladeshis in this country, he's from the Sylhert region.'

'One of the world's wettest climates,' said Shepherd. He grinned. 'Just one of those stupid bits of information I can't forget.'

'Married with four children,' continued Hargrove. 'Runs several *bureaux de change* in and around the Edgware Road.' He tapped the second photograph. 'His older brother, Matiur Uddin. Not British yet, but he has leave to remain through marriage to a Bangladeshi woman who does have citizenship.'

'*Bureaux de change*? Makes sense. They ship in the counterfeit euros, run them through their shops and into the banking system.'

'We're going to put the bureaux under surveillance, see who else they're dealing with. We'll run checks on their banks and contacts, put their whole operation under the microscope.'

'I guess the notes alone aren't enough to bust them.'

'We don't have any evidence that they've opened the cans. Anyway, we'd like them for conspiracy and to bust the French end so that we can find out where the notes are coming from.'

'I'll make a call this afternoon, see if I can get them to bite on the boat plan. If they agree, I'm going to need a crash course in driving the bloody thing.'

'It's in hand,' said Hargrove. He picked up the photographs and slipped them back into his pocket.

Shepherd sipped his coffee. 'I get the feeling there's something else,' he said.

'Something else?'

'Some other reason for you getting me here. Or am I being paranoid?'

The superintendent smiled. 'I'm that transparent, am I?' He exhaled through pursed lips. 'There's no easy way to say this, Spider, but I'm leaving the unit. I'm sorry I couldn't give you more warning'.

'What happened?' asked Shepherd. 'I thought everything was hunky-dory.'

'The unit's being co-opted into the Serious Organised Crime Agency.'

'The British FBI, right?'

'That's the plan,' said Hargrove. 'Targeting drug-traffickers, people smugglers, paedophile networks, international fraudsters. The sort of stuff we do at a local level. SOCA's going to go after the big fish and they want to hit the ground running. They figured the best way to do that was to absorb our unit.'

Shepherd scowled. 'Why fix something that's not broke?' he said.

'We're a victim of our own success,' said the superintendent. 'SOCA's going to need some major successes to justify its funding and they reckon a few good undercover operations will do that.'

'The reason we've been so successful is because we've never blown our own trumpet,' said Shepherd. 'We always let the local cops take the credit. We're never in the papers. We never give evidence.'

'I explained all that,' said Hargrove, 'but the world is changing. The powers that be need to show they're being effective.'

'So we'll be dragged out at press conferences, will we? It doesn't work like that, and you know it.'

'No one's going to blow your cover, Spider,' said Hargrove, 'but SOCA wants to be able to show that it's doing its job.'

'This is madness.'

'It could be a major step up for you,' said Hargrove. 'Bigger operations, bigger targets. Bigger challenges. SOCA will have more resources than my unit. More manpower.'

'The more people involved, the more chance of a leak,' said Shepherd. 'That's why your unit works so well. Hell, I don't even know half the guys who work for you and they don't know me. Once we're part of a bigger bureaucracy, who knows who'll be looking at my file?'

'What do you want, Spider? You want them to put you in uniform? You're still employed by the Met, remember. Officially they can put you where they want you.'

Shepherd's jaw dropped. 'Is that what they're saying? I join SOCA or I start wearing a pointy helmet? Fuck that.' He grimaced, as if he had a bad taste in his mouth. 'No offence.'

'None taken,' said the superintendent. 'But it's a done deal. In two months' time my unit becomes part of SOCA and there's nothing you or I can do about it.'

'And you can't get some form of autonomy for the unit? Special circumstances and all that.'

The superintendent looked pained. 'That's the second bit of news,' he said. 'I'm moving on. Promoted, finally. And I won't be in SOCA.'

Shepherd slumped in his chair. The undercover unit had been Hargrove's brainchild, his baby. He had hand-picked the undercover operatives and had been involved in every assignment. He had personally persuaded Shepherd to join the unit when Shepherd had applied to join the Metropolitan Police, offering him the chance to use his specialist skills rather than pounding a beat. Shepherd had trusted Hargrove from the outset and the superintendent had never once let him down. The sort of work Shepherd did required him to have absolute faith in his controller, and it couldn't be transferred at short notice. 'How long have you known?' he asked.

'It was first raised last year,' said Hargrove. 'As a suggestion. I made my views clear, that we functioned best as an autonomous unit. I was overruled, but they took their time doing it. That was why I was over at the Yard today. You're the first person I've told, Spider.' He smiled ruefully. 'I haven't even told the wife yet.'

'And the promotion was to make the transfer smoother, was it?' said Shepherd, unable to keep the bitterness out of his voice.

'I was due one anyway,' said Hargrove. 'Don't get paranoid on me, Spider. You'll be up for sergeant before long. Look, I didn't expect you to be happy about this, but there was no way I could have told you earlier. Button's appointment won't even be confirmed until this afternoon.'

'Button?'

'Charlotte Button. She's heading up undercover operations.'

'Never heard of her.'

'I'm not surprised. She's MI5.'

Shepherd groaned. 'Oh, terrific! A spook and a woman. Anything else I should know?'

'Only that she's a damn fine operator. I know you SAS boys tend to be disparaging about women and the intelligence agencies, but Charlotte Button has a track record second to none, both in the field and as a controller. SOCA is only recruiting the best, Spider. That goes for you and for her. Between you and me, three guys in my unit won't be joining SOCA. They're not even being considered.'

'Because?'

'Because SOCA's standards are higher. That's all I've been told. I'd put my men up against anyone but MI5 has been positively vetting all of you and three got the thumbs down.'

'But if I move to SOCA I stay as a cop, right?'

'Strictly speaking, no. At the moment you're employed by the Met, same as I am, although the unit has always been answerable to the Home Office. The individual police authorities are funded by local councils. SOCA will be funded by central government.' He smiled. 'You'll become a civil servant, with pay, pension and the like being handled by the new agency.'

'But the work will be the same?'

'My understanding is that the various forces around the country will still be able to call on the resources of the undercover unit by making an application to the Home Secretary, exactly as they do now.'

Shepherd watched a crocodile of Korean tourists walk by, following a tour guide holding aloft a furled red umbrella. 'I suppose I should congratulate you,' he said, 'on the promotion.'

'It's a big hike in salary,' said Hargrove. 'My wife's been hankering for a villa in Tuscany and it looks like she'll get it now.'

'You're not retiring?'

Hargrove shook his head. 'I think she plans to be in the villa on her own, actually. I'm being co-opted on to the emergency planning committee – national disasters and all that. Deskbound until the shit hits the fan.'

'Sounds like fun,' said Shepherd. 'This can't be happening. Why fix something that isn't broke?'

'Think of it as an opportunity,' said Hargrove. 'A bigger playing-field for you.'

'It's a question of trust,' said Shepherd. 'If I put my life on the line, I need to trust my back-up one hundred per cent.'

'You'll be able to meet Button before you sign up,' said Hargrove. 'You'll see that she's sound.'

'You've met her?'

'No, but I know her reputation. She's rock solid, Spider.'

Shepherd put his head into his hands. 'I really don't need this, not now.'

'It was going to happen one day, we all knew that,' said Hargrove. 'Nothing lasts for ever. Especially in the police. They move us around to stop us getting stale.'

'How do you think the rest of the unit will take it?'

'About the same as you, I suppose. No one likes change.'

Shepherd sat back in his seat. 'Maybe it's time for me to move on, too.'

Hargrove frowned. 'What do you mean?'

'I've been spending too much time away from Liam – and there was that business on the trawler . . . If anything had happened to me, Liam would've been on his own.'

'Time for a quieter life?'

'Maybe,' Shepherd said. 'Maybe it's for the best.' High overhead a passenger jet banked right and headed for Heathrow. He stared up at the plane. 'Maybe I need a holiday,' he mused.

★　　★　　★

Shepherd caught a black cab back to Ealing. He went upstairs to change into his running gear. As he took off his jeans he realised he still had the mugger's flick-knife in his pocket. It was about seven inches long with fake pearl insets on either side of the handle and a chrome button on one side. Shepherd pressed it with his thumb. The blade flicked out and clicked into place. It was a vicious weapon, long and sharp enough to kill with one thrust, even in the hands of an amateur. He put it down by the basin. He'd destroy it: a few blows with a hammer would render it useless.

He pulled on an old sweatshirt and shorts, went downstairs and picked up his rucksack. He ran for the best part of an hour, pushing himself harder than usual, and was drenched with sweat by the time he got back to the house.

Katra was in the kitchen, ironing. She laughed as he walked into the kitchen and took off the rucksack.

'What?' asked Shepherd.

'Nothing,' she said.

'You're laughing at something,' he said, as he took a bottle of Evian water from the fridge.

'It's those bricks,' she said.

'Well?'

'In Slovenia they would think you were crazy, running with bricks.'

'They might be right.' He twisted the top off the bottle and drank half of it.

'It makes you stronger?'

'Oh, yes.'

'But you don't look strong.'

Shepherd wiped his mouth on the back of his hand. 'What do you mean?'

'You are not big.'

'Size isn't everything,' said Shepherd, looking at her playfully.

Katra looked perplexed.

'Strength and size aren't the same thing,' he explained. 'A lot of big people aren't strong. I train for stamina. I want to be able to run long and hard, and the bricks help me do that. They make my heart stronger.'

'You trained like that in the army, yes?'

'A lot of the time. Being a soldier is often about moving a lot of equipment from place to place in the shortest possible time. It's all very well being able to run in shorts and expensive trainers, but in the real world you're wearing heavy clothes and boots, and carrying a pack on your back.'

'But you're not a soldier any more.'

'Old habits,' said Shepherd.

'Old habits?'

'It's an expression. Old habits die hard. It means that once you've done things one way for a long time, it's hard to do things differently.'

Shepherd went upstairs to shower and change. He pulled on a denim shirt and black jeans, then grinned as he caught sight of his reflection in the wardrobe mirror: his own taste in clothes pretty much matched Tony Corke's.

The three mobiles were lined up in their chargers by the bedside table. Shepherd picked up the Tony Corke phone, then paced up and down for a few minutes, getting into character. He connected the digital recorder, then hit 'redial'. The Uddin brothers' number was the only one in the phone.

'It's me,' said Shepherd. 'Is that Ben?'

'Yes,' said Salik.

'Everything okay with the cans?'

'They were fine.'

'Still not going to tell me what was inside them?' He kept the tone light, chatty.

'You were paid.'

'Thanks for that,' said Shepherd. 'Though to be honest, it's going straight into the pockets of my lawyer. Look, have you thought about what I said about my boat?'

'I have thought about it, yes.'

'So?'

'We should talk.'

'That's why I called.'

'Not over the phone,' said Salik. 'We must sit down and talk. You and me and my brother.'

'The guy with the money was your brother?'

'I don't want to discuss anything on the phone,' said Salik. 'Today's Monday. Let's say we get together on Wednesday. We'll have dinner. You can tell me about this boat of yours.'

'Excellent,' said Shepherd. 'Where and when?'

'I'll phone you on Wednesday,' said Salik. 'Where are you?'

'Dover,' said Shepherd, 'but I can come in to London, no problem. Call me when you're ready.' He ended the call, pleased with the way it had gone. There was plenty of time for Hargrove to decide how to play the meeting, and Salik had seemed genuinely hooked.

Shepherd put down the Tony Corke mobile and picked up his work phone. He called Hargrove and told him about the conversation with Uddin.

'Well done,' said the superintendent. 'The timing's perfect because I've just got the boat fixed up. Former SBS guy, now lives in Southampton, Gordon McConnell. Ever come across him?'

'No,' said Shepherd.

'He's expecting you tomorrow. I'll text you his number. He'll do a couple of night runs with you – that way you'll be up to speed before your sit-down with the brothers.'

Shepherd went downstairs. 'I'm going to be away tomorrow night,' he said. 'Make sure Liam does his homework.'

'Of course,' said Katra. 'Don't forget you're going to his grandmother's this weekend.'

'I hadn't forgotten,' he said, 'and I can't tell you how much I'm looking forward to it.' He could tell from her blank look that she had made as much sense of his sarcasm as she did of his humour. He winked.

Shepherd drove down to Southampton in the ten-year-old Land Rover. The battered, mud-splattered vehicle was registered in the name of Tony Corke at the Dover address and was full of the sort of gear a sailor might need, including wet-weather clothing, boots, a tool-kit, and various sailing magazines.

He phoned McConnell on the way and they arranged to meet at a pub on the outskirts of the city. 'Keep an eye open for the big man with the beard and a look of bored contempt on his face,' said McConnell, in a Northumberland accent.

Shepherd spotted him as soon as he walked into the pub. The self-description was bang on, although McConnell wore an amused smile as he shook Shepherd's hand. 'So, I'm going to turn you into a sailor in twenty-four hours, am I?' he said.

'That's the plan,' said Shepherd. 'You're Gordon?'

'Gordy on dry land,' said McConnell. 'Skipper when I'm at the helm. Okay, lesson one. We need antifreeze in the system before we go anywhere near the water. What are you drinking?'

'Jameson's. Ice.'

'On the rocks, as the Yanks say,' said McConnell. 'Bad bloody omen for a start.' He pushed himself off the bench seat and ambled over to the bar. He had the rolling gait of a man used to a moving deck rather than solid ground. The beard made it difficult to place his age but Shepherd figured he was probably in his late fifties and that it had been a decade or so since he had last squeezed into an SBS wetsuit.

McConnell returned with a double whiskey and ice for Shepherd, and a pint of beer for himself. They clinked glasses and McConnell drained half of his in one gulp. 'I needed that,' he said. 'So, from the Sass to the cops. Like paperwork, do you?'

'My wife wanted me out,' said Shepherd. 'Too many nights away.'

'Ah, wives,' said McConnell. 'I've had four, bless them.'

'A girl in every port?'

'All local, as it happens. Kids?'

'A boy. Nine.'

McConnell grinned. 'I've got five. Can't remember how old they are.'

Shepherd could see that McConnell was the competitive sort,

but that was generally the way it was with men who had served in the Special Forces. You didn't get into the SAS or SBS by hiding your light under a bushel.

'So, what's your sailing experience?' asked McConnell.

'I did a crash course in trawlers, but as I was only a deck-hand I didn't have to do much. But I'm okay on navigation.'

'And you've used night-vision equipment?'

'Sure.'

McConnell belched loudly. 'Then the rest of it is like driving a car,' he said. 'Why don't we have another round and then I'll show you the boat? We can pop over to France and back to get the feel of it, then do a few night-runs.'

The sea spray blew across his face like a light shower and Shepherd narrowed his eyes. High overhead, seagulls soared on the breeze coming in from the English Channel. Whichever way he looked he saw other boats. A huge cross-Channel ferry heading for France, as big as a skyscraper turned on its side. Flotillas of small sailboats, some barely bigger than bathtubs. Freighters caked with dirt. Gleaming white executive toys with massive outboard engines. Fishing boats with rusting hulls.

'It'll be quieter at night,' shouted McConnell, over the roar of the massive outboard engine behind them. He was standing up, leaning back against his seat, legs planted like trees, shoulder-width apart. His right hand was on the wheel, his left on a chromium-plated throttle lever. 'This is us doing thirty knots.' He banked to the left to avoid a twin-masted sailboat ahead.

Shepherd was standing next to the skipper, his left hand on a grab rail at the side of the boat. Even at thirty knots he could see the high degree of concentration necessary to keep the boat away from trouble. All the craft around them were heading at different speeds in different directions. Working out where they were all going in relation to one's own boat was like some huge mathematical problem that required constant computations.

'You want to divide the sea into three circles around you,' shouted McConnell. 'Far, near, and fuck-me-that's-close. The far stuff, you have to be aware of where it's heading and if it's a potential problem. The near stuff, you need to know its speed and if you're going to pass it to port or starboard. The other stuff shouldn't be a problem, providing you've got the outer two covered. It's all about anticipation. The big stuff is easy – you can see it from miles away. It's the fair-weather sailors in their piss-pot fifteen-footers that you've got to watch out for. Or windsurfers who've gone out too far. Hit one of them at sixty knots and they'll rip right through the hull. There's flotsam and crap all around, too, everything from deckchairs to empty champagne bottles, so you can't let your guard down for a second.' He banked left again and increased the throttle. 'That's forty knots,' he shouted, 'and the engines aren't even breaking sweat.' He pulled the throttle back and the boat slowed to a little over ten knots. He grinned at Shepherd. 'You take the helm, get the feel of it.'

Shepherd put his left hand on the wheel in front of him. McConnell kept a loose grip on it, but Shepherd could feel that he had control of the boat. It was responsive, with far less play on the wheel than he'd had when he was at the helm of Pepper's trawler.

'Take it up to fifteen knots,' said McConnell. 'Nice and slowly.'

Shepherd did as he was told. The boat kept slamming into the crests of the waves and the wheel bucked and kicked in his hand. He kept the speed steady at fifteen knots.

'Okay, that's us just before we start to plane,' shouted McConnell. 'We're slamming into the waves rather than cutting over them. It's a teeth-juddering ride, right?'

Shepherd nodded. He was concentrating on the water ahead of the prow.

'Take it up to twenty knots,' roared McConnell. 'Smoothly as you can.'

Shepherd pushed the throttle forward. As the boat accelerated past sixteen knots the juddering stopped and it carved across the top of the waves.

'That's the planing,' said McConnell. 'You feel it?'

'Awesome!' It felt to Shepherd as if the boat was flying above the water now, barely skipping along the surface.

'Keep it going!' bellowed McConnell.

Shepherd pushed the throttle forward until the speedometer registered forty knots. He was finding it harder to concentrate on all the ships in the vicinity. There was a freighter off to starboard that seemed to be on a collision course and he steered away from it.

McConnell grinned when he saw what Shepherd was doing. 'We'll miss him by a hundred yards, he's only doing twelve knots. The thing to remember is that out here we're the fastest bastards, by far.'

It was like driving a motorcycle, Shepherd realised. Fast and furious, not worrying overmuch about what was behind you. Just keep focused on where you're going and be ready to accelerate out of trouble.

'Ready to put her through her paces?' McConnell shouted.

'Sure!'

'Give it full throttle!'

Shepherd took a deep breath and pushed the throttle forward. The edge of the seat pressed against the small of his back as the craft surged forward, and the air beat against his face like a living thing. He was panting like a dog and fought to steady his breathing. His left hand ached from gripping the wheel too hard and he forced himself to relax.

'See the branch?' yelled McConnell, but Shepherd was already steering the boat to port. 'Nice,' said McConnell, approvingly.

Shepherd kept accelerating. The huge Yamaha outboard roared and the waves beat under the hull. The boat felt as if it was bouncing along the surface like a stone that had been sent spinning across a lake. The speedometer went past fifty knots. Fifty-five. Sixty. The throttle was in the full forward position.

'Both hands on the wheel now!' roared McConnell. 'At this speed you have to steer your way out of trouble, so you need both hands.'

Shepherd did what he was told.

'Try a hard to starboard!'

Shepherd turned the wheel right. The boat banked easily and he felt his body dragged to the left by the force of the turn. His eyes kept scanning the area ahead of the bow. There were a dozen craft close by, all yachts, none going at more than ten knots.

'This is amazing!' shouted Shepherd. 'It's as if everything else is standing still.'

'Compared to us, they are! Come on, let's go to France.' McConnell pointed at the GPS screen mounted between the two wheels. 'Just follow the dotted line.'

Shepherd put a pint of beer in front of McConnell, who grunted his thanks. It was a little after six o'clock and McConnell had insisted that they retire to a pub 'for a drop more antifreeze' before nightfall. He had a sketch-pad in front of him and was drawing a rough map of the south coast and the French shore with a Biro whose end had been well chewed.

Shepherd sat down and took a sip of Jameson's. 'That is one hell of a boat, Gordy.'

'State-of-the-art.' McConnell sat back and swallowed a good third of his pint, then belched.

'Explain the planing thing to me,' said Shepherd.

'It's what gives the rib its edge. That boat lifts up on to plane at between fifteen and sixteen knots, depending on the load being carried. The tilt lever on the wheel sets the angle of the propeller compared with the hull and that has to be right to get up on plane. I'll run you through that tonight. It's a matter of feel more than anything.'

'But what's the science behind it?'

'A rib boat is built like an arrow so that it cuts through the waves rather than bouncing over them. The semi-inflatable bit keeps it out of the water, and they have a very shallow draught. Mine's just eighteen inches, which is nothing. Boats that are built with a displacement design slow to a crawl in rough seas but a rib just punches through. Your old mob has one that's made with metal collars rather than rubber and has an internal diesel engine with a range of four hundred miles. It's all hush-hush, covered with radar-deflecting paint with an electromagnet on the front that lets it stick to hulls until the guys can offload. Now, that bugger is one hell of a boat.'

He took another deep pull on his pint and another third disappeared.

'The shallow draught also gives you an advantage if you want to play hide and seek. The rib can go where most other craft would run aground. If you're being chased you can slip into the shallows off Norfolk or the Thames estuary. It helps with loading and unloading, too. I'll show you tonight. You can run right on to the beach, load and unload at the bow while the engine's still in enough water to pull her away when you're ready. No need to go anywhere near a dock if you don't want to.'

'And no one can keep up with us?'

'You couldn't outrun a fast sports boat with surface piercing props,' said McConnell, 'but only flash bastards who want to be noticed have them anyway. They throw a huge plume of white water out of the back so you can see them for miles. I've had a few races with the local Customs boys for fun and they couldn't come close. The navy have some faster stuff but you'd be bloody unlucky to have them on your tail. Mind you, even if they had the speed, they'd have a bloody tough time tracking you. The beauty of the rib design is that it's virtually impossible to follow. It won't show up on radar, unless it's stern on. Then the engine might give off an echo, but even that's not guaranteed.'

'You keep calling it a rib,' said Shepherd.

'Stands for rigid inflatable boat. Basically an inflatable with a hard hull.'

'It's the perfect smuggler's boat,' said Shepherd.

'Good job I'm one of the good guys, isn't it?' said McConnell. He winked and laughed, a bellowing guffaw that had several heads turning in his direction.

'Do you get asked to bring stuff over?'

'All the time,' said McConnell. 'Usually by guys in sharp suits down from London who think I'll drop my trousers for a few grand. If they really piss me off I pass them on to an undercover Customs guy I know, otherwise I just let them ply me with drink then bid them farewell with a few choice words.'

'What about being followed by planes or helicopters?'

'On a daytime run they could pick you out of all the rest of the cross-Channel traffic maybe, but not at night.'

'Range?'

'At a steady ten knots the engine burns through eight gallons of fuel an hour. Once you're up on the plane, you burn eleven gallons an hour but you're doing forty knots or more. Pretty much four times more efficient. The fuel tank holds fifty-five gallons so you can do two hundred nautical miles or thereabouts. More than enough for a Channel run. And it's no trouble to carry another fifty-five gallons in cans.'

'There's just the one engine?'

'The biggest outboard on the market. Three hundred horse-power. A beast. Fifteen grand's worth of motor.'

'Reliable?'

'Just don't run over anything and it'll be fine.'

'What if it breaks down?'

'It won't.'

'Have you got a manual I can read?'

'If anything does go wrong, I don't want a bloody amateur tinkering with it,' growled McConnell. 'You have a problem, you call me. Now, I've a question for you. What will you be carrying?'

'Hargrove didn't tell you?'

'I wouldn't be asking if he had,' said McConnell. 'I don't play silly mind games, life's too short.'

'Sorry,' said Shepherd, not wanting to offend the man. 'I just assumed he'd filled you in. Cash. Counterfeit euros. Maybe a couple of passengers.'

McConnell nodded. 'At least it's not drugs.'

'Does it matter? Doesn't Hargrove give you a "get out of jail free" card?'

McConnell chuckled. 'It's not as easy as that,' he said, 'but you

know as well as I do that villains who deal in drugs are at the nasty
end of the spectrum. The people-smugglers are a bad bunch, too.
Wouldn't want anything to happen to you. Or my boat.'

'I'm a big boy, Gordy,' said Shepherd. 'Besides, the guys at this
end are sweethearts.'

'And the ones in France?'

'I'm not sure,' said Shepherd. 'Could be Albanians.'

McConnell grimaced. 'Now they can be heavy bastards,' he
said. 'Albanians and Serbs are worse than the Russians.'

'Yeah, but it's currency, not drugs.'

'Still worth killing for,' said McConnell. He gestured at the
notepad. 'Okay, let's run through a few things and then I'll go
over the charts with you.'

After two runs across the Channel in close to complete darkness,
then seeing the dawn come up as they brought the boat back into
Southampton, McConnell decided they needed refuelling, which
meant going back into a pub for a full English breakfast: fried
eggs, bacon, black pudding, beans, potato pancakes, tomatoes
and two slices of fried bread.

'So, have you got any questions?' asked McConnell, through a
mouthful of egg and bacon.

'How do you earn a living down here?' asked Shepherd.

'I meant about handling the rib,' said McConnell. He twisted
the top off a bottle of HP sauce and poured it over his fried bread.

'I'm fine on the boat,' said Shepherd. 'I'm trying to work out
where you stand in the grand scheme of things.'

McConnell scratched his ear. 'I'm a sort of consultant,' he said.
'Your old mob uses me from time to time, and I'm a regular
visitor to Poole.'

Poole in Dorset, headquarters of the SBS. Shepherd had twice
been on courses there during his days as an SAS trooper.

'Ribs are used for all sort of things, these days – interception of
craft at sea, boarding oil-rigs, getting people into places with the
minimum fuss. I do a fair bit of training.' He grinned. 'And in my
spare time, I take merchant bankers out deep-sea fishing.'

'Really?'

'Pays well and I get stock tips to boot. You wouldn't believe the size of my portfolio.'

As Shepherd laughed, his work phone rang and he fished it out of his pea coat. It was Hargrove. 'How are you getting on, Spider?' asked the superintendent.

'Fine,' said Shepherd. He nodded an apology to McConnell and went outside the pub. 'Gordy's a good teacher,' he continued. 'Hell of a crash course he's given me.'

'Think you can handle the boat?'

'I can't guarantee a smooth crossing, but I can get there and back,' said Shepherd.

'On your own, or do you want him with you?'

'I think the brothers are more likely to be spooked if I bring in someone else,' said Shepherd, 'but I'll play it by ear when I speak to them. He's a character, though. No way they'd think he was any sort of law-enforcement official.'

'A maverick?'

'Definitely.'

'You're probably getting on like a house on fire, then,' said Hargrove. 'Are you done there?'

'We did two trips in the dark. We're going back out this morning and then I've asked him to give me a rundown on maintenance and stuff in case I get asked awkward questions.'

'Did he tell you there's a tracking unit on the boat?'

'He didn't, but that's good news.'

'We'll know where you are every step of the way. And we'll have both ends covered.'

'You sound like you're worried.'

'It's a big stretch of water and I didn't want you to think you'd be on your own out there,' said Hargrove.

'I've already proved I can swim,' said Shepherd.

'No question about that,' said the superintendent. 'When you get back to London, Charlotte Button wants to meet with you.'

'A job interview?' said Shepherd.

'A chat,' said Hargrove. 'I'll text you her number. She's expecting your call.'

'Have they said when you'll be leaving?'

'Sooner rather than later.'

'What about this operation? They won't pull you off it before it's done?'

'I can't guarantee that won't happen, Spider. I'm sorry.'

'I'm putting my life on the line here, and some desk jockey decides that my safety-net gets taken away?'

'If I'm pulled off, Button will be fully briefed and she'll take over. I guarantee you won't be put in harm's way.'

Shepherd cut the connection. He waited outside the pub until the text message arrived, then called Charlotte Button. She was brisk and to the point, and asked him to meet her for tea at the Ritz the following day at three o'clock. He smiled as he cut the connection. 'No time for chit-chat, then,' he muttered.

He went back inside. McConnell was waving at a barman and ordering two more slices of fried bread.

Shepherd was an hour outside London when his personal mobile rang. It was Katra, and she was clearly upset. 'Dan, you have to go to the school now,' she said, voice shaking.

Shepherd's stomach lurched. 'What's happened? Is Liam okay?'

'There's some problem, but they won't tell me what it is. The office of the headteacher called and said you have to go to the school right away.'

'He's not hurt, is he?'

'No, but there is a problem. I think he's done something wrong.'

'What?'

'They wouldn't tell me because I'm not a relative or his legal guardian. Only you.'

Shepherd looked at the clock on the dashboard of the Land Rover.

'Okay, I'll go now. I'm on my way back to London anyway – I can easily swing by the school.'

'I'm sorry,' said Katra.

'It's not your fault,' said Shepherd. 'Whatever it is, I'll sort it out.'

Shepherd spent the rest of the drive to Liam's school running through all the reasons why he'd get an urgent summons to see the headteacher. Liam wasn't hurt or sick, and anything to do with his work could have been dealt with by letter. Which left only a disciplinary problem, but that didn't make sense because Liam wasn't the sort of boy to get into fights. He wasn't a coward, far from it, but he had a sharp tongue and a wicked sense of humour and generally preferred to talk his way out of trouble. It was a talent he had inherited from his mother. Sue had always been able to cut Shepherd to the quick with a few well-chosen words.

He had to park several hundred yards from the school and buy a pay-and-display sticker. Then he walked briskly to the school gates, across the playground to the main block and followed a sign that pointed to the administration office. In it he stood at a large wooden counter that bore a strong resemblance to the reception area in many police stations he had been in. The three middle-aged women standing behind it had the same world-weary look of police officers.

Shepherd told them who he was and that he was there to see the headteacher. He couldn't remember her name but as he waited to be called through he scrutinised a noticeboard and eventually found a memo that told him she was Mrs Lucinda Hale-Barton. Shepherd pictured a woman in her fifties with permed hair and a tweed suit, but the woman who shook his hand and ushered him into her office was barely out of her twenties, with shoulder-length red hair, a low-cut top and a figure-hugging skirt. Liam had never mentioned what an attractive headteacher he had, but then he rarely spoke to Shepherd about school.

Suddenly Shepherd realised he was wearing his sea-going gear, that his hands were stained with oil from the outboard engine and that it had been twenty-four hours since he had showered or shaved. He ran a hand through his unkempt hair and opened his mouth to apologise for his dishevelled appearance but the head-teacher had already started to speak.

'I'm so sorry to have called you in like this, Mr Shepherd,' she said, as she dropped down on to a high-backed leather swivel chair behind a chrome and glass desk, 'but we have a problem and I wanted to let you know face to face, as it were.' She opened a drawer and took out a flick-knife. Shepherd recognised it immediately. 'Liam had this with him today,' she said and placed it in front of him. 'It's what they call a flick-knife.'

'He brought it to school?'

'Yes, he did,' said the headteacher, 'and mere possession of a knife like this is a criminal offence.'

'Actually, he's below the age of criminal responsibility,' said Shepherd. 'He isn't ten for another month.'

She flashed him a cold smile. 'Well, strictly speaking, the Crime and Disorder Act of 1998 allows the authorities to bring in a child-safety order and have him placed under the supervision of a social worker or a youth-offending team, even if he isn't yet ten.' She must have seen Shepherd's horror because she put up her hands in a placatory gesture. 'Mr Shepherd, I'm just ex-plaining the law,' she said. 'Trust me, there's no question of the police or social workers being involved. But carrying a weapon in school is not something we can tolerate. On the rare occasions it's happened here, we have excluded the pupil immediately.'

'You mean you want to throw Liam out?'

'We have no choice, Mr Shepherd. We have a policy of zero tolerance and we must show that we act on it.'

'He wasn't threatening anyone with it, was he?'

'That's not really the point,' said the headteacher. 'But, no, he was just showing it to his classmates. Do you have any idea where he might have got it from?'

Shepherd took a deep breath and exhaled slowly. 'It's mine,' he said eventually. 'Well, not mine exactly. I took it from a mugger on the Underground. I was going to destroy it but Liam must have found it. Mrs Hale-Barton, I really can't apologise enough for this, but I'm at least partly to blame. I left it in the house – in my bathroom, actually, but he goes in there all the time. I'm sure he didn't mean any harm by bringing it in.'

The headteacher frowned. 'You took it from a mugger? I don't understand.'

'I'm sorry – I thought you knew that I'm a police officer,' said Shepherd.

'No, I didn't. Liam's file has you down as being in the army.'

'I don't shout about it,' said Shepherd. He took out his wallet and handed her his warrant card. 'I left the army some time ago. I'm not a uniformed officer, I have more of an administrative role.' He gestured at his clothing. 'I was actually on my way back from a friend's boat when my au pair called.'

'You tackled a mugger?'

'Actually, he tackled me,' said Shepherd. 'He didn't know I was in the job – just wanted my watch and mobile. I was in the wrong place at the wrong time.'

'And you disarmed him?' She handed back the warrant card and Shepherd slid it into his wallet.

'That sounds more dramatic than it was,' he said. 'We grappled and I took it off him. I don't know which of us was more scared. Look, this is absolutely my fault, Mrs Hale-Barton. I shouldn't have had the knife in the house. I should have handed it in straight away but it slipped my mind. I've a lot on my plate at the moment, not that that's any excuse. I promise Liam will never do anything like this again – he's a good boy generally, isn't he? He's never been in trouble before?'

'He works hard and behaves well,' said the headteacher. 'Especially when you consider what he's been through, losing his mother.'

'He's a great kid,' said Shepherd, and gestured at the knife. 'He just made a mistake with that. And it's not one he'll repeat.'

The headteacher picked up the knife and grimaced. 'What a horrible thing,' she said. She pressed the button and flinched as the blade sprang out. 'And the mugger was trying to stab you with this?' she asked.

Shepherd nodded. 'He was just a teenager. Only a few years older than Liam.'

The headteacher shook her head sadly. 'I don't know what the world's coming to,' she said. 'Violence within our school is very rare, but I wonder how well we're preparing our pupils for life in the real world. You must see it all the time, doing what you do.'

Shepherd smiled. 'I'm not really in the firing line,' he lied, 'but you're right. Gun crime is at an all-time high. We have drive-by shootings and stabbings and all the other things we used to associate with American cities. These days there's more violent crime in London than there is in New York.'

The headteacher pressed the blade with the palm of her hand, trying to get it back into place.

'Let me,' said Shepherd. He took the knife from her, depressed the chrome button and clicked the blade back into its safe position.

'The council has a facility for disposing of knives, so perhaps I should take care of it,' said the headteacher. She held out her hand and Shepherd gave it back to her. She put it back in the drawer. 'As I said, we have a policy,' she said. 'Zero tolerance.'

'I understand. But I don't see that excluding Liam is going to change anything. He made a mistake. He wasn't carrying a knife out of badness, just curiosity. And I really do blame myself for having it in the house in the first place.'

'Can I ask you something?' she said. 'Do you keep a gun at home?'

'Generally it's the armed-response teams of SO19 who carry weapons,' said Shepherd, 'and they're locked away at the station when the men are off duty.' It wasn't exactly a lie, he thought. He'd just evaded the question. He did keep a gun in the house, but not anywhere that Liam would find it. Sue had always been insistent that he stored any gun under lock and key and that Liam was never to be aware of it.

'Do you think we'll ever get to the stage where our policemen carry guns as a matter of course?'

'Probably,' said Shepherd. 'There are just too many guns in the hands of drug-dealers and the like, these days. You can't expect unarmed policemen to give chase down a dark alley blowing their whistles as they did in the days of *Dixon of Dock Green*. The world has changed, and the police have to change with it. It's like patrol cars – the villains drive faster vehicles so we have to upgrade our transport. There's no point in ours having a top speed of a hundred if the villains are roaring along at a hundred and twenty.'

'I suppose not,' said the headteacher. She sighed. 'Anyway, that's beside the point, isn't it? We have to decide what to do with young Liam.'

'He's very settled here,' said Shepherd. 'I really, really don't want to have to move him. So much of his life has changed recently that he needs the stability school offers him. My wife was killed and then he stayed with his grandparents for a while. Now at least we're a family again.'

'I do understand, Mr Shepherd.' She chewed her lip, then nodded slowly. 'You're right, of course. Excluding him will do more harm than good. I'll speak to him and make it clear that he's had a lucky escape. But you must talk to him too, Mr Shepherd, and there has to be some sort of punishment.'

'His PlayStation and the television set in his room will go. And he'll do housework until it comes out of his ears.'

The headteacher smiled. 'That should be enough,' she said. She stood up and offered her hand. Shepherd shook it over the desk. 'We haven't seen you at any of the PTA meetings, have we?' she said.

'I've been busy,' said Shepherd, 'but I'll make time in future, I promise.'

'Excellent,' said the headteacher. 'And perhaps one day you could come in and give a talk to our pupils – a career in the modern police force, something like that.'

'Sure,' agreed Shepherd, although he doubted that the headteacher would appreciate him giving her pupils a rundown on life as an undercover officer. He'd been shot at more times than he cared to remember, and he'd lied, cheated and conned his way into the lives of numerous villains so that he could put them behind bars. Shepherd loved the job and relished its challenges, but it wasn't the sort of profession that a seventeen-year-old should be nudged towards. And the way the police were going, he wouldn't recommend any youngster to sign up straight from school. Police pay wasn't great, while political correctness and mounting paperwork meant that the job was as much about protecting your back as it was about putting villains away. The only way to make a decent career was to go in as a graduate on the fast-track promotion scheme, but then it was more about climbing the greasy pole than it was about fighting crime. Shepherd had always been happier at the sharp end. As a soldier he had wanted to be where the bullets were flying. As a police officer, he wanted to be head-to-head with the bad guys. But explaining that to a group of impressionable schoolchildren probably wasn't what the lovely Mrs Hale-Barton had in mind.

'Liam's still in class,' she said. 'School finishes in ten minutes. I can have him brought here or you can wait for him at the gates.'

'No problem, I'll wait outside,' said Shepherd. 'I'm really grateful for you giving Liam another chance.'

He waited at the school gates until he heard the bell ring. Thirty seconds later the doors banged open and pupils flooded out, laughing and shouting. On the road a line of four-wheel-drives stretched into the distance as far as he could see, engines running. Shepherd stood with his hands in his pockets, wondering what he should say to Liam. Discipline was the part of parenting he hated most, but kids needed boundaries: they needed to be told what their limits were and kept to them. They had to be taught the difference between right and wrong, and when they did wrong they had to be punished. Shepherd hated punishing his son. He'd never laid a finger on him. Never had and never would. He'd always left the disciplining to Sue when she was alive. Good cop, bad cop. She'd administer the punishments, and Shepherd would flash his son a sympathetic smile when she wasn't looking. It was only after she had gone that Shepherd had understood how much she must have hated the bad-cop role.

Shepherd saw Liam among a group of youngsters, all with their ties at half-mast and their shirt collars open. A grin broke across Liam's face, which vanished when he realised why his father was there. He slowed and stared at the ground, avoiding Shepherd's baleful stare.

He muttered something as he got close.

'What?' said Shepherd.

'I said I'm sorry,' Liam mumbled.

'You are in so much trouble,' said Shepherd.

'I know,' said Liam. 'They're going to exclude me.'

'No, they're not,' said Shepherd. He started walking away and Liam hurried after him. Shepherd held up his right hand, the thumb and first finger almost touching. 'But you were this close to getting kicked out. You're lucky the headteacher decided to give you a break. What the hell were you thinking of?'

'I don't know. It just looked kind of cool.'

Shepherd stopped dead. '*Cool?* There's nothing cool about knives.'

'I'd never seen a flick-knife for real, only on telly.'

'Yeah? Well, the reason for that, Liam, is that they've been banned since 1959. Since before I was born. And since 1988 no one has been allowed to carry any knife with a blade more than three inches long unless they've a very good reason. And why would you even think you could go waving it around at school?' He started walking again.

Liam followed. 'I wasn't waving it, Dad. I was just showing it to my friends.'

'Well, your little show-and-tell has cost you your PlayStation. And the TV comes out of your room. And I want you to help Katra with the washing and cleaning. You're going to be in the garden every weekend, pulling up weeds.'

'Okay,' said Liam.

'You know how dangerous knives are, right?'

'Of course.'

'And flick-knives are just about the most dangerous of them all. You press the button and the blade is there. It serves only one purpose. It's not like a Swiss Army knife. The only thing you can do with a flick-knife is attack someone.'

Liam said nothing.

'Do you know where I got it from?'

Liam shook his head.

'Someone tried to stick it into me. And they weren't playing. The only reason you carry a weapon like that is if you want to hurt someone. And you don't want to hurt anyone, do you?'

'No. I just wanted to show it to my friends.'

'Can you imagine what would have happened if someone had taken it off you and started waving it around? Someone could have been cut – or worse. And it would have been your fault. What were you doing in my bathroom anyway?'

'I wanted some toothpaste and I saw the knife by the basin.'

'You shouldn't have taken it, Liam. Hell, if you'd asked me about it I could have explained what it was and why I had it. Why didn't you ask me first?'

Liam was silent.

'Because you knew I'd say no, right?'

'I guess.'

'So you knew that what you were doing was wrong, didn't you?'

Still Liam said nothing.

'That makes it worse. You were being sneaky.'

'I wasn't, Dad.'

'You thought that if I didn't know you had it you could take it to school. That's being sneaky. I thought you were better than that, Liam.'

Liam muttered under his breath.

'What?' said Shepherd.

'I said I'm sorry,' said Liam.

'Okay,' said Shepherd. 'And I'm sorry, too.'

'For what?'

'For having it in the house. For not locking it away. We both made mistakes, kid, but it's not the end of the world.'

'So will you have a punishment, too?' asked Liam.

Shepherd pointed a finger at his son. 'It's punishment enough being your father sometimes,' he said. 'Don't push your luck. And we'd better get a move on, because you're going to be cleaning the toilet before dinner.'

Shepherd took the Central Line to Tottenham Court Road, walked down Oxford Street, checking reflections in store windows, and headed into the Virgin megastore. He spent a full fifteen minutes in the classical-music section, then wandered round hip-hop, checking faces. There was no overlap.

He took the escalator to the ground floor, then walked along Oxford Street to Borders bookstore. He took the escalator up, then went down in the lift, did a final check at Oxford Circus Underground station then left through the Regent Street south exit and walked as rapidly as the crowd of shoppers allowed to the Ritz Hotel.

He felt underdressed as soon as he entered the lobby. Even the receptionists were better dressed than he was and for a moment he regretted not putting on a suit. He'd known there would be a dress code so he'd forgone his regular jeans and put on grey flannel trousers but he'd decided to keep his leather jacket. He didn't exactly blend in, but here it was more about having the right attitude than about the name on the label inside a suit.

He heard the sound of clinking cutlery and a piano to his left and strode confidently in that direction. Middle-aged women in Gucci and Chanel, wearing Rolex or Cartier watches, were nibbling at finger sandwiches and sipping tea from delicate china cups, trying not to disturb their perfectly applied make-up. He scanned the faces. Botoxed foreheads. Lifted brows. Collagen lips. Bleached hair. Then he saw a face that was smiling naturally, without the benefit of a surgeon's intervention. Dark chestnut hair, brown eyes that were almost black and a well-cut dark blue jacket and skirt that suggested quiet professionalism rather than ostentatious spending. She got to her feet and flashed him a small wave. He wasn't surprised that she had recognised him so easily. Charlotte Button would have had access to his Metropolitan Police file: she would know everything about him and would have seen every photograph, surveillance and official, that had ever been taken of him.

He went over to her and shook her hand. 'I'm sorry I'm late,' he said.

She glanced at the discreet Rolex on her left wrist. 'You're bang on time,' she said. 'I've only just got here myself.'

She sat down and smoothed her skirt. Shepherd sat opposite her. A young waiter in black hovered at her shoulder and she ordered afternoon tea for two, with English Breakfast and Blue Mountain coffee. Shepherd knew that the coffee was for him and she went up another notch in his estimation: that she had remembered he didn't drink tea showed that she was attentive to detail.

'I though we could have a bite as we talk,' she said. 'I've been on the go all day.'

'No problem,' he said. There were only half a dozen men in the room and he was the youngest by a good two decades. It wasn't the sort of place Hargrove would have suggested as a venue.

When he looked back at Button, he was surprised to find her smiling at him. 'I can hazard a guess as to what you're thinking, Dan. I hope you don't mind me being so informal, but I can hardly keep calling you Mr Shepherd.'

'Dan's fine.'

'So, you're probably thinking, tea at the Ritz, she's a fast-track Oxbridge graduate, Cheltenham Ladies' College perhaps, rode to hounds as a kid, father was a lawyer or maybe even a judge, mother spent her time on various charitable committees, family connections got her into Five, silver spoon, playing at a career until she finds the right man to make her happy. Am I close?'

'Close.' Shepherd grinned. 'I'd have said your father was a doctor, though.'

Button smiled. 'No, he was a lawyer,' she said. 'There's the thing, Dan. I've been able to go through your file with a fine-tooth comb and there's almost nothing I don't know about you. But my working life is a closed book. Totally hidden from view to all but those with the highest security clearance.'

She stopped speaking as the waiter reappeared with a laden tray. With a minimum of fuss he put down the pot of tea and the cafetière of coffee, a selection of sandwiches and cakes, then left with a courteous half-bow. 'Isn't the service just out of this world?' she said to Shepherd.

Shepherd figured that the question was rhetorical, so he shrugged. She picked up the cafetière and poured coffee into his cup, then added a splash of milk. Just as he liked it. He glanced at her left hand. No wedding ring. Her nails were short with clear varnish. And there was a faint nicotine stain between the first and second fingers of her right hand. At least she had one weakness.

'I much prefer tea,' said Button, 'and the English Breakfast here is the best there is. I like the sandwiches they do too. And the cakes.'

'So we're at the Ritz because you like cucumber sandwiches,' said Shepherd. 'I get the picture.'

'No, you don't, Dan. You have a perception, that's all. Like you noticed I wasn't wearing a wedding ring. You probably assume I'm not married. But maybe I took off my ring before this meeting.'

'The skin isn't white where the ring would be.'

'The ring, if there is one, could go on and off as often as the Rolex. Or the pearls.'

'Are you married?'

She smiled, ignored the question, and finished pouring her tea. 'Apart from the English Breakfast and the sandwiches, the great thing about the Ritz is that you can be among people but the tables are so far apart you won't be overheard. Planting any sort of listening device would take a huge amount of effort, and there's no guarantee that your target would be in range. Most of the people here are tourists so there's little chance of bumping into someone you know. And the dress code will keep out most of the followers – the ones in the hooded tops and trainers. So, you walk through the Virgin megastore on Oxford Street, wander through Borders, then head here. The contrast will show up all but the most versatile, don't you think?'

Shepherd's stomach lurched. He'd had no inkling that anyone was on his tail. 'You know surveillance.'

She added milk to her tea and stirred it slowly. 'I was trained by the best, Dan, and now I work with the best. The problem is, I can't trot out my CV to prove to you that I'm the sort of person you'd want to work with. And, frankly, we don't have time to build up the sort of trust you and Hargrove have established. We have to hit the ground running, so to speak.'

Shepherd nodded. 'I understand.'

'I know you do,' she said. 'So what I'm doing here isn't playing some silly game, trying to show you what a clever girl I am. I just want you to know that I'm a professional. I've run agents in some very dangerous places and I've never lost a man or a woman. I've never lied to one of my people. And I've never asked them to do something I wouldn't do myself.'

'You had a team on me?' said Shepherd. He wondered if any of her watchers was still in the vicinity. Wherever they were, they were good.

'No team, Dan,' said Button. 'Just little old me.'

Shepherd sat back and stared at her in disbelief. 'But you were here when I arrived.'

'I had to run a little, I admit.' Her smile widened. 'Remember, all I needed to know was where you went. I knew your ultimate destination and that you were meeting me, so even if I'd lost you I'd have been able to pick you up again.'

'But you didn't lose me.'

She smiled. 'No. I didn't.'

'All the way from Ealing?'

'You have a nice house. The garden could do with some TLC, though.'

Shepherd was annoyed with himself. He took pride in his ability to spot a tail, but more than his pride was at stake: his life depended on it. Button was on his side, but there were plenty of men, the odd woman too, who would love to get close to him – close enough to do him harm.

'Now I've hurt your feelings,' she said.

She offered him a plate of sandwiches and he took one. Egg and watercress. 'I'm not used to being followed,' he said.

'If it makes you feel any better, I was never closer than fifty feet.'

'Oh, that's all right, then,' he said, and grinned. 'Sorry. But if you could tail me so easily, so could others. And they might not have my best interests at heart. Hell's bells, they could follow me home. I could put my boy at risk.'

'Dan, you were spot on with what you did. But I knew what to expect. An amateur wouldn't.' She sipped her tea. 'Is there anything you'd like to know about me? My background?'

'You were Five, right?'

'Straight from university. Fast-track graduate entry.'

'You applied to be a spy, is that it?'

'Pretty much. The days of university lecturers having a quiet word with likely candidates are long gone. It's just another branch of the civil service, these days.'

'And you ran surveillance teams?'

'That was part of my work,' she said. 'I was in Belfast for a few years.' She smiled. 'I didn't talk like a Brit bastard when I was there, of course, I had more of the Irish in me,' she said, in a perfect North Belfast accent.

'Counter-terrorism?'

'I wasn't handing out parking tickets,' she said.

'And in the UK?'

'The National Security Advice Centre, working on serious crime investigations. And then, after 9/11, I moved to International Counter-terrorism Investigations, mainly because of my language skills.'

'You speak Arabic?'

'Fluently. And half a dozen other languages, as it happens.'

'Why would Five want to lose someone like you?' asked Shepherd. He took a bite of his sandwich.

'They don't see it as losing me, Dan,' said Button. 'They see it as forging a link with a new investigative organisation.'

'So you'll go back to Five one day?'

'I'm not going to lie to you, Dan. This job is a stepping-stone for me. Sometimes you have to leave an organisation for a while to progress up through it.'

'So, just as I'm getting used to you, you could up and leave?'

'That goes for anyone,' said Button. 'Sam Hargrove is moving up. I will, in due course. What about you, Dan? Do you plan to end your days as a DC?'

'Of course not.'

'So, if you stay with the police, you'll more likely than not be offered a job with another unit when promotion comes. If you agree to switch to SOCA, another opportunity might come up for you elsewhere. So it could be that, just as I'm getting used to you, you'll be the one who ups and goes.'

'So, if I join SOCA, I could still transfer back to the regular police at some point?'

'If you wanted to. Or there might be other options. Five, for instance. Or Six. Special Branch. Customs investigations. There's much more movement between the various law-enforce-ment agencies, these days. Nothing lasts for ever, Dan. That's the only constant in this world. But enough of what might be and what could be. I'm heading up the SOCA undercover unit, and I hope you'll be part of it. You're just the sort of man I need. Your SAS background will be invaluable, and you've proved that you're more than capable of working undercover.'

'And you need a decision from me soon?'

'Sooner rather than later.'

'And if I decline, I stay with the police?'

'It'll be complicated but, basically, yes. At present you're employed by the Met but Superintendent Hargrove is answerable to the Home Office and works for the various UK forces on an ad-hoc basis. Under the new regime, SOCA will handle all roving units, but each individual force will have its own undercover unit for local investigations. If you decided not to join us, a space would be found for you on one of the local units. I'm sure the Met would jump at having you. But, Dan, it would be such a waste of your talents – it really would. We'll be handling all the major undercover investigations, and the local units will be sweeping up the crumbs, nothing more.'

Shepherd sipped his coffee. What Button was saying made sense. It would be a good career move for him. And although she hadn't discussed money yet, he was sure there'd be a hike in salary. There was the challenge, too, the opportunity to pit himself against the country's biggest villains.

'What are your reservations?' she asked. She picked up a slice of cherry cake and put it on to her plate.

'I'm not sure,' he said.

'But you need time to think it over?'

'I guess I'm like most people,' he said. 'Change is always a bit worrying, even if it's change for the better.'

'It's going to be a big move for all of us,' said Button. 'SOCA is new territory, but it's much-needed. Crime has gone country-wide, global even, so the way we tackle it has to change. It's an opportunity for both of us to get in on the ground floor. Frankly, I can see the day coming when the local forces are more involved with crime prevention and motoring offences, and all major crime is investigated by SOCA. Murder, robbery, rape, they'll all be dealt with by a national team. It makes so much sense.'

'I'm not convinced that just because something is handled nationally makes it more efficient.'

'Trust me, Dan. Most of the corruption in this country is at local level. Members of Parliament are lily-white, compared with the men and women who sit in our town halls. Policing is just too big an issue to be dealt with locally. The town halls can't even run our schools properly.' She smiled. 'Anyway, this isn't about politics. This is about you doing what you do best. Being a thief-taker. And you'll be taking a lot more thieves working with me than you will at the Met.'

'What about giving evidence?' asked Shepherd. 'The way things are at the moment, we do the work but the local force takes the credit so the undercover operatives don't have to stand up in court.'

'Same with MI5,' said Button. 'And it'll be the same with SOCA. The undercover unit will be protected. Other officers, from the more visible units, will give evidence under oath. The worst possible scenario for you would be giving evidence *in camera* or with your identity withheld.'

'Weapons?'

'On a case-by-case basis, as now. You have a weapon signed out to you, don't you?'

Shepherd nodded. 'A SIG-Sauer.'

'I'm a fan of the Glock. But I rarely, if ever, carry one.'

'Mine's locked away at home most of the time, but there are occasions when I need one at short notice.'

'Nothing will change there,' said Button.

'I don't want to be signing forms in triplicate and having to justify every round.'

'I hear you, Dan. Loud and clear.'

Shepherd sipped his coffee. It was full and rich, possibly the best coffee he'd ever drunk. But he doubted that he'd pay regular visits to the Ritz. Charlotte Button, on the other hand, seemed at home in the opulent surroundings. He wondered if she was meeting all the SOCA recruits there, or if he had been singled out for special treatment. And if she pulled the same surveillance trick on all her interviewees.

'What sort of time-frame are we talking about?' he asked.

'Weeks rather than months,' said Button. 'Because of the long-term nature of undercover work, people will join gradually, as and when they become available. I gather you're on a counterfeit-currency case at the moment and that you're co-operating with Europol.'

'It's a complicated one, and I'm right in the middle of it,' said Shepherd. 'Albanian Mafia have been using asylum-seekers to bring in fake euros. The euros are being handled by Bangladeshi money-changers in London. We're getting ready to bust both ends.'

'How long before it's wrapped up?'

'A week, maybe.'

'So if you decide you want to come on board, I'll make sure no further work comes your way.'

'I've decided,' said Shepherd.

'And?' said Button, raising an eyebrow.

'I'm in,' said Shepherd. He picked up his cup and held it towards her. She smiled and clinked hers against it. 'I look forward to working with you,' he said.

'And I with you, Dan,' she said. 'Or can I call you Spider now?'

'You know about that?'

'I know everything,' she said. 'Except how you got the nickname.'

Shepherd looked shamefaced. 'Ah,' he said. 'I ate one once.'

'You ate a spider?'

'A big one.' He held out his hand, fingers splayed. 'About that big. When I was doing jungle training with the Sass. Sort of for a bet.'

Button shuddered. 'Must have been horrible.'

'Tasted like chicken, actually.'

Button giggled so much that she spilled tea into her saucer.

The surveillance van was parked in a side-road off Inverness Terrace, less than half a mile from Paddington station. Shepherd knocked on the back door, which opened immediately. He climbed in and Amar Singh pulled the door closed.

Hargrove was sitting on a small stool at the far end, pouring coffee from a stainless-steel flask into a plastic cup. 'Want some?' he asked, offering the flask.

'I'm fine.'

Hargrove screwed the top back on to the flask and put it on the floor. 'Okay, here's the situation,' he said. 'We're not going to put anyone else into the restaurant, but we'll be watching everyone who goes in and out. The main restaurant is on the ground floor and there's another seating area in the basement, but that's rarely used. The floors above are apartments. There's a backyard, which leads out to an alley, and we'll have that covered but, frankly, I don't see that there's anything to worry about, do you?'

'I'm pretty sure they trust me,' said Shepherd. 'If anything was up I don't think they'd have suggested a restaurant.'

Singh handed Shepherd a Nokia mobile. 'We decided against a recording device, as it's only the second time you've met them.'

'Agreed,' said Shepherd. 'They patted me down the first time and might well do it again.' He turned the mobile phone over and examined it.

'Apparently they checked your phone before so it's unlikely they'll look at it again. This one functions as a transmitter as well as a phone.'

Shepherd removed the back cover of his regular phone, took out the battery and slid out the Sim card. He gave the old phone to Hargrove and installed the Sim card in the new one.

'Providing it's switched on, we'll hear everything,' said Singh. 'Range is practically unlimited. It transmits through the mobile-phone system rather than an independent transmitter. We'll be recording here. The microphone isn't great – ideally you'd want it out in front of you but that's up to you. You don't want to draw attention to it.' He smiled thinly. 'Sorry. Didn't mean to start teaching you how to suck eggs.'

'We'll see how it goes,' said Shepherd. 'Back-up?'

'I've got Sharp and Joyce nearby, but we'll keep our distance. What's your rescue phrase?'

'Does anyone have the time?' said Shepherd.

Hargrove wrote it down on a piece of paper in capital letters. It was one of Shepherd's regular phrases. If he used it, Hargrove and his team would move in immediately. 'Ready?'

'As I'll ever be,' said Shepherd. He put the phone into his pocket and climbed out of the van.

The restaurant where Salik had wanted to meet was in a road off Queensway, which ran parallel to Inverness Terrace. While Inverness Terrace was mainly residential, Queensway was a bustling mix of ethnic restaurants, gift shops and bars, and the pavements were packed with tourists and students looking for a cheap meal or heading for the cinemas in the Whiteleys shopping mall. It was the worst possible area to look for a tail:

there were too many people, and too many types – black, white, Asian, Oriental, young, old, male and female, a mass of humanity in which nobody stuck out because everybody was different. The only ones likely to be noticeable were Sharpe and Joyce – middle-class, middle-aged white men in suits.

There were a dozen tables in the restaurant and the Uddin brothers were sitting in the far corner. A big man in a purple suit tried to steer him towards a small table in the window but Shepherd nodded at the brothers. 'I'm expected,' he said. He walked towards their table and Salik got to his feet. He was wearing a grey silk suit and a white shirt with an Asian collar buttoned up to the neck. 'Tony, good of you to come,' he said.

'How's it going?' said Shepherd.

Salik's brother stood up. He was wearing a pale blue suit and a white shirt with a flowery tie.

'You already know my name,' said Shepherd. 'Don't you think it's time I was told who I'm dealing with?'

'I suppose you are right,' Salik said. 'I am Salik. My brother is Matiur.' Matiur nodded at Shepherd.

'The drive from Dover was okay?' asked Salik.

'Traffic wasn't great, but I made it.'

Salik took out his mobile phone and placed it on the table. It was a new Motorola.

'How do you find it?' asked Shepherd, indicating the phone and placing his own Nokia in front of him. 'I've always used Nokias.'

'Very reliable,' said Salik.

Matiur put his phone on the table too, another Motorola. 'We have a supplier who gets them in bulk from Hungary,' he said. 'We can get you one, if you want. Nokia is a good brand but a phone is a phone. They are all the same.'

Shepherd smiled and nodded, although his phone was not an ordinary mobile: if it was working properly Hargrove and Singh should be listening to every word of the conversation and, hopefully, recording it.

'You like Indian food?' asked Salik.

'Sure. I'm a big fan of chicken tikka masala and a pint of Cobra,' said Shepherd. 'It's pretty much our national dish, these days, isn't it?'

'On the phone you said you were as British as roast beef and Yorkshire pudding,' said Salik, with a sly smile.

'You've a good memory.'

'I need it in my business. Let me tell you something, Tony. Chicken tikka masala is British. It was invented here. And Cobra is brewed in the UK. And I'll tell you something you didn't know, I'm sure. Every time you've had an Indian meal in London, the chances are it was cooked by a Bangladeshi.'

'Yeah?'

'We are great cooks,' Salik went on. 'We cook better Indian food than the Indians. Most Bangladeshis are Muslim, as are we, but they still have to work in restaurants where alcohol is served. We are an adaptable people, Tony. We have had to adapt to survive.' A waiter hovered at Salik's shoulder and he spoke to him in rapid Bengali. The waiter moved away. 'I have ordered you a Kingfisher,' Salik said. 'It is more authentic, but only just.'

'You don't drink beer?'

'Muslims don't drink *any* alcohol,' said Salik, emphatically.

'I've seen Arabs in the West End knocking back champagne like there was no tomorrow,' said Shepherd.

'Then they were not Muslims,' said Matiur. 'Or not true Muslims.'

'We have no problem with you partaking,' said Salik, 'but alcohol must not pass a true Muslim's lips. And pork is forbidden, too. That's why you will never see it in an Indian restaurant. The chef would rather die than prepare it.'

'Do you know much about our country?' asked Matiur.

'It has the wettest climate in the world,' said Shepherd, and the two Bangladeshis burst out laughing.

'That is true,' said Salik. 'I am sure that when I was a child it rained every day.'

'It is one of the reasons we love this country,' said Matiur. 'When it rains, it reminds us of home. And it rains a lot here.'

The waiter returned with Shepherd's Kingfisher lager, which he poured into a frosted glass, then placed three glasses of iced water on the table. Salik and Matiur raised one each to toast Shepherd. 'To our new friend,' said Salik.

'To a profitable relationship,' said Matiur. '*Inshallah.*'

Shepherd frowned. He knew what the phrase meant, but Tony Corke wouldn't.

'God willing,' explained Salik.

Shepherd nodded. '*Inshallah,*' he repeated. He put down his lager, picked up his water glass, and clinked it against the brothers'. '*Inshallah,*' he said again.

The two brothers nodded approvingly and Shepherd knew he'd done the right thing in not accepting the toast with his lager. He sipped his iced water.

'So, what else do you know about Bangladesh?' asked Salik, as the waiter tried to hand them menus. He spoke briefly to the man, who hurried off. 'The chef is an old friend. He will take care of us,' Salik explained. 'So, you think Bangladesh is part of India, don't you? Everybody does.'

Shepherd shook his head. 'It used to be part of Pakistan.'

Salik looked surprised. 'You are right. We gained our independence in 1971 after a civil war. Bangladesh means "land of the Bengali people". We should never have been part of Pakistan. Like the British taking over Northern Ireland.'

Shepherd laughed. 'I'm not sure that's the same thing,' he said.

'Oh, it is,' said Salik, seriously. 'You should read your history. The Irish are fighting for what we had to fight for thirty years ago.'

'What about you?' asked Shepherd. 'When did you come to this country?'

'I was three years old,' said Salik. 'My father came over just after I was born, in 1958, and he sent for me and my mother and my three siblings a few years later. He worked as a hotel porter and by the time he died he owned three hotels here in Bayswater and had twenty-four grandchildren.'

'A good life,' said Shepherd.

'A good life, well lived,' agreed Salik. 'I should be as lucky as my father. *Inshallah.*'

'You have a big family?' asked Shepherd.

'Four children,' said Salik proudly. He took out his wallet and unfolded a flap to reveal small photographs of three boys and a girl, all neat in school uniforms, smiling at the camera with bright eyes.

'Nice kids,' said Shepherd.

'And you, Tony? You have a family?'

'Divorced,' said Shepherd. 'It's hard to keep a relationship when you're at sea.'

'My father spent three years in London while my mother stayed in Bangladesh,' said Salik. 'True love never dies.'

'I guess my wife didn't really love me,' said Shepherd.

'Children?'

'A boy. I don't see much of him. She moved up north with her new boyfriend.'

'A boy needs his father,' said Salik. 'He needs his mother when he is a child but he needs his father to show him how to be a man.'

'No argument there,' said Shepherd. He picked up his glass and sipped his lager.

The first dishes arrived, along with an oval stainless-steel plate piled high with rice. 'Ah, the chef's speciality,' said Salik. '*Aloo dom*. Potato curry. The secret is in the yoghurt he adds. My own wife can't cook *aloo dom* as well as he can.'

Another waiter appeared from the kitchen with a tray of more stainless-steel bowls. Salik pointed at each in turn as they were placed on the table.

'*Doi begun*,' he said. 'Aubergine in yoghurt. *Kanchkolar dom*, green banana curry.' He pointed at another dish. 'Now this one I doubt you'll have had before. *Shukta* – it's *lauo* with lentils. One of my favourites. *Lauo* is bottle gourd. Do you know it? Like melon, but not as sweet. It's a difficult flavour to describe. Anyway, you fry cubes of *lauo* with mung beans, then simmer with ginger and turmeric, add peas and a sprinkling of coriander leaves.' He smacked his lips appreciatively. 'What the chef here does is to fry mustard seeds in hot oil, then add the cooked vegetables and bring them to the boil again. It's one of his secrets but I bribed one of the waiters to tell me what he does.' He laughed.

Matiur gestured at something else. 'This is my favourite,' he said. '*Reshmi kebab.* Minced chicken kebab.'

A big Asian man appeared at the kitchen door, his face beaded with sweat. He was wearing grubby white baggy trousers, a white T-shirt and apron. A threadbare chef's toque was perched at a jaunty angle on his head. He was holding a large oval tray and grinning broadly. 'And here's the man himself,' said Salik. 'My very good friend Nasram. Possibly the best chef in London.'

'What do you mean "possibly"?' chided Nasram, setting the platter on the table. A whole fish lay on it, covered with a thick, reddish sauce. He grinned at Shepherd. 'Don't listen to anything this man tells you,' he said. 'This is what I am famous for. *Makher taukari.* My own recipe. You will have tasted no fish curry like it.' He extended a shovel-like hand. 'Welcome to my restaurant,' he said.

Shepherd shook it. 'Tony,' he said. 'Pleasure to be here.'

'Do not let this man lead you astray,' said Nasram, grinning at Salik.

'In what way?'

Nasram patted Salik's ample stomach. 'He likes his food too much, this man. Moderation in all things is the way to a long and happy life.'

'I'll try to remember that,' said Shepherd.

'Enjoy,' said Nasram. He chuckled and headed back to the kitchen.

Salik waved at the food. 'Please, Tony, start.'

Shepherd spooned some of everything on to his plate, picked up his fork and began on the *aloo dom.* He raised his eyebrows. It was good.

'What do you think?' asked Salik.

'Excellent,' said Shepherd.

Salik handed him a platter of naan bread. He ripped off a chunk and dipped it into the aubergine.

'So, tell me about your boat,' said Salik.

'It's called a rib, a rigid inflatable boat,' said Shepherd. 'Virtually invisible to radar, it can cruise at fifty knots.'

'And it can cross the Channel?'

'Easily.'

'Even in bad weather?'

'We'd try to do it in reasonable weather,' said Shepherd. 'It can go out in storms, but why would we?'

'And how much would you want?' asked Matiur.

'That depends on what you're bringing over,' said Shepherd. 'Like I said before, it's all about risk.'

'We should be paying you for the trip,' said Matiur, 'not for what you are carrying.'

'Let me put it another way, then,' said Shepherd. 'How much do you think you'll want to bring over?'

'What do you mean?' asked Salik.

'The weight. The boat can carry about a thousand kilos.'

Salik pursed his lips. 'Probably a hundred kilos. Maybe two hundred. I am not sure.'

'How can you not be sure?' asked Shepherd. 'You buy it by weight, don't you?'

'No, not really.' He said something to Matiur in Bengali and the two men laughed.

'What's the joke?' asked Shepherd. He had to keep playing the part of the slightly stupid sailor. As far as Tony Corke was concerned, the brothers were bringing in drugs.

'We don't buy it by weight, my friend,' said Salik.

'That doesn't make sense,' said Shepherd.

'It makes perfect sense,' said Salik.

Shepherd put down his fork. 'I think I have the right to know what I'm going to be carrying,' he said. 'I'm the one whose balls will be on the line.'

'It doesn't matter what you'll be carrying,' said Matiur. 'You'll get your money anyway.'

Shepherd reached for another hunk of naan. 'I guess that's true.'

'It is, my friend,' said Salik.

'What about more deliveries in future? Can this be a regular run?'

'It is possible,' said Salik. 'But first things first. The men in France want to see you.'

'What?'

Salik smiled reassuringly. 'It is not a problem. They just want to know who they are dealing with.'

'You can tell them I delivered the first load.'

'I have. But I also had to tell them that you charged me thirty thousand pounds.'

'Who are they?' asked Shepherd. Meeting the French end of the currency ring was exactly what he wanted but Tony Corke wouldn't be thrilled at the idea of getting involved with foreign gangsters.

'The men who gave Pernaska the cans to bring over.'

'And they're French, yeah?'

Salik shook his head. 'Albanian,' he said.

'Why are you working with Albanians?' asked Shepherd.

'They have the money,' said Salik.

'What money?' asked Shepherd, pouncing on Salik's slip.

Salik and Matiur exchanged a look. Matiur gave a small shrug. 'Okay,' said Salik. 'We're not bringing drugs over. It's cash. Currency. And the Albanians have it.'

'If it's just money, why not put it into the boot of a car and bring it over on the ferry?'

'Because Customs have the right to impound any money they suspect is from criminal sources. And anyone doing regular runs on the ferries or who takes their car through the Eurotunnel is flagged. And if you fly or take the Eurostar your bags are X-rayed.'

'But the money's good, is it?'

'It's fine. We're just moving it around. We can get a better price for it in London.'

That was a lie, Shepherd knew. But he smiled and nodded. 'That's good. At least I won't be carrying drugs.' He lowered his voice: 'Sixty grand a run, right? That's twice what you paid before but this time I'll be bringing over a lot more for you.'

'Sixty thousand is acceptable,' said Salik.

Shepherd rubbed his hands. 'And where in France do they want to see me? Do I use the boat?'

'They said Paris,' said Salik. 'You can fly over or take the Eurostar.'

Shepherd couldn't make it look too easy: Tony Corke wouldn't want to risk travelling out of the country by train or plane with his upcoming court case. 'You're forgetting one thing,' he said. 'They took my passport.'

'Who did?' asked Salik.

'The police. A condition of my bail. I had to surrender it.'

Salik and Matiur exchanged another look. 'That's not a problem,' said Salik. 'We can get you another.'

'In my name?'

'In any name.'

'I don't want to be travelling on a fake passport,' said Shepherd. 'If I get caught, I'll be in so much shit. Plus it'll look like I'm skipping bail.'

'It won't be a fake passport,' said Salik. 'It'll be in the system. You can even renew it after ten years.'

'What are you talking about?' asked Shepherd.

'We have a friend in the Passport Agency,' said Salik. 'We give him the photographs and you can use whatever name and date of birth you like. Ten thousand pounds.'

'Ten grand?'

'It's a bargain,' said Salik. 'It's a real passport – you can use it to apply for visas in other countries and it'll never be spotted. We can take the ten thousand off the money we will be paying you.'

Shepherd pretended to consider the offer. Then he nodded slowly. 'Okay,' he said. 'A new passport it is. How long will it take?'

'Forty-eight hours after we have the photographs,' said Salik. 'We can take them tonight. There's a photo booth at Paddington station. We can go there after we've eaten.' He waved at the dishes on the table. 'Now, please, enjoy the food.'

The van was still parked off Inverness Terrace. Shepherd knocked three times on the rear door, which opened. Hargrove was still sitting on his stool while Singh was listening to a recording on a set of noise-suppressing headphones.

'Did you get everything?' asked Shepherd.

'Everything in the restaurant, clear as a bell,' said Hargrove. 'The passport stuff was interesting. We didn't do so well at Paddington. Your phone was in your jacket, I guess.'

'They didn't say much, just took the photographs and told me they'd be in touch. I've said I'll stay in London until the passport's ready. You definitely want me to run with the passport thing?'

'Absolutely,' said the superintendent. 'If they've got a man in the Passport Agency doling out the real McCoy, we need to know who he is.'

'And what about Paris?'

'Let me speak to Europol,' said Hargrove. 'I'll see if they can set up surveillance in France.'

'The Albanians are tough bastards,' said Shepherd. 'I'm going to need back-up I can trust.'

'I'll take care of it,' said Hargrove. 'It's starting to look like this is a serious currency ring. There's a North Korean embassy in Tirana, Albania's capital. If the North Koreans wanted to flood Europe with fake euros, the Albanian Mafia could do it efficiently for them, with Albanian asylum-seekers flooding into Fortress Europe. The Uddin brothers are just a small part of it.' He rubbed his knee. 'One thing I won't miss about this job is sitting in the back of this bloody van. Do you want a lift home?'

'I'm parked in a multi-storey down the road,' said Shepherd. 'I'll be fine.'

'How was the food?' asked Singh. 'My mouth was watering hearing that guy run through the menu.'

Shepherd grinned. 'It was bloody good, actually. The guys like to eat.'

'You seemed to be enjoying yourself,' said Hargrove.

'They're easy to relax with,' said Shepherd. 'They're not your regular villains – they don't have that edge so you don't keep expecting them to fly off the handle.'

'Not getting soft, are you, Spider?' asked Hargrove.

Shepherd grunted dismissively. 'They're a pleasant change from the drug-dealing scumbags and blaggers I'm used to dealing with. I didn't say they don't deserve to be put away for what they're doing.' He climbed out of the van. 'I'll call you when they give me details of the meet,' he said, and slammed the door. He turned up the collar of his pea coat and headed towards the car park.

It was Friday morning when Salik rang, a little after nine. Shepherd had just got back from his run. He'd picked up the *Daily Mail* and the *Daily Telegraph* from his local newsagent, with a cappuccino and two almond croissants from the delicatessen but had to leave them untouched as Salik wanted to see him within the hour. Speaker's Corner again.

He showered and shaved, put on Tony Corke's clothes and drove to Marble Arch. He had decided against wearing the bulletproof vest. He phoned Hargrove on the way but the superintendent confirmed what Shepherd already knew: that there had been no time to put any surveillance in place. The meeting would go unmonitored and there would be no back-up.

'It's your call, Spider,' said Hargrove.

'It's in the open – if he was up to something he'd have picked somewhere more private,' said Shepherd.

'Call me when you're through,' said Hargrove. 'If you feel it's necessary, I can get Sharpe and Joyce to head your way.'

'It'll probably be over by the time they turn up,' said Shepherd. 'I'm sure it'll be fine. He probably just wants a chat about the boat.'

'If you change your mind, call me,' said Hargrove.

Shepherd parked in a multi-storey and took a circuitous route to Speaker's Corner. Salik Uddin was sitting on the bench where Shepherd had waited for him. He was wearing a camel coat with the collar turned up and peeling an orange. 'Tony,' he said, 'thank you for coming.'

Shepherd sat down. Salik offered him a piece of fruit but he shook his head.

'Vitamin C,' said Salik. 'It keeps colds at bay.'

Shepherd smiled. 'My mother used to say that,' he said, 'but I had just as many colds as the other kids.'

Salik smiled and popped a segment into his mouth. 'Mothers always know best.' He chewed slowly. 'So, where are you staying in London?'

'A mate's spare bedroom,' said Shepherd. 'His wife walked out too, so we've a lot in common. Thanks for the meal the other night. Best Indian food I've ever had.'

'Bangladeshi food,' corrected Salik.

'Sorry,' said Shepherd. 'Best Bangladeshi food I've ever eaten.'

Salik reached into one of the side pockets of his jacket and took out a brand new British passport. He handed it to Shepherd. 'That was quick,' Shepherd said.

'We get fast-track treatment,' said Salik.

'That's why it costs so much, I guess.'

Salik smiled. 'Ten thousand pounds for a genuine British passport is cheap, my friend. I spent five times that on legal fees for my application and Matiur has spent twice as much and doesn't even have citizenship yet.'

Shepherd opened the passport and flicked to the back. The photograph he'd taken at Paddington station grinned up at him. The date of birth made him thirty-three and the name was Peter Devereux. Place of birth, Bristol. Shepherd ran his fingers over the lamination, and examined the pages.

'Don't worry, it is the real thing,' said Salik, as if reading his mind. 'It's not a copy or a facsimile, or your photograph stuck in someone else's passport.'

'If it's so easy, why doesn't Matiur just buy one? Why does he bother going through the whole legal process?'

'He is already in the system – has been for the past five years. We have only had our contact in the Passport Agency for the past three years. You see, at the moment the only real identifying feature in a passport is the photograph. But soon they'll be biometric, with either fingerprints or retinal scans incorporated. When that happens anyone who is in the system twice will be spotted. Anyway, travelling isn't a problem as Matiur has permanent residency, so he's happy with the way things are. He will get citizenship. It's just a matter of time.'

Shepherd put away the passport. 'Okay, I'll head off back to Dover.'

'Actually, there's something I need you to do first.' Salik's hand disappeared inside his coat again and reappeared with a white envelope.

Shepherd took it and opened it. Inside, a dark blue folder contained a Eurostar ticket. 'What's this?' he said.

'Your train leaves Waterloo at nine minutes past one,' said Salik. 'You have plenty of time to get to the station.'

Shepherd stared at the ticket. It was in the name of Peter Devereux. 'You can't do this!' he exploded.

'What do you mean?' said Salik, evidently confused by his outburst.

'Have me running off to Paris at the drop of a hat.'

'You'll be back by this evening,' said Salik, patiently. 'They will meet you in Paris. You will be there for three hours and you will be back in London by ten o'clock.'

'Who's they?'

'The men who are arranging the shipment. They want to meet you. I have already emailed them your photograph.'

'You did what?' Shepherd was genuinely alarmed. As Tony Corke he had no reason to refuse to go to Paris to meet the Albanians. But as Dan Shepherd, undercover cop, he knew that the Albanians wouldn't think twice about killing him if they knew his true identity. And now they had his photograph.

'Just so they'll be able to spot you. They need to know what you look like.'

'Salik, I've got things to do.'

'A few hours, that's all. Less than three hours there, three hours back.'

Shepherd stood up. 'God damn it, you can't treat me like some sort of servant!'

'You are working for me, remember?' said Salik, quietly. His voice had hardened. 'And the Albanians will not do business with men they do not know. You will go, or we are through.' He stared at Shepherd with unblinking brown eyes.

Shepherd had been backed into a corner. Tony Corke had no valid reason for refusing to go. He needed the money – and Salik was right: he was no more than a hired hand. 'Okay,' he said.

Salik smiled. 'Thank you,' he said. 'It's a formality. Just go over, show your face, and they'll put the consignment together.' He looked at his watch. 'You'd better be going,' he said. 'The traffic's pretty heavy over the river so if I were you I'd get the Tube.'

Shepherd forced a smile. 'I'll call you tonight, let you know how I got on.'

He headed out of the park. He decided against using the Tube and flagged down a black cab. His mobile wouldn't work on the Underground and he had some urgent calls to make.

The Saudi stirred his coffee slowly and looked out of the window. The street outside was filled with housewives loaded with shopping, office workers stealing time from their employers to run personal errands, youngsters in hooded tops smoking cigarettes furtively, planning their next shoplifting trip. A slim leather briefcase stood at his feet.

He sipped his coffee. Strong and bitter, as he liked it. He checked his watch. It was time. He had spent an hour in the coffee shop and was on his third espresso. He was sure that no one was watching the building opposite. He picked up his mobile. The Sim card was new and this was the first time he had used it. It would also be the last: later on that day he would destroy it. The way in which the authorities allowed the liberal use of untraceable phonecards made no sense to the Saudi. Disposable Sim cards were used by terrorists, drug-dealers, money-launderers, by anyone who wanted to communicate without detection. Mobile phones were also used to detonate bombs, but governments in the West allowed anyone to buy a Sim card without identifying themselves. The Saudi had two dozen in his briefcase, not one of which could be traced back to him. It was greed, pure and simple: the phone companies made money, and so did the governments – from tax, and from the licences they auctioned to the phone companies. No one wanted to kill the golden goose.

He tapped out a number. The man who answered didn't identify himself. He said simply, 'Yes?'

'Our meeting for tomorrow is still on schedule?' asked the Saudi.

'The following day would be better,' said the man.

The Saudi ended the call. He finished his coffee and picked up his briefcase, then walked across the street. Between a shop selling bric-à-brac and an off-licence, a door led up to the shabby flats above. There were eight buttons in two rows of four. There had once been paper stickers on the buttons with typed names but now they were all illegible. Someone had written the number '2' on one in pencil. The Saudi pressed it. Almost immediately the door lock buzzed. The Saudi pushed his way in and climbed a set of bare wooden stairs to the second floor. The man he was there to meet had already opened the door. '*Allahu akbar,*' he said.

'*Allahu akbar,*' said the Saudi, and walked into the flat.

The man was a Chechen. He had fought for his own people against the Russians, and in Bosnia. It was while he was fighting Serbs in the former Yugoslavia that he was approached by a representative of a Saudi charity. Two weeks later he was in Pakistan. Initially he was trained in the use of explosives but gradually his instructors realised that Ilyas could be used for greater things. His commitment to the Muslim cause, the fact that he had no living family and hated all things Western made him the perfect candidate to join the ranks of the *shahid*. They began to groom him to sacrifice his life for the *jihad*. He was shown videos recorded by *shahids* who gone to sit in heaven with Allah, then guided through the Koran and shown that there could be no greater glory than to die for Islam.

It was the Saudi who had realised that Ilyas was too valuable to be thrown away on a suicide mission, no matter how important the target. He had fair hair and green eyes, and spoke excellent English, albeit with a strong accent. No one would suspect he wasn't European until they heard his voice. He was fearless, trained in the use of most arms from pistols to rocket-propelled grenades, a skilled driver and mechanic.

The flat where Ilyas had been staying for the past month was small but clean: a cramped sitting room with a futon and a coffee table, tiny bedroom with a single bed, and a cooking area with a double hotplate, a microwave and fridge. A copy of the Koran lay open on the coffee table.

An orange fluorescent jacket hung over a chair with 'NETWORK RAIL' on the back. Next to it stood a large blue metal toolbox with patches of rust on the sides.

The Saudi went to the futon and sat down. He placed his briefcase on the coffee table and opened it. Ilyas picked up the Koran and sat with it in his hands as the Saudi got out eight detonators and put them on the table. There were six triggers in the briefcase, which he laid beside the detonators; only four would be needed but the Saudi had included two spares. There were four nine-volt batteries, with enough wiring and connectors to complete four trigger circuits.

Ilyas studied the components and nodded slowly. 'Perfect,' he said. 'When?'

'Soon,' said the Saudi. '*Inshallah*.'

Shepherd sat holding his mobile phone as the driver of the black cab negotiated the traffic heading south. He had a serious problem and wasn't sure how to deal with it. He'd only taken the Tony Corke mobile with him to the meeting. It was bugged and Hargrove had been listening to the conversation, assuming he'd been able to hear it through the pea coat. But Shepherd needed to talk to him. If he used the phone to call Hargrove, there'd be a record on the Sim card. He could delete the number afterwards but an electronics expert would be able to retrieve it. If the Albanians checked the phone when he arrived in Paris, they might want to know whom he'd called. Worse, they might even check the phone, and if they discovered the transmitter it would all be over.

Shepherd needed to ditch the phone, but he also needed a replacement. And for that he had to speak to Hargrove. He stared out of the window and cursed. Even if Hargrove had got on the case as soon as he'd heard that the Uddin brothers were sending him to Paris, Shepherd doubted he'd have time to arrange anything like adequate back-up. Once he was on the train it would take just over two and a half hours to get to Paris. Men had to be assigned, briefed and put in position. Surveillance equipment had to be requisitioned. He could talk to Hargrove and the bug would pick it up, but he'd have no idea if Hargrove had heard him. Equipment failed, usually at the worst of times.

Shepherd had just decided he would have to use the mobile when it rang. It was Hargrove. 'We're right behind you, Spider,' said the superintendent.

Shepherd resisted the urge to look out of the rear window. 'I've got to switch phones,' he said.

'Sharpe is on his way, on the back of a bike,' said Hargrove. 'He'll be at Waterloo waiting for you. Men's toilet. Swap phones and remove this number from the Sim card. You'll be fine.'

Shepherd smiled to himself. Hargrove, as usual, was way ahead of him – he would be a tough act for Button to follow.

'I've already been on to Paris,' said Hargrove. 'They're getting teams in place.'

'It'll be tight.'

'They promised me at least four men and another monitoring CCTV at the station.'

'Are you going?' asked Shepherd.

'We'll be on the train but we'll keep our distance.'

'Thanks. I'll feel better knowing you're around.'

'It's short notice, but in a way it'll help the case,' said Hargrove. 'The French won't have time to get audio but they'll take pictures and hopefully identify the Albanians. That'll give us a big advantage for when you do the actual run.'

'Agreed,' said Shepherd.

'Is the ticket first or standard?'

'Standard,' said Shepherd.

'In what name?'

'Peter Devereux,' said Shepherd. 'Same as on the passport they've given me.'

'Okay, let me call Eurostar, get myself and Sharpe on board. Be lucky, Spider.'

The superintendent cut the connection. Shepherd bit his lower lip. He hated going into any situation blind. Preparation was everything. Now he was travelling to a city he'd only ever visited as a tourist and would be questioned by Albanian gangsters. He didn't know who they were, or anything about their backgrounds, but they had his photograph and there was an outside chance they might know who he was. That was the big unspoken fear in every undercover operative's heart: that someone out there might know the truth. And if the Albanians did, they'd kill him. Shepherd's heart was pounding and he took several deep breaths to calm himself. He was worrying about nothing; he hadn't worked against Albanians before; this was his first case involving counterfeit currency. All they had was a photograph and a legend that would withstand all but the most thorough investigation. Everything would be fine. In eight hours or so he'd be back in London, asleep in his own bed. He flipped off the back cover of his phone, removed the battery and slid out the Sim card. He put the Sim card into his wallet and reassembled the phone.

The taxi dropped Shepherd outside Waterloo station. He gave the driver ten pounds and told him to keep the change. As the man took it, Shepherd remembered that the station toilets weren't free. 'Sorry, mate, you couldn't give me twenty pence, could you?' he asked sheepishly. 'I've got to take a leak.'

The driver handed him a coin. 'Have it on me.' He laughed.

Shepherd walked into the station and headed down the stairs to the lavatories. He put his twenty-pence coin into the slot and pushed through the turnstiles. All the urinals were unoccupied but two men were washing their hands at the line of basins. There was no sign of Sharpe. Shepherd checked his watch. There was half an hour before the train was due to leave and he still had to go through the Immigration and security checks.

He went over to one of the urinals. Two stalls were occupied, red squares showing in their locks. The rest showed green. Unoccupied. Shepherd urinated, whistling softly to himself. The two hand-washers left.

An elderly man with a walking-stick limped over to a urinal. A toilet flushed and one of the doors opened. Shepherd glanced over his shoulder. It was Jimmy Sharpe. Shepherd zipped up his jeans and went to a washbasin. He put his mobile phone beside it and started to wash his hands. Sharpe stood at the adjacent basin and put down an identical phone next to Shepherd's, nodded curtly and thrust his hands under the tap.

Shepherd shook his hands dry, picked up Sharpe's phone and left.

He slid his ticket into the automated barrier and showed his passport to a bored officer of the French Police Nationale, then walked through a metal detector. It amazed him that there were no checks by British officials on people leaving the country. Virtually every other country in the world examined the passport of anyone leaving, and often punished those who had overstayed their visas. Not the British. The government seemed to take the view that as long as people were leaving, that was the end of it.

The train was boarding and Shepherd took the escalator to the platform. Carriage number eight, midway down the train, a window-seat facing the rear in a group of four. Two students sat opposite, sharing an iPod and nodding in time to tunes that Shepherd could hear only as an irritating buzz. It looked as if the seat next to him might be empty, but at the last moment a middle-aged woman in a fake-fur coat hurried down the aisle pulling a wheeled suitcase after her. She rammed it under the table, banging Shepherd's leg.

Shepherd closed his eyes and rested his head against the seat back. He wasn't looking forward to meeting the Albanians.

The train pulled out of Waterloo. Shepherd asked the middle-aged woman to let him pass so that he could use the toilet and took the opportunity to walk to the front of the train. He hadn't realised how long the Eurostar was. He counted the number of seats in one carriage and did a quick calculation in his head. More than seven hundred passengers on the train – the equivalent of two full jumbo jets. Virtually every seat was taken and there was no sign of Sharpe or Hargrove. He hoped they'd managed to get on because he didn't want to be in France with only the French police behind him.

Just before the train went into the tunnel, Shepherd went in search of the buffet car towards the rear. He bought a chicken-salad sandwich and some coffee, then took them back to his seat. As he was unwrapping the sandwich he saw Hargrove walking through the carriage from the rear of the train. They had the briefest eye-contact and then he was gone. Shepherd relaxed a little. At least he was on board. And, presumably, Sharpe was, too.

Shepherd moved along the platform to the Gare du Nord station concourse, his hands in his pockets. He was fairly sure that Hargrove was some way behind him, but he didn't look round. Ahead, a line of taxi drivers held up handwritten cards, and behind them was a Häagen Dazs outlet, with a scattering of tables. To the left of the ice-cream shop two big men in black leather jackets and blue jeans were staring at him with hard eyes. Shepherd hoped they weren't part of the French surveil-lance team because they were as obvious as hell. He kept walking.

The French station was considerably scruffier than its London counterpart, the concourse littered with discarded fast-food wrappings and crushed cigarette packets. An old woman in a brightly coloured headscarf and a long dark coat flashed him a toothless smile and held out a gnarled hand. Shepherd shook his head and walked past.

The two men in leather jackets were heading purposefully towards him. Not surveillance, then. Shepherd stopped and turned to them, head slightly up, lips tight, playing the hard man.

'You are Tony Corke?' asked the taller of the two. He had jet-black hair that kept falling across his eyes, a narrow, hooked nose and a pointed chin.

'Yeah,' said Shepherd, hands deep in his pockets. He wasn't expecting violence in a public place, but he wasn't going to offer to shake hands.

'We are here to meet you,' said the man. 'I am Ervin. This is Artur.' He nodded at his colleague, a heavy-set man with a square jaw and a five o'clock shadow. 'Our English is not so good. You can speak French?'

'No,' lied Shepherd. He wasn't fluent in the language but he had enough to get by. He didn't want the Albanians to know that, though.

An old man with a wheeled suitcase that must have weighed more than he did banged into Artur and apologised in a gruff Scottish accent. Artur glared at him.

'We have an auto outside,' said Ervin.

'A car,' corrected Artur.

'Yes, a car,' said Ervin.

'Nobody said anything about a car,' said Shepherd. 'We can talk here.'

'We are just here to meet you,' said Ervin.

'You've met me. Now I want to go back to London.'

'Our boss wants to meet you.'

'Your boss can come here.'

'He's in his apartment. He wants us to take you there.'

'Look, Salik said I was to come to Paris because you wanted to see me. You've seen me. I'm just a sailor and I'm working for Salik, not you.'

'My boss doesn't work with people he hasn't met. He doesn't trust people until he has looked them in the eye.'

'Where is he?'

'I said. In his apartment. Please, come with us.'

Shepherd glared at him. He had no way of knowing how good the French surveillance was – or even if it was in place. For all he knew, the two Albanians might have more than a meeting planned for him. 'How far away is his apartment?'

'A few minutes.'

'Walking?'

Ervin shook his head. 'We have a car. I said.'

'No one told me I'd be getting into a car with people I don't know,' said Shepherd. 'Salik didn't say anything about it. All I had to do was come to Paris so that you could meet me. I've done that.'

Artur gripped Shepherd's left arm above the elbow. Shepherd shook him off. 'Don't you touch me!' he hissed. 'Don't you fucking touch me!'

Ervin stepped closer to Shepherd and drew back his leather jacket to reveal the butt of a gun.

'What? I don't come with you so you shoot me in front of a hundred witnesses?' said Shepherd. 'How stupid are you?'

Ervin put his hand on the butt of the pistol. 'You think anyone will stop me?' he said.

'Probably not, but those guys over there might just come after you.' Shepherd nodded at four armed men in black overalls and gleaming black boots standing at the entrance to the station. They were Compagnie Républicaine de Sécurité, the hard men of French law enforcement. They had MAS PA 9mm pistols on their hips and were cradling FAMAS G2 assault rifles. The G2, nicknamed 'the bugle' because of its shape, was a fair to middling weapon, but not a patch on the SAS's MP5. The French could easily have equipped their own men with the MP5, but took a chauvinistic pride in building their own, albeit inferior, weapon.

But while the weaponry was nothing to write home about, the men of the CRS were as hard as they came.

Ervin took his hand off his gun.

Shepherd knew he had no choice other than to go with the two Albanians. If he refused, the deal would be off. And if they pulled out of the deal, everything he'd done so far would have been a waste of time. There wasn't enough evidence to put the Uddin brothers behind bars. And it was the Albanians who had forced Rudi Pernaska to carry the cans containing the counterfeit cash. If Shepherd walked away now, the Albanians would remain free. The only way to make them pay was to go with them. Besides, he was Tony Corke, and Tony Corke had nothing to fear from the Albanians. 'Okay, let's calm down,' said Shepherd. 'There's no need for artillery.'

'We were told to take you to our boss.'

'Yeah, I got that. Okay – but I'm on the afternoon train back to London.'

'We understand that.'

'So I'll be back here in time for the train?'

'Of course,' said Ervin. He looked at the armed policemen, but they appeared to be more interested in a group of schoolgirls than a potential shoot-out on the station concourse.

'Okay. Let's go.' Shepherd pointed a finger at Artur. 'But don't touch me.'

Artur stared at Shepherd, eyes cold and hard. Shepherd stared back.

'Come on,' said Ervin. 'We are wasting time here.' He said something in Albanian to Artur, who grunted, then headed for the exit. Shepherd and Ervin followed.

'No hard feelings,' said Ervin.

'Not so far,' said Shepherd. He glanced around but didn't see Hargrove or Sharpe, or anyone who looked as if they were paying them any attention. Either the French surveillance was top notch or it wasn't there. 'What about Salik? Did you put him through this before you did business with him?'

'We have known him for a long time,' said Ervin. 'We have done business many times.'

'But with me you'll be able to do much bigger runs, and make a hell of a lot more money,' said Shepherd.

'That is why you are here,' said Ervin.

They walked out of the station and into the main street where passengers queued for taxis. They went past the taxi rank. Shepherd saw Jimmy Sharpe buying a copy of *Le Monde* from a newsagent and felt more at ease. At least one friendly face was close by. Sharpe flicked the paper under his arm and ran across the road towards a pavement café. There was no sign of Hargrove.

'This way,' said Ervin. 'We have a car.'

Shepherd fell into step next to him. Artur stood aside to let them go by, glaring at Shepherd with undisguised hatred, then followed. Shepherd knew he'd made a mistake in insulting Artur, but the alternative would have been to let the Albanian man-handle him and he hadn't been prepared to allow that. Tony Corke wasn't an SAS trooper turned undercover cop, but he was a former merchant seaman with a criminal record for violence and it would have been out of character for him to let Artur push him around.

They hurried across the road and away from the café where Sharpe had seated himself at a table, then turned down a side-street where a large Mercedes was waiting, engine running.

As they walked up to the rear of the car, the driver got out. He was a stocky man with a scarred left cheek and, like the other two, was wearing a leather jacket and jeans, but with a blue New York Yankees baseball cap.

Ervin called to him in Albanian. The driver leaned into the car and popped open the boot.

Shepherd stopped. 'Now what?' he asked.

Ervin grinned – and Shepherd realised he'd made a big mistake in turning his back on Artur. He heard a swishing sound, then something hard thumped behind his left ear and everything went black.

★   ★   ★

When Shepherd came to he was lying in the foetal position in pitch darkness. He could hear muffled street sounds and the floor was vibrating. He was still in the boot of the car and his head ached. He reached up with his right hand as a sharp pain lanced his skull. He cursed and groped around with his hands for something he could use to force his way out, but there was nothing. He was lying on thick carpet that smelt of chemicals. As it was a Mercedes, he was pretty sure there was a spare wheel and a tool-kit under the floor, but he didn't know how he could get at it in the confined space. Mentally he went through the contents of his pockets. His wallet. The mobile phone. His keys. Loose change. His Peter Devereux passport. Hardly an arsenal, and certainly no match for three men with guns.

He cursed himself for his stupidity. He should have agreed to go with them in the first place: then at least he'd have been travelling in comfort, not locked in the boot. The big question, Shepherd knew, was what they would do next. If it had been a set-up from the start he would be dead as soon as they opened the boot. If they had any sense they'd pump half a dozen bullets into him first chance they got, because if they didn't he'd come out fighting and a man with nothing to lose could do a hell of a lot of damage. Was he in the boot because he'd been argumentative, or had that been the plan from the start? Shepherd squinted at the luminous dial of his Rolex Submariner. He had only been out for a few minutes, which was another good sign because Artur could probably have hit him a lot harder if he'd wanted to. They hadn't tied him up either. So, all in all, everything was looking rosy.

The car turned sharply to the left, slowed, then took another sharp left turn. It dipped down and the traffic noises died away. They were in an underground car park. Another good sign. If they'd been going to kill him they'd probably have driven out into the countryside.

The Mercedes slowed to a crawl, turned, and the engine died. Shepherd tensed. He was ninety-five per cent sure that this was going to work out all right, but the adrenaline kicked in, his heart pounded and he started to breathe faster.

The boot clicked. Shepherd grunted, kicked it open with his feet and sprang out, hands up, ready to lash out. Ervin was standing a dozen feet away, his gun aimed at Shepherd's chest. Artur stood off to the side, even further away, clasping a Glock with both hands, one finger tensed on the trigger. Shepherd stood where he was, breathing heavily. Ervin smiled. 'Relax, Tony,' he said.

'*Relax?* You fucking poleaxe me and you tell me to relax?'

'What are you going to do? *Kung fu?* Karate? Even Bruce Lee couldn't block a bullet.'

Shepherd glanced over his shoulder. The driver was standing by the open door of the Mercedes, holding a sawn-off shotgun. He looked back at Ervin. 'Now what?' he asked.

Ervin gestured with his gun. 'We're here,' he said. 'The boss is upstairs.'

Shepherd put a hand to his head, and felt his hair wet with blood. 'So let's go.' He wiped his fingers on his jeans.

Ervin nodded, then spoke to the others in Albanian. Artur put away his gun and the driver slid the sawn-off under the front passenger seat. Ervin stuck his weapon into his trouser belt. 'First, we must search you,' said Ervin.

'For what?'

'For anything. Please raise your hands.'

Shepherd did as he was told. Ervin moved forward cautiously and went through the pockets of the pea coat. He examined the Nokia mobile and put it into his own jacket pocket, along with Shepherd's wallet, keys, return ticket and passport.

'I'll want those back later,' said Shepherd.

'You'll have them.' He patted down Shepherd's jeans to his boots. 'I'm going to lift your shirt,' said Ervin.

'Nice of you to warn me.'

Ervin pulled Shepherd's shirt out of his jeans and undid the buttons. He lifted the shirt, peered round Shepherd's waist, then checked his chest.

'Satisfied?' asked Shepherd.

Ervin nodded. Shepherd fastened his shirt and tucked it into his jeans. The driver climbed back into the Mercedes and drove off.

'This way,' said Ervin. He led Shepherd to a lift and tapped in an access code on a console set into the concrete. A few minutes later the doors opened and Shepherd stepped in, followed by Artur and Ervin. It was austere and functional, lined with stainless steel. The doors hissed shut.

The lift was designed to stop at only two floors – the underground car park and the penthouse. There was no way of knowing how many floors it bypassed, but less than a minute later the doors opened and Shepherd walked out into a hallway with a red thick-pile carpet and gilded wallpaper, which featured rushes and long-legged birds pecking for fish. Ornate candelabra hung from the ceiling. At the far end of the hallway there was a pair of ornate Chinese doors. As Shepherd and the two Albanians walked towards them they opened. Shepherd wasn't surprised to see that the man standing there to greet them was also wearing a leather jacket and jeans. It seemed to be the standard uniform: Albanian gangster chic.

He grunted at Ervin and held the door open for them. The room they went into was huge with high ceilings, more candelabra, a massive marble fireplace that was almost as tall as Shepherd, and gilt furniture with overstuffed red cushions. There were ornate statues everywhere – dolphins, lions, African warriors holding spears – and a massive plasma-screen television on one wall with huge speakers. Shepherd stood at the window, which looked out over the Seine and the towers of Notre Dame Cathedral. They were right in the centre of Paris and the apartment must have been worth millions of euros.

A door opened at the far end of the room and a small but powerfully built man came in. He had close-cropped grey hair and a square chin, which he thrust up like a boxer eager to get started. He was wearing a salmon-pink polo shirt, cream trousers and pale tan loafers, as if he'd just stepped off a golf course.

'Nice view,' said Shepherd.

'You don't notice it after a while,' said the man. 'I am Kreshnik.

My men tell me you did not want to accompany them.' He had a thick Central European accent but was obviously fluent in English. He waved for Shepherd to sit down on one of the sofas.

Shepherd stayed where he was. 'Salik said I was to meet you guys in Paris. He didn't say I was going to be thrown into the boot of a car.'

'That was because you didn't go with them willingly,' said Kreshnik. 'Now, please, sit down. Can I offer you a drink?'

'No, thanks,' said Shepherd, and sat on a large sofa. It was nowhere near as comfortable as it looked.

'I have a very nice white wine, perfectly chilled.'

'Fine. Okay, whatever,' said Shepherd.

Kreshnik clicked his fingers and Artur left the room. He clicked his fingers again, this time at Ervin, who stepped forward and put the contents of Shepherd's pockets on to the coffee table. Kreshnik flicked through the passport. 'One of Salik's?' he asked.

Shepherd nodded.

Kreshnik put it down, then picked up the wallet and went through it, examining every card and banknote. He looked at both sides of the driving licence, then laid it on top of the wallet. He picked up the mobile and scrolled through the menu. He frowned. 'There is only one number in the memory?'

'Yes. Salik's.'

'No friends? No family?'

'I only use it to talk to him.'

Kreshnik's eyes narrowed as if he was squinting into a bright light. 'You have no other friends?'

'It's a pay-as-you-go mobile. I have another phone I use to call friends. That one's a business phone. If there's a problem I can throw it away and there's no comeback.'

'You are suspicious of Salik?'

Shepherd laughed. 'I'm suspicious of everyone,' he said. 'Especially thugs who whack me on the back of the head and dump me in a car boot. I don't know, maybe I'm paranoid.'

Kreshnik scrolled through the menu again. 'No calls made, none received,' he said.

'I clear the logs,' said Shepherd. 'You never know when some nosy bastard's going to start searching through it.'

Kreshnik's face hardened. 'That would be your British sense of humour, would it?' he said. 'I'd be careful with that. Not everyone understands the joke.'

'I'm just saying that in this business you have to be careful. The cops can trace every call you make. You must know that. You watch every word you say and you keep switching Sim cards. And whenever you can, you use public phones. That's basic – everyone knows it.'

Kreshnik removed the back of the phone and peered inside, took out the battery, examined it, then reassembled the phone and switched it back on.

He put it down on the coffee table and picked up Shepherd's keys. 'These are for your car?' he said.

Shepherd nodded.

'What sort?'

'A Land Rover.'

'I have a Range Rover,' said Kreshnik.

'Nice car,' said Shepherd. 'Bit pricy for me.'

Kreshnik weighed the keys in the palm of his right hand. 'No house keys?' he said. He had a gold half-sovereign ring on his third finger.

'I left them in the car.'

'And the car is where?'

'In a car park not far from where I met Salik today.'

'You always do that? Leave your house keys in the car?'

Shepherd shrugged. 'Habit, when you're at sea. You don't clutter your pockets with non-essentials,' he said. 'You carry what you need.'

'Yes, that's right,' said Kreshnik. 'You are a sailor.' He laid the keys on the table and watched Shepherd with unsmiling eyes.

'Yes.'

'My father was a sailor. Were you in the navy?'

'Merchant navy. Six years. Five on the cross-Channel ferries.'

'And now?'

'I go where the money is.'

'Why did you leave the ferries?'

'They were cutting back. Competition from the Eurostar.'

Kreshnik held Shepherd's look. His smile hardened. 'I do not believe you,' he said.

Shepherd held his gaze steady. His mind raced. Had he slipped up? 'I had a bit of legal trouble,' he said calmly. 'A fight. I did six months in prison.'

Kreshnik smiled cruelly. 'I knew it,' he said. 'I can always spot someone who has been in prison. There is a smell about them. An odour.'

'I showered this morning,' said Shepherd.

'It's a smell that never leaves,' said Kreshnik. 'All the soap in the world won't get rid of it.' He grinned. 'I have never been to prison,' he said.

'I'm pleased for you.'

'Why is it, do you think, that I have never been behind bars?' asked Kreshnik.

'You pay off the cops?' said Shepherd.

The Albanian wagged a finger at Shepherd, but he was smiling. 'That sense of humour *will* get you into trouble. We don't laugh much in Albania, unless we are drunk.'

Arthur returned with two large glasses of white wine on a silver tray. He gave one to Kreshnik, the other to Shepherd. Kreshnik clinked his glass against Shepherd's, sipped his wine and rolled it round his palate with pursed lips. For a moment Shepherd thought the Albanian was going to spit it out, but he swallowed, smiled and nodded approvingly.

Shepherd drank from his glass then put it on the table.

'The answer to that question, why I have never been to prison, is that I never do business with people I don't know,' said Kreshnik. He picked up the driving licence and waved it in front of Shepherd's face. 'Now I know you, Tony Corke, and I know where you live. Your date of birth. I have all the information I need to track you down.' He slid the driving licence into the back pocket of his golfing trousers.

'I'll need that,' said Shepherd.

'You can get a replacement,' said Kreshnik. 'It's one of the great things about your country. They issue copies of official documents so quickly.'

'I don't know what you're so worried about,' said Shepherd. 'If it wasn't for me, you'd have lost the consignment you gave that asylum-seeker. I've already done you a big favour.'

'Salik told me you demanded thirty thousand pounds.'

'It was more of a commission than a demand,' said Shepherd. 'Can I ask you a question?'

'You can ask,' said the Albanian. 'Whether I choose to answer or not is up to me.'

'I get the feeling you're bigger than Salik. This apartment. The crew you've got around you. You're in the Premier League. Salik, he's Second Division. Hoping for promotion but still a long way behind you.'

Kreshnik smiled. 'That is a reasonable assessment.' His smile widened. 'You know what my dream is, Tony? To buy a football team in your country one day. Like Roman Abramovich. He bought Chelsea. And that American – he bought Manchester United. I want to do the same. Liverpool is for sale, right?'

'In England everything is for sale,' said Shepherd. He leaned forward, fingers interlinked. 'Look, I might be in a position to do some work for you. Salik told you about my boat, right?'

Kreshnik nodded.

'Okay, then. I'm running cash for Salik, but I can carry a thousand kilos of anything over the Channel with next to no chance of being caught. I was working with Pepper on his trawler to learn the ropes, but I could see that his boat was a pile of shit. I can put ten men on mine and have them in the UK in under an hour. I can run them from France to Scotland if you wanted.'

'I don't run asylum-seekers,' said Kreshnik. 'I use them to courier cash, that's all.'

'Right. So I'm doing this run for Salik. You must have other customers in the UK. You could use me more often. A thousand kilos a run. That's a lot of currency.' He lowered his voice. 'Or anything else you wanted to take over.'

'Anything else?'

'Drugs. Guns. I'm like Federal Express. Door-to-door, guaranteed delivery.'

Kreshnik took another sip of wine, his dark brown eyes fixed on Shepherd. He licked his lips. 'Let's see how we get on with this, shall we? Then maybe we'll talk again.'

The Mercedes stopped in front of the Gare du Nord, close to the taxi rank. Ervin twisted round in the front passenger seat. 'No hard feelings?' he asked.

Shepherd grunted. 'Guess not.' He nodded at Artur, who was sitting next to him. 'I'm not so sure about him. I might need stitches in my head.' He climbed out of the car and slammed the door.

As the Mercedes drove away, Artur made a gun with his fingers and mimed shooting at Shepherd. In return Shepherd gave him a friendly wave.

He walked slowly through the station concourse. He had forty-five minutes before the Eurostar left for London. It was only as he passed through Immigration that he remembered he hadn't eaten since the sandwich he'd had on his outward journey.

The train was packed, with every seat in standard class taken. Shepherd's was in a group of four again, the rear-facing window-seat. The three other passengers at the table were Japanese women, chattering in their own language and exchanging their digital cameras with lots of pointing and giggling.

Shepherd folded his arms. He was angry, but couldn't afford to show it. He was angry with the Albanians, for hitting him over the head and dumping him in the car boot. He was angry with Salik, for forcing him to travel to Paris. He was angry with Kreshnik, for the arrogant way he'd treated him. And angry with the French for not having been anywhere near him when he'd been kidnapped at gunpoint.

He saw Hargrove walking along the aisle. They made eye-contact and Hargrove nodded for Shepherd to follow him. Shepherd stood up and gestured to the Japanese woman sitting next to him that he needed to get out. She stood, bowing, and Shepherd followed Hargrove down the carriage.

The superintendent was waiting for him beside an unmarked door. He pushed it open and Shepherd followed him inside. The room was two paces square, with two first-class-sized seats at either side of a small table. Next to one a padded bench seat, with four thick metal hasps, was set into the wall.

'What's this?' asked Shepherd.

'One of the little secrets of Eurostar,' said Hargrove. 'They're used to transport criminals to and from the Continent. There are two on every train. Immigration use them for deportations to France. Saves all those nasty scenes we used to see with failed asylum-seekers trying to kill themselves on planes or throwing themselves off ferries.' He nodded at a metal cupboard on the wall next to the ceiling. 'Guns have to be locked away in transit.'

'The French cops, right?'

'They can carry their guns until they're at the halfway point of the tunnel. Then they have to put them away. Occasionally the UK cops are armed, Special Branch or SO19, but it's mainly for the French.'

Shepherd sat on the bench and stretched his legs. 'That could have turned to shit so easily,' he said.

'There was nothing we could do without blowing the whole operation.'

'It wasn't an operation, it was a disaster. I was unprepared, there was no back-up and no rescue signal.'

'If there had been an opt-out, would you have given it?' asked Hargrove.

That was a good question. If he'd not gone with the Albanians, the whole operation would have been blown. 'I'm not sure,' he said, 'but it would have been nice to have the option.'

'And would you have had time?' said Hargrove. 'The way

Sharpe tells it, they hit you from behind and it was all over before he could do anything.'

'That's not the point,' said Shepherd. 'The point is that I was unprepared and with no back-up. I was on my own with them for more than two hours and if they'd decided to top me it would have been over anyway.'

'The French were at the station. They just weren't geared up for the car.'

'They should have been.'

'Agreed,' said Hargrove. 'But they were there, Spider. And they got everything on CCTV. Do you want to hear the good news?'

'There is some?'

'Lots. Sharpe got the registration number of the Mercedes, and the French got an address and we were outside all the time you were in the apartment. The guy who owns it is a big fish, and Europol are very excited. Kreshnik Zagreda is Albanian but he's had French citizenship for the last ten years. Brings cannabis in from Morocco, runs weapons into Algeria, prostitution, extortion.'

'And untouchable. He told me he'd never been inside.'

'So far. Obeys all the rules. Doesn't go near the illegal stuff, doesn't go near the money, only deals with people he knows.'

'So we're not going to get him on the currency.'

'On his track record, probably not. But it's the first that Europol has heard about him being involved in counterfeiting. It's another piece of the puzzle. The guys who took you in are two of his lieutenants, Ervin Ristani and Artur Veseli. They're working on the driver now. Ristani and Veseli will be under round-the-clock surveillance until you do your run. There's a good chance they'll get their hands dirty and the hope is that they'll roll over on Kreshnik.'

'They didn't seem the type that would roll over,' said Shepherd. 'And Kreshnik didn't seem the type who'd let them.' He rubbed the back of his neck. The tendons were as taut as steel cables. 'I tried luring him on a drugs run, but he was noncommittal. Wanted to wait and see.'

'We might get him on conspiracy down the line,' said Hargrove. 'Send you back with a wire. Or get his place bugged.'

'No wires,' said Shepherd, emphatically. 'They gave me a full going-over and I got the feeling it was standard practice.'

'I'll talk to Europol and see what they say,' said Hargrove. 'The important thing is that you're back in one piece and the operation's still on. The Uddin brothers will organise the currency run and, hopefully, we'll tie up both ends.'

Shepherd took out the passport and offered it to the superintendent. 'It looks genuine to me,' he said.

Hargrove flicked through the pages. 'If it isn't, it's a first-class forgery,' he said.

'Ten grand's expensive for a fake,' said Shepherd. 'I think it's the real deal.'

Hargrove handed it back. 'We'll have it checked. When you get to Waterloo, slip it to Sharpe.'

'The toilets again?'

'You can change phones at the same time.'

'Lucky we did that,' said Shepherd. 'Kreshnik took the phone apart. Checked the Sim card, too.'

'Luck doesn't come into it,' said Hargrove. 'Hopefully the brothers will call you tomorrow. We need to know date and time, pick-up and delivery points.'

'Are you going to bust them, or wait?' asked Shepherd.

'The French will let their end run, I'm sure of that,' said Hargrove. 'I think they want Kreshnik on a drugs charge, if they can get him. And they want to nail the counterfeit euros. It really is starting to become a Europol investigation so that means they're going to be setting the rules. If we bust the Uddins, Kreshnik might go to ground.'

'That's fine by me,' said Shepherd. 'It always gets messy when I get hauled in.'

'But the passport is our investigation, and definitely worth pursuing,' said the superintendent. 'We want to know who their man is, and who else he's fixed up passports for.'

'You think they'll tell me?' asked Shepherd.

'Make them your new best friends,' said Hargrove. 'That's what you're good at.'

After he'd exchanged phones with Sharpe and given him the Peter Devereux passport, Shepherd caught a black cab from Waterloo and had it drop him close to the multi-storey car park where he'd left the Land Rover. It was close to eleven o'clock and he wanted to get home, but there was something he had to check first and that meant driving to Dover. Salik knew where Tony Corke lived. He'd seen the address on the driving licence and Shepherd figured that he would have viewed Corke's trip to Paris as too good an opportunity to miss.

He stuck to the speed limit on the motorway, although there was little traffic. He parked in front of the two-up, two-down terraced house in a quiet street on the outskirts of the town. The door keys were in the glove compartment. Shepherd let himself in and switched on the hall light. The burglar-alarm system began to beep and Shepherd tapped in the four-digit code on a keyboard by the light switch. He looked around slowly. Half a dozen envelopes lay on the threadbare carpet, all bills and all in the name of Tony Corke. On a side table there was a phone and a telephone directory, and on the wall above it a framed photograph of the *Titanic* leaving port on its appointment with destiny. The house had been dressed by experts who worked for Hargrove's unit, two gay men who could furnish a house or apartment to fit any legend. Everything from the food in the refrigerator to the clothes hanging in the cheap, teak-effect MFI wardrobes had been selected to accommodate Tony Corke's personality.

Shepherd walked slowly down the hall. The door to the sitting room was open. A black plastic leather-effect sofa, a wooden coffee table pockmarked with cigarette burns and beer-can rings, an old television set. A handful of letters was scattered across the coffee table, court papers and correspondence from Corke's solicitor, including a bill for legal fees of more than twenty thousand pounds. Shepherd stood looking down at them and flashed back in his memory to the last time he'd been in the room. The bill had been further to the right. Six inches, maybe a bit more. It had been moved.

He walked round the room, looking for other signs that he had been visited in his absence. There was an old gas fire in a cast-iron fireplace, covered with decades of paint. On the mantelpiece, a wedge of rejection letters from various shipping lines, all dated within the previous year, and credit-card statements, all showing substantial debts, was pushed behind a brass ornament of three monkeys – hear no evil, see no evil, speak no evil. A statement from a building society detailed the amount outstanding on Tony Corke's mortgage. They had been moved, too. Someone had rifled through them.

Shepherd went upstairs and opened the wardrobe in the main bedroom. Cheap, well-worn clothes. A lot of thick wool pullovers and denim shirts, work socks in a drawer, a pile of towels, several of which had the logos of ferry companies. It was little touches, like the stolen towels, that added authenticity to any cover story. Shepherd ran his hand along the clothes on the hangers. They'd been moved, too, since the last time he'd been in the house. Now, at least, he knew where he stood. On the surface Salik Uddin might appear to be an easy-going family man but he was shrewd enough to take advantage of Shepherd's absence to check out the house. It had been a professional job: there was no sign of a forced entry, which meant that the lock had been professionally picked and the alarm system dealt with. It wasn't difficult – Hargrove had several operatives on his team who could have got past the lock and the alarm in less than thirty seconds – but whoever Salik had used was an expert. Shepherd doubted that Salik was a locksmith but he clearly had access to someone with the necessary skills.

Shepherd reset the alarm and locked the door. On the drive back to Ealing he phoned Hargrove and briefed him on what had happened.

*   *   *

The Saudi walked up to the three-storey house and glanced at the top floor. A figure was silhouetted at the window, looking down, so the Saudi didn't press the bell. He stood with his back to the door, swinging his briefcase from side to side. He had taken a taxi to the residential street and had it drop him round the corner, then spent the best part of an hour reassuring himself that the area was not under surveillance.

The man who opened the door had light brown hair, a long face and a dimple in his chin. He smiled, showing even white teeth, the result of good genes and a healthy diet. Joe Hagerman was American, a relatively recent convert to Islam.

He'd been in Afghanistan in 2001 where he'd been trained in weapons and explosives at Khalden Camp, close to Kandahar. After the Americans had invaded, he had moved to Bajaur, a mountainous tribal land near the Afghan border, then on to Rawalpindi in Pakistan, which was where the Saudi had met him. Back then, Hagerman had had a long beard and an untidy mop of hair. His skin had been nut brown from the fierce desert sun, his hands ingrained with dirt and oil. The face that smiled back at him now was clean-shaven and considerably paler; the hands were well manicured. 'How's it going?' asked Hagerman, his voice Midwestern American.

'Everything is on schedule,' said the Saudi.

Hagerman led him up a wide staircase to the second floor, then stepped aside to allow the Saudi across the threshold first. The flat was almost monastically bare, with no pictures on the walls. There was no carpet, just gleaming oak floorboards, and only cushions to sit on. A prayer mat lay in one corner, and a copy of the Koran on the window-sill. Hagerman was an American by birth but a devout Muslim by choice, and had nothing but contempt for the ways of the West. He was a vegetarian, drank no alcohol, prayed far more frequently than the five times a day laid down by the Koran, and could quote the Holy Book by heart in its original Arabic.

'Can I offer you a beverage? I have water and fruit juice.'

'Water, please,' said the Saudi. He sat down on one of the

cushions as Hagerman went into the kitchen. Other than the Koran there was nothing to read and no source of entertainment. No television, no radio, no stereo.

It had taken the American more than five years to convince al-Qaeda that he wasn't a CIA plant and another two before they were satisfied that he was indeed suitable to join the ranks of the *shahid*. The Saudi had felt from his first meeting that Hagerman was almost too committed to the *jihad*, too willing to die for Islam. His commitment bordered on a mental illness, but he would be a tool that the Saudi was happy to use.

Hagerman returned with a glass of water, chilled, from the fridge. The Saudi knew that he drank only bottled water, never from the tap.

'I was robbed yesterday,' said Hagerman, as he sat down on a cushion.

'What do you mean?'

'Someone got in through the bathroom window. Climbed a drainpipe. Kids, probably.'

'The case?'

'It's fine. But they took some money and my passport.'

'That's not good news,' said the Saudi. He knew he was stating the obvious, but there was no point in showing his anger. He could not have been told earlier: Hagerman had no way of getting in touch with him. Communication was one-way, once an operation was running.

'I can't travel without my passport,' said Hagerman, also stating the obvious.

'It wasn't your American passport?'

Hagerman shook his head. 'Of course not. I ditched that years ago. I'd be red-flagged at every airport in the world under that name. It was the Bosnian one.'

'And difficult to replace in London?'

'It would take time. And even then it wouldn't have my UK visa in it so I couldn't travel.'

The Saudi grimaced. 'Okay,' he said. He didn't want to

criticise the American, but it had been a stupid mistake to leave his passport in the flat.

'I'm sorry,' said Hagerman.

'It is a problem, but it can be solved,' said the Saudi. 'I know people in London who can get you a passport.'

'A counterfeit?'

'A real passport. A British passport. You'll be able to travel without any problems.'

'And they'll do it quickly?'

'Providing you have the money,' said the Saudi. He opened his briefcase, flicked through the document folders built into the lid and pulled out a manilla envelope. The Saudi never travelled without large amounts of cash. He rarely used credit cards as they left an electronic trail that could be followed. He opened the envelope and removed a wad of fifty-pound notes. He counted out two hundred – ten thousand pounds. 'This will get you the passport,' he said. He counted out another thousand pounds. 'And this is for any other expenses.'

The American took the money, stood up and went into the kitchen where he put it into the freezer compartment of the fridge.

The Saudi scribbled a name and a phone number on a piece of paper and stood up. As Hagerman came out of the kitchen, the Saudi gave it to him. 'Call this number. Tell him what you want and that you have the money.'

Hagerman took it and put it into his wallet.

'Where's the case?' asked the Saudi.

'In the bedroom,' said Hagerman. 'Under the bed.'

'Show me,' said the Saudi.

The bedroom was as bare as the outer room. There was a built-in wardrobe along one wall and a metal-framed bed with a mattress, a single thin pillow and two sheets.

Hagerman knelt down and pulled out a small hard-shell suitcase. He placed it on the bed and clicked open the locks.

The Saudi nodded, satisfied. It had been perfectly constructed and there was no way to tell from looking at it that the shell contained fifteen pounds of Semtex. The case would pass through any X-ray scanner without showing anything out of the ordinary. All that was needed to turn it into a devastating weapon of destruction was a detonator. And the Saudi had plenty of those.

Shepherd was finishing his breakfast when he heard a phone ringing upstairs. He knew from the tone that Salik was calling. 'Work?' said Liam, reading his mind. He was sitting at the kitchen table, eating his favourite scrambled eggs with cheese on toast and reading a comic, in which aliens were being blown apart by wisecracking space cowboys.

'It never stops,' said Shepherd.

'We're going to play football, right?'

'Sure,' said Shepherd, then hurried up the stairs and took the call.

'Where are you?' asked Salik.

'Out and about,' said Shepherd. 'What's up?'

'Are you at home?'

Shepherd couldn't afford to say he was in case Salik was sitting outside the house in Dover. 'I'm talking to some guy about a property in Spain,' he said, 'in case I have to leave the country at short notice.'

'We would like to see the boat today,' said Salik. 'Can you meet us in Southampton?'

Shepherd looked at his watch. 'When?'

'We are in London. We could get to Southampton by three.'

'Okay. Have you got a pen?' Shepherd gave Salik the address of the marina and told him to wait in the car park until he got there. He cut the connection and phoned Hargrove.

'They're hooked,' said the superintendent. 'That's good news.'

'They just want to check the boat out but it looks as if they're going to bite.'

'Excellent,' said Hargrove. 'I'll bring Singh in and we'll get you wired up.'

'I don't think there's much point in recording anything,' said

Shepherd, 'and we wouldn't pick up much on the boat over the noise of the outboard.'

'We'll need something on tape,' said Hargrove.

'Let's see if they pat me down today,' said Shepherd.

'It's your call,' said Hargrove.

'I wouldn't mind Sharpe and Joyce in the vicinity.'

'Do you think the brothers still don't trust you?'

'After what the bloody Albanians did to me in Paris, I'm assuming nobody trusts me.'

'I'm sure they'll appreciate the overtime,' said Hargrove. 'I'll call them.'

'I'm assuming that all the Uddins will want is a look at the boat, maybe a short run out to sea.'

'They wouldn't be planning to pull a fast one on you, like he did with the trip to France?'

'If they do, I'll say no. I'm not doing the proper run unless everything's set up at both ends. I learned my lesson last time.'

Shepherd ended the call and went downstairs. Liam glared at him over his comic.

'What?' said Shepherd.

'I know what you're going to say.'

'Liam—'

'It's not bloody fair.'

'Don't swear!'

Liam threw down his comic and stormed out of the kitchen, pushing past Katra who was carrying an armful of dirty towels.

'I have to work,' Shepherd explained to her.

'He was looking forward to playing with you,' said Katra.

'I know, but this is important,' said Shepherd.

Katra opened her mouth to speak, then changed her mind.

'What?' said Shepherd.

'Nothing,' said Katra.

'What were you going to say?'

'It's not my place, Dan,' she said. 'I work for you. I'm an employee.' She opened the washing-machine and began to push in the towels.

'You're more than that, Katra, you know you are. Now, what were you going to say?'

Katra sighed and closed the washing-machine door. 'Old habits die hard,' she said, as she straightened up. 'That's the expression you used before, right?'

'Yes.'

'It's as if you've got into the habit of letting Liam down, as if he doesn't matter.'

'Of course he matters,' said Shepherd. 'He's my son.'

'But work comes first?'

'Of course,' said Shepherd, and regretted the words as soon as they'd left his mouth. He sat down at the kitchen table as the ramifications of what he'd just said hit home. 'Wow,' he said.

Katra smiled sympathetically, knowing she'd proved her point.

'I really said that, didn't I?' He put his head into his hands. 'What a shit I am.'

Katra sat down opposite him. 'He knows you love him,' she said.

'But he always comes second to my job. What sort of father am I?'

Katra reached across and put her hand on his shoulder. 'It's because when your wife was here it didn't matter so much if you had to be away. He had a mother and a father. Now he has only you.'

Shepherd banged his fist against his head. 'You're right.'

'I can be with him, so it's not as if you leave him on his own, but I'm not his family.'

'And I'm carrying on exactly as I was when Sue was here,' he said. 'I can't believe I said work was more important than my son.'

'It's a demanding job,' said Katra.

'That's no excuse,' said Shepherd. 'I've been such a bastard to him.'

'No,' said Katra. 'He understands. Really. And he's proud of you. He talks about you all the time when you're not here,' she said.

'I didn't know that.'

'You don't tell him much about your work, but he knows you don't have a job like his friends' fathers. He understands you don't work regular hours.'

'I don't think I could do any other sort of job.'

'Even for Liam?'

Shepherd sat back and ran his hands through his hair. 'I want both.' He sighed. 'I want a job that challenges me, and I want to be a good father.'

'Perhaps you can't have both,' said Katra. 'Perhaps you have to choose.'

Shepherd pushed back his chair and stood up. 'You might be right,' he said. He went upstairs and knocked on Liam's bedroom door. When the boy didn't answer, Shepherd knocked again and opened the door a little way. 'Liam, can I come in?' Sue and he had made it a rule since Liam was seven that they asked permission to enter his bedroom. And Liam had to do the same with theirs. It had taught him the value of privacy, and prevented embarrassing interruptions. 'Liam, I'd like to talk to you.'

'There's nothing to talk about,' said Liam.

Shepherd opened the door fully. His son was lying on his bed, gazing up at the ceiling. 'I'm sorry,' said Shepherd.

'You're always sorry.'

Shepherd sat down on the side of the bed. Liam rolled away from him. 'It's a big case,' said Shepherd. 'It's one I've been working on for a long time.'

Liam said nothing.

'Last time I was away, remember? I had to go to France. I was on a boat. I told you, right? Well, it's that case and I'm still working on it. I'll have to go back to France again and this is part of that. I have to go and see some people this afternoon.'

'Why today? It's Saturday.'

'The bad guys don't work office hours, Liam. I can't tell them I'm playing football with my son, can I?'

'Why not?'

Another question to which Shepherd had no answer.

'Do the bad guys have kids?'

'One does,' said Shepherd. He thought of the four photographs Salik had shown him. 'Four. One's a boy of about your age.'

Liam rolled back to face Shepherd. His cheeks were wet with tears. 'So he'd understand. He'd play football with his kids, right?'

Shepherd imagined Salik running around with his children, sweating and panting as he tried to keep up. 'Probably,' he said.

'So?'

'So what?'

'So tell him you promised to play football with your son and that you'll see him next week.'

'It's not as simple as that.'

'Why?'

'Like I said, it's a big case.'

'Is it drugs?'

'No. Fake money.'

'And are they gangsters?'

'The men in France are. But the men in England . . .' Shepherd frowned. He wouldn't have described the Uddins as gangsters. Criminals, of course – they were breaking the law – but they weren't what Shepherd would have called gangsters. 'Not really. They're bringing in the fake money. Smuggling.'

Liam sat up and shuffled back so that he was propped against the headboard. 'Millions?'

'Sure.'

'Millions of pounds?'

'Euros.'

'And how do they smuggle it in?'

'Boats,' said Shepherd.

'And is that what you've been doing?'

Shepherd was telling his son more than he should about an operational matter, but Liam was enthralled. He patted the boy's leg. 'This is top secret, you know that?'

Liam nodded seriously. 'Secret Squirrel.'

Shepherd held out his hand, his little finger crooked. 'You mustn't tell anybody,' he said. 'Pinkie promise.'

'Pinkie promise.' Liam crooked his little finger and linked it with Shepherd's.

'They use boats to bring the money in from France. I'm pretending to be a sailor. That's why I drive the Land Rover with the boat stuff in it.'

'Is it dangerous?'

Shepherd remembered the Albanians. 'No, not really.'

'Do they have guns?'

'Most gangsters have guns,' said Shepherd.

'Do they fire them at you?'

'No, of course not.'

'But you were shot in the army.'

Shepherd's shoulder began to ache. It was his brain playing tricks, he knew, a subconscious reminder of the bullet he'd taken in the Afghan desert. 'That was different,' he said. 'That was a war.'

'But gangsters shoot people, don't they?'

'Not police officers,' said Shepherd. 'If they do, they go to prison for ever. Liam, I'm really sorry about today, but I have to talk to these men and show them the boat.'

'The smugglers' boat?'

Shepherd nodded. 'I won't be more than a few hours. If I get back before it's dark, we can still play football. Okay?'

Liam smiled unwillingly. 'Okay.'

'And I'll owe you one,' said Shepherd.

'So you'll let me have my television back in my bedroom?'

'Don't push it.' Shepherd grabbed him and began to tickle him.

Liam writhed on the bed. 'No!' he screamed. 'I give in, I give in!'

'Are you sure?'

'Yes!'

Shepherd released him and stood up. 'And I want all your homework done by the time I get back,' he said, 'or I'll tickle you again.'

'I'm too old to be tickled.'

Shepherd lunged at him again and the boy squealed. 'Okay! I'll do it!'

The boat was moored at a berth in a small marina on the outskirts of Southampton, rented in the name of Tony Corke and back-dated for twelve months. Salik and Matiur stood on the wooden jetty as Shepherd pulled the faded blue tarpaulin off the boat and rolled it up.

'Come on, climb aboard,' said Shepherd.

'I'm not good on boats,' said Matiur. 'I get seasick.'

'A rib doesn't roll like a normal boat,' said Shepherd. 'It cuts through the waves. It's more like a car than a boat.'

Matiur put his hands up. 'I'll stay here,' he said.

Shepherd looked at Salik. 'What about you?'

'I suppose so.'

'I'll just show you how it works so you can see for yourself how simple it is.' He helped Salik climb in, fired the engine and told Matiur to release the moorings. He coiled the ropes, then eased the boat away from the jetty.

'He liked you,' said Salik, as Shepherd headed out to open water.

'Who?'

'Kreshnik. He said you were professional.'

'Did he tell you what he did to me?'

'What?'

'His men hit me over the head and put me into the boot of a car at gunpoint.'

Salik seemed genuinely surprised. 'They did that?'

'Kreshnik's a heavy guy,' said Shepherd. 'Dangerous.'

'I'm sorry,' said Salik.

'It wasn't your fault,' said Shepherd. 'Okay, sit down and hold on to the rail. I'll show you what this baby can do.'

As soon as Salik had slid on to the seat, Shepherd pushed the throttle forward and the boat accelerated away from the marina, reaching planing speed within seconds. Salik's jaw dropped.

Shepherd guided it through a flotilla of small dinghies, then accelerated to forty knots.

'This is amazing,' yelled Salik, squinting against the slipstream. 'And we can't be seen on radar?'

'We're virtually invisible,' shouted Shepherd.

'Amazing!'

Shepherd put the boat through a couple of tight turns, enjoying the alarm on his passenger's face, then spent half an hour showing off what it could do and eventually took Salik back to the marina.

The brothers helped him tie up and cover the boat with the tarpaulin.

'How was it?' Matiur asked his brother.

'Amazing,' said Salik. 'Like a sports car on water.' He slapped Shepherd on the back. 'We'll do it for real tomorrow.'

'What?' said Shepherd.

'Tomorrow. We have already paid Kreshnik.'

'That's a bit sudden, isn't it?'

'The sooner the better,' said Matiur.

'What about you? Are you coming too?'

'We're not, but we will send someone with you,' said Matiur.

'To keep an eye on me?'

Salik smiled. 'It is a lot of money, Tony. You can understand our reluctance to let you bring it over alone.'

'Just don't make it one of the Albanians,' said Shepherd. 'I don't want a bullet in the head.'

Salik patted his arm. 'Don't worry, they trust you now. As do we. But just because we trust you doesn't mean we stop being careful.'

'Where do I collect the stuff from?'

'We'll tell you tomorrow.'

'And where do I deliver it to?'

'Tomorrow.'

Shepherd smiled. 'You love keeping me in the dark, don't you?'

'Tomorrow,' Salik repeated. He put his arm round Shepherd's

shoulders and hugged him. 'Everything's going to be fine, Tony. We'll make a lot of money and become good friends. We'll meet again here tomorrow, as soon as it gets dark. *Inshallah.*'

Shepherd phoned Hargrove, using the hands-free kit, as he drove the Land Rover back to London. 'They want to do it tomorrow night,' he said.

'You're okay with that?' asked the superintendent.

'Providing the back-up's in place at both ends, I'm easy,' said Shepherd.

'I'll talk to Europol now,' said Hargrove. 'The snag is, we won't know where the stuff's being collected. Are you okay being wired?'

'I guess so,' said Shepherd. 'They didn't pat me down this time.'

'We'll know where the boat is from the tracking device, but not where you're going.'

'You realise they might not tell me in advance?'

'We'll have the Albanians under surveillance, and the Uddin brothers under the microscope here. The wire will be a fallback position.'

'Will it work at sea?'

'Let me talk to Singh,' said Hargrove, 'see what he's got in his box of tricks. We'll meet in Southampton tomorrow at four.'

When Shepherd got home Liam was sitting at the kitchen table with Katra, chewing at a pencil and frowning at an exercise book. 'Dad!' he shouted, throwing down the pencil and rushing to hug him.

'Homework?' asked Shepherd.

'Science,' said Katra. 'Do you know anything about trees?'

'The brown things with leaves on them? Sure.'

Liam laughed. 'Photosynthesis, Dad,' he said. 'They turn sugar into starch in their leaves. I have to write an essay and Katra says I can't use the Internet.'

'Why would you want to?'

'To download stuff. It makes it easier.'

'You're supposed to do it yourself,' said Katra. 'The Internet's cheating.'

Liam looked at his father, hoping he'd contradict her, but Shepherd said, 'Katra's right. The teacher wants to know that you understand the science, not that you can download someone else's work off the Internet. And you're in enough trouble at school as it is.'

'You're so old-fashioned,' said Liam, scornfully. 'Everyone uses the Internet.'

'Yeah, and everyone uses calculators, these days, which is why no one can add up in their heads any more. Remember when I made you do the times tables?'

Liam sighed. 'Yes.'

'And you didn't like doing it at the time, right?'

'It was boring.'

'Sure it was boring. But now you know all the times tables, right? What's nine times seven?'

'Fifteen,' said Liam, straight-faced.

'What?' said Shepherd.

'Just joking,' said Liam. 'Sixty-three.'

'See. You can do that because you learned your tables. Sometimes it's better to do things the old-fashioned way.'

'It's hard,' said Liam.

'Nothing worth having comes easy,' said Shepherd.

'It's okay for you – your memory's perfect.'

'But it never helped me write essays,' said Shepherd. 'The teacher wants to know that you understand what you've learned, not that you can repeat parrot-fashion what someone else has written. Having a good memory doesn't make it any easier to understand things. And being smart is about understanding stuff, not just memorising it.' He pointed at the exercise book. 'So, get writing, yeah?'

Liam sat down.

'Do you want coffee?' asked Katra.

'Please.'

'What about something to eat?'

'I'll make myself a sandwich.'

As Katra made coffee, Shepherd took butter and ham out of the fridge. 'I'll be away tomorrow night,' he said. 'Just for the one night.'

'Dad, we're going to Gran and Granddad's, remember?'

'You and Katra can go,' said Shepherd. 'I'll phone Gran and explain.'

'She won't like it.'

'It's you she wants to see, Liam, not me,' said Shepherd, buttering two slices of bread.

'Can we play football?'

'As soon as you've finished your homework.'

'Can I have my TV back in my room?'

'No,' said Shepherd, slapping ham on to the bread and smearing mustard across it.

'You're really mean sometimes,' said Liam.

'I'm your father,' said Shepherd. 'It's my job.'

Shepherd had breakfast with Liam and Katra, and after they had left for Hereford in the CRV he pulled on his black army boots and brick-filled rucksack. Moira hadn't sounded surprised that he wasn't going with Liam, nor had she seemed disappointed. He understood why they only wanted to see Liam. Sue had been their only child and he was their only grandchild, all they had left of their daughter. They had a right to as much access as Shepherd could give. Moira and Tom would have liked Liam to live with them, but he wasn't prepared to allow that: Liam was his son. They were a family – a family of two, but a family nonetheless. It was a pity they didn't live closer, but Moira and Tom had spent more than half of their lives in their house in Hereford and he didn't think they would consider moving now. It was also the house in which they'd brought up Sue: giving it up would be tantamount to walking away from their memories of her growing up.

He stared at himself in the mirrored door of his wardrobe. He'd told Liam that selling the house in Ealing would be a good idea, but that wouldn't apply to Moira and Tom. Liam wanted a new mother, and there was a good chance that, at some point, he'd have one. Shepherd still missed Sue as much as the day she'd been taken from him, but he was enough of a realist to know that eventually he would find someone else to share his life with. But Tom and Moira would never be able to replace their lost daughter. Memories would be all they ever had of her. Memories, and their grandchild.

Shepherd left the house. He did two laps of his regular five-kilometre route through the streets of Ealing and on to Scotch Common, but it was only when he was towards the end of the second that he began to work up a sweat. He preferred to run out of doors, even when the weather was bad. He'd tried exercising in gyms but the machines were boring, the air was stale, and most were full of middle-aged women waddling on treadmills or men in designer clothes with highlighted hair who seemed more interested in attracting partners than in working on their stamina. Shepherd ran to stay fit, but it also helped him to think. When he was working, more often than not, he was in character. He had to think and act in accordance with whatever role he was playing, not as Dan Shepherd. But when he was running he could be himself: he could think and feel without worrying that he might give himself away. Most of the time he ran on autopilot, barely aware of his surroundings and even less so of his pounding heart and burning muscles.

He thought about Charlotte Button and how his life would change when he worked for SOCA; he thought about the Uddin brothers and how their lives would shortly fall apart; about Liam and his piano lessons; about Moira and Tom and how he ought to let Liam spend more time with them.

He'd taken his work mobile with him, stuffed into one of the side pockets of the canvas rucksack, and it started to ring as he ran down the road towards his house. He stopped. It was Hargrove.

'Not caught you at a bad time, have I?' asked the super-intendent.

'Just running,' said Shepherd.

'The passport they gave you is genuine,' said Hargrove. 'It's in the system. Whoever they've got on the inside has access at a very high level. We need to nail him.'

'Any thoughts?'

'Get them to fix you up another passport. I'll get a name for you, and the Passport Agency systems boys will be watching when it goes up.'

'Before or after the currency run?'

'Do the delivery first. We might get one of the brothers to roll over on the passport guy, depending on how big an operation it is.'

'Ten grand a passport? Even doing a few dozen a year it's not going to be big bucks, is it?'

'It's not about the money, Spider. Anyone on a UK passport has visa-free travel to the States. It would be a terrorist's dream. We need to know how many have been issued and to whom.'

The superintendent cut the connection and Shepherd ran back to his house.

Shepherd drove to a Best Western hotel on the outskirts of Southampton and arrived just before four o'clock. Hargrove and Singh were already there. The superintendent had ordered coffee and sandwiches from room service and was pouring himself a cup when Shepherd walked in.

'Coffee?' he asked.

'Sure,' said Shepherd. 'It's going to be a long night.' He took off his pea coat and tossed it on to a sofa.

'Take your shirt off,' said Singh, 'and drop your trousers.' He had a briefcase full of electrical equipment open on the dressing-table.

'Amar, I never knew you cared.' Shepherd did as he was asked.

Singh held up a small grey plastic box. 'This is the battery pack,' he said. 'No way we can get it any smaller, unfortunately. We need power to transmit over long distances.'

'I'm not putting that up my arse,' joked Shepherd.

'It'll be taped to the small of your back,' said Singh, ignoring his attempt at humour. 'Then I'll run a mike to your chest. It'll pick up everything you say and should give us anyone talking within a few feet of you.'

'Until the engine's on,' said Shepherd. 'You have to shout to make yourself heard.'

'Which is why we'll need you to give us a position before you set off, if at all possible,' said Hargrove.

Singh used strips of tape to fasten the battery to Shepherd's back. Then he held up a metal cylinder the size of a small cigar. 'The transmitter,' he said. 'This we *can* put up your arse.'

'What?'

'Gotchya,' said Singh, grinning. 'The higher this is the better, so I'll strap it to the back of your arm. I'll be running wires from it to the battery and the mike. It's all about transmitting power, so you'll only switch it on when you need it. I'm going to rig an on-off switch under your belt.'

'If they pat me down, I'm screwed,' said Shepherd.

'It's your call, Spider,' said Hargrove. 'If you've any reservations we can do it another way.'

Shepherd watched as Singh ran tape around his left arm. He thought of the last time he'd seen Salik, how the man had hugged him and talked about trust. 'No, it's okay,' he said. 'I'm in with them.'

'Your new best friends?' said Hargrove.

'Pretty much.'

'You're meeting them at the marina, right?'

'At dark,' said Shepherd. 'Seven.' He jumped when he heard a buzzing noise.

Singh was holding an electric razor and grinning. 'Shall I do the honours?' he said.

'Go ahead,' said Shepherd.

Singh shaved off Shepherd's chest hairs.

'We've already got the marina staked out, but I'm guessing all we'll see is you and them having a chat,' said Hargrove. 'We'll be listening in so see if you can get some idea of where you'll be going, and where you'll deliver the cash.'

'Will do.' Shepherd pointed at his chest. 'You missed a bit, Amar,' he said.

Singh grinned. 'The range is good for three miles, maybe four or five if we're lucky,' he said. 'We'll know from the lump where you are and the direction you're heading in.'

'Lump' was police slang for a tracking device.

'Has Europol got the Albanians covered?'

'They've been on them since this afternoon,' said Hargrove. 'Our problem is finding out where the Uddin brothers will be meeting you. We need to see them with the cash. We've got them under surveillance but there's no guarantee that they'll turn up in person. So, you'll have to take it slowly on the return journey, without making it obvious, of course.'

'Got you,' said Shepherd.

Singh taped the microphone to Shepherd's shaved chest, then ran the connecting wires round his body. 'That's you sorted,' he said.

Shepherd pulled up his trousers and slipped on his shirt.

'Do me a favour – put your coat on and nip down to the car park,' said Singh. 'Switch it on and talk to yourself for a bit.'

Shepherd went outside, made sure that no one was within earshot, switched on the transmitter and recited the Lord's Prayer, the first thing that came into his head, as he walked about.

When he got back to the room, Singh confirmed that the transmitter was working. He ran his hands down Shepherd's arm, back and chest. 'You can't feel it,' he said. 'You're fine. Just don't go jumping into the water with it.'

Shepherd picked up a sandwich. 'There's no question of busting them tonight?' he asked Hargrove.

The superintendent shook his head. 'We'll give them a clean run,' he said. 'We'll have all the evidence, but we'll wait until we've got their passport contact before we move in, by which time you'll be long gone.'

★　　★　　★

Shepherd drove the Land Rover into the marina car park and switched off the engine. The Mercedes was already there and the Uddins were standing at the locked gate that led down to the jetties. They were both wearing long coats and gloves and Salik had a thick wool scarf round his neck. He waved and Shepherd raised a hand in response. He reached down and switched on the transmitter, then climbed out of the Land Rover and locked the door.

Salik hurried across the car park and Shepherd sensed he was about to hug him so he stuck out his hand. Salik shook it. 'Everything okay?' asked Shepherd.

'I've spoken to Kreshnik. It's all ready,' said Salik.

Shepherd nodded at Matiur. 'Sure you don't want to come with me?'

Matiur shuddered. 'I'm happier on dry land.'

A big man got out of the Mercedes, wearing a blue waterproof jacket with the hood up and green wellington boots.

'That is Hussain,' said Salik.

'He looks seasick already,' said Shepherd.

'He'll be okay.'

'And when exactly are you going to tell me where I pick up the stuff?'

Salik handed Shepherd a piece of paper. 'Kreshnik gave me the GPS co-ordinates. You can find the place from this?'

Shepherd nodded. 'To within twenty metres,' he said. He studied the numbers on the paper and squinted as he recalled the charts McConnell had shown him. He read out the numbers slowly, as if he was checking them. 'Cap Gris Nez,' he said. 'Good choice. Quiet coastline but the *autoroute* E402 runs close by. Lots of traffic to get lost in.' Shepherd figured that would give Hargrove enough information to go on.

'You know the area?' said Salik.

'I know the charts.'

'You've got a good memory.'

'I get by,' said Shepherd, and put the piece of paper into his back pocket. 'What about coming back? Where do I deliver the stuff?'

'Hussain has the GPS co-ordinates,' said Salik. 'He will give them to you on the way back.'

'Yeah, well, he'd better not lose them,' said Shepherd.

'It's safer that way,' said Matiur.

'Safer for you, you mean,' said Shepherd. 'I'm going to be buzzing around at fifty knots not knowing where I'm going.'

'As soon as you have the cans on board, Hussain will tell you where to go.'

'But it's the south coast, right? I don't want to be running up to John o'Groat's.'

'It's the south coast,' said Salik.

'Which means I won't need to carry extra fuel,' said Shepherd. 'See? That's why it's nice to know these things in advance, Salik. We'd look pretty bloody silly sitting out there with Hussain telling me he wants me to take him a hundred and fifty miles and me having to explain that we don't have enough fuel.'

'It's the south coast,' repeated Salik, 'and I'm sorry if we appear to be keeping you in the dark but there's a lot of money at stake.'

'That's okay. It's not the first time I've been treated like a mushroom,' said Shepherd, 'and it probably won't be the last. Will you be there?'

'Matiur and I will both be there to take delivery,' said Salik. 'Don't worry.'

Shepherd wasn't worried. But at least now Hargrove knew that all he had to do was keep tabs on the Uddin brothers to find out where the consignment was arriving. 'What time did you tell Kreshnik we'd be there?' he asked.

'Eleven o'clock.'

Shepherd glanced at his watch. 'We've plenty of time. Have you arranged any signals?'

'Hussain has a flashlight.'

Shepherd grinned. 'A mobile phone would be better,' he said. His face hardened. 'Is that all he's got?'

'What do you mean?'

'Does he have a gun?'

Salik and Matiur exchanged a look so transparent that he almost laughed. 'It is for security,' said Matiur.

'His or mine?'

'It's a lot of money, Tony,' said Salik.

'And if I try to run off with it, he'll shoot me?'

'Tony, please.'

'If I'd known you were going to send someone to ride shotgun, I'd have worn my vest.'

'If Kreshnik decides to double-cross you, the gun could be useful,' said Matiur.

'If the Albanians decide to double-cross us, we'll both be dead.' Shepherd waved to Hussain and pointed for him to get into the boat. 'We'll head off now,' he said.

Salik stepped forward and hugged Shepherd, surprising him, then kissed his cheek. 'We shall see you later tonight, my friend,' he said. '*Inshallah.*'

'You can bank on it,' said Shepherd. '*Inshallah.*'

Shepherd looked at the GPS monitor. He had turned the brightness right down so that it wouldn't interfere with the night-vision goggles. He slowed the boat to twenty knots and steered to port. 'About a mile to go,' he told Hussain.

Hussain hadn't said much during the crossing: fifteen minutes into the trip he'd leaned over the side and thrown up.

Shepherd followed the course he'd programmed into the GPS navigation unit. There had been a fair amount of traffic, much of it heading to or from Boulogne, but it had all been commercial – ferries or trawlers – no fair-weather sailors or rich men playing with the motor-boats that cluttered the seaway during the day.

Shepherd hadn't bothered giving Hussain night-vision goggles. Out at sea, there was enough of a moon to see by, and all the vessels were equipped with navigation lights. The goggles were a help, but not essential, and he'd told Hussain to warn him if he spotted anything in the water.

The crossing was as uneventful as it had been when Shepherd

had gone out with McConnell, and navigating with the GPS was as simple as driving a train.

He slowed the boat to fifteen knots, still fast enough for it to plane, pushed the night-vision goggles up his forehead and blinked rapidly.

'Are you okay?' asked Hussain.

'I will be in a few minutes, as soon as I get used to the dark.'

'I can't see the land.'

'It's there,' said Shepherd. 'Flash your light.'

Hussain took his torch from his pocket, switched it on and began to wave it.

'Flash it,' said Shepherd. 'On and off. Didn't you prearrange a signal?'

'Salik just said to use a light.'

'Flash it three or four times, then wait,' said Shepherd.

Hussain did as he was told. They stared in the direction of the shore. Nothing.

'They're not there,' said Hussain.

Shepherd turned up the brightness of the GPS screen. They were right on course. He pulled out the piece of paper Salik had given him and cross-checked the reference, which matched. 'We're where we should be.' He pulled back on the throttle and the boat settled into the water, rising and falling with the swell of the waves. 'Flash the torch again.'

Hussain switched it on and off. On and off. On and off. He groaned.

'What's wrong?'

'I feel sick.'

'You'll be fine.'

'I feel really sick.'

'It's because we're not moving forward. You'll be on land in a few minutes. Flash the torch again.'

Hussain did as he was told. 'Where are they?' he whispered.

'Relax,' said Shepherd. 'You're making me nervous.' He frowned as he peered into the darkness. He hoped nothing had happened to spook Kreshnik. Shepherd didn't have as much faith in Europol as Hargrove had. All it would have taken was for one of the French surveillance team members to have shown out and the Albanian would have called off the whole thing. 'Again,' said Shepherd.

Hussain flashed his torch. Almost immediately a powerful single light flashed on and off to Shepherd's right. He applied power gently and moved the boat towards the beam. It flashed again.

'See? You were worrying about nothing,' he said. He increased power and moved closer to the beach where he made out a figure, holding a large flashlight. Some distance behind him, Shepherd could distinguish a squat silhouette, which he assumed was a vehicle. He edged the boat forward until he felt the hull scrape across sand. The man on the beach was wearing dark clothes and a ski mask. Shepherd could see the van clearly now. The rear doors were open and two men, also wearing black clothes, were unloading cans on to the sand. They, too, wore ski masks but from their body shape and the way they moved Shepherd could tell they were Ervin and Artur.

The man with the flashlight went to the van. He tucked the light into his belt and picked up two cans. Shepherd kept the engine ticking over, with just enough throttle to keep the bow on the sand. Hussain jumped off the boat on to the beach, holding the tow rope.

The man with the cans splashed into the water and walked past him. 'Nice night for it,' said Shepherd. The man grunted something unintelligible that he figured was probably an Albanian insult. He shrugged. So long as he wasn't getting his feet wet, he was happy.

Ervin and Artur carried the rest of the cans to the water's edge and left them there, obviously having decided there was no point in them all getting wet. When the man with the flashlight saw what they were doing he yelled at them, but the two Albanians laughed and went back to the van.

This time the man swore in English, then beckoned to Hussain. 'You can help me,' he said, with a strong Albanian accent.

'He has to keep that rope taut,' said Shepherd, 'and I have to keep my hand on the throttle.'

The Albanian swore again as he waded back to the shore to pick up more cans. There were twenty in all. If the three that Rudi Pernaska had brought into the country contained a million euros, the cans on the boat would probably hold closer to seven million. He could see why the Uddin brothers wanted an armed guard on the run.

By the time the last can was in place the Albanian was soaked. Artur and Ervin watched from the beach, their hands on their hips.

'Okay, Hussain, back into the boat,' said Shepherd. He gunned the engine to hold it firm against the sand as Hussain clambered on to the prow, then eased himself over the windshield. It was a far from elegant manoeuvre, accompanied by a lot of grunting and groaning. He sat in his seat, gripped the handrail, and Shepherd put the throttle into reverse to pull the hull slowly off the sand. He kept the boat moving backwards until there was several feet of water under it, then turned slowly so that they were pointing towards England. He pushed the throttle forward, but kept the speed to just under five knots. 'Right, Hussain, where are we going?' he asked.

Hussain took a scrap of paper from inside his waterproof jacket and handed it to him. Shepherd entered the co-ordinates into the GPS. The computer showed the route. It was a beach about twenty miles east of Southampton. He pulled the night-vision goggles over his eyes and pushed the throttle. 'Home, James,' he said, as the boat leaped forward.

'What?' said Hussain.

'Nothing,' said Shepherd. 'Hold tight and enjoy the ride.'

It was just after three in the morning when Shepherd cut the engine and fished his mobile phone out of his pocket. He slid the goggles on top of his head and stared out into the darkness as he pressed 'redial'. Salik answered almost immediately.

'What's wrong?' asked Salik.

'Nothing,' said Shepherd. The rib rose and fell with the swell.

'You're late,' said Salik.

'It took longer than we'd thought to load up,' said Shepherd. 'The Albanians didn't want to get their feet wet. Anyway, are you ready?'

'We've been ready for the last hour,' said Salik.

'Flash your headlights,' Shepherd said.

'Now?'

'Now,' said Shepherd. 'Do it twice.'

Shepherd stared towards the coastline. To his left he saw two beams cut through the night sky, just for a second. Then again. He took a bearing off his compass, then pulled down the goggles and gunned the engine.

He was half a mile from the beach and reached it in less than a minute. He slowed the outboard as he got closer. He could see the Mercedes on the road beyond, and a Transit van. It was the Mercedes headlights that had flashed from the shore. Three men were standing by the van, but they were too far away for him to see who they were.

He repeated the manoeuvre he'd made on the French beach, edging the boat forward slowly. The hull crunched on the pebbles and Shepherd held it where it was. Hussain knew the drill now and climbed over the side with the rope. He held it tight and Shepherd flashed him a thumbs-up.

Salik and Matiur walked over the beach, their shoes slipping on the pebbles. They held their hands out at the sides as they waddled along in their thick overcoats, like a couple of agitated penguins. Two other Asian men, younger and fitter, followed them.

'Tony!' called Salik. 'Everything is okay?'

'Perfect,' said Shepherd. 'Take the stuff off the boat and I'll get the hell out of here.'

Salik said something to the two young men and they hurried over, grabbed two cans each, then jogged back to the van.

'You've done well, Tony, thank you,' said Salik.

'You don't have to thank me. Just have my money ready tomorrow.'

Salik grinned. 'Don't worry, it will be.'

It took about ten minutes to unload the cans, then Hussain tossed the rope into the back of the boat.

Salik waved goodbye. 'We'll see you tomorrow. Our office.'

'I don't know where your office is, Salik,' shouted Shepherd.

'We'll call you.'

'You'd better,' said Shepherd. He put the engine into reverse and edged away from the beach, then turned the boat, pulled on the goggles and made for Southampton.

Shepherd took the boat to its mooring, then drove to the Best Western hotel, where he gave the transmitting equipment to Amar Singh. Hargrove was out with the surveillance team, on the trail of the Uddins.

'You came over as clear as a bell,' said Singh. 'Hargrove called the French and they were there to see the whole thing. Captured it on film with infra-red cameras. Hargrove told me to tell you what a great job you did.'

'Thanks,' said Shepherd, putting his shirt back on.

'You heard he's leaving, right?'

'Onwards and upwards.'

'Hard act to follow,' said Singh.

'No question.'

'You heard about his replacement?'

Shepherd shrugged. Singh was on attachment from NCIS and, as such, wasn't a full member of Hargrove's team so he didn't want to say too much. 'I've only just found out he was moving on,' he said. 'Why? What have you heard?'

Singh stashed the equipment in his briefcase. 'Just that he's going to New Scotland Yard. Office job.'

'Promotion, right?'

'Yeah. Chief super. At least we'll have friends in high places.'

Shepherd drank two cups of coffee and ate a beef-salad sandwich before he drove back to London. It was seven thirty in the morning when he parked in front of his house. Liam was sitting at the kitchen table, eating toast and jam.

'What happened to the cheesy scrambled eggs?' asked Shepherd, dropping on to a chair opposite him.

'I fancied a change,' said Liam.

Katra appeared at the door. 'You're back!'

'Well, if I'm not, a stranger just stole this kid's toast.' Shepherd grabbed a slice off Liam's plate and stuffed it into his mouth.

'Hey!' shouted Liam.

'I'll make more,' said Katra.

'How were Gran and Granddad?' asked Shepherd.

'Okay. They've got a PlayStation Two.'

'What?'

'And a load of games.'

'Well, that must be for your benefit. I can't see Tom and Moira playing video games.' He frowned. 'Hey, didn't I say that losing your PlayStation was part of your punishment?'

'It wasn't my PlayStation, it was Gran's PlayStation,' said Liam, speaking slowly as if Shepherd was hard of hearing. 'Anyway, it was a PlayStation Two, not a PlayStation One.'

'Sounds like you're going to be a defence lawyer when you grow up,' said Shepherd. 'What's happening about the piano lessons?' he asked.

'What piano lessons?' said Liam.

'You wanted to learn the piano, right?'

Liam pulled a face. 'The guitar's better – *bass* guitar.'

Shepherd leaned back in the chair, grinning. 'She likes somebody else, right?'

'I dunno what you mean.'

'The piano girl. She's not as pretty as she was a few days ago. Hey, I'm not complaining. A guitar is a tenth the price of a piano.'

'You're going to buy me one?'

Shepherd held up a hand. 'That's not what I said. You're grounded, remember? But you'll be out on remission by Christmas, so unless you've fixated on the trombone by then, I don't see why you can't have one.'

'Cool!'

'Did your gran say anything about me?'

'Asked how you were.'

'And what did you say?'

'I said you were okay.'

'And am I?'

'What?'

'Am I okay?' asked Shepherd.

'Yes.'

Shepherd leaned over and gave him a hug.

'But you don't half smell bad.'

Kathy Gift's high heels clicked along the walkway as she headed towards the Starbucks outlet. Down to her left were the platforms of Paddington station, and below, harried-looking men in suits with briefcases next to their stools plucked small plates off the Yo Sushi conveyor belt. She smiled to herself. Fast food, literally.

She took off her raincoat and shook it, then went into the coffee shop. A woman in her forties was already getting to her feet. Gift wasn't surprised at the ease with which Charlotte Button had recognised her. As an MI5 high-flyer, she would have had access to Gift's police file, and more.

Button smiled and extended her hand. 'Good to meet you, Dr Gift.'

'Kathy, please,' said Gift.

'Excellent,' said Button. 'Titles do get in the way, don't they? I'm Charlie.' They shook hands. Gift noted the elegantly painted nails and the thin gold bracelet with half a dozen charms. It was a strangely old-fashioned piece of jewellery for an intelligence officer to wear, she thought, especially one who was meeting a psychologist.

'My grandmother's,' said Button. 'She left it to me and I always wear it on her birthday. What can I get you?'

Gift asked for a low-fat latte. As she sat down she wondered if she'd been staring at the charm bracelet. She was sure she hadn't, but even a glance hadn't gone unnoticed. Gift was normally the one who did the observing, picking up on the body language and subtle signals, spoken and unspoken, that gave her the clues she needed to assess the personality of her clients. It made her feel uneasy to be in the presence of someone equally adept at reading people. She was sure that Button had already noticed the Star of David on the gold chain round her neck, and the absence of a ring on her wedding finger.

She watched Button order the coffee. The other woman looked like the naturally slim type. Her heels weren't low enough to be frumpy, or high enough to be tarty. Bally, perhaps. Or Gucci. Good legs, a skirt that ended a few inches above the knee, and a long jacket, a blue so dark it was almost black. Her hair shone glossily, black without a trace of grey. Her make-up was expertly applied, a touch of eye-shadow, mascara and lipstick, which might be Lancôme's Chilled Rose. Gift used the same colour. Button could have been a merchant banker or a sales director: efficient, confident, with an accent that suggested a Home Counties childhood and a public-school education. No wedding ring. A Rolex watch. Her money could have come from her inheritance or she might have a wealthy husband who didn't mind that she didn't wear a ring.

Button returned with the latte and placed it on the table, then sat opposite Gift. 'I'm sorry to ask you to meet me here, but I've got a train to catch and I thought I'd kill two birds, as it were.'

'It's fine,' said Gift. 'Actually, I'm a caffeine addict.' She smiled brightly but kicked herself mentally for the slip. Addiction was a weakness, and she didn't want to show any in front of this woman.

Button raised her mug. 'Me too,' she said. She took a sip and dabbed at her lips with a napkin. 'So, Dan Shepherd.'

'Right,' said Gift.

'Superintendent Hargrove has told you about the new arrangement? The undercover unit is being co-opted into the Serious Organised Crime Agency and he's moving on to pastures new.

I'm taking some of his operatives into the agency. Others will return to regular police work.'

Gift nodded but didn't say anything.

'I'm interested in your assessment of Dan, as a person and as an undercover officer.'

'You've seen my reports.'

'I never rely solely on written reports,' said Button. 'People are always so much more careful when they commit to paper, aren't they?'

'The written word encourages accuracy and precision, of course.'

Button smiled encouragingly. 'Of course. But we both know the world isn't black and white. There are so many shades of grey. And it's the grey I'm interested in.'

'Specifically?'

'You gave him a clean bill of health after your last session,' said Button.

'He was fit for undercover work,' said Gift.

'Your report is pass or fail, isn't it? An operative is either suitable or not suitable?'

'If I have specific reservations, I make a note of them,' said Gift. 'In Dan's case, I had no reservations.'

'He's very intelligent, isn't he? A quick thinker?'

'His IQ is high, and he's helped by having a photographic memory.'

'I read that,' said Button. 'Is it genuinely photographic?'

'Total recall of anything he sees or hears,' said Gift. 'He can remember content but not necessarily context. He could memorise a physics book, for instance, but that wouldn't mean he could explain the laws of relativity to you. Knowing something and understanding something aren't the same thing, which is why he never did especially well academically.'

'Faces?'

'Perfect recall,' said Gift.

'A useful skill in undercover work,' said Button. 'That and his charm would keep him out of trouble, I'd guess.'

'Charm?'

Button laughed. 'Come on, you know what I mean. He's good-looking and he's got that boyish-charm thing going.'

Button was a skilled interviewer and Gift had the distinct impression that she was being tested. From the way the conversation was going, it felt as if she was being assessed as much as Shepherd. 'I'm not sure that his looks have anything to do with his work,' she said carefully.

Button arched one eyebrow. 'Really? In my experience people trust good-looking people more readily than ugly ones. It's not fair, but it's the way of the world. If you're going to lie and deceive, you've a better chance of getting away with it if you're attractive.'

'I suppose so,' said Gift.

'The point I'm making is that, on paper at least, Dan is the perfect undercover agent. His SAS background, his trick memory, his charm.'

'He's good at his job,' agreed Gift.

'Not too good, though?'

'Too good?'

'Over-confidence can be as much of a liability as lack of ability,' said Button. 'Every year we have James Bond wannabes trying to join up, and we go to a lot of trouble to weed them out. They think that joining MI5 means they get a licence to kill.' She looked expectantly at Gift, waiting for her to speak.

Gift was adept at playing the silence game, leaving a long pause so that the other person would speak to fill the gap. It was a standard element in any psychologist's armoury, but she doubted it would be effective against Button. She hated to let the MI5 officer win the mental game, but the alternative was to sit there in silence, which would only make her appear defensive. 'Dan isn't exactly an adrenaline junkie,' she said. 'He'd have stayed in the SAS if that was so. Police work is a lot more restrained than serving with Special Forces.'

'But leaving the SAS was his wife's idea, wasn't it?'

'She thought that it wasn't the right career for a husband and father, and he agreed.'

'Under protest?'

'I don't think he was happy about the move,' said Gift. 'He had visions of pounding the beat, but that's not how it worked out. He didn't even go through basic training.'

'Straight into the undercover unit?'

'Exactly.'

'Which, I suppose, was out of the frying-pan and into the fire?'

'That was how his wife saw it. He seemed to be at greater risk as an undercover policeman than he was in the SAS, where at least he was always with fellow soldiers. Working undercover meant he was alone most of the time.'

'He was undercover in prison when his wife died, wasn't he?'

Gift nodded. It was a curious conversation. Button was telling her things she already knew from Shepherd's file. She didn't seem interested in the facts, more in Gift's interpretation of them. Which meant that the meeting wasn't about him, it was about her. 'He was tasked with getting close to an international drug-dealer who was behind bars. While he was undercover in prison, his wife was killed in a car accident.'

'And he decided to remain in prison to continue with the job, rather than abort and take care of his son?'

'It was his decision,' said Gift.

'Heck of a call to make,' said Button.

'It was an important case. If he'd pulled out, the dealer would have got away with it.'

'So Dan will put job before family?'

'He tries to juggle them,' said Gift. 'Are you married, Charlie?'

'Twelve years,' said Button.

'Children?'

'A girl,' said Button. 'Ten.'

'Then I suppose you can empathise with Dan, trying to mix parenthood with a career.'

Button smiled, showing white teeth so perfect they could only have been the result of good genes or expensive orthodontic work. 'You'll need a much higher security clearance to start debriefing me, Kathy,' she said.

Gift returned the smile. 'I wasn't trying to analyse you,' she said. 'I was just making the point that you and Dan have something in common. I think he's as capable as you are of mixing the two.' She sipped her coffee. 'What happens to me under the new regime? Do I continue to provide assessments on Dan and the rest of the undercover team?'

'Absolutely.'

'And were you as sure of that prior to this meeting?'

'You mean, was this an interview?' Button shook her head. 'No, absolutely not. Dan needs all the continuity he can get. It's enough of a shock to his system that he's losing Superintendent Hargrove. In fact, I'd like to start sending you more of my people. I'm impressed by your work.'

'And will you be needing briefings like this, or will written reports be enough?'

'Didn't Superintendent Hargrove see you regularly?'

'We met occasionally, but he was satisfied with written reports.'

'I'll need written reports, obviously, but I'll also want to talk to you face to face.'

'For the grey areas?'

'Exactly,' said Button. 'A lot of my operatives will be moving into a different league, and I need to know they can take the pressure.'

'I'm not sure I follow you.'

'Take Dan, for instance. Until now he's been working on basic criminal cases. He poses as a drug-dealer, a bank robber, a contract killer, and he gathers evidence against criminals. Hard-core, some of them, but the Serious Organised Crime Agency will go after bigger fish. The IRA's criminal activities, for instance. The Russian Mafia. The Colombians. Al-Qaeda. If I'm putting Dan up against them I need to know he won't crack under the pressure.'

Gift raised her eyebrows. 'He's tough. He'll cope.'

'That's my view, too,' said Button. She glanced at her watch. 'I must go,' she said. She stood up and offered her hand, which Gift shook.

She left the coffee shop and Gift moved with her coffee to a seat by the window. From there she could look down at the platforms below. Button went down the stairs, then walked away from the trains towards the taxi rank. Gift smiled to herself. She'd caught Charlotte Button in a deliberate lie. She wasn't there to catch a train. It had been an unnecessary lie, too, because it was of no concern to her where Button was going. Gift wondered why she had lied. Habit, maybe. Instinct. Or because the lie was simpler than the truth, whatever it was. Perhaps the Lancôme lipstick and the mascara weren't for the office but for a lover. Perhaps there was more to Charlotte Button than met the eye.

A phone woke Shepherd from a dreamless sleep. It was Tony Corke's. He squinted at his watch – just after ten o'clock in the morning. He took a couple of deep breaths to clear his head. He was Tony Corke, seaman, with a son he rarely saw and a court case looming. Early mornings and late nights were always the most dangerous times, when he was most likely to let his mask slip. He ran through his legend, ticking all the mental boxes. Dan Shepherd was pushed into the background. His feelings and memories had to be locked away because they might betray him. He took the call. 'Yeah?' he said.

'Tony, it's me. Salik.'

'Hiya, Salik. How's it going?'

'Very well,' said Salik. 'Very well indeed. We have something for you, Tony.'

'Music to my ears,' said Shepherd. 'So, where do we meet?'

'Where are you?'

'At home,' said Shepherd, 'but I'm coming in to London so it's not a problem.'

'Why don't you meet us at our office at, say, five o'clock? We can have a chat.'

'Fine,' said Shepherd.

'Do you have a pen? I'll give you the address.'

Shepherd didn't need a pen. He knew the address already. It was the *bureau de change* in Edgware Road.

Shepherd walked into the pub. Hargrove was standing at the bar, staring at a television set on a shelf close to the ceiling. A cricket match. Shepherd didn't care for cricket. He wasn't a big fan of games – never had been, even at school. It wasn't that he didn't enjoy being part of a team: the SAS was all about teamwork. The police, too – even on undercover cases, Shepherd was always part of a team. He just couldn't understand what was enjoyable about throwing a ball at three pieces of wood. Or hitting one with a piece of metal at the end of a stick and walking after it. He was even less convinced by the pleasure to be had in watching others play. Spending ninety minutes watching two groups of men chasing a ball seemed to Shepherd a total waste of time. But that wasn't an argument he ever wanted to have with the superintendent, who was a diehard cricket and rugby fan, and always wore cufflinks with a cricket motif.

'Job well done, Spider,' said Hargrove. 'Jameson's and ice?'

Shepherd nodded. Hargrove ordered it, and another pint of lager for himself. He was wearing a tweed jacket with a red waistcoat, dark trousers and brown brogues: his off-duty uniform. When he was working, he always wore a suit.

'We've got all we need to put the Uddin brothers away on currency smuggling, and the French had the Albanians covered at every step of the way,' said Hargrove.

'Are they arresting them?'

'Not yet. They want confirmation that the euros are coming from the North Koreans.'

'And then what? A strongly worded letter to the ambassador? They can't put a whole country on trial.'

'This is bigger than one court case, Spider. It's about destabilising economies. It's political.'

Shepherd shook his head. 'I don't agree. It's about profits. The euro economy is – what? Trillions? Trillions upon trillions? A few million isn't going to hurt economies as big as France and Germany. A few billion could be absorbed without anyone noticing.'

Their drinks arrived. The superintendent paid with a twenty-pound note and waited until the barman had given him his change before he replied. 'You might be right.'

'I know I am. They should do Kreshnik now, take him out of circulation.'

The superintendent sipped his lager. 'There's a problem,' he said.

'Don't tell me,' said Shepherd. 'He never went near the money.'

'His men did. We might get them to give evidence against him down the line.'

'They'll have family in Albania and they know what'll happen if they cross him.'

'Let's look on the bright side, shall we? His men will be jailed so Kreshnik will have to shut down the operation.'

'And start up a new one.' Shepherd grimaced. 'It's always this way, isn't it? The little fish get banged up while the sharks live to fight another day. And the really small fish, like Rudi Pernaska, kill themselves in police custody.'

'Spider . . .'

'I know, I know. I look at the glass and see it's half empty while others see it's half full. But the thing is, the glass *is* half empty. There's no getting away from it. And the world is a shitty place full of shitty people. And there's no such thing as fair any more. The meek will never inherit the world, they'll just get shafted until the end of time.'

Hargrove raised eyebrows. 'Rough day?'

Shepherd smiled thinly. 'Rough year,' he said.

'I'm not saying that Kreshnik won't get his comeuppance eventually, but this time we don't have enough evidence. Europol have him in their sights, though.'

'I won't be holding my breath,' said Shepherd. 'Their resources are as stretched as ours. That's always the problem, isn't it? It costs time and money to nail the big guys, and unless it's a one hundred per cent sure thing the accountants say it's not worth committing the resources.'

'Don't be too sure,' said Hargrove. 'Kreshnik's involved with drugs and if any are ending up in the States the Americans will be on the case and money will be no object.'

'Great. So the plan now is for the Americans to bail us out.' Shepherd drained his glass. 'Another?' he said. Hargrove gestured at his barely touched pint. 'Well, I need one,' said Shepherd. He waved at the barman and pointed at his empty glass.

'What's wrong, Spider?'

Shepherd sighed. 'Nothing,' he said. 'Nothing much.'

'The Uddin brothers? Is that it?'

Shepherd smiled. The superintendent could always tell what was on his mind. That was what made him such a good boss. 'They're nice guys and they're going to go down. They'll be taken away from their families and banged up with drug-dealers, burglars and child-molesters for bringing in paper.'

'Millions of counterfeit euros, actually,' said Hargrove.

'Paper,' repeated Shepherd. 'They haven't hurt or killed anyone – it's as close to a victimless crime as you can get. Yet they go to prison, while lowlifes like Kreshnik live in million-pound apartments in Paris.'

'So, life's unfair,' said Hargrove. 'We know that. But it doesn't mean we don't put away people who break the law.'

Shepherd's second whiskey and ice arrived and he paid for it, telling the barman to keep the change. 'Sometimes it looks like we don't aim high enough.'

'Well, maybe that'll change with SOCA,' said Hargrove. 'I get the feeling that Charlotte Button will choose her own targets. I've always been at the beck and call of the various forces who use the unit, but she's got more autonomy so you might get your wish.'

'Cheers to that,' said Shepherd, raising his glass. The superintendent clinked his against Shepherd's and they drank.

'Which brings me to why I'm here,' said Hargrove. 'As of

today, I'm in my new post. Well, as of yesterday, actually.'

The news took Shepherd by surprise, even though he had known the move was imminent. 'Congratulations,' he said. He heard the bitterness in his voice and forced himself to smile. 'Seriously, congratulations,' he said. 'I'll miss you.'

Hargrove nodded. 'I'll miss you, too. The new job's going to be a hell of a lot less exciting than working with you guys.'

'Until the shit hits the fan,' said Shepherd.

'Well, if we do our job right, the shit won't ever get near the fan.'

'Do you believe that?'

'Who knows? Anthrax from a plane, a dirty bomb in a container on a freighter, a barge of explosives sailing up the Thames to the Houses of Parliament. We can make all the contingency plans we want, but it's like the IRA said when they almost blew up Margaret Thatcher in Brighton . . .'

'The government was lucky, but they have to be lucky all the time,' said Shepherd. 'The bad guys only have to be lucky once.'

'Exactly. And al-Qaeda are way more dangerous than the IRA ever was. The IRA would never have brought down a plane or thought about biological weapons. They had limits. Lines they wouldn't cross. We had some idea of how they thought, how they operated, but al-Qaeda have thrown away the rule book.' He sipped his lager. 'Anyway, hopefully we'll be lucky.'

'*Inshallah*,' said Shepherd.

Hargrove raised an eyebrow.

'God willing,' explained Shepherd.

'*Inshallah*,' said Hargrove. He rapped the bar with his knuckles. 'Touch wood.'

'So, what do I do now?' asked Shepherd. 'I'm working for SOCA as of today?'

'You're in a transition phase,' said Hargrove. 'As always, there's paperwork and human-resources stuff to work through. But Charlotte Button will phone you later today to finalise the transfer.'

'And what about the Uddin brothers?'

'She'll take over that operation. Everyone's keen that we find out who their man is in the Passport Agency.' He smiled. 'I'm going to have to stop saying "we", aren't I?'

'I'm going to see them this afternoon at five to collect the money. Will you be handling that or Button?'

Shepherd's mobile rang. He pulled it out of his jacket pocket and grinned. 'Speak of the devil,' he said.

Shepherd popped a piece of gum into his mouth and chewed slowly. He didn't like turning up to meet his new boss with whiskey on his breath, but Button had said she wanted to see him that afternoon and it had been an order rather than a request. He took a black cab and had it drop him a quarter of a mile from the address she'd given him: a shopping street in Marylebone. He doubted she would pull her tailing trick again, but he didn't want to take the risk. He spent ten minutes making sure he wasn't being tailed, then headed for the office where they were to meet. The entrance was between two shops – a high-class butcher and a florist. There were three brass nameplates by the door, and an entryphone with three buttons. The three firms were a solicitor's, a travel agency and an accountant's. He pressed the button for the accountant and Charlotte Button's voice crackled on the intercom. 'Second floor,' she said.

The door buzzed and Shepherd went in. Button was waiting for him on the second floor in an office lined with filing cabinets and volumes on tax law. There were four desks, and a door that led to another office.

'This is very cloak-and-dagger,' said Shepherd, as Button closed the door.

'I understand Sam Hargrove preferred to meet in pubs or at rugby matches,' said Button. 'Hardly my style.'

'There's always the Ritz,' said Shepherd.

'I can't start pulling out investigation files in full view of the ladies-who-lunch. We have a number of offices like this so I plan to make full use of them.'

She took him through to the interior office, which contained a big oak desk and a high-backed executive chair, with two smaller ones facing it. A large whiteboard bore several dozen photographs, head and shoulders shots.

Button sat down in the big chair and motioned him to a seat. 'Congratulations on the money run. I gather Europol are happy with the way things went.'

'They're not busting the Albanian guy who's running the show,' said Shepherd, 'but, yeah, it went well.'

'We're keen to follow up the Passport Agency angle,' said Button. 'We're not going to pull the Uddin brothers in until we've nailed their contact.'

'Okay,' said Shepherd. 'I'm going in to their office today at five to get my money.'

'I'd like you to wear a wire. You've established enough trust with them, haven't you?'

'They've not given me a second glance at the last couple of meetings.'

'She slid an envelope across the desk. 'Give them these details, and we'll be watching to see who enters them into the system.'

Shepherd took the envelope. 'What happens to the money I get?'

'You keep it,' said Button, and grinned at the surprise on his face. 'Joke,' she said. 'Take it home with you and I'll arrange to have it collected.'

'So that's it?' he said. 'I'm now employed by SOCA?'

'Welcome aboard,' she said.

'I thought there'd be more to it. Paperwork and stuff.'

'That'll be on its way. Your next pay cheque will be from the Met, but after that you'll be on SOCA's payroll.' She smiled. 'With a pretty hefty increase.'

'Thanks for that,' he said.

'Someone from Human Resources will talk to you about pensions, holidays and all that stuff. Any problems, let me know, but I'm sure there won't be.'

'Logistics? Vehicles and equipment?'

'I'll introduce you to our people as and when we need them. But you know Amar Singh from NCIS?'

'He's been working on the currency case.'

'He's on our tech team.'

'That's good to hear.'

'I'll get him to call you later to arrange the wire.'

'And what about the other undercover operatives?'

'The same applies. As and when you work with other team members, you'll be introduced. But there'll be no office parties or group hugs. There might be times when you come up against other members of the team without knowing it.'

'That could be dangerous.'

'On the contrary, it could be a life-saver. The fewer people who know what you do, the fewer people there are who can betray you.'

'What about Jimmy Sharpe?'

Button nodded. 'He's in. First-class operator. You can use him today as back-up.'

'Paul Joyce?'

'Decided he'd prefer to remain with the Met. I wanted him on board – it was his call.'

Shepherd wanted to run a number of other names by her, but there would be time for that later. 'What about cases? Do you have some lined up?'

Button smiled thinly. 'Oh, yes,' she said. 'My bosses have given me a list of targets. High-profile villains they regard as priorities. But one step at a time, Spider. We're hitting the ground running but we're not rushing into anything. The Uddin brothers and their passports are your priority.'

'It's a small deal, financially. Ten grand a passport.'

'But a huge deal politically,' said Button. She stood up and went to the whiteboard. 'Look at this.'

Shepherd joined her and stared at the photographs. There were forty in all; most were in colour but a handful were black and white. All but two were men. A few weren't even photographs but artists' impressions.

'Let me tell you a story,' said Button. 'It goes back to 1992 when the government of Bosnia and Herzegovina held a referendum on independence. The result was a call for independence and separation from Serbia, and the result was civil war, with Bosnian Serbs murdering thousands of Bosnian Muslims. Ethnic-cleansing on a massive scale, just a few hours' flight from London. Muslim fighters from all over the world, America, Russia and Europe, piled into the former Yugoslavia to help. Now jump ahead a few years. The UN peacekeepers are in, the civil war is over. Money is pouring into Bosnia to pay for reconstruction. Millions of dollars. A big chunk comes from Saudi Arabia. Muslims helping Muslims. Nothing wrong with that. King Fahd puts in $100 million from his own pocket. The Saudi government pours in $450 million, restores water supplies, rebuilds schools and mosques, and takes care of seven thousand orphans. A whole raft of Saudi-funded aid agencies and charities moves in. And that's where the trouble starts. Move ahead to 2001. The Americans invade Afghanistan a few weeks after the attacks on the World Trade Center. In 2003, they invade Iraq. Elements of the Muslim world see America as the enemy and want revenge. The *jihad* begins in earnest. Muslim terrorists carry out atrocities around the world. Terror has a new face – Arab men with beards and baggy trousers. The world goes on high alert. Every Arab who gets on to a plane is watched. Every Arab family is regarded with suspicion. Arabs and Asians get stopped more often by the police. Their passports are looked at more closely. It gets harder and harder for Arabs to travel, to apply for visas, to book into hotels, to hire cars. And that's when we come back to Bosnia.'

She walked over to a window and looked down at the street below.

'London is a target. As are most European cities. Our landmarks, our stations, our football stadiums. Al-Qaeda wants to kill, maim and destroy our way of life. And for that they need troops. Warriors prepared to die for the cause.'

'Suicide-bombers?'

'Right. But men and women who can blend, who can move through Western countries without attracting attention, who won't get picked up by racial profiling. Al-Qaeda targeted two groups as fulfilling these criteria. The first are the Invisibles, second or third generation Muslims born in the West, of Asian or Middle Eastern heritage, but with full British citizenship. We think there are up to ten thousand Invisibles in the UK sympathetic to the al-Qaeda cause, and we know up to three thousand have been through some form of al-Qaeda training overseas. And they started looking for non-Arab Muslims, and Bosnia was the perfect hunting ground. Several of the charities there became recruiting centres for the *jihad*. The Americans discovered a stack of terrorist-related material at the offices of one of Saudi Arabia's leading aid agencies, including instructions for using crop-duster aircraft to spray poisons from the air, US State Department identification badges, photographs and maps showing the location of government buildings. Half a dozen charities in Sarajevo have been shut down in the last few years because of suspicious finances. Money that was supposed to be used for the reconstruction of Bosnia has been channelled into terrorist networks. Millions upon millions of dollars.'

Button pointed at the photographs on the whiteboard. 'Those are just some of the men and women we suspect have been recruited to the al-Qaeda cause out of Bosnia. And what makes them so dangerous is that none is an Arab. They can fly under our radar, assuming that their paperwork is in order.'

'And you think they could be using the Uddin brothers for passports?'

'We need to know who their contact is, and who he has supplied passports to,' said Button. 'It could just be that they're helping economic migrants get into the country by the back door. Or something more sinister may be going on. That's what we need to know. And we need to know quickly.'

Shepherd nodded at the photographs. 'And these are all terrorists active in the UK?'

'They're all Muslims, and they were all in Bosnia at some

point. And they're all missing now – or, at least, unaccounted for. The Americans are looking for them. So are we.'

'Isn't there any facial-recognition system at the Passport Agency office same as there is for fingerprints? Cross-check these photographs with photographs submitted for passports?'

'It's been worked on, but there's no system in place yet. Once we have biometric passports, that will change. But it doesn't help us now. We need to find out who the Uddin brothers have supplied with passports and if any are on this board.'

'And how am I supposed to do that?'

'I'm not suggesting you can,' she said. 'But see how much the Uddin brothers know. See if they'll tell you how many passports they've arranged over the years for what sort of customers. Anything you can get will help.'

'When do they get busted?'

'It's still being discussed,' said Button. 'It depends how extensive the passport operation is, and how closely linked the passport guy is to the brothers. What we've got to decide is whether we pull in the passport guy as soon as we identify him, or let him run and watch him. My former colleagues in Five have been informed, and they're pushing to leave him in place.'

'So that we can see who else he's supplying with passports?'

'Exactly. If potential terrorists are using him, there'd be more to gain from watching and waiting. If it's just economic migrants, we can bust him and plug the hole. It could be that we pull the Uddin brothers in for the currency-smuggling but leave the passport guy in place. It's all up in the air.'

'Okay,' said Shepherd.

'I'm sorry if it sounds a bit vague, but it's complex. I know it'd be a lot easier if we were going after a drug-dealer or an armed robber. Catch them in the act and it's on to the next case. As soon as there's the possibility of terrorist activity, the game moves up a notch.'

Shepherd frowned. 'Game?'

'You know what I mean.'

Shepherd knew exactly what she meant. He'd worked with operatives from the intelligence services before, British and American, and they often treated their cases as an academic exercise. They enjoyed pitting their wits against an enemy who was their intellectual equal, took pleasure in every victory and were embittered by defeat. Button had said 'game' and that was what she meant. Her job didn't involve putting herself in harm's way: that was what Shepherd was for. He'd be the one on the ground, risking a bullet in the head or a knife in the gut, lying, cheating and doing whatever it took to take down the enemy. He'd be the one walking into the lion's den with a recording device taped to his back. He didn't regard what he did as a game. He put away criminals because they hurt other people physically, stole from them or plied them with drugs. Each case was a battle, and while he often doubted that he'd win the war, he was determined to win every battle he fought.

Button could sense Shepherd's concern. 'It's an expression,' she said.

It was – but it was more than that: it was an attitude. And when you were facing dangerous criminals, it could be a dangerous one. Generally spies didn't shoot other spies, but drug-dealers most definitely put bullets into undercover cops. When he'd faced Kreshnik in the apartment in Paris, it hadn't been a game, and it was important that Charlotte Button understood that. 'No problem,' he said. He remembered how she'd taken pleasure in telling him she'd followed him to the Ritz. She'd been playing a game then, no question about it.

'I wasn't minimising what I'm asking you to do, Dan,' she said. 'It really is just an expression.'

'It's fine,' said Shepherd. He looked at the photographs and artists' impressions on the whiteboard and wondered how many of those men and women thought of the *jihad* as a game.

Shepherd walked slowly along the pavement, checking reflections in shop windows, more from habit than any fear that he was being followed. The Uddin brothers' *bureau de change* was little more than a booth set in a row of shops, with a staircase next to it that led up to the offices. An Asian youth with slicked-back hair was sitting in a glass-fronted cubicle next to an electronic board that listed exchange rates in red numbers. He was engrossed in a book. Plenty of people were walking by, but no one seemed interested in changing money. It was a busy street. There was an Argos, a Woolworth's, small shops selling electrical equipment and phone cards, and an amusement arcade packed with fruit machines. The bulk of the shoppers were Arabs, and along the street there were several Arab coffee shops with tables on the pavements where men in long white robes sat and sipped strong, sweet coffee and sucked on ornate hookah pipes.

Shepherd crossed the road at a set of traffic-lights. A huddle of women clothed from head to foot in black burkhas, with veiled letterbox slots at eye level, scuttled out of Argos weighed down with bulging carrier-bags. They waved frantically at a black cab and climbed into the back.

The youth didn't look up from his book as Shepherd walked past him and headed up the stairs to Salik's office. He had a tight feeling in his stomach. He always did when he was wearing a wire. He could feel the battery pack and the digital recorder in the small of his back, the wire that wound round his waist under his shirt, the microphone taped to his chest. He hated carrying digital recorders, but sometimes they were a necessary evil. Devices like the transmitting mobiles and long-distance microphones were all well and good but the quality was variable. Stand-alone recorders with good-quality microphones were pretty much foolproof, so long as they remained hidden. Shepherd only used them when he was sure he had the trust of the people he was talking to, and he knew the Uddin brothers trusted him. He had just brought in seven million euros of counterfeit currency for them and he hadn't even insisted on being paid in advance.

On the first floor he came to a white-painted door with a plastic plaque that displayed the name of the *bureau de change* in large capital letters and underneath it half a dozen other company names in smaller type. Shepherd knocked.

An Asian youth opened the door. He might have been the elder brother of the boy downstairs, although his hair was longer and he was wearing horn-rimmed glasses.

'I'm here to see Salik and Matiur,' said Shepherd.

'Tony, don't stand on ceremony, come on in,' called Salik.

The office was spacious, with gunmetal grey blinds covering the windows and desks in three corners, each with a computer and flat-screen monitor on it. There was a bank of half a dozen fax machines on a table under one window and a large oval teak table with eight chairs round it. Salik and Matiur were sitting at the table. A tall, long-spouted earthenware teapot stood in front of them with four handleless mugs.

'Tony,' said Salik. He hurried around the table to give Shepherd a hug. Shepherd untangled himself before the other man could feel the concealed recording device. 'Sunday was perfect – better than perfect.'

The youth sat down at one of the computer terminals and began to tap on the keyboard. Matiur stood up and Shepherd reached out to shake hands. 'You are a good man,' said Matiur. 'A professional.'

'Well, hopefully we can do it again some time soon,' said Shepherd.

Salik sat down and picked up the teapot. 'Have some mint tea,' he said. 'We import it.'

Shepherd joined him. 'You have your fingers in a lot of pies,' he said, taking a cup.

'You have to diversify,' said Salik. 'Businesses are cyclic. If you have only one, there are peaks and troughs.' He reached under the table and pulled out a leather briefcase. 'This is yours, Tony.' He handed it to Shepherd, who put it on his lap and clicked the two locks. The case was full of bundles of banknotes, fives, tens and twenties. 'I hope this is all real,' he said.

Salik and Matiur laughed. 'You have our money-back guarantee,' said Salik. 'Fifty thousand pounds, and it is all real.'

Shepherd took out a bundle and counted it carefully. Tony Corke needed the cash and he'd be sure to count every note. When he'd assured himself that there was fifty thousand pounds in the case, he said, 'Thanks. Now I need to talk to you.'

'What about?' asked Salik.

'My court case.' Shepherd closed the briefcase. 'This is all well and good but my solicitor's costing me an arm and a leg.'

'Lawyers are expensive,' said Salik. 'Does he think he can keep you out of jail?'

Shepherd scowled. 'It'd take a miracle to do that, which is why we need to talk.'

'You want more money? Is that it?'

'I want Tony Corke to disappear.'

'But you said you'd lose your house if you run. You had to put it up as surety for your bail, you said.'

'They'll take the house, sure, but there's a big mortgage on it. With the equity in it and the cash, I'd be running away from eighty grand. If I'm going to be doing more runs for you, money won't be a problem.'

'So?'

'I need a new identity. A new life.'

'You have a passport already.'

'Yes, but I don't have a birth certificate to go with it. Or any other paperwork.' He reached into his coat and pulled out the envelope Button had given him. 'I've got paperwork here on a guy who died a few years ago. He was a friend of a friend. He never had a passport so he's not in the system, but he has a birth certificate, a school record, a university degree and a national-insurance number. With a passport, I'll have a ready-to-use new identity.'

'But if he died, there'll be a death certificate and the national-insurance number will have been cancelled,' said Salik. He took the envelope and examined the papers.

'He died overseas,' said Shepherd. 'He was an oil-worker out in the Middle East. He rarely visited the UK and died in a car accident in Malaysia. He had no relatives and was cremated out there. No death certificate's been filed here – I checked.'

Salik peered at the birth certificate. 'Christopher Donovan?'

'I look like a Chris, don't I?'

'This would make you thirty-seven?'

'So I gain a couple of years. It's not a problem.'

Salik nodded. 'Okay. The fee will be the same as last time. Ten thousand pounds.'

Shepherd opened the briefcase and gave Salik ten thousand pounds. Then he produced his wallet, fished out two passport photographs and gave them to Salik. 'How reliable is your guy?' he asked.

'What do you mean?'

'I'm going to be using the new identity for the rest of my life, hopefully. What if he gets busted down the line? Presumably there'll be a record of every guy he gave passports to.'

'He's careful,' said Salik. 'So are we. We don't keep records. We take the money and we hand over the passports. That's all.'

'I'd like to meet him,' said Shepherd. 'To reassure myself.'

'Out of the question,' said Salik.

Shepherd shrugged. 'I guess I can't force you,' he said. 'I'd just be happier if I knew who I was dealing with.'

'You're dealing with us, Tony, and you have my word that nothing will go wrong.' Salik put the photographs into the envelope with the papers. 'Two days,' he said. 'We'll call you.'

'And what about another currency run?'

'We're talking about it. We'll let you know.'

'The sooner the better,' said Shepherd.

'It's not something we will rush into,' said Matiur. 'Besides, our friends in France require payment in advance. They do not allow us credit.'

Shepherd sipped his tea. 'Can I ask you something about your business here?'

'Of course,' said Salik, waving expansively.

'I see these *bureau de change* places all over London, but I don't understand how they make money.'

Salik frowned. 'What do you mean?'

'Well, they're always in busy shopping streets – Edgware Road, Oxford Street, Knightsbridge, expensive places – but I never see queues of people lining up to change money.'

Salik laughed. 'You are feeling sorry for us, my friend?'

'No, I'm sure you're making a living or you wouldn't stay in business. But the margins are tight, right? You buy a currency at one price and sell at another. It's the margin where you make the profit.'

Salik chuckled again. 'And you think we don't have enough tourists wanting to change their traveller's cheques, is that it?'

'I don't see you'd make big money, that's all.'

'We don't make our money from the tourists,' said Salik. 'If a German wants to change five hundred euros into sterling, of course we make a pittance on the transaction. But there are plenty of people around who need six-figure sums changing, and that's where we make our money. You never see it because, of course, that doesn't happen down on the street. They come upstairs to our office.' Salik said something in Bengali to his brother, who muttered in response.

Salik stood up. 'Come on, let me show you,' he said.

He took Shepherd along the corridor to another office, pulled a key chain from his pocket and opened the door. Inside there was no furniture, just a metal door set into the wall. He used another key to open it. Behind it a space three feet wide and three feet deep was filled with metal shelving on which were stacked thick bundles of banknotes, euros, dollars, pounds and a dozen other currencies that Shepherd didn't recognise, many from the Middle East. His jaw dropped. 'Don't tell me that's one day's takings,' he said.

'This is our float,' said Salik. 'We do several runs a day to the bank.'

'But where does it come from?'

'Cash businesses that want to convert currencies without going through a bank. On large amounts we can give a better deal than the banks. Our overheads are lower.' He smiled. 'And we tend to be less concerned about paperwork.'

'So it's money-laundering?'

Salik looked pained. 'Tony, please . . .'

'But that's what it is, right?'

'We provide a service for people who don't want to go through the banking system,' said Matiur. 'That doesn't mean we have a stream of drug-dealers passing through. Let me give you an example. A Saudi prince is over here and he wants to buy a car for his new girlfriend. The Saudis pay cash for almost everything. Now, if he's just come from the South of France, he might have euros. If he has been in New York, he'll have dollars. He might even have riyals. Do you think the car dealer is going to protest when one of the prince's assistants produces a briefcase full of banknotes, no matter whose face is on them? Of course not.'

'Cash for everything?'

'The Saudis don't use credit cards,' said Salik, 'and they rarely write cheques. In the UK, foreign nationals are only taxed on the money they bring into the country. So if it comes in as cash on a private jet, the Inland Revenue never gets its cut. Now, is that money-laundering? No, not strictly speaking.'

'I suppose you're right.'

'Then there are companies that deal with overseas buyers and need cash.'

'For bribes?'

'For commissions,' said Salik, with a sly smile. 'We get a lot of Nigerians and South Americans. They give us sterling and we supply whatever currency they need. Hookers come to us too. Bayswater and Lancaster Gate are full of prostitutes and escort-agency girls, and they're all paid in cash. Some of them pull in twenty thousand a week, and a lot of that is in foreign currency.' He smiled. 'Not many men are stupid enough to pay for sex with their credit cards.' He patted Shepherd on the back. 'So, you see, Tony, there is no need to feel sorry for us. We do good business. Once the money is ours, we can put it straight into the banking system.'

'What about the ten-thousand-pound limit?' asked Shepherd, playing the Tony Corke role to the hilt. 'I thought all big transactions had to be reported to the cops and you had to prove it wasn't drugs money.'

'People assume that the limit applies to every transaction,' said Salik. 'Of course, that's nonsense. Every shop in Oxford Street takes at least ten thousand pounds every day and the big stores take hundreds of thousands, most of it in cash. Do you think they are interrogated every time they pay in their takings? Of course not. Providing the banks know their customer and where the money has come from, there is no problem.'

'They trust you, and that's enough?'

'Exactly,' said Salik, closing and locking the steel door. 'All business is down to trust.'

Shepherd followed the brothers back to the office. He sat down and took another sip of the fragrant mint tea. 'What about the money I brought in?' he said. 'What happens to that?'

'Some we change. Plenty of businesses need euros, these days. Some we pass on to other companies like ours that need large amounts of euros. Some we pay into our bank.'

'But why go to all the trouble of smuggling the cash in? That's what I don't understand.'

'You don't need to understand,' said Matiur.

'I'm just interested. You buy the euros from Kreshnik, and you use them here in London. But you're paying me an arm and a leg so that can't leave much in the way of profit for you.'

Salik chuckled softly. 'It's good of you to be so concerned about our welfare, Tony, but please believe me, we make money on the deal.'

'I'm glad to hear it,' said Shepherd. He'd pushed it as far as he could – to probe any further might make them suspicious. 'Hopefully, we'll do just as well next time,' he said. '*Inshallah.*'

Salik did a double-take at Shepherd's use of the Islamic phrase, then nodded approvingly. '*Inshallah,*' he said.

'*Inshallah,*' repeated Matiur.

The digital recorder pressed against the small of Shepherd's back. It had recorded everything that had been said.

Shepherd went into the underpass where the Marylebone flyover crossed the Edgware Road. The few shops down there had done decent business until the council had installed traffic-lights above ground that allowed pedestrians to cross in safety. Now the shops were finding it tough going. There was a public toilet, too, now only rarely visited.

The only other person in the underpass was a homeless man with two scruffy collies. He was lying on a sheet of cardboard, snoring loudly, an empty cider bottle clutched in a filthy hand. The dogs wagged their tails as Shepherd walked by.

He went into the public toilet, locked himself into an empty stall and put the briefcase on the floor. He stripped off his coat and pullover and removed the digital recorder and microphone. He flushed the tape that had secured the device to him down the toilet and slid the equipment into the pocket of his pea coat. Then he went back above ground and phoned Jimmy Sharpe, who was sitting in his car round the corner from the *bureau de change*. He told Sharpe that everything had gone according to plan and that he could stand down. His next call was to Amar Singh. The technician was parked in nearby Gloucester Place, close to Marylebone station. Shepherd took a circuitous route through residential streets to the black Cherokee Jeep with wire wheels.

'This is a bloody pimp's car,' he said.

'Pimps drive Beamers, you know that,' said Singh.

'It's a bit high-profile, is what I mean,' said Shepherd. 'This isn't a pool car, is it?'

'Damn right it isn't. It's mine. Bought and paid for.'

'You're a very sad man.' Shepherd took the recording equipment from his pocket and handed it over.

'Anything good on it?' said Singh, twisting to put it into his briefcase.

'Not really. Just confirmation that they're getting the Christopher Donovan passport for me and that they're thinking about another run.'

'All grist to the mill,' said Singh. 'I'll pass it on to Button.' He closed the briefcase.

'Yeah, you kept that close to your chest, didn't you? The Button thing.'

'So did you.'

'How do you rate her?'

'Too soon to say,' said Singh.

'You don't think it's strange that she's not here?'

'What do you mean?'

'Sam Hargrove would have been, that's all,' said Shepherd.

'Hargrove was always hands-on,' said Singh.

'Yeah. He liked the street stuff. Button's more cerebral.'

'You say it like it's a bad thing,' said Singh. 'I think it's an advantage. She'll leave us to get on with our jobs. Hargrove tended to micro-manage.'

'Bollocks.'

Singh held up his hands in surrender. 'I'm not arguing with you, Spider. Like I said, it's too early to say. Now, get the hell out of my pimp-mobile, I've got work to do.'

Shepherd climbed out.

'What happens to the money?' asked Singh, nodding at the briefcase in Shepherd's hand.

'She said I could keep it,' he said. 'As a signing-on fee.' He left Singh staring after him, open-mouthed.

The Saudi sipped his champagne and sat back in the leather armchair. He was in the American Bar at the Savoy Hotel, drinking his favourite champagne, the Pol Roger *cuvée* Winston Churchill 1990. A fitting way to end his last night in London.

'Celebrating?' said a woman's voice to his left. American.

The Saudi hadn't noticed her at the next table, so she must have sat down while he was in conversation with the wine waiter. She was a striking blonde in her early twenties with an impressive figure squeezed into a red dress. She was wearing a gold Cartier watch, diamond pendant earrings, and a slim gold chain round her neck. No wedding ring. 'I suppose I am,' he said.

'You know what Winston Churchill said about champagne?' she asked.

The Saudi did, but he was happy enough to play the idiot.

She grinned. ' "In victory, deserve it. In defeat, need it." Isn't that so true?'

'It is,' said the Saudi. 'Why not join me?'

'Are you sure?' she asked. 'You're not waiting for anybody?'

'It's my last night in town,' he said. 'You can help me drink this.'

'Okay,' she said. She stood up and smoothed down the red dress, revealing several inches of cleavage. The skirt rode up her legs as she sat beside him. 'I do love champagne.' She placed a gold mesh evening bag on the table. An elderly waiter had anticipated her move and was walking over with a second glass. She giggled as he poured the champagne. 'This is my lucky night,' she said.

'Mine too,' said the Saudi. 'I didn't catch your name.'

'I didn't throw it,' she said. She laughed. 'Isn't that a corny line? It's Madison.'

'Like the square?'

She nodded. 'Exactly. Except I'm not. Square, that is.'

'And what brings you to London, Madison?'

'Just passing through.'

'You're on your own?'

'Terrible, isn't it? I'm in swinging London and can't find a man.'

'I don't believe that for a moment,' said the Saudi. Close up, the woman was near-faultless. And exactly his type. Tall, long legs, perfect breasts. She looked like a blonde Nicole Kidman, and the Saudi had always had a thing about the Australian actress.

'Are you here on business or pleasure?' asked Madison.

'A bit of both,' he said. He raised his glass. 'Anyway, to chance encounters.'

'I'll drink to that,' she said. She clinked her glass against his, then drank deeply. When she put it down there was a red smear across the rim. 'Don't you just love the Savoy?' she said.

'It's my favourite hotel,' he said. 'Are you staying here?'

She shook her head. 'No. But I always come to the American Bar – because I'm American, right?' She laughed and patted his knee.

He liked her laugh. It was the laugh of a teenager. Despite that, she looked older now than he'd thought when he first saw her. Twenty-eight, maybe. 'That makes sense,' he said.

She didn't take her hand off his knee. He could feel the heat of her flesh through his trousers and started to harden. She was looking around the bar, almost as if she'd forgotten she was touching him. Her full breasts rose and fell with her breathing. Her skin was flawless, slightly tanned, and he could see now that she wasn't wearing a bra.

She turned back to him. 'What are you thinking?' she asked.

The Saudi smiled. 'I can't tell you,' he said.

'Try,' she said, and looked him straight in the eye as if she already knew what was going through his mind.

He sipped his champagne slowly. 'I was wondering how to get a beautiful woman like you into bed,' he said.

'A thousand dollars would do it,' she said, running a long fingernail down his thigh. 'And for that I'd just about fuck you senseless.'

Shepherd walked into the sitting room where Liam was watching a football match, his feet on the coffee table. 'It's almost nine,' he said. 'Time for bed. You've got school tomorrow. And what have I told you about putting your feet on the table?'

'Dad, can't I watch the end of this?' said Liam, and moved his feet.

'It's late.'

'I can't even watch it in my room, can I?'

'That's not my fault.'

'You took my television away.'

'Because that was your punishment,' said Shepherd. 'You can read a book or something.'

'So reading's a punishment too, is it?' said Liam, slyly.

Shepherd laughed. 'You've definitely got a future as a defence barrister,' he said. He sat down beside his son. 'You know how we were talking about maybe finding a new house?'

Liam nodded.

'How would you feel if we moved closer to your gran and granddad?'

'Really?'

'I'm thinking about it,' said Shepherd.

'Why?'

'You could spend more time with them. We wouldn't have such a long drive to see them. You were happy when you stayed with them, right?'

Liam frowned. 'You're not sending me to live with them again, are you?'

Shepherd put his arm round his son. 'No, of course not. We could sell this house and buy one in Hereford.'

'And I'd go back to the school there?'

'It's a good school, and you had friends there. What do you think?'

'It's up to you.'

'No, it's up to the two of us.'

'And Katra.'

'Sure.'

'Can we get a dog?'

'Excuse me?'

'If we're out of London, we can have a dog, can't we?'

'Maybe,' said Shepherd.

'Okay, then.'

Shepherd grinned. 'Good.'

'And we'll get a dog.'

'We'll talk about that later.'

'Can't I watch the end of the game? Please?'

Shepherd ruffled his son's hair. 'How much more is there?'

'Fifteen minutes.'

'Okay. Fifteen minutes, then bed.' Shepherd kissed the top of Liam's head and went upstairs. He sat down on his bed, picked up the phone and dialled Tom and Moira's number. Tom answered and they chatted for a while then Tom put his wife on the line.

'Daniel, I'm so sorry you couldn't make it,' she said, and sounded as if she meant it.

'Liam had a great time, Moira. Thanks.'

'We'd like to see more of him, you know that.'

'That's sort of why I'm phoning,' said Shepherd. 'The problem is my job – I keep getting sent away at short notice. And it's not as if you're around the corner. Anyway, I've got a new job that's going to change the way I work.'

'Less travelling?' asked Moira, hopefully.

'Probably more, actually.'

'You'll still be a policeman, though?'

'The job's essentially the same,' said Shepherd, 'but because I won't be working for the Met, there's no real need for me to be based in London. I don't see why Liam and I couldn't live in Hereford.' He waited for Moira to reply, but she didn't say anything. 'Moira, are you still there?' he said.

'I'm sorry, Daniel. I'm stunned. You're serious?'

'Sure. Over the last few days I've been up to Newcastle, over to France, down to Southampton. If anything, I think the travelling will get worse in the new job, so I don't see why I shouldn't make Hereford my base. That way you'd be able to see Liam whenever you wanted.'

'I don't know what to say, Daniel.'

'I hoped you'd be pleased.'

'I'm delighted – and I know Tom will be too. But what about his school?'

'He liked the one he went to in Hereford, and it would mean less travelling for him.'

'Daniel, I can't tell you how much this means to me. Really, I can't.'

'It'll be much better for me, too,' said Shepherd.

'I'll talk to the headteacher,' said Moira. 'I'm sure they'll find a place for him. Do you have any idea when you'll move?'

'Let me talk to an estate agent to see how easy it'll be to sell this place. Then we'll talk about it in detail.'

After he'd hung up, Shepherd lay back on the bed and stared up at the ceiling. 'I miss you, Sue,' he whispered. 'I will do until the day I die.'

The limousine was waiting for Madison a short walk from the hotel's entrance. She climbed into the back and sighed. 'I hate fucking Arabs,' she said. 'I mean, I hate Arabs. And I hate fucking them.'

'Was it terrible?' asked the American.

He'd told her he was Dick but he had a funny sense of humour and Madison wasn't sure whether or not he was joking. He was forty-eight, forty-nine maybe, with short grey hair and lips that went really thin when he smiled. He was wearing a dark blue blazer, grey trousers and gleaming black shoes with tassels. When he'd first approached her she'd thought he was a banker or a property developer. He had the confidence that came from handling large amounts of money and knowing that people would always do what he wanted. She didn't want to know what he did or whom he worked for – it would be dangerous. She would just take his money and run. 'They always want to do anal, and I told him I didn't. He kept nagging and nagging and offering me more money.'

'I'm sorry, honey,' said the American.

'He paid me five thousand, so I had to do it, right? But I told him it was under protest. Now I'm bleeding.'

'Was he enormous?'

Madison flashed him a humourless smile. 'He was rough. Kept calling me a bitch, too.'

'Poor baby,' said the American. 'But you have it, right? What I want?'

Madison sighed. 'That's the other thing about Arabs. They always want to do it bareback. He kept upping the ante—'

'Madison,' said the American, coldly, 'please don't tell me you didn't use a condom.'

'Don't be stupid. For what you're paying me, there was no way I wasn't using one. Speaking of which . . .'

'Your money?' The American smiled coldly. 'You show me yours and I'll show you mine.'

Madison opened her evening bag and took out a small polythene bag. Inside was a used condom. The American had supplied the bag and the condom. He took the bag and examined it closely. 'Excellent,' he said.

'What are you going to do with it?' she asked suspiciously.

The American took an envelope out of his blazer pocket and handed it to her. She opened it and flicked through the contents. Twenty-five thousand dollars, in one-hundred-dollar bills.

'You're not going to, like, eat it, are you?' she asked.

'Do I look like a pervert, Madison?' he asked.

She narrowed her eyes. 'Well, yeah, a bit. Sorry.'

The American laughed. 'You're probably right, honey,' he said. 'But don't worry, you're not my type.'

Madison nodded at the used condom. 'What do you want it for?'

The American smiled. 'That, honey, is for me to know. Now, off you go.'

Madison blew him an air-kiss, then climbed out of the limousine and tottered off on her high heels in search of a black cab. Twenty-five thousand dollars from the American, and five thousand from the Saudi. It had been a good night. Apart from the anal.

The Saudi stood in the shower and let the water play over his face. He loved the huge showerheads in the Savoy's bathrooms. It was like standing in the rain. He rubbed the honey-scented soap over his torso and smiled as he remembered the way the American woman had soaped him in the shower. She had been good, and worth every dollar he'd paid her. She'd gone down on him in the shower, taking him in her mouth as the water cascaded over his chest. He'd screwed her in the sitting room of the suite, on the sofa, across the coffee table, and finally in the king-sized bed. He'd paid a lot more for a lot less.

The Saudi loved screwing American women. They always started off so self-assured, so confident, so full of themselves, as if they were doing him a favour. But when they were on their knees and he was behind them, pounding into them, making them gasp and moan, there was no doubting who was in control. He hadn't realised Madison was a hooker until she'd asked for money, but it hadn't been a problem. He was happy to pay for sex and, frankly, where Western women were concerned, he preferred it that way. His smile widened. He doubted that Madison was her real name. Not that he cared. It had been a one-off. He had paid for sexual relief and he had got what he'd paid for.

The doorbell rang. The Saudi rinsed his hair, wrapped himself in the Savoy's thick towelling robe, then headed for the door. 'Room service,' called a waitress.

The Saudi had ordered eggs Benedict, a pot of coffee, and Buck's fizz, with Pol Roger. A leisurely breakfast, a stroll by the Thames, then off to the airport. The Saudi would miss London, but he would be back, sooner rather than later.

He padded across the thick carpet and opened the door. A matronly waitress, with grey hair tied back in a bun and an ample chest that strained at her white blouse, was standing behind a trolley. She had a nametag over her left breast. Amy.

'Good morning, sir,' she said brightly. She smiled, showing greying teeth.

The Saudi nodded. He didn't believe in talking to the hired help. He waved for her to wheel in the trolley.

'How are you this morning, sir?' she asked.

The Saudi ignored her and headed back to the bathroom. He heard a rapid footfall but before he could react he felt a thump in the small of his back and slammed into the wall by the bathroom door. The barrel of a gun was forced under his chin. 'Don't move or I'll blow your head off,' the waitress hissed

There were more footsteps in the corridor outside the suite, then half a dozen men burst in, all armed. Hands grabbed at the Saudi's arms and forced him around so that his back was to the wall. The grey-haired waitress was grinning as she kept the gun rammed against his neck. The Saudi stared at her, but said nothing.

The Labrador growled softly and dropped the tennis ball at Charlotte Button's feet. Button ignored her and carried on flicking through the dozen or so personnel files she had scattered across the coffee table. The dog gave a plaintive yelp and Button sighed. 'What part of working at home don't you understand, Poppy?' she said. 'I'll take you out at lunchtime.'

The dog was panting and Button patted her. Then she picked up Shepherd's file and reread Kathy Gift's most recent assessment. There was no doubt that Shepherd was going to be an asset to SOCA. His Special Forces background combined with his police experience made him the perfect undercover operative. She had been impressed with him when they'd met at the Ritz, and he didn't appear to be the sort who'd have problems working for a woman. The police was still a very male-dominated organisation, especially when compared with MI5 where more than half of the two thousand or so officers were female and the director general was a woman. But Shepherd didn't seem bothered by Button's sex, and she hadn't once caught him glancing at her breasts or legs. Jimmy Sharpe was a different matter. During his interview he'd made some outrageous observations about the role of women in police work, always followed by a gruff 'no offence intended' – although he clearly didn't care one way or the other whether she was offended or not. Button didn't plan to hold Sharpe's sexist views against him. It took all sorts to make up an undercover unit and his assets far outweighed his liabilities.

It had been two days since Shepherd had taken the Christopher Donovan birth certificate and he was due to go in and collect the passport from the Uddin brothers. She picked up her mobile and dialled his number.

'It's Charlie,' she said, when he answered.

'How's it going?'

'I was going to ask you the same.'

'I'm getting ready to go in,' he said. 'Jimmy Sharpe's riding shotgun.'

'Great,' said Button. 'Bag it as soon as possible. We'll need to run a full print and DNA analysis.'

'You know who the contact is?'

'It's all wrapped up,' said Button. Another phone rang. Her landline. 'Dan, my other line's going. Call me when you've got the passport.' She stood up and cut the connection. Poppy raced to the door, tail wagging.

'I'm answering the phone, silly,' she said. 'We'll do the walk thing later.'

At the mention of the word, Poppy's tail wagged even more enthusiastically. Button shook her head. Poppy had been her husband's idea. Given the choice, she would have preferred a cat, but as the house had been her call, as had been the car, their daughter's boarding-school and the cottage in the Lake District, she reckoned he deserved the pet of his choice.

She picked up the phone. It was Patsy Ellis, her former boss at MI5's International Counter-terrorism Branch. Ellis was also one of MI5's representatives on the Joint Terrorism Analysis Centre and was tipped as a potential director general.

'How goes SOCA?' asked Ellis.

Button looked across at the files on the coffee table. 'Slowly,' she said. 'I don't want to make any mistakes with my team. There's a lot at stake.'

'Absolutely,' said Ellis. 'You won't have the Official Secrets Act to hide behind. Everything you do will be followed by every investigative journalist in the country.'

'This is a pep talk, is it?' asked Button.

Ellis laughed. 'You don't need one from me, Charlie,' she said. 'I put you forward for the job, remember?'

'Only because I was after yours,' said Button, only half joking.

'A few years out of the fold will do you the world of good,' said

Ellis. 'And you'll be able to take the credit for your successes, which we're never allowed to do.'

Button knew she was right: SOCA had been a good career move – if she made a success of it.

'Before you get too settled in, we've had a request for your assistance,' said Ellis.

'We?'

'It came from the DG's office. Not for you personally but the DG decided you were the perfect candidate.'

'Because?'

'Your Arab language abilities, as it happens. And your inter-rogation skills. Oh, and your sex, which makes it even more intriguing.'

'My what?'

'They wanted a woman. Ideally a pretty one. I was going to cry sexism when I heard, but there is a method to their madness.'

'Patsy, you're talking in riddles. Who's "they"?'

Poppy nuzzled the back of Button's legs.

'The Americans. The request came from Homeland Security, which, as you know, now covers a multitude of sins. But it came at the highest level. Actually phoned the DG at home at five o'clock in the morning, and you know how she relishes her beauty sleep. Seems they've got someone in their embassy they need interrogating.'

'They've got their own Arab speakers, surely?'

'They want some UK involvement, because although the embassy is effectively on American soil it's still our country. Just about. And apparently the only Arab speakers they have *in situ* are Muslims, and that's not what they want.'

Button looked at her watch. 'When?'

'Now,' said Ellis.

The windows overlooking the garden rattled.

'It's going to take me a while to get to Grosvenor Square,' said Button.

The rattling intensified. The trees at the end of the garden bent over as if they were being pushed down by invisible hands.

'Not as long as you think,' said Ellis.

Button heard the whup-whup-whup of the helicopter's rotor-blades, then saw its shadow flash across the lawn.

'Must be important,' said Button.

'Oh, yes,' said Ellis. 'Very.'

Button replaced the receiver and looked down at the Labrador. 'Your walk will have to wait, Poppy.'

The dog's tail beat a tattoo on the carpet.

'You really are a stupid animal,' said Button. She headed for the kitchen door. She'd phone her husband when she got to Central London. When all was said and done Poppy was his dog.

Jimmy Sharpe lit a cigarette and blew smoke out of the open window of the Vauxhall Vectra. Shepherd coughed pointedly and Sharpe flashed him a tight, but non-apologetic, smile.

'When did you start smoking?' asked Shepherd.

'When I was twelve,' said Sharpe.

They were sitting in the car a short walk from the Uddin brothers' Edgware Road *bureau de change*. It was just before eleven o'clock, an hour before Shepherd was due to collect his new passport.

'Haven't seen you smoke before.'

'Don't read anything into it,' said Sharpe. 'I just felt like a cigarette.'

'Okay.'

'And, Hargrove never allowed smoking on the job.'

'Ah, so while the cat's away . . .'

'I just felt like a cigarette.'

'Fine. Makes a change from you farting.'

'Hey, you don't have to wait in the car,' said Sharpe. 'There's a Starbucks over there. Or you can go sit with the sand jockeys and have a hubble-bubble pipe.'

'Not very politically correct, Razor.'

'Well,' said Sharpe, 'take a look round you. Arab cafés, Arab shops, Arab banks and half the shops here have got Arabic signs. You wouldn't think this was England.'

'You're Scottish, remember?'

'So?'

'They've as much right to be here as you.'

'Yeah, but look at them, the way they walk around in their white dresses with those tea-towels on their heads. Making their women wear black from head to foot. I'm Scots, sure, but you don't see me walking around in my kilt scratching my sporran, do you?'

'And your point is?'

'I don't know what my point is.' He took another long drag on his cigarette. 'Maybe there is no point.'

'What do you make of Button?' asked Shepherd.

'Ah, a loaded question if ever I heard one,' said Sharpe. 'Not wearing a wire, are you?'

'You know I'm not, you prat. And I'm serious,' said Shepherd.

'Have you had a run-in with her already?'

'Have you?'

Sharpe laughed. 'I love talking to you, Spider. Your defences are never down, are they? You're always in character.'

'That's bollocks.'

'Have I ever spoken to the real you in all the years I've known you? I get the feeling that all I ever talk to are the roles you're playing.'

'That's not true.'

Sharpe narrowed his eyes and puffed at his cigarette. He held the smoke deep in his lungs, then exhaled it in a tight plume through the window.

'Razor, piss off, will you?' said Shepherd.

'I'm your back-up, remember? I can't piss off. If I piss off who's going to haul your nuts out of the fire if it all goes tits up?'

'Like you did in Paris?'

'Cheap shot. Anyway, Paris worked out all right, considering it was kick, bollock, scramble all the way.'

'I was bundled into the boot of a car at gunpoint,' said Shepherd.

'I know.'

'I could have been killed.'

'Could've, would've, should've,' said Sharpe. 'Anyway, what's that got to do with Charlotte Button?'

Shepherd tilted his head back and stared up at the car roof. 'Nothing,' he said.

'Paris wasn't even her operation,' said Sharpe. 'That was Hargrove, God rest his soul.'

'Why didn't Joycie join SOCA?'

Sharpe grinned wolfishly. 'What did you hear?'

'That he wanted to stay with the Met.'

'That's the gist of it. He's moving to the Drugs Squad.'

'Button said she wanted him in the SOCA unit.'

'Apparently.'

'So?'

'I think his exact words were "I'm fucked if I'm gonna take orders from a tart" – or something like that.'

'Because she's a woman?'

'Come on, Spider, when was the last time you took orders from one? There's none in the SAS, right, and precious few in the army. The only time we use women in undercover units is in honey-traps, pretty much.'

'That's not true, Razor. There's plenty of women cops around. Good ones, too.'

Sharpe shook his head. 'The big villains are all guys. Crime is an XY chromosome business.'

'Doesn't mean you can't use women to get close to them.'

'That's what I said. Honey-traps.'

'Racism and sexism in one day. You're on a roll.'

'Don't get me started on religion!' laughed Sharpe. He flicked the still-burning cigarette butt through the window.

'Racism, sexism and littering,' said Shepherd.

'No biggie,' said Sharpe. 'We're not cops any more, we're civil servants, remember? You having second thoughts about Button?'

'Not because she's a woman,' said Shepherd. 'That didn't even enter the equation.'

'What, then?'

'Her background.'

'You don't like upper-class, university-educated, Home Counties, riding-to-hounds types, then?'

'It's not about liking. It's about trusting. It's about knowing your back's being watched.'

'You think she should be here today? You're only collecting the passport. No need for her to be around for that.'

'I don't need babysitting,' said Shepherd. He took a deep breath. 'Okay, let me tell you what I think's wrong about her. She thinks this is a game. Good against evil, cops against robbers. She's spent her whole working life in MI5, most of it behind a desk, and when she wasn't behind a desk I'm damned sure she wasn't getting her hands dirty. She thinks it's like some huge game of chess, where she sits there like a grandmaster—'

'Mistress,' interrupted Sharpe. 'Grandmistress.'

'Screw you,' snarled Shepherd. 'If you don't want to talk seriously, go fuck yourself.'

'Just trying to ease the tension,' said Sharpe. 'Besides, the vision of Charlotte Button in thigh-length boots and a whip was too good to pass up.'

'And what's that got to do with chess?'

'Okay, I'll put my hands up. I was focusing more on the mistress aspect.'

Despite himself Shepherd laughed.

Sharpe lit another cigarette. 'You think she's just an academic, is that it?' asked Sharpe.

'I think she treats it like a game of chess, and that we're just pieces she moves around. And if a piece or two have to be sacrificed to win, then so be it.'

'She said that?'

'It's just my take on it. But she did say it was a game.'

'In what way?'

'She said "The game moves up a notch" when terrorism's involved. How can anyone call terrorism a game?'

'It's an expression. Like raising your game. Or living to play another day.'

'That's what she said. I don't know, Razor . . . She's never fired a gun in anger, never faced a thug with a knife, never walked into a room with half a dozen villains who'd gouge your eyes out if they knew you were a cop. You walked a beat in Glasgow before you were in plain clothes. You've been in pubs when fists and bottles were flying, you've looked down the barrel of a gun and known that only your ability to bullshit would stop the other guy pulling the trigger. Hargrove had been there, too.'

'Back when dinosaurs walked the earth, maybe,' said Sharpe. 'But, yeah, I know what you mean. Hargrove's old school.'

'She isn't old school. She's Oxbridge, fast-track promotion, management courses and human-resources bullshit. I don't think she even knows what it's like to be hurt. Maybe the odd manicure injury or a twisted ankle when she was getting to grips with high heels, but she's never killed anyone.'

Sharpe coughed and exhaled a cloud of smoke. 'Neither have I, truth be told,' he said. He made a vain attempt to wave the smoke out of the window.

'I didn't mean it that way. It's about understanding how the real world works. She's no idea how violent men can be to each other. The damage they can do. I was shit-scared when they put me in that boot, Razor. Logically, I'd talked myself into believing that they had no reason to hurt me, but on a purely physical level, I was scared. I know the damage a bullet can do.'

Sharpe scratched his chin. 'I've no reason to defend the woman, but just because she hasn't been where the bullets are flying doesn't mean she's not up to the job. We should at least give her a chance, right?'

'Yeah, maybe.'

'Plus she's got magnificent breasts.'

'Razor . . .'

'I'm just saying, Hargrove was a great boss, but there wasn't much in the way of a cleavage, was there?'

As Button walked away from the helicopter, two marines in flak jackets and helmets brandished M16s and one practically screamed at her to show her identification. Button smiled sweetly and produced her MI5 pass. 'Charlotte Button,' she said. 'I gather I'm expected.'

The older of the two marines studied the photograph, compared it with her face, nodded grimly, then handed it back to her. 'Follow me, ma'am,' he said. He led her away from the helicopter landing area towards a steel door set in a concrete wall. A third marine already had it open.

As she stepped inside the building, the helicopter's turbine roared and it clattered up into the afternoon sky. A man was waiting for her in the corridor. He was in his late forties, with short bullet-grey hair and thin lips. He smiled and offered his hand. 'Richard Yokely,' he said, with a slight Southern drawl. There was large ring on his right ring finger, and a small gold pin held his dark blue tie in place. 'Thanks for coming, Ms Button.'

'It's Charlie,' said Button.

'Then it's Richard,' said Yokely. 'I'm glad you're not one to stand on formalities. If you don't mind, we'll talk as we walk.' He headed down the corridor. He was wearing a grey suit and black loafers with tassels, which worried Button. Her mother had once warned her never to trust a man with tassels on his shoes. Her mother had been a housewife, and had never wanted to do anything other than raise her family and keep house for her husband, but she was an astute judge of character and had rarely offered her children bad advice.

'This morning we pulled in a Saudi by the name of Abdal Jabbaar bin Othman al-Ahmed,' said the American. 'We have reason to believe he's planning a terrorist incident here in the UK. Under normal circumstances we'd put him on a plane to Guantanamo Bay but there's a time issue so we want to start the questioning here.'

'Okay,' said Button, cautiously.

'Now, you're probably wondering why we wanted you on board,' said Yokely.

'I'm told you wanted a good-looking female to be part of the interrogation team,' said Button. 'In another life, I'd be flattered.'

'You're a fluent Arabic speaker,' said Yokely. 'That's why you're here.' He grinned. 'But, yes, we wanted a woman because although he's Western-educated he's still a Saudi, and Saudi men are somewhat chauvinistic.'

'If you call not allowing women to vote and stoning them for adultery, yes, they can be somewhat chauvinistic,' said Button.

Yokely pulled open a fire door and stepped aside to let her go through first. 'We took the view that a woman – and, dare I say it, an attractive one? – would put him on the wrong foot and keep him there.'

'How's this going to work?' asked Button.

'I'd like you to handle the interrogation,' he said. 'We'll have him in an interview room and you'll be asking the questions. I'll be in radio contact with you and two of my operatives will be there to assist.'

'With the questioning?' said Button.

'With the physical side of it,' said the American. The corridor came to a T-junction and he steered her to the left.

'Physical side?'

'From the intelligence we have, he's not going to want to talk,' said Yokely. 'Of course, you might prove us wrong, in which case I'll happily eat whatever item of headwear you have available.'

'I don't follow you,' said Button. 'If I'm running the interrogation, what exactly will your men be doing?'

Yokely looked pained. 'Charlie, the man you'll be talking to might well be responsible for the deaths of hundreds of people. And may be planning to kill hundreds more. We won't be using kid gloves. I don't want you going in there under any illusions. The interrogation is going to be quite robust.'

'Robust?'

'Hard core,' said Yokely. 'We're going to do whatever it takes to get him to talk.'

'Within the law, right?' said Button, apprehensively.

Yokely smiled without warmth. 'Let's just see how it goes,' he said.

'And I conduct the interrogation in Arabic?'

Yokely shook his head. 'No. English. But show him that you speak Arabic. I want him to know that you understand the way he thinks. You don't become fluent in a language without understanding a country's culture.'

'So I'm a Western woman, but one who understands Arab ways?'

'Exactly.'

'If he's with al-Qaeda, he's not going to respond to questioning.'

'That's a distinct possibility,' said the American. 'But we should give him the opportunity to co-operate. He knows we'll never let him go now that we have him so we can offer him a way out. A new identity. Money. Whatever it takes.'

'But again, if he's al-Qaeda that's not going to work. They're fanatics. Most of them are prepared to die for their cause. Their religion promises them eternity in heaven if they die as martyrs.'

'Agreed.'

'So if he won't talk, and he refuses to be bribed, what then?'

'Then we get robust,' said Yokely. 'Don't worry, my men are experts. You'll just watch, and learn.'

'What about playing him the Barney song? Isn't that what you do in Guantanamo Bay?'

'You can mock, Charlie, but it works. It takes time, but exposure to banal music over long periods can bring on disorientation. And disorientation is half the battle. Problem is, we don't have the time. You can try talking to him, but I think you'll find that we'll have no choice other than to get physical.'

Salik smiled and passed a brand-new UK passport to Shepherd. 'So, now I suppose I should call you Christopher,' he said.

'That's the idea,' said Shepherd. He opened the passport and examined the photograph and details. It was as perfect as the last passport Salik had given him.

'What are you going to do?' asked Salik.

'I'm not sure,' said Shepherd. 'I can't sell the house until the court case is over. I might just have to walk away from it.'

'Your fingerprints will always be on file,' said Salik. 'If ever you get caught by the police again, they'll know you're Tony Corke.'

'I don't plan to get caught again,' said Shepherd. 'I've got the money you've given me and that's enough to start over. Spain, maybe. Or France.' He grinned. 'Maybe I'll go and work for Kreshnik.'

Salik's smile evaporated. 'I hope that's a joke, Tony,' he said. 'Kreshnik is a dangerous man.'

'You introduced me to him.'

'No, he said he wanted to meet you. It wasn't my idea for you to go to Paris, you know that. I do business with him, but at arm's length. Anyway, he's happy now. We can do more business together, Tony. You and Matiur and me. We trust each other, and we won't let each other down. You can make serious money, enough to start a new life anywhere in the world.'

'What we do is safe,' said Matiur. 'It's clean. We're not hurting anybody. We're not dealing with drugs, or arms, or profiting from the misery of others. And we can pay you well.'

Shepherd nodded, but didn't say anything. He slid the passport into the top pocket of his shirt. He had a plastic Ziploc bag in his jacket pocket and he'd transfer the passport to that when he was outside.

'What are you doing at the weekend, Tony?' asked Salik.

'Why? Are you ready for another run?'

Salik laughed. 'It's always work with you, isn't it? No, it's my wife's birthday on Saturday and there's going to be a big party. It's supposed to be a surprise but I'm pretty sure she knows what's happening. It'll be in the afternoon and there'll be lots of children. Bring your boy.'

Shepherd pretended to consider the offer. Then he nodded. 'I'm not sure if my ex-wife will let me have him for the weekend but, yeah, I'll be there.'

'Excellent,' said Salik. He gave Shepherd a printed invitation. 'Don't bother with a present or anything, just come.'

Shepherd thanked him and put the card into his coat pocket.

He stood up, suddenly feeling guilty at what he was doing. He shook hands with Salik. 'See you,' he said.

'On Saturday,' said Salik.

'On Saturday,' repeated Shepherd, although he knew he would not be at the party.

Matiur stepped forward and hugged Shepherd, patting his back.

Shepherd stiffened, but relaxed when he remembered he wasn't wearing a wire. Button had only wanted him to collect the passport. They already had everything they needed to put the Uddin brothers away.

He went downstairs. Part of him was relieved that he wouldn't have to see them again, but another part was sorry he wouldn't be going to the party. He liked Salik, and under other circumstances he could imagine them being friends. But Salik liked Tony Corke, and Tony Corke was only a role Shepherd had been playing. After today he would cease to exist. In a few weeks, or months, Salik's world would collapse around him, and it would all be Shepherd's fault. He didn't want to dwell on his betrayal of Salik Uddin.

As he walked out of the stairwell and into the street a man in a beige raincoat stepped aside to let him go by.

'Thanks,' muttered Shepherd.

The man grunted. He had his head down but Shepherd caught a glimpse of his face. Light brown hair, a long face with a dimpled chin, brown eyes. It was a face Shepherd had seen before. He looked over his shoulder but all he saw was the man's back disappearing up the stairs.

Shepherd walked down the road and stopped outside a mobile-phone shop. He stared into the window, unseeing, as he flicked mentally through his memory files, searching for that face. It wasn't someone he'd met, or spoken to, he was sure. And it wasn't a computer file he'd seen. It was a photograph – but where? And when? Then the correct neurones fired and Shepherd remembered. He took out his mobile and phoned Sharpe. 'Razor, are you in the car?'

'What's wrong?'

'Nothing. Where are you?'

'Still parked up. Did everything go okay?'

'I've got the passport, but something's cropped up. I've just seen a face I recognise.'

'Who?'

'That's the problem,' said Shepherd. 'I recognise the face but I don't know the name. It's a terrorist that Button's on the lookout for. She had his photograph up on some sort of hit list.'

'What sort of terrorist?'

'Al-Qaeda.'

'Shit.'

'Exactly. Look, you hang fire there. I'm staying put until I've spoken to Button.'

Shepherd cut the connection and phoned Button.

Yokely and Button gazed through the glass window at the man sitting in the room next door. He was an Arab in his early thirties, good-looking with jet-black hair and piercing black eyes. He was wearing a well-cut suit and a crisp white shirt, buttoned with no tie. He sat with his legs crossed at the ankles, arms folded across his chest.

'He can't see us, but he probably knows he's being watched,' said Yokely. The American nodded at a manilla file on the table behind him. 'I've printed out some of the information we have. See what you think.'

Button sat down and opened the file. There were a dozen or so surveillance photographs of the Saudi, taken with a long lens.

'Can I get you some coffee?'

'Tea would be nice,' said Button, setting the photographs to one side and picking up a computer printout. 'Low fat milk, if you have it.'

Yokely went out of the room and reappeared a couple of minutes later. 'On its way,' he said.

'There's nothing in the file that says you arrested him,' said Button.

'He's not under arrest,' said Yokely.

'Just helping you with your enquiries, I suppose,' said Button.

Yokely flashed her a cold smile. 'This isn't a police investigation,' he said. 'We're not bound by the usual rules of interrogation. He stays here as long as need be. And if he refuses to co-operate, he sits in a cell in Cuba for as long as we deem necessary.'

'But what evidence do you have?'

Yokely sat down at the table and adjusted the cuffs of his shirt. 'Your Forensics boys found a DNA sample on a glass in a safe-house used by one of the suicide-bombers who hit the Tube last year. They drew a blank but we gave it to our guys.'

'And they had him on file?'

'Not exactly,' said Yokely. 'We knew it wasn't the bomber because the bomber's DNA was all over the place. It matched the DNA of the guy your man Shepherd shot in the Tube station. But we couldn't get a match on the other DNA on any of our databases, and there were no prints other than the bomber's. All we had was the DNA from saliva on the glass and no match. That's when we got creative.' He grinned. 'We ran a check through all the available databases looking for a close match. Not a perfect match, but enough of one to suggest a family relationship. And we got a hit, from Baltimore of all places. There was a guy there, a Saudi, who'd been accused of rape back in the nineties. He was a Ph.D. student at Johns Hopkins. The alleged victim was a secretary. She claimed the guy had doped her with Rohypnol, then raped her. She vaguely remembered the rape and a video camera, but there was no physical evidence.'

'He used a condom?'

'He did indeed. But he left his fingerprints all over the place, so off the back of that the police took DNA and blood samples to cross-check with other unsolved rapes. Nothing came up, and the case never went to trial. The Saudi left the country and the secretary was driving around in a brand-new Porsche.'

'He paid her off?'

'That's what it looks like, and we couldn't get her to press charges. But the guy's DNA stayed on file, and it was a close match to the saliva sample we found in the bomber's flat. Not close enough to be a sibling, but definitely a first cousin or a nephew. We had enough information to start tracking down all the members of his family. Two hundred or so names, as it turned out. Then we started cross-checking them with visas issued for the UK in the six months running up to the London bombings. That gave us a handful of hits, but by then we'd realised that quite a few of them had British passports.' Yokely smiled. 'You do make it easy for them, don't you?' he said. 'The way you hand out citizenship to almost anyone who asks for it.'

'Don't look at me,' said Button. 'You need to take it up with our home secretary.'

'Your capital city is now so foreigner-friendly they call it Londonistan, you know?'

'Yes, I know,' said Button patiently. 'It's part of being a multicultural society.'

'Anyway, the ones with British citizenship wouldn't be recorded entering or leaving the country, so we started to look further afield,' said Yokely.

There was a discreet knock at the door, which was opened by a young blonde woman carrying a tray with a mug of coffee, a pot of tea, a jug of milk and a bowl of packets of sugar and sweetener. Yokely smiled at the woman and took it from her. He put it on the table, waited until she had closed the door behind her, then resumed. 'We looked for countries where there had been terrorist incidents and started cross-checking the coming and going of the family members. As you can imagine, it took time. Milk and sugar?'

'Just milk,' said Button.

'Am I right that the Queen puts the milk in first?'

Button smiled. 'I've heard she does, yes.'

'And why would that be, do you think? Doesn't it make sense to put the tea in first so that you can see how strong it is before you add the milk?'

'I think it's to do with the flavour,' said Button. 'If you add cold milk to hot tea, the milk scalds and tastes bitter. If you add the hot tea to the cold milk, the temperature of the milk rises slowly, so it doesn't scald.'

Yokely nodded as he added a splash of milk to Button's cup. 'Okay, but if that's the case, why does everybody add milk to coffee? Coffee's just as hot as tea, isn't it?' He poured tea into the cup, then handed it to her.

'Thanks,' she said. 'Tea has a subtle flavour that can be spoiled by scalded milk. Coffee is more . . . robust.'

'I've always been a coffee-drinker,' said Yokely. He sipped and smacked his lips. 'I can't function without a high caffeine level.'

'There's more caffeine in tea than there is in coffee,' said Button.

Yokely arched an eyebrow. 'I didn't know that,' he said.

'Well, you live and learn.'

'And then you die and forget it all,' said Yokely. He chuckled and put his mug on the table. 'Anyway, enough chit-chat. The family are all well travelled. Rich Saudis like to stay away from their own country during the really hot season, and there are perks to being on the move during Ramadan. Like no fasting. Anyway, we came up with several possibilities, so then it was a matter of getting DNA samples on the quiet. That was fun, I can tell you. We had guys posing as waiters, garbage-collectors, hairdressers. No stone unturned, as they say.' He gestured with his thumb at the two-way mirror. 'I have to hang my head in shame and admit that we used a lady of the night to get Abdal Jabbaar bin Othman al-Ahmed there. I won't bore you with the details but we took a perfect sample from him last night. Anyway, we struck gold. He was in the bomber's flat, no question. And as you'll see from the file there, he's been in and out of countries where some pretty heavy stuff has gone down. Madrid. London. Bali. And the kicker was that he was in Australia just before the bombings there.'

Button's mobile rang and she smiled apologetically at the American. She looked at the screen: Shepherd. 'Do you mind if I take this?' she asked.

'Please,' said Yokely. He gestured at the door. 'Do you need some privacy?'

Button shook her head and accepted the call. 'Dan, I'm in a meeting, can I get back to you?'

'It's urgent,' said Shepherd.

'Go ahead.' She mouthed, 'Sorry,' to Yokely. He waved away her apology.

'I've just spotted one of the faces on your board,' said Shepherd, 'going in to see the Uddin brothers.'

'Which one?'

'It was one of the pictures with no name. Colour. Light brown hair, long face, brown eyes. Dimple in his chin. It wasn't a surveillance picture, more official, head and shoulders staring at the camera.'

Button knew there was no need to ask Shepherd if he was sure. His memory was near-photographic and he had not hesitated when he gave the description. 'On his own?'

'Just him. He definitely knew where he was going so I'm figuring he'd been there before. My guess is that he's picking up a passport.'

'Okay. I'll get a colleague to send the photographs to your mobile. Tell him which man you've seen. He'll give you a name and let me know who it is. It might take half an hour or so, but stay there. Is Sharpe with you?'

'Yes. He's got his car.'

'I'll get other surveillance around there ASAP. If he moves, stick with him.' She ended the call. 'I'm sorry, Richard, one of my people has spotted someone on our watch list. Give me a minute, will you?'

'No problem,' said Yokely. 'I could do with a visit to the men's room anyway. You go right ahead.'

The American left the room while Button phoned her number two in the SOCA undercover unit. David Bingham was in his early fifties and had moved with her from MI5. Like Button, he had worked closely with Patsy Ellis and had been her number two in Five's Belfast office for two years. He was a safe pair of hands, trustworthy and a good friend. She told him what she needed and Bingham promised to get on to it immediately.

'Call me as soon as you have a positive ID,' she said. She glanced through the window at the Saudi, who was frowning at the four plasma screens. 'David, my mobile might well be off. Leave a message or text me if it is, okay?'

'Will do, Charlie. Talk soon.'

As Bingham cut the connection, Yokely came back into the room. 'Everything okay?' he asked.

'Everything's fine,' she said. 'Sorry about the interruption.' She nodded at the Saudi in the next room. 'All you've got at the moment is a link between him and the bomber. Nothing concrete.'

'Absolutely,' said Yokely. 'But this isn't about making a case against him. That's for later, if we ever decide to put him on trial. Here's the clincher, Charlie. When we busted him in the Savoy early this morning, we found a first-class ticket to Dubai for a midday flight. Today. Which means that whatever he's got planned is almost certainly under way. The clock, as they say, is very much ticking.' He put a Bluetooth headset into his ear and handed a matching one to Button. 'Okay, let's get started.'

Shepherd looked at the picture on the screen of his mobile phone. It was a white male, brown hair and brown eyes, but he wasn't the man who'd walked into the Uddin brothers' office. He sent a text message to David Bingham. NO. He sipped his coffee and waited for the next photograph. So far he'd rejected three. There couldn't be too many more because most of the men on the whiteboard had black hair and Shepherd was sure about the dimple in the man's chin.

He was sitting in a coffee shop overlooking the row where the *bureau de change* was. He had a seat by the window and a copy of the *Evening Standard* in front of him. There was no doubt in his mind that the man he'd seen was one of the faces on Button's whiteboard. Shepherd was annoyed to have to deal with Button's number two, whom he'd never met. Al-Qaeda terrorists, Button had said. Men and women who moved under the radar of the intelligence services. Now Shepherd had found one, and she had switched off her phone. Hargrove would never have acted so unprofessionally.

Shepherd tensed as he saw the man walk out of the doorway at the side of the *bureau de change*. He phoned Sharpe as he walked out of the coffee shop, leaving behind his newspaper.

'Razor, he's on the move. Heading north on the Edgware Road.'

'Got that. What do you want me to do?'

'Stay put,' said Shepherd. 'He's heading against the traffic but he might jump into a cab.'

'No sign of our back-up?'

'Bingham says it's on its way,' said Shepherd.

'Promises, promises,' said Sharpe.

Shepherd kept on his side of the road, matching his pace to that of his quarry. He kept the phone pressed to his ear. 'Still heading west.'

'I should leave the car, Spider,' said Sharpe. 'One on one always comes to grief, you know that.'

'Let's make sure he's not heading for a vehicle or a cab,' said Shepherd.

'At least I should start driving your way,' said Sharpe.

'Okay, but steer clear of the Edgware Road. It's backed up to Marble Arch and if you get stuck there you'll be screwed.'

The phone clicked in Shepherd's ear. 'I've got a text message, I'll call you back,' he said. He cut the connection and called up the message. Another picture from Bingham. He texted back NO.

Shepherd called Button's number and was put straight through to her voicemail. He left a brief message saying that the man was on the move and that he was following. Then he redialled Sharpe. 'Where are you, Razor?'

'Praed Street. I'll hang a right and cut back down Sussex Gardens. Where's your man?'

'Still heading along Edgware Road. Shit.'

'What?'

'The Tube. There's two stations, Circle and Bakerloo. If he goes down one I won't be able to use the mobile.'

'There's nowhere to park here. I'm stuck with the car.'

'I know.'

Shepherd hurried across the road and quickened his pace. The man was striding purposefully ahead. He looked at his watch as he walked so Shepherd decided he had a deadline, wherever he was going.

'Razor, listen. If I go underground and lose the signal, keep your phone clear and I'll call again as soon as we surface. Call Button and tell her what's happening. Put the rest of the surveillance team on standby. He's crossing under the Marylebone flyover now. That rules out the Circle Line station. He's still walking against the traffic so it's either the Bakerloo Line or he'll stay on foot.'

'Are you sure you shouldn't just bust him now?'

'For what? Buying a passport? If he's a terrorist, Button will want to know where he's going and who he meets. SO13 will want to know exactly what he's up to.' SO13: the Anti-terrorist Branch.

Ahead of him the man hurried across the road. The traffic-lights were red but the green man was flashing. Shepherd cursed under his breath. It was a busy intersection with the traffic gearing up to drive onto the A40. If he got caught on the wrong side of the lights he'd be stuck for several minutes.

He ran across the road just as the traffic started to move. A van driver banged on his horn and the man Shepherd was following turned. Shepherd stopped running and turned sharp right, head down, the mobile phone pressed to his ear.

'What happened?' asked Sharpe.

'Just making a twat of myself,' said Shepherd. 'I'm having to pull back.'

Shepherd headed back to the Edgware Road, more cautiously this time. There was no sign of his quarry and he hurried down the road towards the Tube station, slowed and looked into it. The man was taking a ticket from the machine.

Shepherd ducked back. 'He's on the Tube,' he whispered into the phone. 'I'm going after him.'

'Any guess if he'll go north or south?'

'Hell, Razor, toss a coin. Or stay put. I'll phone you as soon as I'm above ground again. Call Button and tell her where I am.'

Shepherd cut the connection and slipped the mobile into his coat. He dug out a handful of change and walked into the station. The man he was following had passed through the ticket barrier and was heading for the lift. Shepherd selected a day ticket that would cover all six zones of the Tube system, then fed the coins into the machine.

As the machine spat out his ticket he heard the lift doors rattle shut. There were emergency stairs to the left of the lift, and a notice warning that there were 125 steps to the platforms. Shepherd had no choice – by the time the next lift arrived his quarry might be on a train. He ran down the spiral staircase, three at a time, covered by CCTV cameras every thirty feet or so. He wondered if anyone was watching and what they thought about the crazy guy running hell for leather down the stairs.

Heading down didn't require too much physical effort but he had to concentrate: one wrong step would send him tumbling. He tried to keep track of the number of stairs as he hurtled down. Sixty. Eighty. A hundred. He wondered how quickly the lift would descend – it had probably been designed for reliability and passenger numbers rather than speed. A hundred and twenty-five.

Ahead of him a sign indicated the direction of the two platforms. To the left, Harrow and Wealdstone. The North. To the right, Elephant and Castle. The South. Shepherd stood still and listened. He heard a rumble to his right and walked in that direction. He reached the platform as the train roared into the station. He caught a glimpse of the driver, a ginger-haired man with square-rimmed spectacles, then the carriages whizzed by. Fewer than a dozen passengers were waiting to board and Shepherd quickly scanned their faces. The man wasn't there. The train stopped and three middle-aged women got off with five young children in tow. Shepherd waited until the train doors had closed, then walked away. That left the northbound platform. He took out his mobile even though there was no signal so far underground. He tapped out a message to Sharpe, NORTH, then put the phone back into his coat. It would keep trying to send the message until there was a clear signal.

He waited where he was until he heard the rumble of a train on the northbound track, then moved on to the platform. A breeze from the tunnel to his right heralded the imminent arrival of the train and a few seconds later it appeared, brakes screeching as it slowed to a halt. Shepherd's quarry was at the far end of the platform, at the rear of the train. Shepherd walked slowly down the platform, hands deep in his pockets, and boarded the second carriage from the end. He sat close to the door that linked the two carriages so that he had a good view of the man, then ignored him as the door shut. There was no need to keep him under observation; all Shepherd wanted to know was at which station the man left the train.

At Paddington, Shepherd glanced across as the doors opened but the man was still seated, arms folded. The doors opened and passengers poured off, then more piled on, mainly businessmen with briefcases. Shepherd tensed in case the man made a last-minute dash as the doors closed, but they slammed shut and the train moved off.

An overweight woman in a dark raincoat was standing in the other carriage with her back to the connecting door, obscuring his view. It was a nuisance but not a major problem: while the train was moving, there was nowhere for the man to go.

The next stop was Warwick Avenue. The man stayed where he was, arms still folded, chin on his chest, almost as if he was asleep.

Maida Vale. The woman in the dark raincoat got off so Shepherd had a clearer view of his quarry.

Kilburn Park. The train slowed. The doors rattled open. Shepherd looked at his watch. Out of the corner of his eye he saw movement. The man had stood up and was peering at the signs on the wall of the station as if confused as to where he was.

Shepherd stood up, and as he did so the man hurried off the train. Shepherd followed – narrowly missing being caught in the closing doors.

He followed the man up the escalator to the surface, keeping close enough to him to see which way he went on leaving the station. The man passed through the ticket barrier, Shepherd behind him.

The Saudi folded his arms and stared at the woman. She stared back with unblinking brown eyes. She looked like a secretary in her dark blue two-piece suit. A woman trying to be a man, he thought contemptuously. 'You have no right to keep me here,' he said quietly. He had no need to raise his voice: he had the law on his side, and he knew his rights to the letter.

'You're absolutely correct,' she said brightly.

The Saudi said nothing. He turned his head slowly and stared at his reflection in the large mirror to his right. There would be a man on the other side, he knew. The woman's boss. Watching to see how he reacted to being questioned by a female. They were assuming that because he was an Arab he would be uncomfortable facing a woman in a position of authority, but they were wrong. She had a Bluetooth headset on her right ear and the Saudi was certain that her boss was relaying instructions to her. She was a robot, nothing more, a machine carrying out her master's instructions.

The only furniture in the room was the metal table and the two chairs they were sitting on. The floor was tiled and the walls were concrete, painted pale green. To his left there were four plasma screens, all blank. Above them a large white-faced clock ticked off the seconds. Two small speakers were set into the ceiling.

'I don't have to say anything,' he said.

The woman wore no wedding ring but she had the look of one who had been married. Her hands were together on the table, nails glistening with colourless varnish. Her lipstick seemed to have been freshly applied and her hair brushed. A typical woman, thought the Saudi. She needed to look her best, even for an interrogation.

'I want a lawyer,' he said, more firmly this time.

'I'm sure you do,' she said. She glanced at the clock and checked the time against her wristwatch. A Rolex, the Saudi noted, but a cheap one. Steel. The Saudi had half a dozen Rolexes, all gold, and four were studded with diamonds, but he rarely wore them. 'I'm so glad it's got a second hand,' she said.

'What?' he said, frowning.

The woman nodded at the clock. 'I always feel that unless a timepiece has a second hand, it's not really performing its function. I do hate those digital models, don't you? You have no real sense of time passing.'

'Who the hell are you?' hissed the Saudi. 'Have you brought me here to talk about clocks?' A brief smile flickered across her face and the Saudi realised that she regarded his flash of temper as a victory. 'Who are you?' he said. 'At least I have the right to know the identity of my interrogator.'

'Actually, Mr Ahmed, you have no rights at all. Not in here.'

'I am a British citizen. I travel on a British passport. I am entitled to all the rights and privileges of a British citizen, and I am covered by the European Convention on Human Rights.'

'Let me tell you what we know,' said the woman. 'And then I will tell you what we want to know.'

'*Anta majnuun,*' said the Saudi contemptuously.

'No, I am not crazy, Mr Ahmed.'

'I demand to see your superior,' said the Saudi.

'I am in charge of this investigation.'

'But you won't even tell me your name.'

'You do not need to know my name.'

The Saudi scowled. 'Man ta'taqid annaka tukhaatib?'

'I know exactly who I am talking to, Mr Ahmed. Now, if you would just remain quiet while I run through what we already know, I'd be most grateful. Your name is Abdal Jabbaar bin Othman al-Ahmed although the name on your UK passport is just Abdal Ahmed.'

Her accent, when she said his name, was perfect, the Saudi noticed. She was refusing to speak to him in Arabic but he had no doubt that she was fluent.

'Abdal Jabbaar – Servant of the Compeller. A religious name,' she said. 'You father is Othman bin Mahmuud al-Ahmed. For many years he was a facilitator for the Saudi Royal Family, and became very rich as a result. Now he is semi-retired, although he still acts as a consultant when required.'

'My father is a well-respected businessman,' said the Saudi, but the woman held up a hand to silence him.

'Please let me finish, Mr Ahmed. We need to get this out of the way as quickly as possible. Your father was granted British citizenship thirteen years ago, as were you, your mother and your siblings. You were educated at Eton, and the London School of Economics. A first-class degree. Well done.'

'I suppose you got a first, too,' said the Saudi.

'A double first, actually,' said the woman. 'Cambridge. I was a bit of a bookworm at university. Since then you have been in effective control of your father's business but, as we both know, it is his partners who do the work. You remain a figurehead. And you travel a lot.'

The Saudi shrugged. She was wasting her time, and his. There was no proof that he had ever done anything wrong. Over the last five years he hadn't acquired so much as a parking ticket. He was careful and covered his tracks well. They had nothing on him, so all he had to do was wait for his lawyer.

'You hit all the hotspots, don't you? The South of France, the Bahamas, Aspen. Spending your father's money.'

'I do a lot of entertaining,' said the Saudi.

'Oh, we know all about the entertaining, Mr Ahmed. The girls. The boys. The drugs.'

The Saudi leaned forward. 'Hayyaa natakallam bil-'arabiyya,' he said.

'No, Mr Ahmed, we shall stick to English. I have no desire to question you in your own language.'

The Saudi shrugged, but said nothing.

'It's not the entertaining that concerns us,' said the woman. 'In December 2002 you visited Bali and stayed in a suite at the Oberoi Hotel. While in Bali you met with two members of the Jemaah Islamiah network. You checked out on the seventh of December. Two days later a bomb went off killing two hundred and two people. One of the men you met was involved in the attack on the Australian embassy in Jakarta in September 2004.'

The woman waited for a reaction. The Saudi stared at her stonily. They had nothing. Anything they did have was circumstantial, and in Britain that wasn't enough. They would have to let him go eventually.

'In August 2003 you arrived in Madrid. You stayed at the Melia Castilla Hotel. You were there for two weeks, but returned again in February, this time staying at the Ritz.' She smiled. 'I'm a big fan of the Ritz myself.' The smile vanished. 'You left Spain on the eighth of March 2004. On the eleventh ten bombs went off on commuter trains killing a hundred and ninety-one and injuring fifteen hundred. Do you sense a pattern, Mr Ahmed? Because we do.'

The Saudi said nothing. He tried to swallow but his mouth had dried.

'Later that year you were sighted in Sumatra. You weren't observed in contact with anyone from Jemaah Islamiah, but they have been pretty low-key since the Bali bombing. But we do believe that the network's main bombmaker, Azahari Husin, was in the area. And Indonesian police, who raided a house in West Java, discovered a list of possible targets, including Western-owned hotels, along with the names of twelve operatives who were willing to become martyrs.'

The Saudi felt sweat trickle down his back. He shivered. He knew there was no evidence against him. They might have suspicions, but suspicions could not be used against him. All he had to do was refuse to answer their questions, and eventually they would have to call his lawyer. 'Laa uriid an atakallam ma'aka,' he said, and folded his arms.

'Whether or not you want to talk to me is immaterial, Mr

Ahmed,' said the woman. 'We will be here until you tell us what we want to know. Just over a year ago you were in London when four suicide-bombers mounted an attack on the Underground. Two succeeded, one above ground, one below. Forty-seven people died and more than a hundred men, women and children were injured.'

The Saudi stared sullenly at her but said nothing.

'A few months later you were in Thailand, staying at the Oriental Hotel in Bangkok. You left just before the tsunami hit in the south. A quarter of a million people dead.' The woman smiled. 'Not that we think you were responsible for the tidal wave but we do wonder what you were doing in Thailand. Phuket, of course, has been a possible target ever since the Bali bombing. Lots of wealthy tourists. Sun, sea, sand, sex and all that. A few bright boys of mine think you were putting together an operation that was disrupted by the tsunami. One of life's awful coincidences.' She smiled and took a sip from a glass of water. She left a smear of lipstick. He remembered the American girl he'd been with the previous night and how she'd left lipstick on her champagne glass. When the men with guns had burst into his suite he'd thought at first that he was being arrested for using a prostitute. But it had soon become obvious that they weren't policemen and that they had bigger things on their minds.

'We have no evidence of what you were planning in Phuket, of course – the tsunami washed everything away. But we do know that three men and one woman were staying at one of the beachfront hotels and travelling on Bosnian passports. Do you know much about the former Yugoslavia, by any chance?' She placed her hands on the table, palms down.

'I want my lawyer,' said the Saudi, quietly. 'Now.'

She ignored him. The Saudi had a sudden urge to stand up and slap her face. He hated her superiority, her arrogance. She was treating him with contempt, and he was not used to that from a woman. He forced himself to stay calm. He was sure that they had used a woman to unsettle him, and it was important not to show that the ruse was working. He tried to smile but his lips dragged across his teeth.

'In May you were in Sydney, Australia. You stayed at the Four Seasons Hotel. You had a suite on the tenth floor. Not long after you left for London, a hundred and seven people died when three bombs went off at Circular Quay. You see why we're more than a little concerned, Mr Ahmed. Terrible things seem to happen after you have paid a visit. People die. A lot of people. Including women and children. I've never understood the way al-Qaeda so happily kills women and children. Doesn't the Koran say something about not murdering innocents? Or does the end always justify the means?'

The Saudi said nothing.

'The right to silence is overrated,' said the woman. 'You will tell us why you're in London, Mr Ahmed. You will tell us and you will tell us quickly.'

'I want my lawyer.'

The woman smiled. 'At this point I am prepared to offer you a million pounds sterling for the information we require, and for your future co-operation. We will not require you to give evidence in court, and once we have everything we need from you we will provide a new identity for you in a country of your choice.'

'I do not need your money,' said the Saudi, 'and I do not want it. I want you to release me now. I demand it. I am a British citizen. I have rights.'

The woman stood up and walked to the whiteboard by the door. She picked up a blue marker pen and wrote '£1,000,000' at the top. 'I'll put it there to remind you that my offer is still on the table,' she said. 'At any stage you will be able to bring a halt to these proceedings by accepting the offer and co-operating.'

'What proceedings?' snapped the Saudi. 'What are you talking about, you stupid woman?'

The door opened and two men walked in. They were in their early thirties, with close-cropped hair and hard faces. They had the look of soldiers but they were wearing casual clothing – dark sweatshirts, jeans and heavy workboots. They had Bluetooth headsets that matched the one the woman was wearing, earpieces in their right ears and stubby microphones that reached the corner of the mouth. They stood at either side of the woman and stared at him. The one on the woman's left had a broken nose, the one on the right a scar above his lip. The Saudi had seen such men before, and he had made use of them. They were men who would kill without conscience – he could see that in their eyes.

'I am asking you again, Mr Ahmed. Would you please tell me what you have been planning while you have been in this country?'

'I have nothing to say to you,' said the Saudi. 'Nothing at all.'

'Well, then,' she said, as cheerfully as a Girl Guide leader. 'Let's get started. Please remove your clothing.'

The man walked up to a three-storey house that seemed to have been converted into small flats or bedsits. There were twenty-odd bells by the front door, but he had a key. Shepherd watched from the pavement as he let himself into the house. He had walked from Kilburn Park station to Kilburn High Road, then headed north, turned off on to Willesden Lane, then right into a residential street. As Shepherd had followed him, he'd checked that the phone had sent the text message to Sharpe. It had. And as the man went inside the house, Shepherd dialled Sharpe's number.

'Got him,' said Shepherd. He gave Sharpe the address.

'Should be there in fifteen minutes,' said Sharpe. 'I headed your way as soon as I got the text. Traffic's hellish, though, and back-up's still on the way.'

'Do you know where?'

'Button's mobile is off. I've left a message.'

'What the hell is she playing at? Doesn't she realise how serious this is?'

'Don't shoot the messenger, Spider. I'll try again. Are you staying put?'

'There's probably a back way out but he's not on to me so I'm thinking he'll come out the front, if he comes out at all. I've got to go, Razor. I'll call you back. Try Button again. Tell her what's happening. I'll call Bingham.'

There were three text messages on his mobile, all from Bingham. Shepherd checked the first. The picture was of a man with brown hair but he was a good ten years older than the one he'd followed to the house. Shepherd sent a message back. NO. He opened the second message and his heart raced. It was the man. No question about it. He pressed the button to call Bingham, who answered on the second ring. 'You've got him?'

'Second of those last three you sent,' said Shepherd.

'Give me a minute,' said Bingham. Shepherd walked away from the house. There was nowhere in the street where anyone would have reason to loiter. He'd have to keep moving. He heard Bingham rustling paper. A file, maybe. Or a notebook.

'Interesting,' said Bingham. 'He's a Yank.'

'No way.'

'Joe Hagerman,' said Bingham. 'The Americans have been after him ever since he was sighted in Afghanistan during the war there. He was in a training camp in Pakistan, then disappeared under the radar two years ago. You have him in sight?'

'He's just gone inside a house in Kilburn,' said Shepherd. 'Jimmy Sharpe's on his way and there's supposed to be back-up coming.'

'There are two cars heading your way but they're stuck in traffic.'

'Is Button stuck in traffic too?'

'She's otherwise engaged, I'm afraid.'

'She should be on top of this,' said Shepherd.

'She's handed it to me until she's available,' said Bingham.

'Yeah, well, with respect, I don't know you. I barely know her. Sharpe tells me her phone's off.'

'That's true. I've been trying to update her on your progress but I'm not getting through.'

'That's not good enough. This guy's a terrorist, a possible al-Qaeda operative, and she's not contactable?'

'Look, Dan, I'm not in a position to tell you what Charlotte's doing, but you have my word that she won't have turned off her mobile lightly.'

Shepherd stopped walking, then turned back to the house. He cursed.

'What's wrong?' asked Bingham.

'Hagerman's just come out and he's got a suitcase with him.'

Hagerman had exchanged his raincoat for a hooded duffel coat. He was holding a medium-sized hard-shelled case. It had an extendable arm so that it could be pulled along on its built-in wheels, but he was carrying it. He started to walk briskly along the main road.

'He's on the move,' Shepherd said, into the phone. 'Back towards Kilburn High Road. I'm going to have to talk to Sharpe.'

Hagerman was carrying his case, alternating it between his left and right hands. Shepherd was about fifty feet behind, matching his speed, stopping occasionally to look in shop windows. He dialled Sharpe's number. 'Razor, where the hell are you?' he said.

'Maida Vale, should be with you in five minutes.'

'He's heading for the Tube. Two black cabs have gone by and he ignored them. He's got a heavy case so I'm thinking he can't be walking too far, which means he's back on the Tube. If he goes to Paddington he can be at Heathrow in fifteen minutes. Where the hell's the back-up?'

'Stuck in traffic,' said Sharpe.

'This is a monumental cock-up.'

'Where are you?'

'Kilburn High Road. Three minutes from the Tube station.'

'What do you want me to do?'

Shepherd cursed. Once they went underground again he'd lose contact with Sharpe. 'Are you near Maida Vale Tube station?'

'Just passing it.'

'Okay. Stop the car. You've got to get on the train. Let me run the numbers. Three minutes to the station. One minute to get tickets, one minute down to the platform. Three minutes for the train to get from here to you. You get the first train that pulls into Maida Vale after eight minutes from now. I'll be close to the centre of the train.'

'Got you.'

'Call Bingham and tell him what we're doing.'

'What about the back-up?'

'What fucking back-up?' Shepherd cut the connection. Ahead of him, Hagerman had quickened his pace. Shepherd cursed and hurried after him.

'It doesn't look that painful, actually,' said Button. She sipped her tea. She was looking through the two-way mirror into the next room where the Saudi was sitting naked on the floor with his legs apart at a thirty-degree angle, his face pressed to the ground, his neck tied to his calves with webbing strips. The two men stood behind him, arms folded.

Yokely smiled thinly and adjusted the cuffs of his starched white shirt. 'You should try it some time, Charlie,' he said. 'It's known as "Stewed Chicken with a Bent Neck" by the guys at the Zhangshi Education and Reformation Camp. Believe me, it hurts.'

'The technique is used at Guantanamo Bay, is it?'

'Sadly, no,' said Yokely. 'I suggested it but was overruled.' He took off his jacket and hung it on the back of a chair.

Button had taken off her Bluetooth headset. It was uncomfortable and made her ear sweat. 'How long do we leave him like that?' she asked Yokely.

'In an ideal world, eight or nine hours. But this isn't an ideal world.' He picked up his mug, took a sip of coffee and grimaced. 'It's instant,' he complained.

'So drink tea,' said Button.

'I hate tea more than I hate instant coffee. After this is over we should go for a walk in Hyde Park. There's a place by the Serpentine that does a great cup of coffee.'

Broken Nose kicked the Saudi in the side, hard.

'I can't believe I'm doing this,' she said quietly.

Yokely walked over to the observation window and watched as Scarred Lip kicked him in the left thigh. The Saudi screamed. 'You're not doing it, Charlie,' said the American. 'You're supervising. There's a difference. It's important that he sees his fate is in the hands of a woman.'

'Because he's a Saudi?'

Yokely shook his head. 'Because he's a man,' he said. 'With same-sex torture, there's always an element of competition. The subject wants to prove he's better than the man who's causing his pain. His adrenaline kicks in and he becomes determined to take as much as he can.'

'And with a woman it's less competitive?'

'You're not happy doing this, are you?'

'Of course not,' said Button, briskly.

'I'm not saying that's a negative. It's in our favour. He'll pick up on it. The fact that you find it so distasteful will make him realise how terrible his predicament is.'

'I get it,' said Button. 'Sort of the ultimate good-cop-bad-cop?'

'As a woman you can say you sympathise and he'll believe it. If a man tries it, he'll assume he's faking it.'

'You're telling me that women fake it better than men, Richard?' said Button, with a smile.

The American chuckled. 'It's a science – it always has been, ever since the days of the Inquisition,' he said.

'I hate to think where you learned all this.'

'I've been around,' said Yokely. 'Do you know what the US Army's field manual defines as the object of interrogation?'

Button smiled. 'To obtain the maximum amount of usable information possible in the least amount of time.'

Yokely raised his eyebrows. 'I'm impressed,' he said.

'I've been on courses,' she said. 'The manual lists sixteen approaches, but I seem to recall that it explicitly prohibits torture, mental or physical.'

'The manual was written a long time ago,' said Yokely. 'Long before 9/11.'

'But the Geneva Convention still applies, last I heard.'

'Really?'

'And I seem to recall article three forbidding violence to life and person, in particular murder of all kinds, mutilation, cruel treatment and torture.'

'You know, Charlie, it's always struck me as a pity that the Geneva Convention never said anything about flying airliners full of civilians into office buildings. But that's just me.' Yokely nodded at the Saudi, who was now being kicked by both men. 'Trust me, if there was a better technique I'd be using it. What we're doing in there has been shown to work. Often the threat of pain is more effective than the pain itself. But first we have to show that we're serious. Once he knows we're willing and able to inflict pain, he'll believe us when we tell him we're going to hurt him even more.'

'And the offer of money gives him a way out?'

'Threatening death on its own is worse than useless,' said Yokely, warming to his subject. 'One of two things happen. It could be that the guy assumes he's going to be killed whether or not he's compliant. He figures he's going to die anyway so might as well get it over with. He just clams up and waits to die. Or he realises that it's an empty threat because death defeats the whole point of the torture, assuming that the point is to extract information. So he calls the torturer's bluff and says, "Okay, kill me." If the torturer doesn't carry out the threat, he loses the initiative. So either we kill him, or we torture him. There's no reason to move from one to the other.'

'So we tell Ahmed that the offer of money is there for him whenever he wants it?'

Yokely flashed her a grin. 'That's what we tell him.'

'And after he's talked, what then? Does he walk away with the money?'

'Do you really want to know, Charlie?'

Button held his gaze for several seconds. The American had the glistening-hard eyes of a freshly killed fish. 'I suppose not.' She took out her mobile. 'Do you mind if I check my messages before I go back in? I'm in the middle of a few things.'

'Go ahead,' said Yokely.

Button switched on the phone and checked her voicemail. She had nine messages.

The first was from her husband, letting her know that he was in meetings all afternoon and had a pre-arranged dinner with a client so wouldn't be able to get back for Poppy, but that he'd call June, their three-times-a-week cleaning lady.

The second was from David Bingham, confirming that he had started sending photographs of the al-Qaeda suspects to Shepherd's phone and that he was arranging to send surveillance teams to back him up.

The third was from Shepherd, letting her know that the suspect was on the move and that he was following.

The fourth was from Jimmy Sharpe. Shepherd had followed the man into the Underground and was out of contact.

The fifth was from Bingham, confirming that surveillance back-up was on the way and that, so far, Shepherd had not been able to identify the suspect.

The sixth was from her husband saying that June was at a local hospital visiting an aunt with a broken hip and wouldn't be able to let Poppy out. She could tell that he was annoyed.

The seventh was from Sharpe. He explained that Shepherd had followed the man to an address in Kilburn and wanted Button to call him back.

The eighth was from her husband. He apologised for being short with her earlier and said that one of his afternoon meetings had been cancelled so he'd be able to pop back to the house to take care of the dog.

The ninth and final message was from David Bingham saying that Shepherd had identified the man. Joe Hagerman. An American. Button smiled to herself. Yokely was going to love that, an American-born terrorist on UK soil and it had been the British who spotted him. Hagerman had left the house in Kilburn and Shepherd was following on foot.

Button exhaled deeply.

'Problems?' asked Yokely.

'There's a lot going on.'

'I need you in there, Charlie,' said the American, nodding at the two-way mirror.

'I have to make a few calls,' said Button.

'Do you need privacy?'

'I wouldn't mind, Richard, thank you.'

'I have to stay in here,' said Yokely. 'The toilets are along the corridor, why not use them?'

Button headed down the corridor and pushed open the door to the toilets. She scrolled through her contacts book and called David Bingham. He briefed her on the current position. Shepherd had just gone back underground. Sharpe had gone to Maida Vale Tube station and was attempting to board the same train. Two back-up surveillance teams were on the way but stuck in traffic.

'What's your reading of the situation, David?' asked Button.

'I think Hagerman's leaving the country. Probably through Heathrow.'

'I'll speak to Patsy. It'll probably be best if we let the Americans handle this. Strictly speaking, we've nothing to pick him up on. I'll call Patsy and get Five to make the approach.'

'How are things going on American soil?'

'They've a strange way of doing things,' said Button.

'Can I help?'

'Sadly, no. Just keep on top of the Hagerman thing for me. Okay, let me call Patsy.'

Button ended the call and phoned Patsy Ellis. Button quickly outlined the situation to her former boss.

'There's no doubt that it's Hagerman?' asked Ellis.

Button explained about Shepherd's near-photographic memory.

'And he's on the move?'

'With a suitcase. He took the Bakerloo Line so we're thinking Paddington, then the Heathrow Express to the airport.'

'Okay. But where's he off to? He can't fly to the US on anything other than a US passport without being fingerprinted.

And he's on their watch list so he'd be lifted as soon as he landed.'

'I agree,' said Button. 'The Uddin brothers supply British passports. They've no American connections, as far as we know. So if he's got a UK passport, he could be going anywhere except the US.'

'I suppose it's possible that he could have been picking up passports for someone else,' said Ellis. 'I think we just watch and wait. I'll notify my opposite number in Homeland Security, but we'll run with the ball until we know for sure where he's going. How about getting a name on the passport? It'd make tracing an itinerary easier.'

'The only way to do that is to bring in the Uddin brothers and their Passport Agency contact straight away,' said Button.

'How's your investigation going?'

'All done and dusted. Shepherd collected his passport today. We followed the passport on to the system and we've identified the man. A Bangladeshi, he's been with the Passport Agency for ten years. David Bingham has the details. We were going to let him run for a while longer.'

'Would you have any problems if I called David and had them pulled in now?'

'No, of course not.'

'Thanks,' said Ellis. 'Are you still at the embassy?'

'Unfortunately, yes.'

'Not pleasant?'

'No, not really,' said Button.

'There's an echo on the line, I do hope our cousins aren't listening in.'

'I'm in the loo,' said Button.

'Lovely,' said Ellis. 'Call me when it's over. We'll have a drink.'

'I'll need one,' said Button.

She ended the call, then stood for a while staring at her reflection in the mirror above the washbasins. She looked tired, and regretted leaving her bag in the room with Yokely. Her make-up needed refreshing, and her hair could have done with a brush.

She tidied it with her fingers, then practised her smile. But she didn't feel like smiling, not with what they were doing to the Saudi down the corridor.

Hagerman stood on the right-hand side of the escalator, holding the suitcase in front of him. He'd carried it all the way from the house and hadn't once used the towing handle.

Shepherd waited until the man was close to the bottom, then stepped on to the escalator and followed him down. He had taken off his pea coat, rolled up the sleeves of his shirt and slung the coat over his shoulder, in case Hagerman had seen him when they'd travelled up from Edgware Road. More often than not it was clothing or posture that gave away surveillance teams, rather than faces.

Shepherd was pretty sure that Hagerman would be taking a southbound train. The suitcase meant he was going away for a while and all the mainline stations and airport connections were to the south. He wandered on to the platform and made a point of looking at his wristwatch, as if he was in a hurry. Hagerman was sitting on one of the plastic seats fixed to the wall, elbows on his knees, deep in thought. He seemed unaware of his surroundings, and Shepherd felt a bit happier about the one-on-one surveillance.

He stood next to a chocolate-vending machine and looked at his watch again. Providing Sharpe had gone straight to Maida Vale Tube station, he shouldn't have any problem getting on the same train.

Yokely looked up as Button walked back into the room. He put down his coffee mug. 'Everything under control?' he asked.

'Everything's fine,' said Button. 'Sorry about that. As you can appreciate, I was pulled in here at short notice and we've got a lot on at the moment. Now, where were we?'

In the adjoining room, Broken Nose bent down and punched the Saudi in the side of the head. Yokely spoke quietly into his headset. 'Not the face,' he said.

Broken Nose straightened up and kicked the Saudi's ribs.

'The thing about threats is that they have to be carried out,' the American said. His voice was flat and emotionless, almost as if he was giving dictation. He didn't look at Button. Instead he stared at the Saudi through the mirror. 'Talk or we'll beat you. He doesn't talk, he has to be beaten. Talk or we'll cut off your finger. He doesn't talk, he has to lose a finger. Talk or we'll castrate you. We'll electrocute you. Drown you. Burn you. First the threat. Then the pain. Once he knows that the pain will follow the threat, the anticipation can be as crippling as the pain. But if at any time the threat isn't followed up, further threats will become ineffective.'

'And the level of pain is increased as time goes on?' asked Button. She was repelled by what was happening in the next room, but fascinated too. The American was right: it was a science, one she knew nothing about.

'That's the true skill,' said Yokely. 'Self-inflicted pain is the most effective.'

'Self-inflicted?'

'Spreadeagled against a wall. Standing on a stool for extended periods. Crouched. Any of those positions adopted for long periods causes pain, but the source of the pain is the guy's own body. He can't be angry with the interrogator because the interrogator isn't causing the pain. But it takes time, and we don't know how much we have.'

'But why don't you just use the torture that causes the maximum pain?'

'Like what?' asked the American with an amused smile.

'I don't know. Red-hot needles in the eyes. Something like that.'

Yokely chuckled again, and Button felt a flash of embarrassment. 'Here's the thing, Charlie. Intense pain, real, searing, life-threatening pain, is so crippling that the subject will say literally anything to stop it. You get an immediate false confession. Now, you can work through that but you'll get a second fake confession. He might even tell you what you want to hear just because he wants an end to the pain. And each time he tells you a lie you have to stop and check it. During the checking, he has time to regain his strength and think up a better lie. Intense pain slows down the process.'

'So, less pain is better?'

'It's the anticipation of greater pain that does the damage,' said Yokely. He put his hand to his headset and frowned. Then he smiled. 'Let me know as soon as you have the satellite link,' he said. He flashed Button a thumbs-up. 'We have a cousin,' he said. 'I need you back in there.'

Button placed her mug on the table and clipped her Bluetooth headset over her ear.

The train slowed as it emerged from the tunnel into Maida Vale station. There were fewer than a dozen passengers scattered along the platform. Jimmy Sharpe was the only one to get into Shepherd's carriage. He had his hands in his coat pockets and kept them there as he sat opposite Shepherd. Shepherd looked to his left, then at the floor. Sharpe cleared his throat, face impassive. Hagerman was staring at an advertisement on the carriage wall, his hands on his suitcase.

The doors closed and the train accelerated into the tunnel.

Broken Nose untied the webbing straps and hauled the Saudi into a sitting position. 'Stand up!' he screamed, then dragged him to his feet. 'Stand to attention!' The Saudi tried to comply but he could barely move. Broken Nose grabbed him by the hair and pushed him face-first against the wall.

Button shuddered. She was sitting at the table, trying to appear calm, as if she watched men being tortured regularly. 'Tell us what you know and this will end, Mr Ahmed,' she said.

The Saudi said nothing. His left leg buckled beneath him. Broken Nose pushed him upright again.

'Do you know what waterboarding is, Mr Ahmed?'

Broken Nose spun the Saudi so that he was facing her. Scarred Lip grabbed his left arm to help keep him vertical.

'I said, do you know what waterboarding is?'

The Saudi stared at the floor.

'I'm told it's in common use in the Abu Ghraib prison in Iraq and in US prisons in Guantanamo Bay and Afghanistan. It's a form of controlled drowning. If you don't tell us what you know, these men are authorised to use the technique on you. I'm told it's incredibly painful.'

The Saudi refused to look at her.

'What have you been doing in London?' she asked.

The Saudi said nothing, eyes on the floor.

Button could see that he had no intention of answering any questions. Obviously he knew that silence was the best defence in any interrogation. To be able to tell if someone was lying, one had to know how they behaved when they were telling the truth. That required conversation. It didn't matter what the subject was, as long as Button could observe the man's mannerisms. Then when he lied, hopefully she'd spot the telltale signs: the breaking of eye-contact, lip-biting, a hand moving up to the mouth or nose, a change in the blinking pattern, eyes moving up and to the right as the brain created images. There were numerous signs that a suspect was lying, but none came into play if they refused to speak.

'What was the purpose of your visit to the UK?'

The Saudi sighed.

Button nodded at the two men and they half carried, half dragged the Saudi to the door. She followed them out of the room and down the corridor to another room. A square-jawed marine stood to attention beside the door, an M16 carbine cradled in his arms.

Inside, a plank of wood lay on a metal support – like a seesaw except for the webbing straps at one end. It was next to a child's plastic paddling pool illustrated with Disney cartoon characters and filled with water. Two CCTV cameras covered the window-less room.

Button watched as Broken Nose and Scarred Lip laid the Saudi on his back on the plank and fastened him down with the webbing straps. Then she went back along the corridor to the observation room. Yokely was sitting at the table, watching a small flat-screen monitor that showed what was going on in the room down the corridor.

'You're allowed to do this?' she asked as she sat down next to the American.

'It's been approved by the Defense Department,' said Yokely.

'Will it work?' she asked.

'It's painful, no doubt about that,' said Yokely. 'But wait until they start the pumping. That really hurts.'

'Pumping?'

'They'll use a garden hose to pump water into his stomach. "*Tormento de toca*", as they used to call it in the Inquisition. It's reckoned to be the most agonising pain that visceral tissue can experience. And the beauty is that it doesn't leave marks.' He grinned. 'Not that that's an issue here.'

'It doesn't worry you?' asked Button, pacing up and down as the American stared intently at the monitor.

'In what way?'

Broken Nose and Scarred Lip slowly lowered the plank so that the Saudi's head dipped into the paddling pool. He shook his head from side to side as his hair went under the water. The two men toyed with him, letting the water play over his face.

'It's torture, pure and simple.'

'It's robust interrogation,' said Yokely. 'He comes from a society where torture is used routinely. We haven't done anything yet that wouldn't have been done to him in his own country. They stone women to death for adultery, Charlie.'

'Just because they behave like savages doesn't mean we should fall to their level.'

'Al-Qaeda wrote and published a manual to tell their people how to deal with interrogation if they got caught. It detailed the torture they could expect if they were captured in Middle Eastern countries sympathetic to the US. And then there was a section on GTMO.' He smiled. 'That's what we call Guantanamo Bay. Anyway, the thrust of the al-Qaeda manual was that in GTMO all they had to do was ride it out. The Americans were not warriors and the interrogators were not allowed to inflict harm. They could lie or they could stay silent, because other than keeping them incarcerated and feeding them three meals a day, there was nothing the Americans could do.' Yokely's smile widened. 'We've moved on since then, I can tell you.' He stared at the monitor. 'What's happening now is about control as much as pain,' he said. 'He has to learn that his life is in our hands. Whether he lives or dies is up to us. We decide when he breathes and when he doesn't.'

'Where did you learn this stuff, Richard?' asked Button.

The American grinned. 'That's classified,' he said. 'I could tell you . . .'

'But you'd have to kill me. Yeah, it's an old joke.'

'I got started in South America where there are fewer concerns about human rights than there are here. But I was there as an observer. I cut my teeth in Afghanistan. The hunt for bin Laden. We had to get intelligence and we needed it quickly.'

'Forgive me, but aren't we still looking for bin Laden?' said Button.

'We got close,' said Yokely, 'and we got a lot of his people. And that was as a direct result of the information obtained by the coercive techniques we employed. Then I was in the Abu Ghraib prison in Iraq for a while.' He smiled. 'Incidentally, there are no interrogators in Abu Ghraib. They're all human-intelligence collectors now.'

'A rose by any other name?' said Button, drily.

'Exactly,' said Yokely.

Button stepped closer to the monitor. Broken Nose had moved to stand by the paddling pool while Scarred Lip let the plank drop so that the Saudi's head dipped under the water. His feet drummed on the plank and his shoulders and chest strained against the webbing straps. His cheeks were puffed and his eyes bulged as he fought to hold his breath. It wasn't a battle he could win. Broken Nose was peering at him, waiting for the moment when the Saudi had to give in.

Button was appalled. The Saudi's chest heaved. Then there was an explosion of bubbles from his mouth and his head thrashed as he breathed water.

Broken Nose made a chopping motion with his right hand and Scarred Lip put all his weight on the raised end of the plank. The Saudi's head and shoulders burst out of the water and he coughed.

Broken Nose nodded and Scarred Lip let the plank fall back. The Saudi's head disappeared under the water again.

'And this works?' asked Button.

'It's part of the process,' said the American. 'Under normal circumstances we wouldn't be under so much time pressure so we wouldn't get to this stage until we were well down the line. We'd start with disorientation and sleep deprivation. Then we'd move on to standing.' He grinned. 'You'd be surprised how effective that is.'

'Just standing?'

'On a stool. Or a brick. For hours on end. It's painful, but it's the pain of the body working against itself. The Gestapo perfected the technique. They had cells built just big enough to hold a standing man. Like an upturned coffin. A week was enough to drive a man mad. I tell you, forced standing is one of the most effective tortures there is. But, like I said, it takes time.'

The Saudi was bucking and kicking and Scarred Lip lifted him out of the water. He spat out water and groaned.

'Can't we use drugs or something?' asked Button.

'There's no such thing as a truth serum,' said Yokely. 'People can lie as easily when they're doped as they can when they're sober. Trust me, Charlie, I know what I'm doing.'

Scarred Lip let go of the plank and the Saudi fell back into the water.

'You should go back in there,' said Yokely. 'Keep the pressure on him.'

Button sighed.

'You're okay, yeah?' asked Yokely.

'I'm fine.'

'You look a bit pale.'

'I'm fine,' repeated Button.

'We need you in there.'

'I'm going.'

Yokely turned back to the monitor and watched the Saudi drown again.

The train slowed as it approached Paddington. Shepherd was standing by the carriage door. He'd go first, get ahead of Hagerman, and Sharpe would bring up the rear. Then they'd play it by ear. If Hagerman was heading for the airport they'd board the Heathrow Express with him. If he got on to another train, it might be more complicated, but they'd be above ground and could be in phone contact with Bingham and the back-up teams.

The train juddered to a halt and the doors clattered open. Shepherd glanced to his left. Hagerman hadn't moved. He was still sitting with his elbows on his knees, hands clasped on his suitcase as if he was in prayer. Shepherd looked at Sharpe, who shrugged almost imperceptibly. Their quarry was staying on the train.

Shepherd stepped off and walked down the platform, away from Hagerman. He passed one carriage, then got into the next and sat down.

The train lurched off and, within seconds, was roaring into the tunnel once more. There was a map of the Tube network above the door. Marylebone station was on the Bakerloo Line. So were Charing Cross and Waterloo. Liverpool Street, King's Cross and Victoria were on the Circle Line, so Hagerman would have changed at Paddington if he'd been heading for any of them. But if he was only making a rail journey, why the rush to pick up a passport from the Uddins? Shepherd studied the map. Waterloo. The Eurostar. Hagerman was leaving the country, but he wasn't flying. He was going by train.

He counted the stations between Paddington and Waterloo. Eight. At about two minutes between stations, it would be sixteen minutes at least before they could phone Bingham. And depending on where the back-up had got to, there might not be enough time for them to get to Waterloo before Hagerman boarded the Eurostar.

Shepherd's eyes flicked across the stations on the Bakerloo Line. The line was one of the deepest on the underground system. He wouldn't get a mobile signal until they arrived at Waterloo. On the bright side, if Hagerman was aiming to travel on the Eurostar, he'd be a lot easier to tail. There was only one way in and one way out. Europol would have plenty of time to mount a surveillance operation at their end. Shepherd started to relax. From where he was sitting he couldn't see Hagerman but he had Sharpe in vision and he didn't have to move until Sharpe did.

The train rattled south. Oxford Circus was the busiest station and so many shoppers crowded on that Shepherd gave up his seat so that he could stand and see through the connecting door. He made brief eye-contact with Sharpe, and then his view was blocked by a housewife struggling with half a dozen Debenhams' carrier-bags.

By the time the train reached Embankment the carriage was half empty and Shepherd was back in his seat. There was only the dip under the Thames and then they'd be at Waterloo.

The train left Embankment and snaked through the tunnel. There was no sense of what was above them, or even how far below the ground they were. Shepherd disliked all forms of public transport: trains, buses, planes, even taxis. It wasn't because he was worried about safety – he knew that he was a thousand times safer in the Tube than he was at the wheel of his CRV – it was a matter of control. And he didn't mind admitting, to Kathy Gift or anyone else, that he preferred to be in control.

As the train slowed on its approach to Waterloo, Shepherd pushed himself out of his seat and stood by the door. He looked to his left and saw Sharpe get up, which meant that Hagerman must be preparing to leave the train.

The train stopped, the doors opened, and Shepherd stepped out onto the platform. He strode confidently towards the exit, following the signs for Eurostar, his coat slung over his shoulder.

Sharpe would follow Hagerman, while Shepherd got above ground fast to make contact with their back-up.

He hurried up the escalator, snatched a glance over his shoulder as he reached the top and saw Hagerman. He pushed his ticket into the slot in the barrier, retrieved it and walked through. He took out his phone. Still no signal.

He followed the Eurostar signs to a second escalator that opened out into a coffee shop full of suited businessmen drinking cappuccinos and barking into mobile phones. As he walked into the main Eurostar departure area, the signal returned to his mobile. He called Charlotte Button and went straight through to voicemail. He left a brief message, then phoned Bingham. He sighed with relief when the man answered. At least someone was taking calls. 'David, it's Shepherd.'

'Where are you?'

'Waterloo. Bear with me a few minutes.'

'You're following Hagerman?'

'He's right behind me, I hope. I'm at the Eurostar terminal.'

'He's on the train?'

'I'm pretty sure that's where he's heading. Wait a minute and I'll know for certain.'

Shepherd saw Hagerman emerge from the Underground, still carrying the suitcase.

'Yeah, he's going on the Eurostar. That's definite. I have eyeball now.'

'I'll phone Europol. Do you know which train?'

Shepherd turned to the departure board. The next train was the 16.39 to Brussels, the one after it the 17.09 to Paris and the next the 17.42 also to Paris. Next to the departure board a huge clock with a yellow hand sweeping off the seconds. There was still thirty minutes before the Brussels train was due to leave. 'It looks like Brussels, the sixteen thirty-nine, but we won't know until he's passed through check-in.' Sharpe walked out on to the concourse. He'd picked up a newspaper from somewhere and was swishing it as he walked, a businessman in a hurry. 'As soon as we know for sure we'll call you.'

'We? Is Sharpe with you?'

'Yes. He's got his warrant card so we'll be able to get on to the train.'

'There's no doubt about this, Dan?' Shepherd could hear the uncertainty in Bingham's voice.

Hagerman walked towards the check-in desks.

'He's getting ready to board now,' said Shepherd.

Sharpe went across the concourse, away from Check-in.

'So this is a straightforward surveillance operation?' said Bingham. 'He's not behaving suspiciously? There's nothing we should be worried about?'

'He seems tense, but that might be because of the passport. He doesn't seem to be concerned about tails, other than the odd glance over his shoulder.'

'Good work. You and Sharpe follow him over. Stay in touch. The mobiles are only inoperative for the twenty minutes or so that you're under the Channel. The rest of the time you'll be able to reach me.'

'But not Button?'

'She's still uncontactable. Sorry.'

'Yeah, well, "sorry" doesn't cut it. But that's for later.'

'Agreed,' said Bingham. 'It's between you and the boss.'

'Your boss,' said Shepherd. 'Not mine. I've got to go.'

Shepherd put away his phone and hurried to the side entrance of the departure area, where Sharpe was talking to two uniformed British Transport Police officers.

'Everything okay?' asked Shepherd.

'This is DC Shepherd,' said Sharpe. 'Don't bother asking for his warrant card because he's undercover.'

The two uniforms nodded at Shepherd, unsmiling. One was in his late thirties and might have been in the army. The younger man was scrawny with a rash of acne across his forehead.

'The trains aren't full so there's no problem with us getting seats,' said Sharpe. 'But I don't have a passport.'

'I do,' said Shepherd. 'But that shouldn't be a problem, right?

You don't have to get off the train at the other end. And you didn't have a passport last time, did you?'

'The guys I saw last time were more flexible,' said Sharpe. 'They let me and Hargrove on with our warrant cards. These jobsworths are insisting on passports.'

'French territory starts at the mid-way point of the tunnel,' said the younger of the two policemen, as if he was answering an exam question.

'Okay, so he can get off when we're halfway there. Guys, come on. This is important.'

'There's nothing we can do,' said the other cop. 'It's not us, it's Immigration.'

'Either of you guys know Nick Wright? He'll vouch for me. We worked together a while back.'

The two men shook their heads. Shepherd could see there was no point in arguing with them. He walked away, pulling his mobile out of his pocket and hitting 'redial'. He told Bingham what had happened, and Bingham promised to sort it out.

Shepherd went back to the cops. 'Assuming we can get his passport, we'll need tickets.'

'You can show your warrant card,' said the younger cop.

'First, I don't have my card. He just told you that. Second, I don't want to have to explain myself to ticket inspectors or Immigration officers or anyone else who decides he wants to stick his nose into my business. I want a ticket.' He nodded at Sharpe. 'And he wants a ticket. In fact, we want tickets for the next three trains because we still don't know which one he's on. And we want them now.' He nodded at the departure board above the entrance to the boarding area. 'We've got twenty minutes to get on to that train.'

The older cop's radio crackled and he walked away to talk into his microphone. A few seconds later he was back and nodded at his colleague. 'Get the tickets now,' he said. He looked at Shepherd. 'First or standard?'

'Whatever,' said Shepherd.

The younger cop hurried off.

'Sorry,' said the older cop. His cheeks were red and he was smiling nervously now.

Bingham must have swung some heavy artillery their way, Shepherd thought. 'Can you walk me through?' he asked. 'We're still not sure which train he's on so I want to get eyeball on him before he boards.' To Sharpe, he said, 'You follow with the tickets, yeah? I'll phone you when I know which train.'

The transport cop walked Shepherd through passport control and the security check. The waiting area was packed. Every seat was taken and passengers unable to get seats were standing in groups around their suitcases. Upwards of a thousand people were crammed into an area about a third the size of a football pitch. 'Where's the CCTV control room?' asked Shepherd.

'Through there,' said the cop, indicating a grey door with 'Staff Only' on it.

'Can you take me in?' asked Shepherd.

The cop swiped a card and pushed open the door. Shepherd followed him through. The CCTV room was fully computerised with two men in shirtsleeves in front of large, flat-screen terminals.

'Guys, sorry to burst in on you. I'm DC Shepherd. I need to find a passenger quickly.'

One of the men pulled over a chair and told him to sit down.

'Thanks,' said Shepherd. 'I'm assuming he's in the waiting area. Can you run through the different cameras?'

'Do you need me for anything?' asked the uniform.

'No,' said Shepherd. 'I can handle it from here. Can you tell my colleague where I am? And thanks.'

The uniformed cop left the room as the various CCTV pictures flashed on to the screen. With so many people packed into the waiting area, Shepherd needed a minute or so to study the faces on the screen. Once he was satisfied that Hagerman wasn't in view, he nodded at the operator to switch viewpoints. He spotted Hagerman on the fifth camera, at the end of a row of seats next to a bank of payphones. 'That's him,' he said. 'Where is it?'

'At the far end of the waiting area,' said the operator. 'Close to the bottom of the escalators.'

'When do they let the passengers up to the platform?'

'Fifteen minutes before departure,' said the operator.

'I don't suppose there's any way of knowing which train the guy's going to get on, is there?' asked Shepherd.

'If you know his name, sure.'

'That's the problem,' said Shepherd. 'I don't. At least, I don't know the name he's travelling under.'

'Then you'll have to wait for him to move,' said the operator.

Shepherd stood up and clapped him on the shoulder. 'Thanks,' he said.

He phoned Sharpe and arranged to meet him at the security-check area.

'Get a move on, Razor,' he said. 'They'll be boarding the first train in the next ten minutes.'

The older uniformed cop appeared again – he'd walked Sharpe through Immigration and the security check. Sharpe was holding half a dozen tickets. 'Where is he?' he asked.

'I'll show you,' said Shepherd. He thanked the uniformed cop again for his help then took Sharpe to the coffee shop that overlooked the area where Hagerman was sitting. It was called Bonaparte's. Someone's attempt at humour, no doubt, but Shepherd wondered how the French felt to be offered coffee in a bar called Bonaparte's at a station named Waterloo. He ordered two cappuccinos and they sat down.

Sharpe turned casually. 'I see him,' he said.

'Looks tense, doesn't he?' said Shepherd.

'Probably because he's travelling on a fake passport.'

'The passport's genuine, remember,' said Shepherd, 'and he's already gone through Passport Control. He won't be checked again.'

'Drugs, maybe?'

'No one smuggles drugs out of the UK,' said Shepherd.

The departure of the Brussels train was announced in English and French, and passengers rushed for the escalators.

Hagerman sat where he was, hunched forward, fingers inter-linked as he watched the passengers stream up to the platform.

The queue stretched back more than a hundred yards, and most of the passengers were pulling wheeled suitcases or carrying rucksacks. Shepherd and Sharpe were almost the only people without luggage.

The queue had shrunk to just a dozen or so when Hagerman got up. He stretched his arms above his head and rotated his neck. 'Here we go,' said Sharpe. 'I wonder why he's going to Brussels. Nobody hates the Belgians, not even al-Qaeda. The Belgians never did anything to anyone.'

'They gave the world Tintin,' said Shepherd.

'Yeah, but that's not worth killing people for, is it?'

'And salad cream with chips.'

'Again, a minor transgression,' said Sharpe.

'According to Button, he's al-Qaeda. And al-Qaeda don't fuck about.'

Hagerman sat down again, this time with his arms folded.

'There you go,' said Sharpe. 'It's not Brussels. Maybe he's not a Tintin fan.'

'It's got to be Paris, then,' said Shepherd.

'Can I smoke in here?'

'No. The train's no-smoking, too.'

Eventually all the Brussels passengers had gone up the esca-lator. More people were coming into the waiting area all the time. Families, students, married couples, businessmen.

Shepherd took out his mobile phone and called Button. Again, he went through to voicemail and swore.

'What's wrong?' asked Sharpe.

'Her phone's still off.'

'Maybe she's having her hair done.'

'She's supposed to be running the unit and every time I call her the bloody phone's off. Hargrove was always available. Twenty-four–seven. You needed him, he was there. I've met Button twice, and both times she was playing cloak-and-dagger. Tea at the Ritz. Some fake office in the middle of nowhere. It's a game to her, Razor.' He phoned Bingham. 'It's definitely Paris,' he said. 'They've finished boarding the Brussels train and the next two are both to Paris. One goes at seventeen oh-nine and I'm betting he'll be on it. The one after is at seventeen forty-two.'

'I'll tell the French,' said Bingham. 'Call me as soon as you know for sure which one he's on. I've already sent his details to Europol so they're ready and waiting.'

Shepherd cut the connection.

'Fancy a sandwich?' asked Sharpe.

'We can get something on the train.'

'I want something now.'

'So get something.'

Shepherd toyed with his coffee as Sharpe went off to buy a sandwich. He didn't bother keeping a close eye on Hagerman. There was only one way to get to the platform and that was up the escalator.

Sharpe came back with his sandwich and a newspaper. Eventually the Tannoy announced the departure of the Paris train. Two Eurostar staff removed the barrier to the escalator and passengers started to head up to the platform.

Hagerman didn't move.

'Maybe he's planning to sleep here,' said Sharpe.

Shepherd sipped his coffee, which had gone cold. As he put down the cup, Hagerman stood, picked up his suitcase and made for the queue.

'We're off,' said Shepherd. 'He never wheels it,' he remarked, almost to himself. 'What is it with him?'

'Maybe the wheels are broken,' said Sharpe.

'So get a new case,' said Shepherd. 'What's the point of wheels on a suitcase if you don't use them?'

'My phone does a hundred things I never use,' said Sharpe. 'Technological overkill.'

'We're talking wheels on a suitcase, Razor,' said Shepherd. 'It's hardly hi-tech.'

Hagerman walked to the end of the queue. 'So, Paris it is,' said

Shepherd. 'I'll call Bingham. Do you want to find out what carriage he's in?'

Sharpe stood up and waved the tickets in Shepherd's face. 'We're in first class,' he said. 'Whoever Bingham called really put a rocket under those guys.' He gave one to Shepherd. 'See you on board.'

Shepherd phoned Bingham. 'He's on the seventeen oh-nine.' He watched as Sharpe joined the end of the queue, a group of American teenagers between him and Hagerman. Sharpe had taken off his coat and slung it over his shoulder.

'Great,' said Bingham. 'I've already warned the French but I'll call them to confirm. You and Sharpe are on the train?'

'We will be soon,' said Shepherd. 'Thanks for clearing the way. The transport cops were being decidedly unhelpful.'

'No problem,' said Bingham. 'I enjoy throwing my weight about occasionally. And SOCA carries a fair bit. Make sure he gets on the train and stays there until Paris. Keep your phone on and I'll call you to confirm that Europol's done its bit.'

Shepherd finished his coffee, then joined the queue. He was one of the last passengers to board the train. Sharpe was already in his seat. They were in carriage number eleven. There were eighteen carriages in all, with five standard-class carriages at either end, the first-class section in the middle. Their seats faced each other across a small table. Sharpe was studying a menu. He looked up as Shepherd sat down. 'They've got steak,' he said.

'Great,' said Shepherd.

'Bingham on the case?'

'He is, Button isn't.'

'Let it go, Spider,' said Sharpe.

'Where's Hagerman?'

'Second carriage from the front. The cheap seats.'

'On his own?'

'There's a woman next to him but they don't appear to be together. Relax. He's not going anywhere for the next three hours and we're going to be waited on hand and foot.'

'You don't get out much, do you?' said Shepherd.

★   ★   ★

The Saudi's eyes were tight shut and his mouth was a straight line. His chest was pulsing as he fought the urge to breathe. Button realised she was holding her own breath as she watched him struggle against the bonds holding him to the plank. She forced herself to relax. How long had his head been under water? A minute? Ninety seconds?

She knew the routine now. She'd watched Scarred Lip and Broken Nose run through the procedure half a dozen times. They submerged his head and waited until he couldn't hold his breath any longer. The Saudi would open his mouth and suck in water. They'd let him breathe it for two seconds, maybe three, then push down on the plank and lift him out. They'd give him a minute or two to recover, then drop him in again. It didn't matter how long the Saudi held his breath. They wouldn't let him up until he'd started drowning.

'We have the cousin,' prompted Yokely, in Button's ear.

The two men torturing the Saudi must have heard the same transmission because they pressed down on the end of the plank. The Saudi's head came out of the water. He gasped for breath, eyes wide, watery green snot trickling from his nose.

Scarred Lip bent down and untied the webbing straps.

The Saudi choked. His chest heaved in and out and his arms went into spasm. Scarred Lip put his hands under the man's armpits and yanked him to his feet. Broken Nose slapped him on the back, hard. The Saudi retched and watery vomit sprayed across the floor.

'Better out than in.' Broken Nose laughed. It was the first time that Button had heard him speak, and she was surprised by his West Country accent. Bristol, maybe.

The two men seized the Saudi's arms and dragged him out of the room. Button ran a hand through her hair. She felt emotionally drained by what she'd seen and heard.

She took a deep breath and exhaled slowly. It had been three weeks since she'd stopped smoking, but she would have given anything for a cigarette.

★   ★   ★

Ilyas parked the hire-car and climbed out. To his left he heard the shouts and screams of children at play. He opened the boot, took out the metal toolbox and placed it on the ground. He pulled out his fluorescent orange jacket and put it on over his overalls, then a woollen hat. He looked around, but no one was paying him any attention.

He closed the boot and walked towards the wire fence that separated the road from the railway lines. A section of fence had fallen down and he stepped over it. It had been in this damaged state for months, but even if it had been repaired he had a pair of wire-cutters in his toolbox. He walked over the strip of wasteland towards the railway lines, then beside the tracks towards Ashford International station. He glanced at the live rail: one touch would kill him instantly.

Ahead, about a hundred yards away, he could see the station platforms. Three and four were for Eurostar trains. Ilyas walked confidently. No CCTV cameras covered the track, but even if he had been observed, Network Rail maintenance workers were always walking up and down it.

He checked his watch. The Eurostar would arrive in two minutes. The timing was perfect, but that was as it should be. The operation had been planned to the smallest detail.

He reached the end of the platform and walked up the ramp. There was a security man at the top, white shirt, black trousers, black tie and black epaulettes on his shoulders, a transceiver in his hand. There was another official at the far end of the platform. They were there to watch over the passengers, so they wouldn't give a second look to a maintenance worker.

The passengers were allowed down from the holding area eight minutes before the train was due to arrive. They were already lined up along platform three, all watching for the approaching train. Ilyas walked behind them, along platform four; signs marked where the various carriages would be when the train had stopped. The passengers whom Ilyas was there to meet would be waiting for carriages seven and twelve. He didn't know their names but he had been told the style of their suitcases.

He walked along platform four, out of sight of the two security officials. He saw the passenger with the dark blue hard-shell suitcase and slid his hand into his pocket. He took out the two packages. Each was about eight inches long and two inches wide, wrapped in black plastic. As he passed the passenger he handed them over.

He slipped his hand back into his overalls as he walked. There were two more packages in his pocket.

The train arrived at platform three, its long, low nose coasting by the waiting passengers.

The man waiting opposite carriage seven also had a hard-shell suitcase, but his was dark green. He was looking at Ilyas and nodded almost imperceptibly. As Ilyas passed him, he slipped him the remaining two packages, then walked on, whistling softly. His job was done.

Shepherd frowned as the train came to a halt. 'I thought it was non-stop,' he said.

'Nah – calls at Ashford before it goes into the tunnel,' said Sharpe, picking at his prawn-couscous starter. 'It's only here for a few minutes.' He gestured at the food. 'This is horrible.' He picked up his glass of white wine and drank half of it.

Shepherd gazed out of the window at the passengers lining up to get on to the train. 'Don't eat it, then.'

'Why aren't you eating?'

'Because I'm not hungry.'

'Well, when they bring the steaks round, get one and give it to me.'

Shepherd frowned. A man had just walked from the next platform holding a dark green hard-shell suitcase.

'Now what?' said Sharpe, stabbing at a prawn.

The man's face was familiar, but this time Shepherd knew immediately where he'd seen him before. He picked up his mobile phone and scrolled through the pictures Bingham had sent him. He called up the second and held out the phone to Sharpe. 'This guy's just got on to the train.'

'What?'

'Another of the guys on Button's hit list has just got on to the train.'

The fork stopped on the way to Sharpe's mouth. 'Shit. What are the odds?'

'Exactly.'

'Where?'

'Up front. A few carriages ahead of us. And he was carrying a case just like Hagerman's. Different colour but the same style.'

'Shit,' said Sharpe.

'Yeah,' said Shepherd. 'Deep, deep, shit.'

Charlotte Button flinched as the two men stamped on the Saudi's feet. The Saudi screamed and she winced as she heard a bone snap. The Saudi went quiet. The two men straightened, breathing heavily.

The Saudi lay perfectly still, curled in the foetal position. 'Is he all right?' Button asked.

Scarred Lip put his fingertips against the Saudi's neck, felt for a pulse, then nodded. Broken Nose unzipped his fly and began to urinate over the bound man. Button gasped. Her nose wrinkled and she put a hand over her mouth.

'We have the sat link,' said Yokely, in her earpiece.

The men untied the Saudi and dumped him heavily on the chair.

He groaned and Scarred Lip slapped his face. The sound echoed in the room like a pistol shot. One of the plasma screens flickered into life. The picture was jerky, but clear. It looked like a hotel room – ornate furniture, gilded mirrors, chandeliers.

Two men in dark suits, black ski masks and black leather gloves came into view holding a young man who was wearing a pale blue polo shirt and khaki chinos. He was clearly scared and his mouth was moving, but there was no sound so Button couldn't hear what he was saying.

The men thrust him into an armchair. One produced a roll of duct tape and wound it around the man and the chair.

Broken Nose grabbed the Saudi's hair and yanked back his head. Scarred Lip pulled up the Saudi's eyelids with his thumbs, examined his pupils, and nodded. He was conscious.

'Please watch the screen, Mr Ahmed,' said Button.

On the screen the man finished binding the captive to the chair. The Saudi blinked as he tried to focus. 'Husayn,' he whispered.

'That's right, Mr Ahmed. Your cousin, Husayn bin Musa al-Ghamdi. Currently in Nice. I'm sorry for the lack of sound, but you'll get the drift of what's happening.'

On screen, one of the men produced a large automatic and pressed the gun against Husayn's head.

'You can't do this,' said the Saudi.

'We can,' said Button.

'He is just a boy,' said the Saudi.

Yokely's voice crackled in Button's ear. 'He's twenty-two.'

'He's twenty-two, Mr Ahmed,' said Button. 'He's a man.'

'He's not part of this,' said the Saudi.

'Part of what?' said Yokely, in Button's ear.

Button glared at the mirror and pulled out her earpiece. She didn't need Yokely to tell her how to conduct an interrogation. 'We need to know what you're doing in London,' she said. 'Tell us, and Husayn will be released. You will get your money and your new identity, and we will all move on.'

The Saudi's eyes were filled with tears. 'He is just a boy,' he repeated.

'Mr Ahmed, I take no pleasure in putting you through this. Tell us what we need to know and it will all be over.'

'I demand you stop this now,' said the Saudi, his voice trembling. 'This is against all international law. Against all human-rights laws. You cannot do this.'

'We have moved beyond laws, Mr Ahmed,' Button told him. 'This is about the survival of our way of life. It's about the safety of the seven million people living in this city. We put their rights above yours, Mr Ahmed. Now, stop being so silly. Co-operate with us, and we can put an end to it.'

'You will go to hell for this,' said the Saudi.

'I dare say,' said Button.

She looked at the plasma screen. The boy was shaking but the tape held him tightly to the chair. The gun was just inches from his head. It was a 9mm Beretta 92FS, used by the US Army, the Italian police and armed forces, and the French Gendarmerie Nationale. It was a good weapon: she had fired one herself many times in MI5's underground range. The safety was off. Husayn's mouth was moving and tears streamed down his face. As Button watched, the gun kicked in the gloved hand. The side of the young man's head exploded in a shower of brain matter, blood and bone.

Button screamed. 'No!' she yelled. Husayn's mouth locked wide open and blood trickled through his teeth as his head slumped forward. Button whirled round and stared at the mirror. 'What have you done?' she screamed. 'What the fuck have you done?'

Shepherd cursed as once again his call went through to Button's voicemail. 'This is unreal,' he said to Sharpe. 'What the hell is she playing at?'

'Phone still off?'

Shepherd scrolled through his call list and phoned Bingham, who answered almost immediately. 'Dan, everything okay?' he asked.

'No, everything is not okay,' said Shepherd, acidly. 'Everything is as far from okay as it could get without falling off the edge of the world. Button is still incommunicado.'

'What do you need?' asked Bingham.

Shepherd took a deep breath. There was no point in antagonising her number two. 'We're pulling out of Ashford station,' he said. 'I've just recognised another face on the platform from Button's hit list.'

'He got on the train?'

'Yes. And he was carrying a suitcase similar to the one Hagerman had.'

'I don't think there's any need to panic,' said Bingham. 'All the luggage—'

'I'm not panicking,' interrupted Shepherd. 'I'm calling in with a sitrep. And the reason I'm doing that is because in ten minutes we're going to be in the tunnel and I'll be out of contact so I want to know now what I'm supposed to be doing.'

'My apologies, Dan. I didn't mean it to come out that way. I meant to say that we don't have to worry overmuch, do we? All luggage is scanned before it's allowed on to the Eurostar, and all the passengers go through metal detectors. There's no way guns or bombs or even knives can get on the train, is there?'

'True.'

'So the most likely scenario is that they're just travelling together. Which guy is it?'

'The second one you sent me. I don't know his name.'

'Okay. I'll inform the French. We'll have them both tailed when they reach Paris. In the meantime carry out a quick recce. Find out if they're sitting next to each other.'

'Negative on that. There's already a woman sitting next to Hagerman.'

'Okay. But sweep through anyway. See if there's anyone else you recognise. Whatever happens, call me back before you enter the tunnel. I'll try to track down Button.'

'Do you know where she is?'

'The American embassy.'

'A bloody cocktail party?'

'Not exactly,' said Bingham.

Button's hands were shaking and she could barely breathe. Her discomfort was intensified by the smug smile on Yokely's face. 'You killed him,' she said.

Yokely shook his head. 'No, I didn't. The man who pulled the trigger did.'

'You ordered it.'

'Someone had to.'

'Why the hell didn't you tell me what you were going to do?'

'Because I needed your reaction,' said Yokely.

Button sat down and put her head into her hands. 'What do you mean?'

Yokely sat opposite her. In the interrogation room, Broken Nose and Scarred Lip had the Saudi on the floor again. Broken nose was squatting on his back, pushing his face to the floor, while Scarred Lip bound his neck to his calves. They were putting him back in the stress position.

'You were horrified, right? Disgusted?'

Button's face was screwed up in disbelief. 'Of course I was horrified!' she shouted. 'You had an innocent man killed.'

Yokely put up a hand. 'Steady, Charlie. We've an assignment here, and that assignment is to make the bastard in there tell us everything he knows. Let's not forget who the enemy is here.'

'That boy wasn't the enemy,' said Button.

'It was his call, not mine. All he had to do was to talk and that boy would have been released, unharmed. We gave him the choice.'

'Richard, we can't go about executing people!'

Yokely smiled amiably. 'Actually, we do it quite a lot in America.'

'The boy you had shot wasn't guilty of anything. You had him killed . . .' She was lost for words.

'Listen to me, Charlie, and listen to me carefully. We are running out of time.' He took a deep breath. 'You didn't see it, did you?'

'See what?'

Yokely shook his head in mock-reproach. 'You were too busy looking at the screen, weren't you?'

Button wanted to swear at the American and tell him not to be so bloody condescending, but she bit her lip.

'He was looking at the clock,' said Yokely. 'His own cousin was about to be killed, but he kept looking at the clock.'

'There's a deadline.'

'Yes. Minutes or hours. Because if it was days he wouldn't care what time it was.'

'Oh, Jesus,' whispered Button. He was right. She'd broken one of the prime rules of an interrogation: always watch the subject's reactions. Often it wasn't what they said that gave them away but their body language.

'I don't think Jesus is going to help us,' said Yokely. 'This is something that's been left up to us.'

'Frankly, I'm not sure I can take much more,' she said.

'Which is why you have to be in there.'

'I want a cigarette.'

'This is a non-smoking building,' said Yokely. 'Sorry.'

'Damn you, I want a cigarette and I want one now!' she shouted.

Yokely put up his hands to placate her. 'Okay, okay,' he said. 'I'll get a pack brought in. What brand?'

'Any brand,' hissed Button. She sat down and sipped some water.

Yokely took out his mobile phone and asked for a pack of cigarettes and a lighter. 'I don't know,' he said. 'Whatever you can get.' He put away the phone. 'It's on its way,' he said. 'Look, as I said before, we mustn't get into a competition with this man. He's as hard as they come, a committed terrorist who's prepared to die for his cause. He's not a suicide-bomber – I doubt he believes that seventy-two virgins are waiting for him in heaven and that Allah has a place reserved for him in temples of gold, but he's prepared to die for what he believes in. If he's put under pressure by someone who hates him, he'll react by hardening himself. He'll make it a point of principle not to give in. But he can see in your eyes the horror of what's been done to him. He'll see you empathising, and that will make it much worse for him.'

'It's sick,' said Button.

'It's technique,' said Yokely. 'If we had more time there'd be other options, but, as I keep reminding you, time is the one thing we don't have. So I need you in there, showing him that you're upset by what's happening, that you'd help if you could but you can't.'

Button shuddered. 'How far do we go?'

'As far as we have to.'

'You'd kill him?' She corrected herself: 'You'd have him killed?'

'If he dies without telling us anything, we'll have lost,' said Yokely.

'Now you're the one making it sound like a competition,' said Button. 'A game, with winners and losers.'

'There will be a winner,' said Yokely. He gestured at the interrogation room. 'And I'm damned if it'll be him.' He put his hand to his earpiece and listened intently. Then he looked at Button. 'We have a brother,' he said. 'They're setting up the sat link now.'

Button could feel a headache building and rubbed her temples with her fingertips. 'Who the hell are we to be doing this?' she whispered.

'We're the good guys,' said Yokely. 'And don't you forget it.'

Joe Hagerman was sitting in a double seat, next to the aisle, facing the rear of the train. A middle-aged Frenchwoman was beside him, snoring softly and smelling of garlic. Hagerman was in a standard-class carriage where any passengers who wanted food or drink had to go to the buffet car in the sixth carriage. He stood up and headed for the rear of the train.

He bought a bottle of water and stood at a circular table, sipping it. He wore a cheap plastic digital watch on his left wrist. Another man was standing at another table, drinking coffee, wearing an identical watch. Two businessmen were at a table close by, drinking red wine and chattering in French, briefcases at their feet. A small queue was forming at the counter as more passengers arrived, eager for refreshments.

Hagerman carried his water across to the man with the coffee, who placed a black plastic-wrapped package on the table, and walked back in the direction of the first-class section. Hagerman slipped the package into the pocket of his duffel coat and went back to his carriage. It would soon be time.

*   *   *

Shepherd hurried back to his seat. Sharpe was starting on his steak. 'You missed the main courses,' he said.

'Hagerman's not there,' said Shepherd.

Sharpe put down his knife and fork. 'What do you mean?'

'His seat's empty. The woman's there, snoring like a chainsaw, but he's not.'

'Buffet car?'

'I had to go through it to get to his carriage. He's not there and neither is the guy who got on.'

Sharpe frowned. 'They're both missing?'

'They might have decided to go to the toilet at the same time, but it seems like one hell of a coincidence.'

'What do you think's going on, Spider?'

Shepherd sat down. 'I don't know, but I've got a bad feeling,' he said.

'They couldn't be planning something on the train, could they?'

'All the bags are X-rayed and everyone has to go through the metal detectors. And they can't hijack the bloody thing, can they?'

'Poison? Anthrax? Gas? Remember the attack in Tokyo by those religious nutters?'

Shepherd took out his phone. 'I'll call Bingham,' he said.

Scarred Lip untied the webbing from round the Saudi's neck and tossed it on to the table. Broken Nose helped him to his feet. Button stood by the door, arms folded across her chest, eyes on the plasma screens.

Scarred Lip used a piece of webbing to tie the Saudi's hands behind his back. His legs buckled and Broken Nose hurried to support him. The two men carried him to the chair and dropped him on to it.

As Button sat down, one of the plasma screens flashed white, then black. A test card appeared. It stayed up for a few seconds and was replaced with a view of what appeared to be the inside of a warehouse or factory. There was a bare concrete floor, prefabricated steel walls and, overhead, a metal roof criss-crossed with girders. Fluorescent lights hung from the girders, and there was a skylight off to the left.

'Please look at the screen, Mr Ahmed,' said Button.

Broken Nose grabbed his hair, twisted it savagely and forced him to confront it. The Saudi gasped in pain.

A man appeared on the screen, short and squat in a leather bomber jacket that stretched tight across his shoulders. He was wearing a black ski mask and gloves, and holding a length of chain in his right hand. He threw one end over a girder above his head. Button realised she could hear the chain rattling. This time there was sound.

The Saudi tried to turn his head away but Broken Nose punched him and forced it back.

The man in the ski mask waved at someone out of view. Two more men in ski masks appeared, holding an Arab man in his early thirties. He was struggling but the men holding him were big and powerful and had already bound his wrists behind his back. He was wearing a blue sweatshirt, shorts and training shoes and looked as if he had been jogging when they had taken him. His struggles intensified when he saw the chain but there was nothing he could do.

The two men threw him to the ground and tied one end of the chain round his ankles. The masked man in the bomber jacket pulled at the other end, and all three hauled the Arab into the air feet first. He was screaming in Arabic – Button caught the gist: he was begging for his life.

Button was staring open-mouthed at the screen and moved to stand by the door so that she could see the Saudi. She caught sight of her reflection and was shocked by how pale she was.

The Saudi was muttering under his breath, praying. It wouldn't help, Button thought. Begging and pleading wouldn't help. The only way out for the Saudi was a full and immediate confession.

The three men moved out of vision. They must have been

tying the free end of the chain to something because they reappeared a few seconds later.

'Your brother,' said Button. 'Abdal-Rahmaan. Servant of the Merciful. Another illustrious name.'

'I know who it is,' said the Saudi. He started to cough.

A wet patch appeared at the bound man's groin.

'Tell us what you have planned and it ends now,' said Button.

'I have nothing to say. I have done nothing wrong.'

The masked man in the bomber jacket walked off screen.

The Arab was begging in English now, his words distorted by the satellite link. 'I haven't done anything,' he sobbed. 'Who are you? Why are you doing this to me?'

'Please, Mr Ahmed. You saw what they did to your cousin.'

The Saudi shook his head.

'They are serious,' said Button.

'You think I don't know that?'

'You will talk eventually so you might as well talk now and save your brother any further pain.'

'You will kill him anyway.'

'That's not true, Mr Ahmed. You have my word.'

'You are not in control,' said the Saudi. 'You are a pawn. A minion. A dog crawling at the feet of her master.'

On the screen, Bomber Jacket reappeared, holding a red metal can with a black plastic spout. He started to splash its contents over the Arab, who started screaming again.

Button swallowed. She couldn't drag her eyes away from the screen. Petrol dripped down him, over his face, through his hair and on to the concrete floor.

The Saudi groaned. 'You cannot do this,' he said. 'My brother has done nothing. He works for my father, nothing more.'

'He has been involved in arms deals for the Saudis,' said Yokely, in Button's ear.

'Abdal-Rahmaan is an arms-dealer,' said Button, but even as she said it she knew it was no excuse for what they were doing to him. He wasn't about to be burned alive because he dealt in weapons but because he was related to the Saudi.

'He is a businessman,' hissed the Saudi. 'My brother has never hurt anybody.'

'No, but you have,' said Yokely, in Button's ear.

Button didn't like the American putting words into her mouth. 'Tell us what you are planning, Mr Ahmed, and your brother goes free. You go free, too. You have my word.'

'I am British. You are British. You cannot do this to me,' said the Saudi. 'You cannot do this to me in Britain. It's not allowed.'

Button smiled sadly. 'We're not in Britain, Mr Ahmed.'

The Saudi frowned, not understanding.

'We're in the basement of the American embassy in Grosvenor Square. You are on American soil.'

The Saudi stared at her. Then he sneered. 'You are a lapdog of the Americans. Same as your prime minister.'

The Arab had stopped pleading and was breathing heavily, almost hyperventilating.

'Tell me what you have planned,' said Button. 'Tell me, and your brother will be released.'

The Saudi pulled back his face and spat across the room. Bloody phlegm splattered across Button's face.

Broken Nose stepped forward and stamped on the Saudi's bare foot, grinding his boot into the flesh. The Saudi shrieked. Button took a handkerchief from her top pocket and calmly wiped her face.

Yokely's voice crackled in her earpiece. 'Tell him we have his sister.'

Button's stomach lurched. But before she could say anything, she saw the Saudi's eyes dart to the clock. Yokely was right: time was running out. She hardened her heart. 'Mr Ahmed,' she said, 'we have your sister.'

'What do you mean you can't find them?' said Bingham. 'They can't have disappeared.'

'They're not in any of the carriages,' said Shepherd. 'The only place they can be is in the toilets. And if they've both gone to the toilets at the same time, there must be something up. I know their luggage has been scanned, but this is too much of a coincidence. And they had similar suitcases. That's what worries me.'

'I agree,' said Bingham. 'But why did one get on at Waterloo and the other at Ashford? Security is the same at both stations, so it can't be that.'

Shepherd kept his voice to a low whisper. He didn't want anyone else in the carriage to hear what he was saying. 'We were thinking maybe chemical,' he said.

'It's possible,' said Bingham. 'Confined space like the tunnel.'

'Look, I'm going to be in the tunnel in seconds. What do you want me to do?'

'It's got to be your call, Dan.'

'What are you saying?' asked Shepherd.

'You're going to have to do whatever you have to do,' said Bingham. 'I'll back you up, I swear.'

'I'm not armed, you know that?' The train plunged into the tunnel and the phone buzzed in his ear. The line was dead.

Shepherd put the phone down and looked at Sharpe.

'Now what?' said Sharpe.

'Now it gets interesting,' said Shepherd.

Button paced up and down in front of the two-way mirror. The Saudi was sobbing quietly, his arms wrapped round his chest. Blood was dribbling from his nose, down his chin and on to the floor between his feet.

'Mr Ahmed, please . . . *min fadlik.*'

The Saudi shuddered. '*Hill 'annii,*' he spat. The literal translation was 'Get out of my sight', but it was closer to 'Fuck off' in meaning.

Button pointed up at the plasma screens. The Saudi's brother was on the top left screen, still hanging from the girder. On the bottom right screen, a woman in a black burkha sat on a wooden chair, back ramrod straight, hands on her knees. Behind her, a man in a ski mask held a baseball bat.

'Mr Ahmed, they are your brother and sister,' said Button.

'You know what's going to happen if you continue to refuse to co-operate. Please. It doesn't have to be like this.'

'Laa tastatii' an taf'al dhaalika,' he said quietly.

'They can do what they want,' she said. 'You must have realised that by now.'

A second man appeared next to the woman. He was also wearing a ski mask. He grabbed the headpiece of the burkha and ripped it off. The woman shrieked and covered her face with her hands.

'No!' shouted the Saudi.

The earpiece crackled. 'Tell him we have a list of all his family and friends. Tell him we'll—'

Button pulled out the earpiece. She went over to the Saudi and put her hand on his shoulder. 'You have to talk,' she said, her voice trembling. 'They're not going to stop until everyone you love is dead. Do you understand that?'

The Saudi wailed and rolled off the chair on to the floor. Broken Nose and Scarred Lip moved to pick him up but Button waved them away. 'Leave him alone!' she shouted. She pointed at the door. 'Get out – get out now! Both of you!'

The two men stopped dead and stood, watching her. Then Scarred Lip put his fingertips to his earpiece, frowned, and nodded at Broken Nose. The two men left the room, faces impassive.

The Saudi scuttled backwards across the floor, like a frightened crab, and sat with his back to the wall, his knees under his chin. His body was racked with spasms and he stared at the screens.

Button walked over to him slowly and knelt by his side. She touched his arm, but he flinched as if he'd been stung. 'Abdal-Jabbaar, please. You can stop this now,' she whispered.

His trembling intensified and his eyes flicked from screen to screen.

'Whatever you are, whatever you believe in, it can't be worth this,' said Button. Tears filled her eyes. 'They're going to keep on until they kill everyone you've ever cared for. They're relentless, these people. Relentless and uncaring.'

The Saudi began to sob and tears ran down his cheeks. Button realised she was crying, too. She sat down next to the Saudi and pulled her legs up against her chest, instinctively adopting the same posture. They were both hugging their knees, tears streaming down their faces.

The Saudi's brother was babbling now, Arab phrases mixed with English, a stream of words that made little sense. He was close to passing out.

The man in the ski mask threw more petrol on to him – some went up his nose, making him cough and choke.

A second masked man stepped forward with a bronzed Zippo lighter. He held up the lighter to the camera and flicked back the lid with his gloved thumb.

The Saudi started to mutter an Arabic prayer, his lips barely moving.

'Please, don't let them do this,' whispered Button. Her mouth was completely dry and the strength had faded from her limbs. 'Just tell them what they want to know and it'll be over. There are others who can take over from you – you know that. You're a soldier in a huge army – no one will blame you if you talk now. You've given enough. You've done enough. No one will blame you, Abdal-Jabbaar. Please. *Min fadlik.*'

The Saudi's breath was coming in short, sharp gasps and he was staring at his brother. 'A'tinii waqtan lit-tafkiir bidhaalik,' he whispered.

'We don't have time,' said Button. 'If you don't talk *now*, you know what they'll do.'

On the other screen, the Saudi's sister was glaring defiantly at the camera, a gun pressed to her temple. She steadfastly ignored it. She was brave, thought Button, but the men hadn't started to work on her yet. Once they did, they'd see just how brave she was.

The man with the Zippo flicked the small wheel at the top of the lighter. It sparked but did not light.

The Saudi screamed in terror.

Button could barely breathe. She couldn't believe that the men in ski masks would set the man alight. It was inhuman. Worse than inhuman. But Yokely's words echoed in her head: 'The thing about threats is that they have to be carried out.' And so far he'd carried out every threat he'd made.

She turned to the Saudi. 'Abdal-Jabbaar, listen to me,' she said. 'Don't let your brother die. If he dies they'll start on your sister. And once they've killed her they'll find someone else. End it now. Please. End it now.'

The Saudi didn't appear to hear her. He continued to stare at his brother and mutter under his breath.

'You can end it. Just tell me you'll co-operate.' She leaned closer to him so that her mouth was close to his ear, but she kept her eyes on the screen. The masked man flicked the Zippo's wheel again. Sparks, but no flame. 'Just tell them, even if you don't mean it,' she whispered. 'They'll stop. Tell them anything. For God's sake, man, lie. Tell them anything.'

The Saudi ignored her.

Button grunted in frustration. She sat back and rested her head against the wall, then banged it twice, hard. She gritted her teeth and relished the pain. She banged her head again, harder this time. This wasn't why she'd joined MI5. She'd joined because she'd wanted to do a job that meant something, a job that made a difference. After she'd graduated with her double first, all sorts of doors had been open to her. Stockbroking, banking – any firm in the City would have hired her. But she'd applied to join the Foreign Office, envisaging a career in embassies around the world, and had been soaring through the interviews when she was asked if she'd consider something more challenging, with the country's intelligence service. She'd accepted, and until today she had never regretted her decision. But nobody had said she'd be involved in torture and murder. And if they had, she would have turned them down flat. What was happening went against every-thing she believed in. It made them no better than the enemy. No better than al-Qaeda. No better than any terrorist or serial killer. And they had forced her to be part of it. She banged her head again.

On the screen, the man in the ski mask flicked the Zippo again.

It burst into life and the man waved the inch-long flame at the camera.

Button stopped banging her head. 'Tell them,' she whispered. 'Please, tell them.'

The Saudi continued to mutter, eyes fixed on the screen. He was talking in Arabic but so fast she couldn't follow what he was saying. She heard 'Allah' and 'Abdal-Rahmaan' but the rest was incomprehensible. The Saudi's eyes were blank and he'd stopped crying.

'Please,' Button implored him. 'Whatever your beliefs, it can't be worth this. It can't be worth the deaths of your brother and sister. You know that blood means more than anything. More than friends, more than country, more than politics. You know they will do it. You know they will kill and keep killing. And they will keep torturing you until you talk. So stop it now. Tell them why you're in London. Tell them what you're planning to do.'

The Saudi's mutterings intensified. His hands were clenched into tight fists, knuckles white.

'It's your brother, God damn you,' said Button. She wiped her eyes with the back of her hand. 'Just tell them.'

On the screen the man in the ski mask turned away from the camera and walked over to the bound Arab, who had closed his eyes and, like the Saudi, was muttering a prayer.

The man with the ski mask put his left hand up to his ear and Button realised he was wearing an earpiece. Yokely was in contact with them, wherever they were. The man nodded, then went back to the camera. 'Last chance,' said the man. A Mid-west American accent. He waved the Zippo in front of the camera and the flame smoked. Even beneath the ski mask, Button could see that he was grinning. Her stomach churned: he was enjoying it.

'Abdal-Jabbaar, please . . .' she begged.

She slumped back against the wall and put her hands over her face, fingers splayed, as she had when she'd watched horror movies with her brothers when she was a child. One had died of leukaemia when he was eleven and she was nine: she'd never forgotten the pain, and life had never been the same. Ricky's death had been unavoidable, a case of nature going wrong, but the loss to Button had been almost unbearable. What the Saudi was going through now was infinitely worse, though. Abdal-Rahmaan's death would be horrific and the Saudi knew that it was within his power to stop it. Button remembered that, as a child, she had knelt at the foot of her bed and prayed to God, promising anything if he'd let Ricky get better. But Ricky had died and Button had stopped believing in God. She wondered how strong the Saudi's faith was. Was he prepared to let his brother die an agonizing death for no other reason than that he wanted others to die? All that the Saudi stood to gain was another terrorist atrocity. But he faced losing his entire family and eventually his own life. It made no sense to Button. If her family was about to be slain, Button had no doubt that she would say whatever it took to save them.

The man with the Zippo walked away from the camera. As Button watched though her fingers, he seemed to be moving in slow motion: each step took an eternity.

'Don't let this happen,' she whispered.

Part of her wanted to believe that everything on the screens had been faked, that Yokely was using special effects to make it look as if the Saudi's loved ones were being killed. But the shooting of the cousin had been real, she was certain: the look on the boy's face, the shower of brain matter and blood, the way the body had slumped forward. None of that had been faked. So what was about to happen to the Saudi's brother was real, too. And Yokely had made her a part of it.

The man in the ski mask reached Abdal-Rahmaan and turned for what Button knew was the Saudi's last chance.

'Please tell them,' she said, her voice a hoarse whisper. She could barely speak. She pressed her hands hard against her face, but was still watching through her fingers: she had to see for herself what happened next, even though she knew the image would stay with her for the rest of her life.

The man in the ski mask grinned and ran the flame round the Arab's waist. There was a whoosh of blue and the man's legs were engulfed in flames. He screamed and writhed as the fire spread upwards. He bucked and jerked, and his shrieks got louder and more frantic. Now Button put her hands over her ears. The smoke turned black as the clothing burned, and the screams continued. Even through her hands the sound chilled her blood.

When the body was engulfed in flames from chest to feet, the fire spread further down, inch by inch. The Arab's screams echoed from the speakers. Button wanted to shout at Yokely to turn off the sound but she knew that even if she did he wouldn't. This wasn't about the effect the killing was having on her: what mattered was how the Saudi reacted.

Button knew there was nothing the Saudi could do or say to save his brother now – he had third-degree burns over most of his body. Within seconds his face would be on fire, then his mouth and lungs, and it would all be over. Button was sure she could smell burned flesh and singed hair. She turned to the Saudi. His face was a blank mask, but his cheeks were wet with tears.

The screams stopped and Button looked at the screen. The Arab's face had bubbled and turned black, the eyeballs had popped, the flesh along his legs had split into red fissures, and thin smoke plumed from the open mouth. Abdal-Rahmaan was dead.

The three men stood behind the body, their arms folded across their chests, feet shoulder width apart, masked heads jutting arrogantly. There was no shame in their stance. Button felt a wave of revulsion wash over her. What Yokely's men had done was every bit as evil as what the Muslim terrorists did to their hostages in Iraq. There was no difference. No difference at all.

Sharpe followed Shepherd down the swaying train. 'What exactly are we looking for?' asked Sharpe.

'A secure room,' said Shepherd. 'If we're lucky, there'll be cops on board. We're going to need all the help we can get.' The first they tried was in carriage ten. There was no one inside. The

Eurostar staff were using it for storage and it was full of bottled water, boxes of fruit and old newspapers.

'What's the plan?' asked Sharpe. 'Pelt them with oranges?'

Shepherd pulled the door shut and headed on down the corridor. The second secure room was in carriage eight. Shepherd turned the handle and pushed open the door. Two French policemen were sitting in the room, wearing blue shirts with police insignia badges and black trousers, handcuffs and empty holsters on their belts. A teenager with a shaved head and a swastika tattoo on his neck was on the bench seat, handcuffed to metal securing hoops on the wall.

One of the men stood up as Shepherd opened the door. There was just enough room for him to step into the room. Sharpe had to stay in the doorway.

'Hiya, guys. Do you speak English?' asked Shepherd. The two policemen looked at him blankly. 'Okay,' he said. 'How about this? Nous sommes des police Britanniques. Il y a des terroristes dans le train. On a besoin de vos armes.'

The other cop stood up and scowled at Shepherd. 'Vous n'avez pas la dégaine de poulets,' he said.

'Show him your warrant card, Razor,' said Shepherd.

Sharpe did so. The cop barely glanced at it. He thrust up his chin and waited for Shepherd to speak.

'On est bien des flics,' said Shepherd.

The cop shrugged. 'Vous pouvez être ce que vous voulez, mais sans nos flingues.'

'On a juste quelques minutes pour arrêter ces mecs, on a pas le temps pour faire des discours,' said Shepherd, trying to keep his cool.

'Y'a pas à discuter,' said the cop. 'Nous sommes seuls autorisés à se servir de ces armes, c'est nous. Et on n'a pas l'intention d'y toucher.'

'Vous ne pouvez pas vous en servir,' said Shepherd. 'On est du côté anglais du tunnel, de plus moi je connais ces types mais vous et vous non.'

The cop shook his head. 'Vous n'utiliserez pas nos flingues.'

'Je réquisitionne ces armes immédiatement,' said Shepherd.

'Allez vous faire foutre!'

'What's he saying?' asked Sharpe.

'He's just told us to fuck off.'

'Maybe he doesn't understand what we want.'

'I'm pretty sure he understands perfectly,' said Shepherd. He shook his head. 'We don't have time for this,' he said. He stepped forward and punched the cop in the solar plexus. The air exploded from the man's lungs and he doubled over. Shepherd punched him in the side of the head and he slumped back in his seat.

Shepherd pointed at the other policeman. 'Sit down unless you want the same,' he said, speaking English this time. The man clearly understood because he obeyed. 'Where's the key?' he asked.

The cop pointed at his unconscious colleague.

'Your English is getting better by the minute, isn't it?' said Shepherd. He leaned over and went through the pockets of the unconscious policeman, found a key and slotted it into the locker. Inside were two 9mm Beretta automatics and four loaded magazines. Shepherd took one of the Berettas and handed it to Sharpe. 'Don't shoot yourself in the foot,' he said. 'Where are the rifles?' he asked the Frenchman.

'We don't have rifles,' he said. 'Just the Berettas.'

Shepherd slotted a magazine into the pistol. 'Are you ready, Razor?'

'What's the plan?'

'We start at the rear of the train and we go through every carriage. I'm pretty sure they're in the toilets.'

'Which means they'll be locked from the inside.'

Shepherd cursed. Sharpe was right. They could hardly start blasting away at the locks. 'There must be some way of opening them from the outside?' he said.

'Let's check,' said Sharpe.

'We can't leave him like this,' said Shepherd, nodding at the seated cop. 'He'll scream blue murder as soon as we go.' He pulled the handcuffs off the belt of the unconscious cop. He handed them to the seated cop and told him to handcuff himself.

'We could gag him,' said Sharpe.

'We could,' said Shepherd. He punched the cop on the side of the chin and the man slumped in his seat. He grinned at Sharpe. 'But that's so much quicker.' He looked at the prisoner, who had stared open-mouthed from the moment they had opened the door. 'Am I going to have to hit you too?' he asked.

The man shook his head. 'I'm cool, mate,' he said, in a nasal Liverpudlian accent.

'You're British?'

'Yeah, mate. The fucking Frogs are taking me in on some trumped-up assault charge. Can you let me go, yeah?'

Shepherd stared at him in disbelief. 'You know we're cops, right?'

'Yeah, but you're English, aren't you? Us English have to stick together.'

'I'm Scottish,' said Sharpe. 'So that pretty much fucks up your theory.'

'Are you going to keep quiet?' Shepherd asked the prisoner.

'Just hit him,' said Sharpe.

'Hey, I'm cool as a cucumber in December,' said the man. 'I'll just sit here.' He held up his shackled wrists. 'It's not like I'm going anywhere, is it?'

'I hear one peep from you and I'll come back and knock you out,' said Shepherd.

Shepherd and Sharpe held the guns inside their coats as they left the room. Shepherd pulled the door shut. There was a toilet a couple of paces away. It was unoccupied, and had steel buttons to open and close it.

Near the roof a socket was set into the door. Sharpe pointed at it. 'The crew will have a key for that,' he said.

'Let's get one, then,' said Shepherd.

Joe Hagerman put down the lid of the toilet and sat on it. His duffel coat was hanging on the back of the door. He opened the suitcase and piled the contents under the washbasin. A few shirts, a pair of jeans, basic toiletries. An empty case would have aroused suspicion. It had been X-rayed but no one had asked him to open it. The Semtex was spread evenly around the shell and was protected by the plastic lining. It could not be detected by the security scanners.

The door was locked. Hagerman picked up his sponge bag, took out a small can of shaving foam and shoved it between the lock and the door. Now the lock couldn't be moved.

He ripped open the black plastic-wrapped package to reveal two detonators, a battery, a trigger, a wiring circuit and a screwdriver. He used the screwdriver to prise off the lining of the case.

Shepherd and Sharpe walked into the buffet car. A young man with gelled hair was serving drinks. 'We need to speak to the chief steward or whoever runs the show,' said Sharpe, discreetly flashing his warrant card.

The young man picked up a phone on the wall behind him and spoke in rapid French. A couple of minutes later a middle-aged man with a receding hairline and a sweeping moustache walked up. Sharpe showed him the warrant card and explained what they wanted.

'There is a problem?' asked the man, in heavily accented English.

'We are looking for someone, and we believe he is hiding in one of the toilets.'

'Is he dangerous?'

'We don't think so,' lied Shepherd, 'but we would like to have him in custody before we arrive at the Gare du Nord.'

The man pursed his lips, then shrugged and pulled a small T-shaped key from his jacket pocket. 'I want it back.'

'Of course,' said Shepherd.

'Do you need any assistance?'

Shepherd smiled confidently. He could feel the Beretta sticking into the small of his back under the pea coat. 'No, we'll be fine.'

Shepherd and Sharpe headed to the rear of the train. Now that it was in the tunnel, yellow fire doors had sprung closed between the carriages in addition to the normal doors. They were an extra safety measure but could be opened manually. Shepherd's ears were popping from the change in pressure as the train hurtled beneath the English Channel.

The toilet in carriage number fourteen was unoccupied, as was the one in fifteen. The doors were different from the first type they'd seen – they had a lever, which had to be pushed to the left to open them while the key was inserted close to it to open the door from outside.

The toilet in carriage sixteen was occupied. Shepherd knocked on the door. 'Billets, s'il vous plaît,' he shouted. 'Tickets, please.'

There was no reaction from whoever was inside. Shepherd nodded at Sharpe, who took the key and slotted it into the hole. Sharpe held up three fingers. Then two. Then one. He twisted the key and shoved the door to the left, moving out of the way to give Shepherd a clear view.

Shepherd stepped forward. A man was sitting on the toilet. At first he thought he'd made a mistake but then he saw that the man's trousers weren't down and that he was holding something metalic. Shepherd's finger tightened on the trigger but then he saw that it wasn't a weapon but a slim metal cylinder. A detonator. The man gaped at him. A hard-shell suitcase lay open at his feet, another detonator inside it. Clothes were piled on the floor under the washbasin.

Shepherd stepped forward and slammed the butt of his pistol hard against the man's temple. He collapsed without a sound. The detonator clattered to the floor.

'Get in here and shut the door.'

Sharpe did as he was told. They stood shoulder to shoulder, staring at the unconscious man sprawled on the toilet. Blood trickled down his cheek from the head wound.

'He's not Hagerman,' said Sharpe.

'I can see that,' said Shepherd. He bent down and picked up the detonator.

'What's that?' asked Sharpe.

'The thing that makes bombs go bang,' said Shepherd. He put it into his pocket, then knelt down to examine the suitcase. The lining had been pulled away. He swore softly.

'What?'

'Semtex,' he said. There was a mess of wires in the case and a nine-volt battery. He studied the circuit. 'There's no timer,' he said. 'Just a trigger.'

'Which means?'

'He was going to detonate himself by pressing it. He was going to go up with it.' Shepherd picked up the second detonator and straightened up.

'A suicide-bomber?'

'We're in deep shit, Razor. Hagerman is somewhere on the train, and his case is pretty much a match for this one. And there's the guy who got on at Ashford. If there are no timers, they must be preparing to detonate at the same time. And if there are three bombers, there might be four. Or more.'

'How did they get the detonators on board? They should have shown up at the security check.'

'They must have found a way through. The explosives in the suitcases wouldn't have shown up, but they've got the circuit in separately. That's what he was doing – putting the final touches to it.' Shepherd looked at his watch. 'We're going to have to move, Razor. Tie him up, then we'll check every toilet on the train. Fast. We'll do the last two at this end of the train, then we head forward.'

Button stared at the plasma screens. Three were blank. The fourth still showed the woman on the wooden chair. The man behind her was slapping his baseball bat into the palm of his left hand.

The Saudi was still sitting with his back against the wall, his knees drawn up to his chest. 'She's pregnant,' he whispered.

'What?' said Button.

'My sister. She's pregnant. Her first child.'

Button's earpiece crackled. 'We know,' said Yokely. 'Five months.'

'We know,' repeated Button. 'Five months.'

The Saudi sniffed and wiped his nose with the back of his hand. 'You know, and still you let this happen? You're a woman, how can you do this?'

Button said nothing.

'Do you have children?'

'I'm not here to answer your questions.'

The Saudi put his head into his hands and began to cry.

Button sat and watched him. 'You can end this at any time,' she said. 'Just tell us what you were doing in London.'

The door opened and Broken Nose reappeared with a red and white pack of Marlboro cigarettes and a cheap disposable lighter. He put them in front of her, then went to stand with his back to the door. Button yelled at him to get out. He put a hand to his headset, nodded, and left the room.

'Tell him to look at the screen,' said Yokely, in her ear.

'Abdal-Jabbaar, you must look at the screen,' said Button.

The Saudi kept his head down.

'Tell him he has to watch,' said Yokely. 'If he wants his sister to be raped, the least he can do is watch.'

'No,' whispered Button.

'Tell him, Charlie.'

Button swallowed. Her mouth had gone dry. 'Abdal-Jabbaar, listen to me. You know what they're going to do. You must co-operate.'

The Saudi glared at her. 'Do what you have to do,' he said.

On the screen, two men in ski masks had pulled the Saudi's sister off the chair and were ripping off the burkha. She was wearing a grey blouse underneath and a long brown skirt. The men ripped those off too until she was standing in her underwear, the swell of her pregnancy pushing over the top of her briefs.

'Abdal-Jabbaar, you can't let this happen.'

'Do what you have to do,' he repeated.

One of the men had a knife and he used it to cut off the woman's bra. Her breasts swung free. The men in ski masks were laughing now, taunting her.

Button stood up. 'I need a break,' she said.

'Charlie, we're on a schedule here,' said Yokely in her ear.

'I need a break. It's either that or I piss myself. Your call.'

Button heard Yokely take a deep breath, then mutter something.

'I didn't hear that,' she said.

'Five minutes,' he said. 'Then we continue.'

Button picked up the cigarettes and lighter and walked out of the room.

The toilet in carriage fifteen was still empty as Shepherd and Sharpe made their way from the rear of the train. When they got to number fourteen, a young father was taking his toddler son into the toilet. The one in thirteen was empty, in twelve it was occupied. Shepherd knocked on the door. 'Billets, s'il vous plâit,' he said. 'Tickets, please.'

'Can't you wait?' said a woman. She had a central European accent that Shepherd couldn't place.

'I'm sorry, madam, can we see your ticket, please?' said Shepherd.

'I'm on the toilet,' said the woman.

'Just a look, madam. It will only take a minute.'

Shepherd put his head against the door. He heard rustling. He motioned for Sharpe to unlock the door.

Sharpe frowned. 'Are you sure?' he mouthed.

Shepherd glared at him and gestured for him to use the key.

Sharpe inserted the key, twisted it, and pulled open the door.

The woman was in her twenties, olive-skinned with dark curly hair tied back in a ponytail. 'What do you think you are doing?' she asked. She was wearing a pale blue padded body-warmer over a white polo-neck sweater and an ornate crucifix. She stood with her right hand behind the door, her ticket in the left.

'I'm sorry,' said Shepherd. He pushed himself away from the door.

'Don't you want to see my ticket?' she said. She held it out.

Sharpe looked at it. 'That's fine, madam. Sorry to have bothered you.'

She started to close the door, but there was a mirror above the washbasin and in it Sharpe saw a hard-shell suitcase perched on the toilet. 'Just a minute, madam,' he said.

'Come on, Razor.' Shepherd was heading for the next carriage.

Sharpe pushed the door, harder. He could see the woman's clothing on the floor under the washbasin. 'Spider!' he shouted.

She took her hand away from the door and it slid to the side. Sharpe lost his balance and cursed. The woman's right hand appeared, clutching a red-handled screwdriver. She plunged it into Sharpe's neck and he lurched backwards. She rushed out of the toilet and stabbed him again, this time in the shoulder.

Shepherd whirled round, pulled the gun from his coat and fired once, hitting her in the throat. She staggered back into the toilet, leaving the screwdriver stuck in Sharpe's shoulder, then fell back against the washbasin, a gurgling sound bubbling from her windpipe. She slumped to the floor and lay still.

Shepherd knelt beside Sharpe.

'Sorry,' said Sharpe.

'Don't be stupid,' said Shepherd. He took a quick look at the neck wound, which was only a small puncture, from which a little blood was seeping, and knew that it wasn't serious. 'You'll be okay,' he said, then went into the toilet, grabbed a shirt from the woman's clothing, rolled it up and pressed it to his colleague's neck. 'Keep the pressure on,' he said. Then he opened Sharpe's coat. His shirt was soaked with blood from the shoulder wound but again there was only minor damage.

He picked up the key and put it into his coat pocket.

'I've got to go, Razor,' he said, and ran towards the next carriage.

Button closed the door behind her and leaned against the wall. Her heart was racing and she felt as if a steel band had been clamped round her chest. Sweat was trickling down her back. She took out a cigarette and lit it. The marine with the carbine looked at her and she glared at him as she drew the smoke deep into her lungs, then blew it up at the ceiling. She could barely believe what was going on in the room behind her. A man was being tortured and people were being murdered in the name of the war against terrorism. And Yokely had made her part of it. She knew that, no matter how the day ended, she would never be the same again.

She walked into the observation room. Yokely was standing at the two-way mirror, watching the Saudi. He turned to her but she held up a hand. 'Don't talk to me,' she said. 'I don't want to hear anything you've got to say.'

'He'll talk,' said Yokely. 'We're nearly there.'

'You've murdered two people,' she said. She went to the table and took out her mobile phone. 'And now you're threatening to kill a pregnant woman.'

'He can end it at any time,' said Yokely.

'There are going to be repercussions, I promise you that,' said Button, switching on her phone. She took another drag on her cigarette.

'First things first,' said Yokely. 'I need you back in there.'

'Screw you.'

'Charlie, you've been seconded to me and you're to follow my instructions. To the letter.'

Button nodded at the two-way mirror. 'After what's been going on in there? I don't think so. We're through. And if I get my way, you're through too.'

Yokely smiled. 'I think you'll find that you're the one who's through if you walk away now. Why don't you phone your bosses, see what they say?' He turned away to stare at the Saudi again.

Button checked her voicemail. The first was from Shepherd, telling her he was at Waterloo. He sounded annoyed. The second was from Bingham, confirming that Hagerman was on the Eurostar and that Sharpe and Shepherd were also on board. The third message was Bingham: he had spoken to Europol and the French were arranging surveillance at the Gare du Nord. The fourth was from her husband. He'd got home to find that the dog had soiled the carpet in the sitting room. It was clear from his tone that he blamed her. The fifth was Bingham again: Shepherd had reported that a second face on her hit list had boarded the train at Ashford International. The man was an Armenian who had fought in Bosnia and had been spotted in Afghanistan fighting with the Mujahideen. The final message was from Bingham again, and this time he sounded worried. Shepherd and Sharpe had lost sight of Hagerman and the Armenian. They had to be on the train somewhere, but what were they doing? Bingham asked Button to phone him back as soon as she could. The train was in the tunnel, so Shepherd and Sharpe would be out of contact for twenty minutes.

Button watched the Saudi as she listened to the final words of Bingham's message. He was staring up at the plasma screen.

'The Eurostar,' she said.

'What?' said Yokely.

'The Eurostar,' repeated Button, and rushed for the door.

Shepherd kept the gun inside his coat as he walked briskly down the centre aisle of carriage eleven. He went past his seat. Sharpe's half-eaten steak was still on the table with his wine glass, which had been refilled. The toilets in that carriage were unoccupied.

Two stewardesses were wheeling a trolley down the aisle in carriage ten. Shepherd squeezed past. He pointed back towards the rear of the train.

'A man down there's been hurt,' he said. 'Can you get a first-aid kit, then go and deal with him?'

The women seemed paralysed.

'Now!' hissed Shepherd. He hurried along the aisle, pushed open the yellow fire doors and went through to carriage ten, where the toilets were empty. Carriage nine: occupied. Shepherd tapped on the door. 'Billets, s'il vous plâit. Tickets, please.'

The toilet flushed and an elderly man opened the door. Shepherd excused himself and hurried on to the next carriage.

The door to the secure room in carriage eight was still closed.

Shepherd didn't have time to check on the two French cops and their Liverpudlian prisoner. The toilet next to it was unoccupied.

Shepherd went into carriage seven. The train was swaying and he had to steady himself on the headrests as he hurried down the aisle. A group of Indian women were playing cards. Businessmen were tapping away on laptop computers or fiddling with their Palm Pilots. Others were holding mobile phones, waiting impatiently for the signal to return, annoyed that their lifeline to the outside world had been cut.

Shepherd pushed through the doors at the end of the carriage and checked the toilet. Occupied. He knocked on the door. 'Billets, s'il vous plâit. Tickets, please.'

There was no answer. Shepherd pressed his ear to the door. He could hear someone moving inside and knocked again. That the woman had attacked Sharpe with a screwdriver suggested the terrorists had no firearms. 'Billets, s'il vous plâit,' he repeated. He inserted the key into the lock, took a deep breath, twisted it and pushed open the door. The man was sitting on the toilet, with an open hard-shell suitcase, gaping at Shepherd and showing several gold teeth. It was the man he'd seen at Ashford.

'Don't move!' snapped Shepherd. His eyes flicked to the suitcase: two detonators had been inserted in the body of the case. The wires had been connected to a nine-volt battery and a trigger. There was a screwdriver on the floor.

The man lunged forward. Shepherd realised he was going for the trigger, and fired his weapon twice. A double tap. Two shots to the head. The first entered the man's left eye and tore off the top of his skull. The second ripped through his mouth, splintering teeth and severing his spine. He pitched forward and fell across the suitcase. The body twitched and was still. Shepherd shut the door and ran towards the next carriage.

Button helped the Saudi to his feet. He could barely walk so she supported him as he staggered to the chair. He slumped down on it, blood trickling from his nose. She gave him a plastic tumbler of water but he threw it away.

Button walked round the table and sat down. She interlinked her fingers and leaned forward. 'Look at me, Abdal-Jabbaar.'

The Saudi wiped his nose with the back of his hand again. His entire body was shaking.

'Abdal-Jabbaar, look at me.'

Slowly the Saudi lifted his head.

'We know everything,' she said quietly.

The Saudi said nothing.

'We know about Joe Hagerman. We know about the Eurostar. All this is for nothing.'

The Saudi's eyes flicked to the clock on the wall.

'It's over,' said Button. 'We caught them before they got on to the train.'

The Saudi sagged in his chair. 'Then let my sister go,' he said.

'That's not my call, Abdal-Jabbaar. It's out of my hands. They want details. They want names. They want a confession. And this will continue until they get that confession.'

The Arab eyed her suspiciously. 'How did you find out?'

Button looked at him with a slight smile on her face. 'We were on to Joe Hagerman,' she said. 'The Uddin brothers work for us.' The lie came easily and she forced herself to smile confidently.

The Arab cursed.

'You can't trust anybody,' said Button. 'You know that. Hagerman is talking and talking fast. He doesn't want to be sent to Guantanamo Bay and he knows his only chance is to be prosecuted here.'

The Arab looked up at the plasma screen. 'Let my sister go,' he said.

'Confess,' said Button.

'You already know everything,' said the Arab.

Button looked at the two-way mirror. She could only see her reflection, but she knew that Yokely would be on the phone. She glanced at the clock and prayed they would be in time.

Shepherd ran down the aisle, holding his gun under his pea coat. His ears popped again and he swallowed to equalise the pressure.

Frowning faces turned to him, but he ignored them. He had no idea how many more bombers there were or when the deadline was, but he was sure that the explosions would take place in the tunnel because that was where the bombs would do the maximum damage. He looked at his watch as he ran. They had been in the tunnel for eight minutes.

Carriage six was the buffet car. Half a dozen French students were drinking bottled beer. He pushed past and one swore as Shepherd jogged his drinking arm.

Carriage five was the first of the standard-class accommodation. There were two seats on each side of the aisle, while in first class the configuration had been two on one side and single seats on the other. The toilet in carriage five was empty. An overweight man with a walking-stick was blocking the aisle and Shepherd shoved him out of the way. The man waved the stick at him, lost his balance and fell against an American tourist. Shepherd reached the fire door and hit the handle to open it. He pushed through the gap and opened the next. The toilet in carriage four was occupied, but as Shepherd was about to knock on the door an elderly woman came out, apologising in French. Shepherd hurried into the next carriage.

The toilet in the third from the front was empty and Shepherd went through to the second. He stared at the small red oblong in the door. Occupied.

He pressed his ear to it. He couldn't hear anything. Then a click. Metal against plastic, maybe.

He knocked. 'Billets, s'il vous plâit,' he said. 'Tickets, please.'

There was no reaction. He knocked again. 'Billets, s'il vous plâit.' He pressed his ear to the door. This time there was silence.

Shepherd inserted the key and twisted. It met resistance. Shepherd frowned. Whoever was inside had interfered with the lock.

He took a step back from the door and held the gun with both hands. Time was running out. If the person in there was an ordinary passenger, they would have reacted to his knock. It must be Hagerman. It couldn't be anyone else. And if it was the

American, he'd be in there with his suitcase full of Semtex and the trigger circuit.

Shepherd aimed at the lock. He wasn't sure how many shots it would take to destroy it. He had slotted in a fresh magazine so he had more than enough rounds – but how far had Hagerman gone in arming his bomb?

He tightened his finger on the trigger. Then he hesitated. If Hagerman had armed the bomb, he would detonate it as soon as Shepherd started shooting. There was no time to shoot out the lock. No time to slide the door open. His only option was to kill Hagerman before he had chance to press the trigger. Shepherd slowly raised the gun. The toilet was a confined space: there were only a few places where Hagerman could be and, more than likely, he was sitting on the toilet. Shepherd had twelve rounds in the magazine. More than enough.

Joe Hagerman was sitting on the toilet, suitcase open on the floor in front of him. He'd inserted the detonator into the Semtex and was attaching the battery when the ticket collector had knocked at the door. He looked at his watch. It was less than a minute before he was due to detonate. He didn't have time for any interruptions.

He picked up the trigger, took a deep breath and cleared his mind. He had no doubts, no reservations and no regrets. He closed his eyes. There would be no pain. He wouldn't be aware of the explosion. It would all be over for him the instant he pressed the trigger.

He jumped as a shot rang out. A piece of plastic had been ripped out of the wall in front of his face. There was a small hole in the door. Someone was shooting at him. Something had gone wrong. Something had gone very wrong.

He heard another loud bang, felt a thump in his right shoulder and saw a black hole in his duffel coat. The trigger dropped from his fingers. He felt blood soaking into his chest, then a dull ache.

His peripheral vision started to go and he seemed to be looking down a long tunnel. He bent to grab for the trigger and found himself smiling, even though he knew he was about to die.

Then his head exploded.

Button walked into the observation room, her mascara streaked. Yokely was on his mobile phone. He flashed her a thumbs-up. 'Absolutely,' he said, into the phone. 'As soon as it's done I'll get back to you.'

He cut the connection and beamed at Button. 'Charlie, you were brilliant,' he said. 'Absolutely first class. You're a natural.'

'The train?'

'Your man Shepherd came through. It's safe. What you did in there was superb. You played him like a one-string fiddle. I couldn't have done it better myself.'

Button wiped her face, then ran damp hands through her hair. She took two steps towards Yokely. The American reached out to her, anticipating a hug, but Button punched him in the face. She felt a surge of satisfaction as the cartilage shattered in his nose and blood spurted over his lips. He staggered back against the table. Without thinking what she was doing, Button kicked him between the legs, hard. Yokely bent over, gasping for breath, blood-flecked hands clasping his groin.

'You bastard,' she said. She raised her hand to hit him again, but managed to hold herself in check. 'You're not worth it,' she said, and stalked out of the room.

The female doctor smiled reassuringly at Shepherd. 'Your colleague will be fine,' she said. She was French but spoke English with an American accent. 'He lost a lot of blood and we'll keep him here for a day or two but there's nothing to worry about.'

'Thanks, Doc,' said Shepherd. Sharpe was lying in bed, bandages round his neck and shoulder. He was pale and weak but he smiled.

Shepherd looked round to see Charlotte Button standing in the doorway. She smiled at him and gave him a small wave.

Shepherd walked over to her. He didn't want to shake hands

with her. He didn't even want to talk to her. She was wearing a fawn raincoat and carrying a Louis Vuitton shoulder-bag.

'Is he going to be okay?' she asked.

'Yeah,' said Shepherd.

'You did good work today, Dan.'

'Where the hell were you?' he snarled.

'It's complicated,' she said.

'No. Quadratic equations are complicated. A boss being there when her team needs her, that's basic police procedure. Hell, it's common fucking sense.'

Button's face hardened. 'I know you've been through a lot today, but I won't allow you to verbally abuse me, DC Shepherd.'

'We don't use ranks,' said Shepherd coldly. 'Ever.'

'You work for me, Dan. I don't work for you. Remember that.'

'Yeah, well, that could change,' said Shepherd. 'I needed you today.' He jerked a thumb at Sharpe. 'He needed you.'

'I hope you're not suggesting that I'm responsible for what happened to Jimmy.'

'There were two of us, unarmed, on a train with four suicide-bombers. We should have had back-up. There should have been armed cops with us.'

'Dan, let's not start off on the wrong foot.'

He flashed her a tight smile. 'We're not dancing here. It's not a question of right foot or wrong foot. Four terrorists with bombs could have killed a hell of a lot of people on that train, and you had your phone switched off.'

'I don't have to justify myself to you,' said Button. 'But I can tell you that I was at the American embassy for most of today, interrogating the man who planned the bombs on the Eurostar. And a lot more.'

'Who is he?'

'A Saudi. I was involved in his interrogation and I have to say it was pretty fucking unpleasant.' She smiled thinly. 'I've had a pretty shitty day myself, Dan. But, unlike you, I don't come out of it covered with glory.'

Shepherd nodded slowly. 'Okay. You're right. I wasn't aware

of the big picture.' He ran a hand through his hair. 'I need to get home.'

'I've arranged a plane,' said Button. 'There's a car outside that'll take you to the airport. I'll stay here and arrange Jimmy's transport back to the UK.'

'What's happened to the Uddin brothers?'

Button looked uncomfortable. 'They're out of the picture.'

'They were arrested?'

'We took them in, along with their contact in the Passport Agency.'

'Will I be giving evidence?'

'There isn't going to be a trial. Not in the near future, anyway.'

Shepherd frowned. 'Why not?'

'They're being taken to Guantanamo Bay.'

'What?'

'They provided passports to Hagerman. The Americans want to know who else they supplied. They're putting them on a military flight tonight.'

'They could be questioned here. Why the hell take them to Cuba?'

'The Americans wanted them, and the way the world is just now, the Americans get what they want.'

'The brothers probably don't even know who Hagerman is,' said Shepherd.

'I agree,' said Button.

'They're not terrorists.'

'In which case they'll be released.'

'When? After three years? Five? Ten?'

'When they've proved they're not terrorists.'

'How do you prove a negative?' asked Shepherd. 'They're just guys who broke the law. Okay, prison here, that's fair enough, even though we both know of men who've done things a thousand times worse and never been behind bars. But they don't deserve to be clapped in irons and kept in cages.'

'I'm not the enemy here, Dan.'

'Then who is? The Yanks?'

'It's the way of the world. The Uddins provided terrorists with passports. That puts them in the terrorist camp. It's like Bush said, you're either with them or against them. There's no middle ground any more.'

'They probably thought they were helping asylum-seekers,' said Shepherd.

'So they can explain that.'

'They shouldn't have to explain it to military interrogators in Cuba,' said Shepherd. 'We made the case. They should be put on trial here and, if they're found guilty, a judge decides on a fair sentence. That's their right, laid down by the bloody Magna Carta. The right to a fair trial. And not to be punished until they've had one. It's bugger all to do with the Police and Criminal Evidence Act or the European Court of Human Rights. It's what our ancestors fought and died for hundreds of years ago.'

'The world has changed, Dan,' said Button, quietly.

'Too bloody right it has.'

'I'm sorry,' she said, and patted his shoulder as if she was comforting a bereaved relative.

Shepherd twisted out of her grasp and she flinched as if she'd been struck. 'It's okay, I'm not—' he started to say, but saw from the look of sympathy on her face that explanations weren't necessary. She understood. But there was nothing she could do. Shepherd walked away without looking back.

When Shepherd got home the house was dark. He went upstairs and opened the door to Liam's bedroom. His son was fast asleep so he went back downstairs, threw his pea coat on to the sofa and went over to the bookcase. A bottle of Jameson's stood there and he picked it up. He rarely drank whiskey at home, and never when he was alone. He'd drunk wine with Sue, usually chardonnay or pinot grigio, and usually as a prelude to an early night. The Jameson's was for visitors, especially Sue's father, Tom, who was a great fan of Irish whiskey.

Shepherd unscrewed the top and raised the bottle to his lips. He held it there, knowing that what he was doing was out of character. He never used alcohol as a crutch. He'd known lots of men, in the SAS and the police, who turned to the bottle in times of stress, but he had always found relief in other ways. He put it down. It was time for a run. A long, punishing run. A run that would leave him bone-weary and aching.

He was about to head upstairs when he heard a mobile phone ring – the Tony Corke phone in the pea coat. He bent down and fished it out. The call was coming from a blocked number. Shepherd accepted it and put it to his ear.

'It's Richard,' said an American voice. Shepherd knew only one American called Richard. And only one American who would have the technical expertise to get hold of the number of the pay-as-you-go mobile.

'Yes,' said Shepherd. Yokely was the last person he wanted to talk to.

'I just called to say congratulations,' said Yokely.

'Congratulations?' Shepherd knew what he was alluding to, but he could feel resentment and hostility building in him with each second that the man was on the line.

'The Eurostar,' said Yokely. 'You saved the day, I'm told.'

'I had help,' said Shepherd. 'A colleague was with me. He was stabbed.'

'But you took care of all four of the bastards, didn't you? Even left us with one to question.'

'Jimmy's fine, thanks for asking,' said Shepherd, frostily. 'Nearly bled to death, but, hey, plenty more cops where he came from, right?'

'Dan, you did what needed doing. You neutralised a threat. God damn it, you saved more than seven hundred lives today. I assumed you'd be pleased, basking in the glory and all that.'

'I killed three people,' said Shepherd. 'Two men and a woman who were prepared to die for their beliefs.'

'Exactly,' said the American.

'You don't get it, do you?' asked Shepherd.

'I get it, Dan. You went up against four hardened terrorists and you won. And you even managed to do it all on the British side of the tunnel so that the French can't try to fuck things up for us.'

'Why do you people always talk as if it were a game?' said Shepherd. 'It wasn't a bloody game and I didn't win anything.'

'Yes, you did. If they'd succeeded, seven hundred innocent men, women and children would have died today. Civilians who were just going about their daily lives. Innocents, Dan. And they're alive because of you. Because of what you did. You should be proud.'

'If that's what you want to hear then, yes, I'm proud. But I still killed three people and I'll have to live with that.'

'It's not so bad,' said Yokely. 'And it gets easier.'

Anger flared deep within Shepherd that someone could be so casual about the taking of human life. 'Not for me, it doesn't,' he said.

'Really? Are you saying it wasn't easier after what you did down the Tube? Wasn't it just that little bit easier to pull the trigger this time?'

'Are you saying I'm getting desensitised to killing?'

'I'm just saying that there are people in Washington who've heard about what happened today and have been on to me asking why you've not signed with us.'

'Because I'm not an assassin.'

There was a long pause, and for a moment Shepherd thought he'd lost the connection. 'Are you sure about that, Dan?' Yokely said eventually, his voice little more than a soft whisper. 'Are you one hundred per cent sure about it?'

Shepherd cursed and flung the mobile at the wall. He found himself looking at the bottle of Jameson's. He stared at it for several seconds, then went upstairs to change into his running gear.

The Saudi rested his head against the fuselage and looked out of the window at the lights of London far below. They had beaten him, drowned him, abused him. They had killed his cousin. They had burned his brother alive. They had done their worst and they thought they had triumphed. The English woman had thought she was so clever. He could see it in her eyes: the contempt as she questioned him, so sure that she was his intellectual superior. The Saudi would have given almost anything to see her expression when she discovered he had outsmarted her.

The plane banked to the left as it climbed. The Saudi was manacled, hand and foot. He was wearing a white paper suit and paper slippers. Sitting next to him was a marine, square-jawed with a crew-cut and hard blue eyes. A typical American, thought the Saudi, big-boned and stupid. He regarded the Saudi with undisguised hatred. The Saudi didn't care. There was nothing else they could do to him.

He didn't know who else was on the plane. He'd been taken from the embassy in a van with a hood over his head. Once he was seated on the plane the hood had been removed and the marine had told him not to turn round. There were definitely other passengers on board, though. As he'd been helped up the stairs to the plane he'd caught a glimpse of black loafers with tassels. The Saudi didn't know if they belonged to one of the Americans or to another prisoner.

He'd heard shouts as they'd boarded the plane, an Asian man insisting he was British and that they had no right to be taking him out of the country. The Saudi hadn't bothered protesting. Citizenship no longer counted for anything in a world dominated by the United States.

No one had told him where he was being taken, but the Saudi knew they were going to Cuba. Guantanamo Bay. The interrogation would go on for years. Followed by imprisonment. Execution if he was lucky. The offer of money and a new life had always been a lie, even if he had been prepared to co-operate. The Americans had him and they would never let him go. But they hadn't beaten him. The Saudi smiled to himself. They hadn't won. They thought they had, but they were wrong.

Shepherd slept badly. He tossed and turned and didn't fall asleep until the early hours of the morning. Even then he was plagued with nightmares about what had happened on the train. He had reacted instinctively – his training had taken over as it always did when he was in combat – but that didn't make it any easier to deal with the taking of life. And he'd killed a woman. That she'd been a woman hadn't occurred to him as he'd pulled the trigger. He'd seen her stab Sharpe, the blood, the screwdriver in her hand, and he'd fired. He'd been aiming for her head but the bullet had caught her in the throat, and even if he'd had all the time in the world he'd still have gone for a killing shot. In his dreams he wasn't firing a single shot, he was blasting away with both hands on his gun. And the woman he was shooting wasn't the terrorist on the Eurostar. It was Charlotte Button. Then it was Katra. Then it was Moira. Then it was Kathy Gift. And even though he recognised the faces in his dream, he kept firing.

When he woke, it was almost eleven o'clock and sunlight was streaming through the curtains. His leg muscles ached from his late-night run and he had a throbbing headache. He grabbed his towelling robe and ran downstairs. He made himself a cup of coffee, went into the sitting room and switched on the television. He sighed and put his feet on the coffee table as he flicked through the channels. He frowned as he stared at the pictures on the screen. Police in yellow fluorescent jackets were cordoning off a section of a London street. The picture changed. Ambulances were arriving at a city-centre hospital. A sombre Sky newscaster summed up what had happened. Three bombs had gone off in the Tube system. A fourth had destroyed a London bus.

The city had ground to a halt. The Tube system had been closed, buses had stopped running, the police were advising everyone not to travel unless it was absolutely necessary.

Shepherd flicked to BBC1. There had been a bomb on a Circle Line Tube near Liverpool Street station. On the Piccadilly Line between King's Cross and Russell Square. On the Circle Line at Edgware Road. A fourth had destroyed a bus in Tavistock Square.

Shepherd stared at the screen in horror. A news reporter said that no one had claimed responsibility for the carnage, but Shepherd knew it wouldn't be long before al-Qaeda took the credit. Innocent men, women and children had been murdered, and the terrorist organisation would claim that they were casualties of war.

Shepherd felt sick. He'd done his best – he'd given everything he could – but he hadn't stopped the killing. He'd taken out one terrorist cell but there had been another in place, who had carried out their murderous mission and would already be in hiding. He'd won one battle and saved lives – Yokely had been right on that score – but the terrorists were winning the war. There had been dozens of deaths, and hundreds of casualties. Maybe the American was right. Maybe the only way to beat the terrorists was to take them out before they committed atrocities. But Shepherd wasn't sure if that was a line he was prepared to cross. Not yet, anyway. He was sure of one thing, though: he'd made the right decision to move out of London. The capital city would not be safe for many years to come.